WINTER'S SPELL

What Reviewers Say About Ursula Klein's Work

Enchanted Autumn

"Klein's lovely debut paranormal romance showcases the value of friendship and authenticity in the face of scheming exes and magical mayhem. The novel's greatest strength is the unshakable friendship between Hazel and Roxy, who find ways to support each other even while pining for the same woman. The healthy communication keeps the love triangle from dragging, and the grounded magic system delights. Klein should win plenty of fans with this."—*Publishers Weekly*

"*Enchanted Autumn* by Ursula Klein is a spellbinding, slow-burn romance. Set in a mysterious hometown, it's the perfect cozy read. Klein does a fabulous job of painting a New England autumn. Each time I opened the book I felt like I was in the cool, drizzly town myself."—*Lesbian Review*

"This story was so much fun! Filled with magical moments, comedy, drama, and pesky otherworldly beings in Salem that can't help but interfere in things where Hazel's personal life is concerned. Each new chapter brought wonder and a new element the story that had the potential to mess with things in a way that only magic can. …A great debut from Ursula Klein that has left me really excited for what she'll bring next."—*LESBIreviewed*

Visit us at www.boldstrokesbooks.com

By the Author

Enchanted Autumn

Winter's Spell

WINTER'S SPELL

by

Ursula Klein

2024

WINTER'S SPELL

ISBN 13: 978-1-63679-503-4

THIS TRADE PAPERBACK ORIGINAL IS PUBLISHED BY
BOLD STROKES BOOKS, INC.
P.O. BOX 249
VALLEY FALLS, NY 12185

FIRST EDITION: JANUARY 2024

CREDITS
EDITOR: CINDY CRESAP
PRODUCTION DESIGN: SUSAN RAMUNDO
COVER DESIGN BY INK SPIRAL DESIGN

Dedication

To my mother,
who first introduced me to all things magical

CHAPTER ONE—ROXY

Roxy's breath caught in her throat as she gazed at her best friend, Hazel, in her wedding dress. It was like she was seeing her for the first time, even though they'd known each other since grade school. She'd never seen Hazel looking so absolutely beautiful.

"That bad, huh?"

"What? No. Oh my gosh, Hazel, you look gorgeous."

Hazel blushed with pleasure and her eyes became bright with tears. "Hey! You're going to make me cry and then I'll be a raccoon bride."

"Sorry. Let me put it another way: you look totes gorge and Elizabeth is going to cream herself when she sees you."

"Ew." Hazel laughed, and Roxy felt her own tears recede a bit. She knew if either of them started crying, the other would too, and they shouldn't be crying, because it was a happy day—wasn't it?

Stop it. Today is about Hazel, not you and your pathetic love life. Roxy forced herself to smile at Hazel before giving her a quick hug. "You look amazing."

"Thanks, Rox." Hazel turned to the mirror in the room to inspect herself one more time. "Do you really think she'll like the dress?" Her voice shook a little at the end of the question, and Roxy realized for the first time how nervous Hazel must be. She and Elizabeth were so in love, Roxy was sure Hazel could show up with a garbage bag on her head and Elizabeth wouldn't care. But she didn't say that.

"Hmmm, I dunno," she said, feigning uncertainty. "You'd better spin around a few times so I can see the full effect."

The ghost of a smile showed up on Hazel's face. She stepped away from the mirror and into the center of the small room they were using as a staging area. Elizabeth had her own room, as the two brides had decided to keep their wedding day clothes a secret until the moment of the ceremony. Roxy was glad of it because it gave her some final moments together alone with Hazel before she left her forever for Elizabeth.

Okay, that was being a little dramatic, but lately, it'd felt that way.

Again, Roxy forced herself to move her thoughts away from her own issues and focus on Hazel, who was slowly spinning in front of her, the bottom of her beautiful white dress flaring out. It was a deceptively simple dress. Roxy was terrible with the names of fabrics and styles, but she'd gone dress shopping with Hazel back in September, and she remembered the saleslady saying this was a classic "A-line" dress with a soft tulle skirt that skimmed the ground. The real showstopper element, though, were embroidered flowers all over the bodice and neckline that, from one angle, looked pink and blue, and from another looked purple and red. It was a stunning effect, and now, while Hazel twirled, it was especially breathtaking.

Of course, it was magic. Hazel and Roxy had found the dress in a shop in Boston, and then Hazel's mother had taken over and enchanted it to change colors. Hazel's mother, like Hazel, was a bona fide witch, and it so happened that her spellcasting abilities were specialized in enchanting objects and materials, like fabrics. Hazel, by contrast, had magical abilities more refined in the area of potions, like her father, so she'd been more than happy to let her mother charm the dress.

This was her first time seeing the full extent of the spell, and Roxy felt her mouth open involuntarily in awe. The effect was simply perfect—simple enough to fool the uninformed, who would attribute the color change to LED lights or a holographic effect, but so subtle, unusual, and stunning that those of the wedding party who knew Hazel's family well would appreciate the skill necessary to create such a beautiful spell.

"Your mom did an amazing job," said Roxy finally. "You should twirl in front of the big mirror to see it better."

Hazel stepped gingerly across the room, making sure not to trample the train of the dress, and twirled in front of the full-length mirrored closet doors. She spun again and gasped when she saw the effect herself. Her eyes filled with tears again.

"How am I ever going to get through today without crying?" she said. Hazel smiled, but her lower lip was still trembling a bit.

Roxy gave her a big bear hug from behind as they both looked into the mirror.

"You're not. We're both gonna cry. It's a wedding! That's what happens, kiddo," she said. She felt certain that if she started crying, it wouldn't be pretty. It really did feel like she was losing her best friend.

"Okay, but it's too soon for that," said Hazel. She shook her head a bit as if she could shake away the emotions of the day. She turned to face Roxy. "Let me straighten your bowtie as a distraction."

"Have at it," said Roxy. The bowtie had been a bone of contention between them—or a bow of contention, as Roxy liked to joke. She'd been thrilled when Hazel asked her to be her best maid at the wedding, and even more so when Hazel said she could wear whatever she wanted. Roxy had elected to wear a teal-colored velvet suit jacket with a crisp white shirt and narrow black dress pants. Hazel's new shop manager, Jazz, had helped Roxy find everything at a deep discount on Black Friday, since Roxy hated shopping and was perpetually penny-pinching.

Roxy had planned to wear a thin black tie with the outfit like John Travolta and Samuel L. Jackson in *Pulp Fiction*, one of her favorite movies. She was somewhat dismayed when both Jazz and Hazel suggested she wear a black velvet bowtie instead. It was not nearly as badass as a skinny black tie, but it wasn't her wedding, so she'd relented.

It'd helped when Jazz showed her some pictures of the king of cursing, Samuel L. Jackson himself, wearing a velvet jacket and matching bowtie to an event. She had to admit it looked pretty sharp. Too bad she had no clue how to tie a bowtie and hers was constantly going askew.

Hazel tugged and tightened the loops of the bowtie until it looked perfect again.

"Ready for the red carpet," she said to Roxy with a wink.

There was a knock on the door and the hotel's event coordinator popped her head in.

"We're ready for you, Roxy. Five minutes, Hazel."

The two of them looked at each other, and Roxy felt a tremble of anticipation and sadness pass through her. This was it. Another half hour and her best friend would be married. She reached out to squeeze Hazel's hands, but instead, she found herself in a giant hug. They clung to each other for what felt like forever, and then finally they broke apart.

"You've got this," said Roxy.

"I'll see you out there," said Hazel. Her voice was barely more than a whisper.

"Hey, it's going to be perfect. And then we're going to party the night away," said Roxy. She mustered all the courage and excitement she could while giving Hazel her trademark wink and an enthusiastic two thumbs up.

Hazel's mother came into the room. She would be walking Hazel down the aisle since her father had passed away some years ago. It was clear she was excited for her daughter's big day, and Roxy was glad of the distraction. She slipped out of the room in the commotion of last-minute prep between mother and daughter and followed the event coordinator to the hall where the ceremony would take place; she took her spot at the front, next to the officiant and across from Elizabeth's matron of honor.

The room was still buzzing with excitement and murmurs of discussion. Roxy checked that she had the ring Hazel had chosen for Elizabeth in her left breast pocket, which she did. She took a deep breath to steady herself and avoided looking out into the crowd for fear of her nerves getting the best of her. She was used to public speaking when she gave ghost tours up in Salem, but those rarely had more than twenty people; there was easily triple that in attendance at the wedding that day in Provincetown.

All of a sudden, the crowd became quiet and the music started up. Roxy looked over at the entrance and her heart gave a squeeze. This was it. She had to try not to cry. It was Hazel's big day—it was her beginning. *And our ending*, she thought with a pang.

Much later, Roxy found herself alone at an empty table, surrounded by the detritus of the end of the night—empty glasses, dirty plates, scrunched up napkins. At least the centerpieces still looked nice. The ones that remained, that is. Several guests had already claimed the centerpieces, at the brides' insistence, and taken them home with them.

Roxy was sipping on an IPA and was, in actuality, quite content to be alone for a while. The day had been a whirlwind. The ceremony had been a bit of a blur. She'd managed to hand Hazel the ring at the right moment without dropping it, for which she'd been extremely grateful. She'd also managed to deliver her toast at dinner with the right mix of good humor and gravitas. Everything had gone smoothly, and when it turned out the bakery had mixed up the cake orders and brought them the wrong flavor—coconut instead of vanilla—there had been no dramatics. Hazel and Elizabeth had shrugged it off, but Roxy, as part of her best maid duties, made sure to call up the bakery and demand a refund. She'd gotten them a fifty percent off discount in the end, but she was proud she'd done right by her best friend.

And Hazel *was* her best friend. She knew in her heart of hearts that nothing would change that. Even when Hazel and Elizabeth had first been dating, a little over two years earlier, Roxy had never felt purposely excluded by them. She'd always had plenty of opportunities to be with Hazel alone and continue their routines. Logically, she knew that. And of course, it'd been a lot easier to see Hazel happy and in love when Roxy had also been happily in love. Or at least in like, if that was a thing.

But ever since her last relationship had ended a couple of months ago, she'd felt like things were getting a bit hopeless. She would never find anyone. She'd be alone forever.

That was silly and likely not true either. But what if she simply continued to date one woman after another, caught in a repetitive cycle of infatuation, lust, happiness, and heartbreak? That wasn't good either.

Seeing the happiness Hazel and Elizabeth shared should have been a reminder that true love exists and can find a way, but instead, their happiness made her heart ache with what she so desperately wanted but couldn't have. It made her bitter, and she didn't like it one bit.

The beer was getting warm in her hand; she set down the bottle and took a swig of water instead, trying to refocus her attention. Hazel and Elizabeth were dancing a slow dance to one of the final songs of the night. Roxy knew it was nearly the end because she'd helped Hazel finalize the playlist herself. There were only a few songs after this one: "At Last" sung by Etta James. It was a stunningly beautiful ballad even if the words stung Roxy to the core with their ode to finding love at last.

The two brides had their arms around each other loosely enough that they could look each other in the eye. Elizabeth's cool blond beauty complemented Hazel's shorter, curvier, darker looks. Roxy thought for sure Elizabeth would go for a suit, as she'd said many times she was considering it, but in the end, she'd chosen a beautiful, simple white sleeveless gown that, in the back, had an insert of deep navy accentuated with silver embroidery. And while both brides swore up and down that they hadn't shared details of their wedding day wear, somehow the dresses complemented each other as if they'd been bought to match. The way they looked at one another, lovingly, with complete trust and easy joy—it was clear to anyone how in love they were.

Of course, Roxy was glad of it, but right then, she would have done anything, just anything, for it to be her in the white dress—and she never wore dresses, so that was really saying something. The sense of longing for someone special to hold in her arms was overwhelming, and she felt her throat tighten and her eyes get teary. She'd wanted to find true love more than anything else, and she felt consistently denied. She gritted her teeth to stem the flow of tears.

That was it, she decided. Today was January first. It was a new year and a fresh start. She made a resolution right then. Or maybe it was more of a wish. She wasn't going to date anymore. No more casual flirting. No more fuck buddies. The next relationship was going to be the One, the one that sticks—even if it meant being single for a while. She knew she had a bad habit of jumping from relationship to relationship, and that ended now, she resolved.

She toasted her resolution and finished the last swig of beer in the bottle as she heard a voice behind her.

"Excuse me? Don't I know you?"

Roxy had been so deep in her own thoughts that she jumped at the sound, and the last sip of beer went down the wrong pipe. She started coughing convulsively and the person, whoever they were, slapped her on the back before going over to the bar and getting her a glass of water.

She sipped the proffered water and tried to get control of her breathing. She felt like an idiot; she wiped her face with her sleeve and saw that Hazel and Elizabeth were looking over at her in concern and several other wedding guests had paused in their conversation to look over at them. *Typical...I made a fool of myself at this wedding after all.*

"It's all right, folks, we got it," said the person who'd handed Roxy the water.

Roxy turned to face the person who'd startled the bejeezus out of her, and her breath caught in her throat.

The woman was seriously hot. She wore a finely tailored navy suit with a silver blouse and, of all things, a skinny black tie. She had dark, almost black hair, wavy and styled in a very chic asymmetrical chin-length bob with hot pink and electric blue highlights mixed in. She had a series of tiny hoops up and down one of her earlobes, and although she was wearing some intense eye makeup, she wore it effortlessly. It wasn't overdone; in fact, it was quite sexy. Roxy wondered how this mysterious person had eluded her during the rest of the wedding reception given how striking she was. She was still taking in the full effect of this gorgeously androgynous wedding guest, and had zero sense of what to say, now that she was capable of saying anything.

"I'm so sorry I startled you," said the stranger. "Hi, I'm Tessa." She held out a hand, and Roxy shook it, still somewhat in a daze.

"Hi, I'm…"

"You're Roxy, I know." Tessa looked her up and down carefully. "I'm guessing you don't recognize me?"

"What?" Roxy was confused. Was she supposed to know her? She was fairly certain she would one hundred percent remember if she'd ever seen such a striking person before. Although Tessa was only of average height and build, she was truly a commanding presence. Her sense of style, her confidence, even her posture made her someone Roxy would not soon forget.

Tessa looked a bit sheepish, self-consciously scratching the back of her neck with one hand before catching Roxy's eye again.

"I don't suppose you remember your college roommate? Freshman year? Kinda pimply brunette, super awkward, always in sweatpants?"

Roxy racked her brain for her college memories. By and large, she tried not to think about her brief stint at university since she'd never finished. But yes, now it was coming back to her. Of course, she knew she'd had a roommate, but she could hardly square the person standing in front of her with the awkward, shy, glasses-wearing girl with a long ponytail. She didn't remember the zits, but she definitely remembered the sweatpants.

Suddenly it all fell into place, and she saw the resemblance.

"Teri!?"

The woman in front of her smiled sheepishly and nodded. "Yep. But I go by Tessa now."

"Holy shit, it's been a million years." Roxy was still reeling from the glow up right in front of her. "You look amazing."

"Aww, thanks. Yeah, I may have changed a few things since freshman year of college."

"You can say that again. You look…" Roxy struggled for a moment for a word that was more appropriate than "smoking," "hot," or "smoking hot." She settled on, "really good." Tessa blushed and looked away.

"Thanks," said Tessa finally. "You look really good, too. I love that velvet jacket."

Roxy was about to invite Tessa to sit down at her table when the final song of the night came on: The Beatles' "All You Need is Love."

"Shit, I'm sorry. It's the last song of the night. I have to go to Hazel."

"Oh my gosh, yes, of course. Go. Go." Tessa smiled encouragingly. "It was nice to see you."

Roxy wanted to say, "it was nice to see you, too," but already Hazel was pulling her onto the dance floor. Pulling both of them in fact.

Soon everyone still at the reception was on the dance floor, screaming "all you need is love," laughing, hugging, dancing, and Roxy was delighted to find herself next to Tessa in the final circle of dancers on the dance floor. When it was Tessa's turn to take to the center of the circle, Roxy felt herself salivating at the sight of Tessa twirling and lip-syncing the words to the song. Everyone was laughing and cheering even as the song faded out.

Roxy, who was doubling as emcee, remembered to grab the mic and turn off the playlist before making the final announcements about transportation back to hotels, breakfast the next day, and thanking all the guests for coming.

Just like that, the wedding day was over. She found herself hugging Hazel, then Elizabeth, then Hazel again, then Hazel's mom, and then Elizabeth's parents as well, as they seemed to have an inexplicable instant connection with Roxy. Soon she found herself in the swirl of end-of-the-night tasks as they gathered the remaining centerpieces, purses, bags, and coats, in addition to grabbing several bottles of champagne from the bar for the after-party.

Only as they were all about to head to the wedding party's hotel suites did Roxy think to look for Tessa. Somehow in the midst of the hubbub, she'd made her exit, and Roxy felt disappointed she hadn't thought to invite her. It would have been fun to catch up with an old roommate. She was eager to know how she'd gone from awkward college freshman to the chic, sexy, sophisticated woman at the wedding.

Stop it, she chided herself. There was no use in thinking things like that. *You'd just want to get into her pants, and we're not doing that anymore.* Besides, tonight was Hazel's night. There was no way she was getting sloshed and making the moves on another wedding guest. Best not to be tempted.

CHAPTER TWO—TESSA

Tessa Flowers couldn't stop thinking about Roxy.
    To be fair, she'd kind of always had a crush on her—even in college when she wasn't out yet. She could smile at it all now, to an extent. Their first year of college was nine years ago. She'd dated and had girlfriends since then, including a serious relationship that had very nearly turned into an engagement. She was single now, but she didn't mind it so much. She had a job she loved, wonderful friends, and she'd gotten the opportunity to pursue one of her lifelong dreams.

And yet.

As soon as she'd seen Roxy at the wedding, her heart started pounding as if those nine years were nothing. Roxy was even sexier than she'd remembered—the suit with the velvet jacket and bowtie alone were enough to make Tessa hot under the collar. Now, her dark corkscrew curls styled short, cropped at the back and sides, but with longer tendrils at the front that framed her elfish features, Roxy was a total babe magnet.

To be honest, Tessa had been avoiding her all night. As soon as she'd seen her, up at the front of the room during the wedding ceremony, she'd felt her heartbeat speed up. Her mouth had gone dry, her mind a jumble of feelings. She'd been glad she'd decided to sit toward the back of the room along with some of Elizabeth's other work colleagues.

She'd met Elizabeth a year and a half ago when Elizabeth had started teaching history at the same prep school in Boston where Tessa taught acting and theater arts. They'd immediately hit it off, and Tessa had been excited to introduce Elizabeth to all her favorite colleagues: Britt in media studies, Calvin in sociology, and Elsa, the women's volleyball coach. All of them had subsequently been invited to the wedding and had accepted. After all, who didn't want to go to a beautiful lesbian wedding in Provincetown—even if it was in the middle of frigid New England winter?

Tessa spent most of the wedding at her table with Britt, Calvin, and Elsa, along with Elizabeth's friends from the UK who'd made the effort to come to the US—a friend from undergrad and her husband, two friends from their doctoral program who'd stayed in close contact with Elizabeth, and a former colleague from the job she'd had right before coming to teach in the US. They were a fun and friendly group; Tessa had always found British people to be hilarious in their creative swear words and, in general, to be rather jolly at events like weddings, and Elizabeth's friends were no exception. It was easy to keep her distance from Roxy and focus on the people at her own table.

By the end of the night, she finally got the courage to speak to Roxy. It was both damning and kind of exciting to realize Roxy didn't recognize her. She was conscious of how much she'd changed since college—and a lot of those changes went more than skin deep. She was a much more confident and successful person now, though apparently her confidence did not extend to talking to a former crush.

It was disappointing, then, that they'd barely had time to exchange pleasantries before the last song of the night played, and they were both pulled into the last dance of the night—a joyful, emotional group dance to "All You Need is Love."

Afterward, she watched the wedding party laughing and hugging but kept her distance. Elsa had already started the drive back to Boston, as she had a young family at home. Britt and Calvin, like her, had elected to spend the night in Provincetown; the two of them were putting their coats and hats on to trudge over to the apartment the three of them had rented together for the occasion. The plan was to do some wine tastings the next day and have a leisurely day out.

They'd just left the wedding hotel when Tessa realized one of her gloves must have fallen out of her coat pocket. She told her friends she'd catch up with them before running back inside the venue.

She nearly bumped into Elizabeth's father, Jim, who'd clearly been heading out the door for a cigarette break.

"Sorry," said Tessa.

He smiled cheerfully. "No problem, love. Say, aren't you Liz's work colleague? Tess, is it?"

"Tessa," she corrected him gently. "Yes, Elizabeth and I are work colleagues at the school."

"The Shakespeare fanatic, is that right?"

"Indeed, that's me." Tessa was impressed. In her experience, few people at a wedding took the time to remember the details of the guests' connections to the happy couple.

"Were you about to head out?" asked Jim. He was a tall, portly man with a jolly demeanor. He was playing with his cigarette lighter. If Tessa had to cast him, she'd say he'd make a perfect Sir Toby in *Twelfth Night*.

"Oh, yes. I came back in to find one of my gloves."

"You should stay! Stay for the after-party," said Jim. "Elizabeth speaks very highly of you. And any friend of hers is a friend of ours, especially one so talented and beautiful."

"You're laying it on awfully thick," said Tessa. "But I wouldn't want to interrupt a family affair."

"Pish tush," said Jim. He waved away her concerns. "You'd be most welcome. All her friends from home will be joining us, too."

"Well, if that's the case…" Tessa's heart started pounding in her chest again at the thought of spending some time with Roxy in close quarters. Maybe they could chat a bit more? Maybe this was their chance to finally connect and make good on Tessa's crush—either crush it finally and completely, or see if there really could be something between them? She'd tried to forget about Roxy for years and years, but there was still a tiny flame of desire within her that was waiting to be explored.

Jim was effusive in his encouragement to join the after-party, and Tessa let herself be convinced. She found her missing glove on the floor of the event space cloak room and rejoined Jim to keep him company while he puffed on his cigarette. Together, they walked down the hallway into the hotel lounge and past it down another hallway and up the stairs to where the honeymoon suite was doubling as the scene of the after-party.

Even though it was well past ten in the evening, everyone was in high spirits. Hazel and Elizabeth had already changed out of their wedding gowns and were now wearing matching Christmas pajamas. Hazel was setting up what looked to be a karaoke machine for everyone to use while Elizabeth busied herself pouring champagne into clear plastic cups. Roxy was smiling and chatting with her while setting out snacks for everyone. It was a real honest-to-goodness after-party.

Nearly all the folks from England who'd been at her table were there too, as Jim had said. The couple from London had already gone to bed, apparently, but Jeff and Lisa, her friends from the doctoral program, and Alexis, the colleague from her last job, were all yucking it up in a corner.

They responded with enthusiasm when they spied Tessa and waved her over. It was impossible to feel like an outsider in this group.

"Ahem!" came a voice from the sitting area of the suite. It was Elizabeth's mother, trying to get everyone's attention. She looked like an older version of Elizabeth, but still elegant and neat as a pin without a hair out of place. Her hair was a mix of blond and gray, pulled back into a sleek chignon, and she still wore her stylish mother-of-the-bride-style navy dress and bolero jacket, though she'd evidently traded in her heels for fuzzy slippers that made Tessa smile. Helen Cowrie could be intimidating, even cold, upon first meeting, but the slippers suggested there was a warmth to her, too. Tessa could tell even from observing the wedding party from a distance, that Elizabeth's mother was extremely proud of her daughter and enjoyed the role of mother of the bride immensely.

She was quite different from Hazel's mother, Rose, who, like Hazel, was on the shorter side, hair still dark brown without a sign of gray to be seen. Her style was softer, more approachable. She wore a deep emerald green chiffon dress with a long flowy skirt and sleeves, with a bodice embroidered in silver and gold lace that mimicked the flowers on Hazel's wedding gown, but in a much more toned down manner. Tessa couldn't imagine how much it must have cost to get custom embroidery done on a wedding gown, much less matching embroidery on a second dress. The effect, in any case, was spectacular.

The two mothers of the brides stood together now and were handing out cups of champagne to everyone. Tessa and the others each took one and stood by quietly, as it was evident some speeches were coming. Hazel and Elizabeth stood side by side next to their mothers, with Elizabeth's father, Jim, nearby as well. The brides looked a little tired but very happy, and soon tears gathered in their eyes as Helen and Rose took turns thanking everyone who played a role in planning the wedding and toasting their daughters' happiness yet again. Tessa felt a little woozy herself—and it wasn't because of the bubbly.

She scanned the room for Roxy until she saw her, way at the back of the suite, next to the sliding doors to the balcony. Once the toasts were over and people began drifting toward the snack table, Tessa followed Roxy to the balcony where she'd stepped out into the night.

The hotel overlooked the bay, with the lights of Boston a mere glimmer in the distance. It was cold, of course, but not dreadful; they'd been lucky that the day of the wedding had been a rather balmy forty degrees, and the temperature now was still in the thirties with little to no wind.

"I hope you don't mind my ambushing you here." Tessa tried to balance apology with playfulness. The cool winter air felt delicious on her hot face; she was mere steps away from Roxy out on the small balcony.

Roxy's face was in shadow as the moonlight backlit her features. It made it hard to read her expression. If Tessa had to guess, she'd say it was an expression of thoughtfulness mixed with concern and maybe something else. Something darker.

"Oh," said Roxy. After a moment, she relaxed into a smile. Even though the smile didn't quite reach her eyes, it still lit up her face and made Tessa feel warm all over. "Glad to see you made it to the after-party. I should have mentioned it earlier."

"No worries. Jim caught me and practically twisted my arm."

That comment made Roxy genuinely laugh, and it was a beautiful sound. Tessa had gotten the impression that Roxy had been rather sad a moment ago. Now, she looked happy again.

"That's Jim. One hundred percent. I'd call him a bully except he's so damn nice."

"He seems pretty different from his wife."

"True. Helen takes a while to warm up. No idea why she loves me so much." Roxy winked roguishly and Tessa felt her heart flutter. She wanted to reply with some flirtatious banter, but it seemed a bit soon for that.

"That's great to hear you get along."

"Definitely. They told me they'd put me up over in England if I ever came to visit."

Tessa racked her brains with what to say next. She had so many questions crowding her head. She wanted to know if Roxy was dating anyone? Where was she living these days? With whom? What was she up to? Was there any chance they would run into each other again soon?

"Will that be anytime soon?" She settled on the most innocuous question possible, and Roxy rewarded her with more information.

"I don't think so," said Roxy. She sighed, leaning on the balcony railing and looking out into the distance. "I don't even have a passport."

"You could get one."

"That would presume I have enough money to go anywhere with it." Roxy's voice turned bitter unexpectedly. She was still looking out into the distance, but Tessa had the impression she was looking more inwardly than out at the water.

"I'm sorry."

Roxy continued as if she hadn't spoken. "I'm twenty-seven. I work seasonally. Sure, I like giving ghost tours and kayak tours and whatnot. I'm good at it. But I don't exactly have savings. I can't travel. No sugar mama to pay my way." She gave Tessa a rueful smile.

"Looks like you've got an amazing friend in Hazel," said Tessa.

Roxy huffed in frustration. "Feels like I'm losing a friend right now," she murmured, and suddenly Tessa understood. Roxy was sad because Hazel was getting married. Moving on. And Roxy felt left behind.

They stood a moment, together, sharing the peace of the evening, even as Tessa was finally starting to feel the chill of the night air starting to penetrate her suit jacket.

"I know I'm being dramatic," said Roxy, "but it feels like the end of an era, you know?"

Tessa nodded. She wanted very much to put her arms around Roxy and give her a big hug and tell her it would all be all right, but she felt that would not be a good idea right then. Clearly, Roxy was laying her heart out to her because she was in the right place at the right time, not necessarily because they had a connection—yet. But it gave Tessa hope. Maybe they could develop a connection. After all, Tessa knew a lot about heartbreak and starting over.

Back in the hotel suite after-party, she could hear people singing karaoke and laughing, but they felt a million miles away from that. At any moment, though, they would be missed and pulled back inside to the noise and celebration.

Now was the time to be bold, make a move.

"What are you doing after the wedding?"

"Hmm?" Roxy was still off in the world of her own thoughts.

"Do you have any plans or place to be? It's just that I'll be staying on here in Provincetown for the winter to put on a play at the theater. I can always use extra help if you're interested. It would be great having a friend here in town to hang out with after work, too." She smiled at Roxy.

"It's funny you should say that. I'm staying in Ptown over the winter, too. Normally, I do ski lessons in Vermont, but I did something to my knee in October and decided to skip it. A friend of a friend knows the owners of the brewery in town, and they agreed to let me work part-time over the winter. I've always thought it would be cool to learn how to brew beer."

"That's amazing," said Tessa. "What a fabulous coincidence." She couldn't help smiling like a fool.

Roxy nodded in agreement. "Coincidence? Or Fate?" She wiggled her eyebrows at Tessa and chuckled. "Who knows?"

"Absolutely," said Tessa, who had been thinking exactly the same thing. "I'll be here through March. I got a grant to put on a Shakespeare play here in the theater. We'll need help building and painting sets, stage crew, things like that. I don't suppose you'd be interested in helping out? If your schedule allows it of course." *Please, please, please say* yes.

"That sounds rad," said Roxy enthusiastically. "I did a little bit of that in high school. Sounds like fun. Though…I don't know anything about Shakespeare." She appeared embarrassed to admit such a thing.

Tessa put a reassuring hand on her arm—mostly so she could touch Roxy. The velvet of her jacket tickled her fingertips. She gave her arm a squeeze and smiled.

"That's kind of the point. A lot of people think they don't like Shakespeare. Or don't understand his plays. But I'm kind of sort of on a mission to change that." This time it was her chance to wink playfully at Roxy. "I swear, it'll be fun. And you'll get paid. We have money in the grant to pay for anyone who helps put on the show in whatever capacity."

Roxy looked impressed. "Sounds like a heck of a grant."

"It is." Even now Tessa could hardly believe her project had been picked. Only six percent of requests were funded. It was so prestigious that the school principal had had no qualms about approving a three-month leave for her to complete the project and hire a long-term sub to teach her classes. She was pretty certain that the school's website had already updated her bio to say, "award-winning drama teacher." She felt a thrill of pride mixed with concern. She hoped the project would live up to the hype.

"Congratulations. That's amazing. And I'd love to help. I'll have to check the schedule at the brewery, but it's pretty part-time."

Tessa made sure to exchange phone numbers with Roxy right then and there. She wasn't about to let another opportunity pass them by. Later, much later, she would open up the listing in her phone with Roxy's number and stare at it. It really was the workings of Fate or magic or destiny that she and Roxy would be spending an entire winter together in Ptown. As a hedge witch herself, Tessa was well aware of the powers of the natural world around them and the dormant magic inside all living things. There was nothing random about this meeting, she was sure of it.

She felt a thrill of anticipation and desire as she pulled the covers up under her chin, and it was a long, long time that night before she could finally slip into sleep.

CHAPTER THREE—ROXY

R oxy couldn't sleep that night.
    By the time the after-party was over, she was amped up again.
The karaoke had sucked her in, and as a best maid, she couldn't refuse,
especially when a somewhat buzzed bride who also happened to be her
best friend told her they *had to* sing Indigo Girls' "Galileo" as a duet. It'd
been fun, even if Roxy wasn't normally the karaoke type.

She couldn't help noticing that the whole time she was standing next
to Hazel singing, Tessa's gaze hadn't left her face even for a moment. It
made her hot just thinking about it. She'd been looking at Roxy with an
intensity that was difficult to forget, and it made Roxy want to kiss her.

In fact, that was why she was out after midnight on a cold winter's
night on Cape Cod. When she'd finally found herself alone in her room at
the inn, all she could think about was taking Tessa's face in her hands and
landing a deep kiss on her pretty pink lips.

The image was so intense and alluring, she had to go for a walk to
cool off. She walked the empty streets of Ptown at a brisk clip, hoping
the chilly night air would cool her down and calm her mind. Even as she
trudged the streets as fast as she could, a cold wind whipping at her face,
all she could think about was Tessa. A million questions crowded her mind.
Was Tessa a lesbian? Had she been hitting on her at the after-party? Was
she looking for a hookup while she was in Ptown over the winter?

The idea of a hookup was extremely appealing at the moment,
knowing as she did that Hazel was leaving on her honeymoon the very
next day and starting a new chapter of her life with Elizabeth. In fact,
Hazel and Elizabeth would be gone for several months, as Elizabeth had
gotten a sabbatical from her job and a giant grant to go to a bunch of

archives all over Europe. They would be traveling a lot and having a grand old time seeing all the places Roxy could only dream of: London, Paris, Florence. Would Hazel even have time for a phone conversation to catch up? Meanwhile Roxy would be alone in a new place all winter.

Plus, wasn't the perk of being best maid that you got to have a hookup at the wedding?

Something light and easy and fun with Tessa sounded like the perfect balm to cure her wounds and distract her from the loneliness and despair of having no one special in her life.

Or would it?

Wasn't this the same logic she'd been using for ages in her dating life? She'd resolved that very day to stop the vicious circle of one-night stands, meaningless hookups, and casual dating, and here she was, hardly a few hours later, already thinking about breaking her resolution.

What was she to do? The intensity of Tessa's gaze, the look of longing that Roxy felt sure she'd seen painted across her features as she'd looked at her that evening, suggested that it would be very, *very* difficult to keep her resolution if indeed they were going to spend the winter together in Ptown.

As her mind turned these thoughts over and over again, she found herself getting closer to the inn again. She wasn't ready to turn in yet, though, so she found her way to the beach nearby instead.

Her boots immediately sank into the sand, making it difficult to walk, and it was incredibly dark out. The moon was obscured by dark clouds, the beach full of shadows.

She was beginning to regret her decision to come to the beach lest she end up with a twisted ankle in the dark when she heard the sound of someone or something thrashing in the water near to shore.

She looked carefully at the shoreline, barely able to make out the water from the night sky; it was pitch-black at this time of night. After scanning quickly, though, she managed to make out the disturbance in the water. To the right of where she was, north along the beach, she saw frothing water and the unmistakable signs of a person, a human being, thrashing for their life.

Without a second thought, Roxy sprang into action.

She began to run toward the thrashing person, her mind focused on that person who was in grave danger. She didn't even think for one moment about how cold the water would be, or the fact that in the dark, she could indeed twist her ankle on something hidden in the shadows.

Instead, all she could think about was saving this person, whoever they were.

She splashed straight into the cold waters of Cape Cod Bay, the adrenaline in her veins momentarily making her unaware of how freezing cold it was. As luck would have it, the person thrashing in the water was very close to shore, and the water was only at Roxy's thighs when she grabbed hold of the stranger and hefted them up.

Everything was a blur as Roxy felt the weight of the person slam against her and then almost immediately slip out of her hold again. She lost her balance momentarily and fell backward into the cold embrace of the bay.

The icy waters enveloped her chest, knocking the breath out of her. She wheezed, trying to inhale; darkness edged in on the sides of her vision and she saw stars. Finally, her legs found the bottom again and she hefted herself up, looking around frantically for the drowning person.

For a second, everything was calm and silent, and Roxy began to shake with cold, her teeth clattering in her mouth. And then the splashing and thrashing resumed right next to her.

In the dark, Roxy bent over and managed to find arms and armpits, and she slid her own arms under the other person's arms, locking hands in front of their torso, and heaving them up.

The other person inhaled loudly, desperately, before falling backward limp. This time, Roxy held her ground and managed to catch this person—a woman, she could tell now—before they both fell back into the water.

The woman was utterly naked, Roxy realized with a start, and her large breasts glowed strangely in the moonlight, which illuminated the entire shore as the clouds parted. She looked away, ashamed of having seen what she'd seen.

She realized with a start, though, that she was going to have to move soon or they would both freeze there in the water. The woman had fainted from exertion or cold or both, and Roxy maneuvered her around so that she could pull her to shore.

Finally, they were on the cold beach, her clothes soaked, the woman's skin frigid with cold and her body exposed. The woman was tall, very tall, with a substantial bust and hips. Roxy was also tall, but rather spare by comparison. Her mind was working slowly, as if her brain was frozen too, but she realized through the haze of cold that she should call emergency services.

She lay the stranger down gingerly on the sand and began patting down her soaked pants and jacket pockets, a sharp poke of panic cutting through her when she couldn't find her phone. It must've fallen into the water; she'd never be able to find it—

No, that's right. The phone wasn't with her. She'd left it safely in the apartment, charging, since it had been almost dead after all the photos and videos she'd taken at the wedding.

She looked up and down the length of the deserted beach, trying to quash the feelings of panic and dread clawing up her chest from her stomach. It was after midnight on January first, no one was out and about, and there were no houses or hotels along this stretch of the beach.

Fuck. I'll have to take her to my place. But how?

It came to Roxy that she could take the woman to her apartment if she draped her across her back, as she'd seen once in a movie. It was the only method she could use to carry the woman, who was still unconscious, back to her apartment. It was imperative to get there so she could call 9-1-1 and get help.

It took quite a bit of effort to heave this person onto her back and drape her properly so she wouldn't immediately slide off, and Roxy had to stop several times to catch her breath. Never in her life had she been more grateful for her regular workouts back in Salem with Jazz. All those squats were finally paying off.

It felt like years, but eventually they made it back to Roxy's apartment.

The warm air of the little studio engulfed her completely, and she shivered violently. The woman on her back shifted awkwardly, and her wet, stiff legs barely managed to keep her upright. Roxy staggered to the bed and let the body slide off her. Every part of her felt frozen, including her brain. She could hardly think straight, her mind focused on warming up.

Through the painful cold in all her limbs and mind, she forced herself to focus on the woman she'd pulled from the water. She knew that she needed to revive this person. What if she were dying? What if she had water in her lungs?

Before these thoughts overwhelmed her, Roxy noticed the phone hooked up to the charger in the kitchenette of the studio. *Oh, thank goodness.*

She bounded over to the phone and picked it up.

Nothing.

Black screen.

Roxy's numb fingers were clumsy, thick-feeling, as she pushed all the buttons and tapped frantically at the screen.

Still nothing.

"Fuck!"

She looked around, moving her fingers from the cord that was, indeed, snugly fitted into the phone charging port, up to the plug. There, with an involuntary groan, she realized that the plug had not been fully pushed into the outlet. The phone hadn't been charging the whole time she was out. It was dead.

She heard the woman sigh as though in pain, and she nearly jumped out of her skin. What on earth could she do? She had to act fast.

Thankfully, she had to do a CPR and first aid training every year as a kayaking and ski instructor, so after checking to make sure the woman was still breathing (she was), and whether she was conscious (she wasn't), Roxy toweled her dry and wrapped her up with warm blankets. The woman was oddly okay-looking. There were no signs of hypothermia that Roxy could detect; even her fingernail beds were pink and healthy looking, with no signs of the blue or purple that Roxy could easily see in her own nails.

She cranked up the heat in the apartment and pulled her freezing cold, wet clothes off and wrapped herself in a blanket. She paused.

What now? Should she go looking for someone who could call emergency services for her?

She looked again more carefully at the stranger in her bed. She looked like she was...sleeping. But what if she was in shock?

Before she could make a decision about what to do next, the woman moaned. It was evident that she was waking up, albeit fitfully, pushing the sheets and blankets away.

The woman's eyes fluttered open, and she looked around the room and at Roxy, her expression frantic. When she opened her mouth, the sounds that came out were...inhuman. It was like no language Roxy had ever heard—and she'd heard quite a few as a tour guide and ski instructor.

"It's okay! It's okay!" Roxy tried to reassure the stranger. "Do you speak English?"

The fear in the woman's eyes subsided only a fraction, but she was listening to Roxy carefully. Roxy tried again. "Are you okay? I'm here to help you. I pulled you out of the bay and brought you to my house. I'm not going to hurt you. I promise."

The skin along the woman's throat moved in a way that looked unnatural, as though the vocal chords underneath were moving and rearranging themselves. Roxy was nauseated at the sight of it, but she was soon distracted as the woman began to speak again—this time in English, and with a human-sounding voice, albeit low and weak.

"Water…I need water…" The words came out slowly, but they were clear and comprehensible.

"Sure, of course. Hold on." She ran to the kitchen to get a glass of water and handed it to the woman, who had now pushed herself up into a seated position and was looking around the room with curiosity and confusion.

The woman took the glass from Roxy and did something strange. She tried to stick her whole face into it. Only her mouth and nose fit—sort of. Then she dipped her other hand into the water and began smearing it over her face and shoulders. Finally, before Roxy could stop her, she proceeded to pour the rest of the water over her legs.

"Stop! What are you doing?"

"*More…water.*" The woman shoved the now empty glass at Roxy and tried to push herself up to standing. Her movements were clumsy, though, and soon she was falling back onto the bed, clearly frustrated. "Water…please…more."

Roxy's thoughts were still slow from the cold, in spite of the warm blanket around her. Finally, an idea came to her—the tub.

She started a bath for the stranger, trying to keep the temperature warm but not hot. She stood up and turned to go back to the stranger, only to find she was right behind her.

The woman pushed her out of the way and stuck her hand under the faucet, then winced.

"No. Must be…cold." She struggled for the words, and then began fiddling with the knobs, turning them every which way.

"Wait, wait," said Roxy gently. "Here. Let me."

She turned the knobs to cold and let the woman feel the water again. "Better?"

"Yes," said the woman emphatically, climbing into the tub with gusto and sitting down in what was now quite chilly water coming from the faucet. Roxy tried not to shudder at the cold, but maybe the woman was right? Maybe this cooler water was better at preventing a sudden temperature shock that came with hypothermia?

The woman's expression of contentment had soured as she observed her legs and ran her hands over them, as if searching for something that should be there but wasn't. She looked at Roxy again, her face screwed up in concentration and then, finally, comprehension.

"Salt. Please." She indicated the water with one of her fingers. "Salt." Her voice was stronger now, demanding but also pleading.

"Salt? Gosh, okay," said Roxy, trying not to think too hard about the fact that there was an almost-drowned, entirely naked woman sitting in her clawfoot tub, full of icy tap water, who was now demanding salt. She must be delirious. The cold water must've affected her brain, that was it.

In the kitchenette, she checked her phone. It was up to five percent now. Enough to call nine-one-one. She reached out to pick it up and make the call, but she hesitated.

If the woman was experiencing symptoms of shock, it would be better for her to be in the hands of professionals, right? Then again, how would it look if she called in the emergency now, and not as soon as she'd gotten her home? And what if the woman was here illegally? English was clearly not her first language, and her washing up on shore, naked in the middle of the night on January first was strange and suspicious indeed.

"Salt!" The woman's voice cut through Roxy's thoughts.

She decided to get the salt and see what happened next. Roxy rummaged through the cabinets and found a small saltshaker. Back in the bathroom, she handed it to the woman, and watched with surprise as she turned the top to the spout setting and poured the entire contents in the tub.

"Hey! That's all the salt I have here." Roxy realized afterward how silly it sounded. She could afford some more salt, after all. Things weren't *that* desperate.

The woman swirled the salted water around, and as she did, something strange happened to her legs.

They completely disappeared.

In their place, there was a shimmering, green, scaly fish tail that took up nearly the length of the tub.

From the waist up, the woman was the same. She leaned back in the tub, closed her eyes, and heaved a long sigh of relief.

Roxy rubbed her eyes. Was this real? No, she must be asleep and dreaming. This was all a dream, that was it. This could not be real...a *mermaid*? Was it really possible?

Her sleepy brain reminded her that witches, vampires, and fairies were all real, so why not mermaids? Very true, Roxy replied to her internal monologue.

The mermaid sighed again, deeply, and stretched her arms out and above her head. Only then did Roxy remember that the mermaid had nothing to cover up her ample bosom. She blushed and started fumbling around the small bathroom, finally deciding on a couple of wash rags.

"Here, take these…to cover up, you know…" Her voice trailed, and she tried to keep her focus on the woman's (the mermaid's?) face.

She opened her eyes and took the rags from Roxy.

"Ah yes, good idea!" She dipped the rags into the water and laid them on her chest. "Feels very good, thank you." She lay back in the tub again, closed her eyes, relaxed, then rewetted the rags and placed them, this time, on her face.

Roxy supposed if she had no qualms about being bare-chested, who was she to judge?

"So…uh…hmm." She wasn't sure what to start with. A name? An identity? Why she'd been in the bay that evening? She settled on a name. "What's your name?"

"Hmmm?" The mermaid was clearly in a reverie of contentment after her ordeal. Roxy cleared her throat and tried again, this time louder and slower.

"Name? Do you have a name?"

The mermaid exhaled deeply again before removing the rags from her face and looking at Roxy curiously.

"Name?"

"Yes. What are you called?" Roxy paused, trying to think how else to explain it. "I'm Roxy. What are you?"

Comprehension lit up the mermaid's bright blue-green eyes, and she smiled and nodded. "I'm Mo."

A mermaid named Moe? Roxy couldn't believe it. It didn't sound like a magical creature's name at all!

"Moe? That's your name?"

The mermaid nodded, but then added almost as an afterthought, "This is how you say it in your language. For easy."

"Oh. I see. Like a nickname," said Roxy. "I get it. So…what is your name in your language?"

After a moment, the mermaid spoke again, this time with her inhuman voice, her real voice, Roxy supposed. The first syllable of the name was, indeed, something that approximated "Moe," but the rest was a jumble of sounds that went beyond what human vocal chords were capable of. It sounded beautiful and musical but indeed…unsayable.

"That's pretty but I think you're right. Let's stick with Mo." Roxy smiled, and Mo nodded happily.

"Good. You Roxy," said Mo, and Roxy nodded.

"So…do you want some privacy?" said Roxy, realizing all over again how awkward it was for her to be with this naked stranger—even if now some of her nakedness was decidedly less human. "Should I leave?"

"No, no. Not necessary," said Mo. She was more serious now. "How did I come here?"

Roxy folded a towel and sat down next to the tub. She felt exhaustion threatening to overtake her again, and it felt good to sit. Slowly, she recounted the details of how she'd found Mo in the bay, thrashing and later unconscious, and how she'd managed to bring her here. She could feel Mo listening to her carefully, and she noticed that Mo was both listening to her words while also studying her lips and throat. The longer Roxy talked, the more natural Mo's English became. Was it possible she was learning to speak English merely by watching Roxy talk? It certainly appeared that way.

"How did you end up in Cape Cod Bay?" asked Roxy, when she'd finished her side of the story. "What do you remember from before?"

Mo crossed her arms over her chest and considered the question, her eyebrows knitting together. Her hair had started to dry over the course of their conversation, and Roxy could now tell that her hair was bright green. Her eyebrows, however, were a mix of light green and dark brown, while her skin, which had originally seemed nearly translucent, had now darkened to almost a bronze color. Her eyes were a deep, deep blue-green. She was unusual looking and incredibly striking, even without taking the tail into consideration.

"I remember…not much. I remember swimming and feeling a current pulling me in a direction. It was an unusually warm current, so I followed it. I thought maybe it would lead to a new food supply…but when I was caught in it…" She shivered from the memory.

"What was it?"

"It was…magic. Bad magic." Mo's expression was now one of fear and confusion. Realization dawned on her features. "Evil magic. Like a magic net to catch me."

"Are you sure?" Roxy had never heard of a magic fish net to catch mermaids, but again, she was learning a lot of new information that night. She was not one to deny the possibility though; she'd seen enough strange things, what with having a witch for a best friend, to know that there was more to the unseen world than most people knew about.

Mo nodded vigorously, her large green curls shaking violently around her face. She raked her hands through her hair in frustration. "Yes. Evil magic." She caught Roxy's gaze, her eyes now full of fear.

"Are you a witch? Did you try to catch me?"

"What! No! Never. I'm not a witch. I swear."

Mo grabbed her wrists in her own, water sloshing out of the tub and onto Roxy's legs and the bathroom floor.

"Swear to me you are not a witch, you mean me no harm."

"I swear." Mo's grip tightened on her wrists so tightly, Roxy felt pain shooting up her arms. "I *swear.* I swear on my grandfather's grave. I'm not a witch. I'm not magical at all." Roxy felt a little pang inside her as the words came out, as if her heart was skipping a beat. She had always tried to suppress those feelings of jealousy. Of being a mere mortal. Someone with no magic.

But Mo was not appeased.

"You *are* magical. I can feel it. I feel the magic inside of you. Tell me the truth!" Her voice was desperate, like a growl, and Roxy wondered if her life was in danger. Mo's features were distorted and angry.

"I'm *not* magical!" There was that little pang again, like a tiny electric shock deep inside of her as she said those words. As if it was a lie and Mo was right that there was some magic in Roxy. But how could that be? "I'm not. But I have a friend. Who is a witch. We hang out a lot. Maybe you're smelling her on me." *Was that even a thing?* "But she's a *good* witch. She'd never set out a net for a mer—"

Mo let go of her right arm and clamped her hand over Roxy's mouth. Her hand smelled salty, but also a little bit like sand and sun.

"*Don't say it.*"

"Don't say mer—I mean, uh, what you are?"

"Exactly. Don't say it." Mo settled back into the tub. It seemed she had accepted Roxy's explanation. "If you are not the one who intended to entrap me, or your witch friend, then there is someone else. Someone evil here. And they will use that word to catch me."

It took Roxy a moment to figure out what Mo was saying, but finally she cottoned on. "Ohhh, so like, saying *that word* will somehow alert the person who's trying to catch you?"

"It's possible. I have heard of such magic nets. My mother has told me about them. That our…people…hold special magic and there are some evil sorts on land who would like to harvest that magic from us."

The word "harvest" made Roxy shudder. How exactly did a magic practitioner *harvest* the magic of a merperson?

"That sounds horrible," said Roxy. "Is there any way you can get in touch with your people from here? To help you?"

Mo considered the question for a moment before shaking her head. Her eyes shone brightly with tears. "No, I don't think so."

They sat in silence for a moment. Roxy's mind was spinning. If someone, or some people, had set a magical net in Cape Cod Bay to lure a merperson, to harvest their magic, *and* they were also capable of including a magical alarm on the word "mermaid" to help locate this being, then they were surely incredibly powerful magicians. Perhaps more than a witch, even. Roxy had read some of Hazel's histories of magic, written by other magical folk, and there were mentions in there of other human and human-like magical practitioners—sorcerers, wizards, enchanters. Perhaps they were right here in Provincetown and Roxy had somehow muddled their plans...

Mo's mind was evidently going in the same direction.

"Roxy, you have *saved* me from a fate worse than death." She grabbed one of Roxy's hands in her two large, elegant ones and gave it a kiss, her voice full of gratitude. "In the water, I remember now, I lost my tail. The net...it forced me to have my legs there on the shore, to keep me from swimming away. And you saved me." Tears now ran down her cheeks.

"Okay, but what now?" Roxy tried to pull her hand away unsuccessfully. Mo was overcome with gratitude.

"You don't know what could have happened. It was luck...it was *fate*...that brought you to the beach today. I am forever in your debt."

"What? No. Not at all," Roxy protested. "I did what any normal, kind person would do."

"No, that's not the case at all," said Mo. "You know this to be true. Not all people are as brave as you."

Roxy felt herself blushing. It *was* true. How many people would jump into freezing cold water to save a stranger in the middle of the night?

"Roxy."

"Yes?" Roxy met Mo's gaze, and saw how earnest and grateful she was, and her heart squeezed a bit. There was fear at the edges of Mo's voice, and the gravity of the situation hit Roxy all over again. There was evil lurking on Cape Cod that winter, and Mo was in danger. And maybe Roxy was too, for helping her.

"What is your heart's desire?"

The question was startling and out of the blue, and yet Roxy answered almost without thinking.

"To find the love of my life. My soulmate."

"I will help you do this." The intensity of Mo's gaze increased, and, incredibly, Roxy felt a strange sensation pass between her hand and Mo's, which were still clasped together. It was almost as though an invisible ribbon was sliding around their clasped hands, binding them together. "I swear, as long as you protect me, I will help you find your heart's desire."

Something like a small shock of electricity sizzled between them, and then their hands were sundered.

"It is done," said Mo, a certain finality in her voice as she lay back into the cold, salty water of the tub.

"What is done?" Roxy was unable to keep a bit of panic out of her voice.

"We are bound now," said Mo, her eyes closed, as if it were the most logical thing in the world. "You help me, I help you. Now, if you don't mind, I need to get some rest."

In a daze, Roxy stumbled out of the bathroom and back into the rest of the apartment. She felt exhaustion wash over her again as she lay down on the bed, careful to avoid the wet spot left by Mo when she'd poured the water all over her legs. Her mind was too numb to think about what had happened, but oddly enough, she felt relieved. Perhaps all she needed to find happiness was a mermaid sworn to help her find true love.

CHAPTER FOUR—TESSA

Three long days had passed since the wedding night. Three long days without bumping into Roxy anywhere in Provincetown, despite her best efforts. Tessa had gone to a different coffee shop each morning, eaten lunch out twice at the brewery where Roxy said she was working, and gone for several late afternoon walks around town, hoping she'd bump into Roxy, but no dice.

She'd tried throwing herself into the work at the theater, but as materials and people were still only beginning to arrive, there wasn't much to distract her.

It was in this moment that Tessa was grateful for her hedgecraft.

She tried to remember what her mentor Freya had taught her—hedge witches worked to become one with nature, to see themselves as part of nature and the natural cycles of life. Hedgecraft was there to help her center herself and take a break from the pressures of the world as well as her own anxieties.

Tessa had discovered hedgecraft when she'd needed it most—after her big breakup. She'd moved from New York City, away from her shared apartment with her ex, to a small cottage in Amherst, the same town where she'd gone to college.

There, the owner of the cottage, who lived across the garden from the cottage in a slightly larger cottage, had recognized her as a spirit in need of solace. Freya had taken her under her wing and introduced her to the life of a hedge witch. She'd shown Tessa that everyone had magic within them that simply needed awakening. With the right tools and mentorship, Tessa had recognized that power within her, though it had been significantly weakened, according to Freya, by the stresses of her life until then.

It had felt like the most natural thing in the world to Tessa, who had grown up with stories of Baba Yaga and Aladdin's lamp, the humpbacked pony, and the (original) little mermaid. Magic had been in all the stories Tessa's mother and grandmother had whispered to her in Polish at her bedside. She'd fallen asleep every night to these magical tales—what could be more natural than learning to do magic herself?

Hedgecraft was not a very flamboyant magic, Tessa had found. It was built on the foundation of working with nature and with one's own instinct. It had a practical side to it, with herbal remedies for various ills, but Tessa had found herself attracted to the tenets of spiritual healing. She'd realized, by working with Freya, that she'd abandoned her own instincts while in a relationship with someone whose personality had come to dominate her own. She'd set aside her own wishes and interests in that relationship, and slowly, through her hedgecraft, she'd started to understand all that she'd given up.

In addition to this journey of self-discovery, Tessa found solace in the practice of everyday magic and ritual. It was especially useful in a situation where things were out of her control—like with Roxy. She wanted to see Roxy again, talk to her, get to know her. She was desperate to spend more time with her. It had irked her that Roxy was there, so close, somewhere in Ptown, and yet their paths weren't crossing.

This morning, Tessa woke up early and pulled out her hedgecraft journal from the bottom of her suitcase and looked through it until she found the spells and rituals she needed.

After drinking some of Freya's personal blend of calming tea, Tessa leaned back in her chair and closed her eyes. She imagined a beautiful forest right after a rainstorm. The sun was beginning to peek through the tree branches. Tessa imagined that the rays of sunshine were her magical powers, shining down on her and soaking into her skin. She felt magic within her begin to grow, like a spark coaxed into a small flame.

She let the flame flicker within her, trying to hold onto that sensation. Her magical abilities were still minor, she knew that. Freya had told her that it would take time and practice to develop them to the next level, without losing too much energy each time.

Tessa decided not to try to call on more magic. She used the magic she had to perform a new home ritual to cleanse the space of her rented apartment and to imbue protective powers into some wards she'd created for her home and the theater. Inside each linen sachet, she placed dried lavender from Freya's garden, shells from the beach in Provincetown, and an evil eye protection charm.

She felt better afterward. Taking several slow steady breaths like her therapist had recommended didn't hurt either, she thought to herself with a smile.

Tessa placed the wards in her bag and checked her watch. It was time to go to the theater, where she would finally get to see Roxy. The night before, she'd texted Roxy a second time, unable to hold back her excitement, and invited Roxy to the theater for a tour and dinner after, and, amazingly, Roxy had accepted.

Tessa put on her coat and hat and walked to the theater, even though it was still another hour before she was supposed to meet Roxy there. Tessa's body was buzzing with excitement, and she needed the movement to distract her.

As she'd expected, it was quiet in the theater; so far, it seemed she was the only person there. She used the opportunity to hang up her wards as unobtrusively as possible.

When she was finished, she went to the greenroom to check herself. She'd chosen her outfit for the day extra carefully, wanting to strike the right combination of sexy, casual, and warm, as the old theater was very drafty. She'd settled on some classic thespian wear—black turtleneck, black cigarette pants, and her high-top Docs. They weren't the warmest shoes, but she couldn't resist how they added a bit of edginess to what otherwise appeared to be a rather conservative outfit.

Finally, she heard the side door doorbell go off, and she jumped out of her chair as if stung. This was it. She was here.

She nearly ran the length of the hallway and down the last couple of steps to the side door entrance and pulled it open. A sharp winter wind blew in and Roxy stepped inside quickly.

"Brrr! Cold out there," said Roxy as Tessa closed the door with some difficulty. The wind was putting up a fight. But at least the sun was shining. Roxy stamped her feet to warm up and took off her coat, hat, and scarf. Tessa showed her where she could hang them on some hooks in the hallway before leading her into the theater.

"Glad you could make it." Tessa tried not to let her voice betray the nervous energy that was coursing through her.

"Absolutely," said Roxy with her trademark giant grin—the smile that made Tessa get all melty inside.

They stepped into the theater from the back of the house entrance. Tessa had purposefully led them back to the front of the old theater so Roxy could get the whole effect.

As they stepped inside, their steps and voices were immediately muffled by the soft red carpeting and velvet-backed seats. That magical hush of a theater was palpable in that grand old lady of a building.

"This is it," said Tessa. She gestured expansively. "What do you think?"

She watched as Roxy looked around and took in the beautiful, heavy red velvet curtains, the well-worn boards of the stage, and the beginnings of a set—thus far, a few flats that were in the midst of being painted white—then Roxy turned to look at the side balconies with their carved wood decorations painted in cream and gold. The theater was in an older style that was absolutely Tessa's favorite kind, and she hoped Roxy liked it too.

"It's amazing," said Roxy. "I feel like I'm back in high school. The good parts."

Tessa chuckled. "I know what you mean. I've been a drama geek forever." Tessa gestured for Roxy to follow her to the stage.

The old wooden floors creaked in welcome, and, under the bright lights, Tessa could fully appreciate Roxy's physical attributes all over again. She was tall and lean, but clearly strong and muscular under her maroon and gray plaid flannel shirt and slate-colored work pants. She had an oblong face, with small pink lips and bright shining brown eyes. Her short curls were all chaos after pulling her ski hat off, but the disheveled look only made her that much more rakishly attractive. Tessa felt her heart flutter. She could only imagine how sexy it would be to feel those strong arms around her, pulling her close.

She felt her cheeks blaze with a heat that had little to do with the stage lights.

"Come on," she said finally. "I'll give you the backstage tour."

They exited stage right, through a door, and then walked through several backstage areas full of old sets, music stands, racks of costumes and tables full of various props.

They continued their conversation as they walked.

"Drama geek, eh?" said Roxy. "I had a bit of that myself. But I never wanted to act. I like all the behind-the-scenes stuff better. What about you? Are you going to act in the play?"

Tessa shook her head. "It's not my main passion, and I'm okay at it. I used to think that was what I wanted, but after a lot of trying and failing at that, I realized I always wanted to direct. In high school, I did small parts, tech, and directing. I did some acting and a lot of directing in New York, but it was super stressful all the time. Teaching gives me the chance to direct but without the stress. It's a ton of fun." It felt good and right to say that, Tessa realized. So many people had criticized her for "giving up" on her dream of being a professional theater director in New York or London, that she'd started to doubt herself. Saying it all out loud to Roxy, though, she realized it was all absolutely true. She loved working with her students and watching them blossom on the stage.

They arrived at a door where they were greeted with the sharp, pleasant smell of cut wood that always made Tessa feel right at home. She fished out a key and opened the door, flicking on a light switch that revealed several saws, lengths of wood, and a large worktable covered in various tools and smaller pieces of wood.

"Whoa," said Roxy. "I feel like I'm back in shop class."

Tessa chuckled again. "I hope that's a good thing. I'm terrified of saws, so this is not my domain, but if you're into it, I know Chayo would love some help."

The door opened behind them with a squeak.

"Did I hear my name?"

They both turned to see Chayo entering the workshop, and Tessa couldn't help smiling to see her best friend arriving even as a shiver of anxiety thrummed through her. What would she think of Roxy after listening to Tessa wax poetic for years about her?

"Chayo, meet Roxy. She's going to be helping out with the play. And she loves tools, apparently."

Chayo held out a hand to Roxy and they shook.

"Nice grip," said Chayo with genuine admiration.

"Thanks," said Roxy. "You're not so bad yourself." They grinned at each other in unabashed butch admiration. Chayo was a large butch Latina with a stylized pompadour haircut whose presence filled the room, with a style completely distinct from that of Roxy, but Tessa was pleased to see that they were hitting it off so quickly. She and Chayo were super close after their experiences in New York together, and she had really hoped Chayo would like Roxy. After all, she'd certainly heard enough about her. "Are you working on the sets in here?"

Chayo nodded, handing a cup of coffee from the tray she'd been carrying to Tessa and offering one to Roxy, who took one also. Chayo set down the beverage carrier and walked over to the worktable.

"Sets, props, all sorts of stuff. I love building things, and for this play, our set designer Nick has some really rad ideas."

Tessa watch as Chayo showed Roxy some of the designs for the play and was delighted by Roxy's positive impressions. She'd been collecting ideas for this project for years, and of course Chayo had a lot of good suggestions too. She was easy to work with, and Tessa had been thrilled that Chayo was available to work on the project.

She couldn't help but feel a thrill of anticipation completely unrelated to her feelings for Roxy as Chayo showed her the plans for the sets and major props. There was a boat that would be built for the production, two different sets, a throne, as well as various tables and stools. This was her baby, and she couldn't wait to see it all come together.

Soon enough, Roxy and Chayo were deep in conversation about the throne, Chayo's first project in the wood shop, and Tessa was starting to feel like a third wheel. Still, she was glad that Roxy was so interested in the project.

She heard the doorbell and left them together to talk wood grains and stains. She hated to leave Roxy, but soon enough she was busy with signing for packages, talking to the costume mistress about new fabrics that had arrived, and answering some phone calls.

Tessa was getting off the phone when her assistant director came in. Joy was petite with a personality, and voice, in inverse proportion to her stature. She was high energy, though, and hilarious, and absolutely one of her favorite people working on the show with her, old enough to be her mother, but with the energy of someone half her age.

"Got some news you're going to want to hear," said Joy. A giant smile painted itself across her face as she handed Tessa what appeared to be another contract. The financial side of putting on a play with an actual budget was somewhat terrifying, and Tessa was eternally grateful that all that kind of stuff was in Joy's domain. "Look carefully, sweets."

Tessa scanned the contract, looking for the slot where someone's name was usually typed in.

Lisa Collins.

"We got her!" shouted Joy with evident glee. "We got 'Broadway's newest shining star'!"

Tessa had to hide her emotional turmoil as she processed the news. She smiled as big as she could and hugged Joy. "It's great news. Amazing."

"This is going to put us on the map. Congrats, hon." Joy kissed her on the cheek before dashing out the office door again to pass along the information to the costume mistress and props master.

Tessa, meanwhile, sat back down hard in her office chair. She and Lisa had a…complicated history. At one point, they'd been engaged, though only for a week, before Tessa broke it all off. It had been one of the worst experiences in her life. Lisa was demanding, controlling, and narcissistic. All the things that made her a terrible life partner, though, were exactly what would make her perfect for the part Tessa had in mind for her. They'd entered a tentative post-relationship friendship, but Tessa wondered how well Lisa would keep up her end of the friendship. She wasn't known for forgiving and forgetting. Tessa hoped Lisa would keep things professional. She was going to be the star of the show, so that would, she hoped, keep her happy and manageable.

What about Roxy?

Somehow Tessa hadn't really thought the whole plan through until just that moment. Having Roxy work on the show meant bringing her, inevitably, into contact with Lisa. Ptown was not a big place. They would have to interact. And Lisa knew what Roxy meant to Tessa.

She had a sinking feeling that maybe this wasn't the best idea she'd ever come up with.

CHAPTER FIVE—ROXY

The past three days had been a blur for Roxy. Between learning the ropes at the brewery, babysitting a lost mermaid whose life was in danger, and trying to make plans to spend time with Tessa at the theater, Roxy was too busy to feel sorry for herself and her singleton status.

So far, Mo had been content, for the most part, with staying in the apartment and taking cold saltwater baths as needed—usually two or three times a day so far. They appeared to comfort her, and it was the only way she could return to her natural state. She was somewhat taller than Roxy, but only slightly, so for now Mo was wearing Roxy's clothes around the apartment. Her chest didn't quite fit into Roxy's shirts, though, as Roxy was very flat chested, so Roxy had ordered some more clothes online—with input from Mo. They'd just arrived that morning and Mo had been in a visibly better mood after putting on a fluffy sea-green sweater that reminded her of home.

Feeding Mo had been a bit more challenging. Mo insisted on raw fish and seafood; canned tuna had been a bust, unfortunately. Roxy wasn't used to shopping at the fish counter, and she'd worried it would be expensive, but one of the perks of feeding a mermaid out on Cape Cod was that fresh and rather inexpensive seafood was not too hard to come by.

Watching her eat the food, however, was another story. Mo ripped into the fish and swallowed raw shrimp whole. It was enough to turn Roxy's stomach. After making that mistake twice, she started making sure she was in another room while Mo was eating.

She'd been nervous to leave Mo in the apartment alone, even after the first twenty-four hours. Finally, though, she had her first shift at the brewery and there was no more putting it off. She'd been nervous the whole time at the brewery, wishing Mo had a cell phone so she could call her periodically and check in, but so far, at least, it appeared that her fears were unwarranted. Mo was still getting used to life on land and was fearful for her life. She had no reason to leave the apartment.

That morning, though, she'd been anxious to get out of the house, bored even. She'd begged Roxy to let her walk with her to the theater. Roxy had refused. They still didn't know what kind of danger Mo was in and it was safest to wait at least three days. Three had special meaning to magical creatures, Roxy knew, and this mention of the number three did the trick. Mo stayed put.

As always, just in case of emergency, Roxy wrote down the name of the theater and the address on the same sheet of paper where she'd written her phone number and the name and address of the brewery. She wasn't sure what kind of emergency Mo might have without her, but better safe than sorry.

The time passed quickly working in the wood shop, and Roxy enjoyed the companionable quiet there. Chayo was friendly and knowledgeable, and she made Roxy feel useful right away. She'd forgotten how much she loved working in a theater; it reminded her of some of her favorite memories in high school. She was a little disappointed that Tessa had to leave, but she'd enjoyed seeing her in her element, and she was glad she'd agreed to come and work on the show. It would be a good way to find out if there was something more to this spark between them.

Eventually, a couple more crew members joined them in the wood shop, and they had to pause in their work on the throne. The props mistress and the lighting director needed to consult with Chayo on the colors for the throne and the paints they would use for maximum effect. Roxy, whose knowledge of theatrical lighting was limited to working the lights during the show, rather than designing effects, felt distinctly out of place. Right then, though, Tessa showed up again, and she gestured for Roxy to follow her.

There was a sparkle in her eye that Roxy noticed yet again. Her enthusiasm was catching.

"Well, don't you look like the cat that swallowed the dairy," said Roxy. Seeing Tessa again, she couldn't help but notice how her turtleneck hugged her curves perfectly. She felt a little tug of desire deep inside. How hadn't she noticed how hot she was back in college? She had no idea how she had lived in close quarters with this woman and not made a move on her.

"What?" Tessa's expression changed to one of puzzlement.

"I mean, you look really pleased."

Recognition dawned on her. "Yes. Yes! I found out that the actor we want to play Leontes has agreed to take the part."

"Isn't it usually the other way around?" asked Roxy. "Aren't the actors the ones hoping to get cast?" She thought of high school days and the drama, pun intended, of looking at the cast list, the joy of those cast, and the despair and disappointment of people like her, who hadn't gotten a part.

"Sometimes, yes. But in this case, I wanted a really big name, which meant convincing someone already successful to take a job that won't pay as well as her usual offers."

"In that case, congratulations," said Roxy with a smile, and Tessa smiled back so big she thought her face would crack. It made Roxy want to hug her—but she supposed it was too soon for that familiarity. That would be weird, right?

They had been walking down a winding hallway that, Roxy realized, probably wound around the back of the theater. They arrived at a door painted bright green and walked through. Inside, Roxy saw a bunch of mismatched furniture, the kind found in a hotel or bank lobby in the 1990s, and all of it outfitted with green upholstery. Three of the walls had mirrors with lights along the sides, and there were doors leading to bathrooms as well. The dedication to green was confusing for a moment until she recalled that the actors' prep area was often called "the greenroom."

"Dontcha love it?" said Tessa, and Roxy did. The whole effect was homey rather than sterile, and she noticed that there was even a small refrigerator in a corner for people to store their snacks during rehearsals or shows.

"It's really nice."

Tessa looked so damn proud of herself, it was adorable.

From the greenroom, Tessa showed Roxy the quickest way to the wings, and then over to the costume and props area, and some rehearsal rooms. Eventually, they ended back outside the shop room where Roxy had been working with Chayo.

"That's the tour," said Tessa cheerfully. "Are you still up for drinks and dinner tonight?" There was a small tremor in her voice and the smile was quickly replaced with a look of concern.

"Sounds good to me," said Roxy. There was nothing necessarily romantic about drinks and dinner. Not if it was with an old college roommate, right? "How about you come to the brewery? I'd love to introduce you to the owners. I haven't had a chance to try their food yet."

Plus, she knew she'd get an employee discount on the food, which was important. She'd blown a lot of her winter savings on wedding stuff, and she was low-key broke at the moment, especially with all the recent fishy expenditures. It wouldn't last long, she knew, as she was still waiting on her last paycheck from the tour company she worked with in Salem, and soon enough she'd get paid from the brewery, but still. Best to be careful with her wallet for a while.

"That sounds perfect," said Tessa, with real enthusiasm. "I'd love to."

Roxy spent the afternoon working on a rather simple, though large, table that would be used for a banquet scene. Chayo was working on part of the throne, but she checked Roxy's work periodically and refreshed her memory on how to work the different saws and sanders. They fell into an easy work routine, and Roxy found herself enjoying the company. Occasionally they'd talk about some technical element of the work or make a little joke, but mostly they worked in friendly silence, and when it came time to break for the evening, Roxy invited her to join them at the brewery, to which Chayo readily agreed.

Later on, as Roxy walked to the brewery to meet her new friends, she wondered if she'd done right by inviting Chayo. After all, Tessa had invited *her,* so it was really her decision to invite others, wasn't it?

Then again, it wasn't a date. There hadn't been any kind of discussion of it being a date. They were meeting as friends, and friends only. Roxy reminded herself of her resolution yet again. Even *if* she wanted to pursue Tessa romantically, it had to be serious. She had to take it slow. And nothing slowed the course of a romance than bringing along a third wheel. Plus, Mo was clearly an added complication to any romantic pursuits Roxy might have at the moment. Hiding a fugitive mermaid in her house—how could she ever explain that to Tessa? Mo had made it very clear that the fewer people knew of her situation, the safer she'd be, and that was another reason not to race into a relationship.

Pleased that she'd rationalized her decision so well, Roxy stepped into the brewery—this time, from the restaurant and tap room entrance rather than the employee entrance. She'd been in the tasting room already. Henry and Jack had done a tasting for her on her first day. It was important that she knew what kinds of beers they brewed and their philosophy on tastings, they'd said.

The tasting room was just as pleasant and inviting as she remembered, perhaps more so now that there were other customers there and the sounds of conversation and cutlery on dishes filled out the space. The tables and chairs were of dark wood with brass elements throughout the space, plus several "snugs," upholstered stools, and a dark patterned carpet that gave the room the feel of an Irish pub. Much of the décor on the walls was typical for Provincetown—paintings of nineteenth-century whaling ships, old whaling hooks, and fishing gear. Sprinkled in between, though, were photos of Pride parades, framed leaflets for things like the Lavender Menace and the Bluestockings, and multicolored buoys arranged in rainbow order.

She supposed it was to be expected for a brewery called the Pride of Ptown. It was a neat little pun that she enjoyed.

"Hey." A voice called out to her from one end of the bar, and she saw that Henry was over there putting away some pint glasses. He waved her over.

Henry was very tall and pale, with a shock of bright red hair and dark red beard. His seaman's dark navy sweater perfectly showed off his trim physique, and a small gold hoop in one of his ears glinted even in the dim pub lighting. He smiled broadly at her as she walked over and slid onto a barstool. She had some time to spare before Tessa and Chayo were due to show up. Henry, as well as his brother and co-owner Jack, were friendly and easy to talk to; soon enough she was telling Henry all about the different saws she was going to be using for the play. Henry, as it turned out, was a bit of a woodworking geek himself.

When Tessa showed up, she sat next to Roxy on one of the stools. Jack showed up behind the bar as well, and introductions ensued. Jack was quite a bit shorter than Henry, with hair that was more of a dark auburn, also cut short. He had no facial hair, but his eyes and nose were clearly similar to those of his brother, and they both shared a fair Irish complexion. Together they made a good-looking pair, and though Roxy's romantic interests leaned another way, she could recognize that their looks would contribute to the success of their business, especially in a place like Ptown that was so popular with gay men as well as lesbians.

"Hi, it's nice to meet you," said Tessa, leaning over the bar to shake hands with Henry and Jack. She looked around the pub and took in the décor, including a large stained-glass mosaic behind the bar depicting a rainbow and the phrase "All are Welcome." "I love that you really take the 'pride' part seriously. That's great."

"Oh yeah, definitely," said Henry. "I mean, if you can't be out and proud in Ptown, what's the point?"

Tessa nodded vigorously in agreement. "I agree. That's why when we stage *The Winter's Tale* in March, Leontes will be played by a female actor as a female character. We're doing a major gender swap." She practically beamed with pride.

"Really? That's an amazing idea," said Jack. "I read that play in college, and Leontes always kind of freaked me out. He's so intense and scary. Making him a woman sounds way more interesting. It totally changes—"

"—the whole pregnancy narrative," finished Tessa enthusiastically. "I know. It just hit me one night as I was researching the play."

The two of them continued to discuss the implications of the casting in a way that made Roxy feel completely clueless. She'd never liked Shakespeare, mostly because she'd struggled to understand one word of his plays in school. Diagnosed with dyslexia later on, after dropping out of college, she'd understood better why she'd struggled with reading so much. The diagnosis had come too late for her, though, and now she only associated Shakespeare's plays with a sense of personal failure and frustration. Aside from that, she had never even heard of *The Winter's Tale*. Hearing Tessa and Jack enthuse about it made her feel a bit of FOMO. Maybe she should try to read it? She was working on the sets after all. And their enthusiasm for it made her want to know more. She *had* learned some strategies now for reading that might help, too. She'd have to think about it.

She turned back to Henry, who had finished with the glasses and was now putting the finishing touches on that evening's drinks list. The tasting room featured a full bar with an extensive cocktail and mocktail list in addition to their beers.

"That looks great." Roxy admired the rainbow chalk art on the signage.

"Thanks." Henry gave the sign one last look before turning back to Roxy. "What can I pour you?"

"How about some more of that Gose?" said Roxy. She'd loved that beer in particular at her initial tasting.

"No problem," said Henry. He was so easy to work with, and a little less intense than his brother. Roxy felt an immediate kinship with him. Maybe it would be easier to make new friends in Ptown than she'd expected. And queer friends, too. Henry was gay, Jack was trans, and Chayo was clearly also queer…it was the opportunity of a lifetime to get to hang out with so many cool queer people.

Just then, Chayo showed up. She spotted them at the bar and Roxy waved her over.

"So, should we get a table or sit at the bar?"

Roxy glanced over at Tessa to see what her preference was, and if she wasn't mistaken, she thought she saw a look of disappointment and confusion pass over Tessa's features. Roxy felt a pang, yet again. Had she been wrong to invite Chayo? Had Tessa's invitation truly been for a date?

The moment passed, though, and Tessa smiled. Maybe Roxy had imagined her disappointment.

"Let's sit at a table. It'll be easier to talk."

"Sit anywhere you like. It's self-seating," said Jack. "But I recommend one of the snugs while they're still available."

Tessa and Roxy grabbed their drinks and walked over with Chayo to one of the snugs, which even had its own little door. It was like entering a tiny private room in the pub. The noise of the other patrons faded into the background as they shut the door behind them.

The conversation bounced lightly between the three of them, moving from the play and the sets, to the schedule of rehearsals, which began the following Monday, to the latest television shows and movies they were watching. After a while, Henry and Jack showed up and crowded in with them with a couple of flights of tasters with both current offerings and some experimental ones the brewery was working on. Their regular evening bartenders had showed up, and the two of them had some time to spare before things got busy.

"Mmm, these beers are wicked good," said Chayo with an expression of deep appreciation as she took another sip of a piña colada porter. "Damn."

"You know, we almost called the brewery that," said Jack.

"What?"

"Wicked Good Brewing."

Everyone chuckled at that.

"That would've been a great name for a brewery around here," said Tessa enthusiastically.

Roxy nodded in agreement. "Why didn't you go for it?"

"We really thought about it," said Henry. "But in the end, we really wanted to embrace the Pride side of Ptown. It's so meaningful to us and to so many people who come to Ptown."

"Absolutely," said Chayo. "I used to work summer jobs here as a teenager and it opened my eyes to how life could be. Living openly, you know?"

Henry and Jack both nodded enthusiastically.

"Absolutely," said Jack. "There's something so special about having a business in Ptown and one that is queer and trans owned at that. We wanted to make sure that we helped keep Ptown queer."

"Do you ever get complaints?" asked Tessa. "From straight or cis patrons, I mean?"

"A few, here and there, but not a lot," said Henry. "We make sure to fly our Pride flag out front in the high season so folks know what the 'pride' in the name is referring to."

"That sucks about the complaints," said Roxy. "This is such a cool place. And the beers are so good."

"So good," echoed Tessa and Chayo.

"Thank you," said Jack. "It means a lot. And the complaints haven't made a difference in how we run things. Some people will complain about anything."

Jack's last comment launched them into a discussion of one-star reviews of national parks that Tessa had seen online, and the conversation moved on. Soon enough, their food arrived, and Jack and Henry excused themselves to see to the running of their business. It had been so nice to have them there, chatting all together, Roxy thought. She hoped they could all hang out again soon. She had managed to forget about Hazel and her own feelings of loneliness; instead, she felt warm and included.

She couldn't help noticing Tessa's gaze lingering on her every so often when she thought Roxy wasn't looking. She was intrigued, and she had the feeling, yet again, that Tessa's interests went beyond friendship. She was flattered, of course, but she was trying her hardest to keep her own feelings in check. The old Roxy would have found it oh so easy to slide into something fast and fun with Tessa, but the new and more mature Roxy didn't want that. She wanted to know there was more than just sexual potential. There was no point, for example, to starting something with Tessa, if she'd never see her again after the show production. That's not what she wanted.

She was brought out of her reverie by a knock at the snug door. Before anyone could say anything, the door swung open. On the other side stood a strikingly beautiful woman with brilliant green eyes and long, platinum blond hair. The woman's gaze swept over them imperiously. It finally landed on Tessa.

"Here you are!" she said in a mixture of frustration and ownership. "I've been looking all over for you."

Roxy glanced over at Tessa and was surprised to find her blushing deeply.

"Lisa, this is Chayo, our head carpenter—I think you already know one another. And this is Roxy, one of our stage crew." Tessa took a deep breath. "Roxy, meet Lisa Collins, our Leontes."

Lisa's gaze lingered uncomfortably on Roxy's face before settling back on Tessa.

"And your ex, don't forget," said Lisa, with a snarl of a smile.

Roxy's mouth fell open. This was Tessa's ex-girlfriend? A sinking feeling nestled into the pit of her stomach. How could she have thought she had any chance at all with Tessa? She felt very silly for entertaining romantic notions about Tessa or her interest in her. Clearly, she was used to dating gorgeous celebrities and her glances at Roxy meant nothing.

She realized with a start just how much she'd taken for granted that Tessa was interested in her romantically, and now she found herself surprisingly disappointed. She was also confused about Lisa's cool, appraising look. If looks could kill, Roxy was very sure she'd be dead.

Chapter Six—Tessa

Tessa felt her whole throat go dry even as the rest of her was sweating profusely.

Lisa.

Lisa freaking Collins, her ex-fiancée, the Broadway starlet, the star of her show, was standing there in the door of their snug, looking as arrogant as ever, and an entire week early in Ptown.

She'd only *just* had her agent fax over the signed contract. There was no way Tessa had been expecting her to arrive the same day. Not when rehearsals hadn't even started. Not when she'd been hoping to use that week to hang out with Roxy, if she was very honest with herself.

"*Well?*" Lisa's cool, clear tones rang out with the trademark imperiousness that would make her a perfectly terrifying Leontes on stage and a perfectly terrifying person off stage. "Aren't you going to invite me to sit down? I'm *famished.*"

"Oh, yeah, um, of course," sputtered Tessa. She was sitting with Roxy across from her and Chayo next to her, so Lisa slid in next to Roxy. *How awkward.*

An uncomfortable silence fell over the table that Tessa didn't know how to break. Finally, Chayo handed Lisa a menu.

"We just ate," she said. "The food came out super fast and it's all delicious. I'll raise our little flag here to signal the server."

Each snug had a small switch that when engaged, would lift a little flag on the door to let the server know that the table needed something.

Lisa took the menu and studied it for all of a minute. French onion soup and Caesar salad, guessed Tessa. It was her standard order.

There came a knock on the snug door before it opened.

"What can I get you?" asked the server.

"French onion soup and Caesar salad," said Lisa, and Tessa felt her stomach clench. Something about that order brought back a cascade of complicated feelings—their past shared intimacy, their past arguments, the horrible breakup… She avoided Lisa's gaze and carefully studied the wood grain of the table, certain she could feel Lisa's eyes boring into her head.

"Anything else?"

"I'll have an eight-ounce pour of the cherry pie porter," said Roxy.

"I'll do a pint of the chocolate gingerbread stout," said Chayo.

"I'll have a glass of Chardonnay," said Lisa after a pause.

The server left and Tessa felt it was safe to lift her gaze again.

Wrong.

Lisa was looking right at her. Another silence stretched out between them at the table. This time it was Roxy who tried to rectify the situation. Tessa felt utterly tongue-tied.

"So….not much of a beer drinker, huh?" said Roxy to Lisa.

"No."

Another awkward silence. Chayo coughed.

Finally, Tessa ventured to speak directly to Lisa again.

"I wasn't expecting you here for another week," she said. "We only just got your signed contract today."

"That explains a lot," said Lisa, rolling her eyes. "It figured Ramón was behind with everything. I suppose he also didn't inform you that I was arriving tonight?"

Tessa shook her head. Unless Joy had gotten the news and simply forgotten to pass it on to her, which seemed unlikely.

"I'm so sorry. Neither I nor the assistant director, Joy, got any forewarning. Obviously! Otherwise I hope you know that I would have come out to meet you. Did you take the ferry? Or fly in?"

"I drove," said Lisa. "Fortunately, I suppose, otherwise I really would have been up shit creek with no one knowing I was coming."

The server returned with the drinks and Lisa's food. It was a relief to Tessa that there was some activity at the table to distract them from how awkward the situation was. She took the opportunity to order a hot toddy. Her body had quickly gone from hot to cold again, and she found herself shivering under her many layers.

Why, oh why, did Lisa still have this effect on her? Like she wasn't good enough. Like she was just an appendage to Lisa's success. Like she was a little kid with dirt on her face.

Next to her, she could feel how annoyed Chayo was. Chayo had been one of her closest friends in the New York theater scene, and she'd helped Tessa realize that her relationship with Lisa was unsustainable. Many late-night discussions with Chayo had revealed to Tessa that Lisa had taken advantage of her and controlled her in their relationship, and she knew that Chayo hated Lisa for what she'd done to Tessa. It was a true testament to their friendship that Chayo had agreed to work on the show, knowing that Lisa would be the star.

Across from her, Roxy sat quietly, evidently cowed by Lisa's appearance. And Lisa had been sizing up Roxy when she first arrived. It was so awkward Tessa could hardly stand it. As soon as Lisa finished her food, she had to find a way to break up their evening. The tension was getting to her. How on earth was she going to get through the show? She was beginning to doubt the logic of inviting Lisa to be the star.

"I'm so sorry, Lisa, that I didn't get the news in time. You must be tired after that long trip. Luckily, your lodgings are very close to here and very comfortable. I'm not sure they are ready for check-in, though, so we'll have to put you up in a hotel."

Lisa looked at her as if searching for something in her face. Tessa wondered what she was looking for. Signs that she was still in love with her? She hoped not. She was done with all that. She knew better now.

"That won't be necessary. Ramón already made a reservation at a boutique bed-and-breakfast for this week somewhere around here." She paused. "This Chardonnay is surprisingly decent." She looked around the table, her expression unreadable. "I'd love to hear more about the preparations for the set." Her gaze landed on Chayo, her eyes full of an unspoken challenge.

Tessa wondered if Lisa remembered Chayo at all. She was one of the friends who'd come to their shared apartment after the breakup to gather up Tessa's things. She'd been too nervous to go back for them herself after their final argument.

She probably did. Lisa never forgot a face.

Chayo, realizing that Lisa was directing her inquiry to her, as head carpenter, launched into an overview of the sets and major props and where they were in the process of making everything. It was a much more detailed and technical overview than what she'd outlined for Roxy earlier in the day. Her tone of voice was authoritative and knowledgeable, and Tessa hoped to goodness it would be enough to establish Chayo's authority on the tech side of things. Lisa was known around theater circles for having lots of her own "suggestions" for all aspects of shows. She was a bona fide diva.

Lisa appeared satisfied with Chayo's relation of things, however, and she turned her gaze to Roxy, sitting next to her.

"And you? How did you get involved in the show?" There was a quiet edge to the question.

"Um, well, you know, I'm not an actual theater professional or anything. But Tessa and I went to college together, and we met recently at my best friend's wedding. Turned out that we were both going to be spending the winter in Ptown and she invited me to help out. I can always use the money," she added, and then looked like she immediately regretted it. Lisa cocked an eyebrow.

"And what are your theater credentials?"

"You don't have to answer that," interrupted Tessa. Lisa was clearly trying to make Roxy feel bad, and Tessa felt her temper flare. "I invited Roxy to help. She's a jack-of-all-trades, with plenty of amateur theater experience. Certainly, more than enough for what she'll be helping out with backstage. The point of my grant is to get the public involved in putting on a Shakespeare production. This is meant to be a community-facing project."

"Roxy's got a great handle on the tools," added Chayo, sensing Tessa's annoyance. "She's going to be a great addition to the crew." She smiled warmly at Roxy, and Tessa was grateful. Roxy smiled at both of them.

Lisa looked nonplussed. "No offense meant."

Oh sure.

"None taken," said Roxy gallantly, finishing off the rest of her beer as though to show just how little offended she was.

Lisa's Chardonnay was nearly gone, and Tessa was just about to suggest asking for the check, when the door of the snug flew open and a stranger appeared in the doorway.

The person who stood at the entrance to the snug was stunning—and in a completely different way than Lisa.

Her features were open and friendly, with a heart-shaped face, large blue-green eyes, a curvaceous body, and shockingly bright green curly hair that cascaded down her back. Her skin shimmered in the dim light of the pub, somewhere between bronze and copper. She was unusual and fascinating. Tessa could feel her jaw drop open.

"Roxy!" said the stranger, her voice melodious and low, with a hint of a foreign accent. "Here you are!"

"Mo!" Roxy looked white as a sheet.

Tessa was shocked. She didn't think Roxy knew anyone else here in Ptown. All of a sudden, Tessa was filled with certainty that this must be Roxy's latest conquest. She was a player, after all. Wasn't that what Elizabeth had told her a million times? And this beautiful creature must be her most recent. It figured she was only in Ptown three days and she'd managed to find the most beautiful woman on Cape Cod to bed.

Her thoughts flew to this conclusion in mere seconds, and the accompanying emotions filled her with disappointment, confusion, sadness, and anger. Yes, anger. She was angry with herself for even thinking she had a chance with Roxy.

"Please to let me in," said Mo unceremoniously, gesturing to Lisa to get up.

Lisa, apparently utterly confused at being ordered around by a stranger, got up automatically and Mo slid into the booth. She then gestured back at Lisa to sit down again, which she did.

All of them at the table were immobilized by the appearance of this unusual and stunning stranger who appeared to be quite comfortable in the snug between Roxy and Lisa. Tessa was on pins and needles to know who this person was and her relationship to Roxy. Were all her plans to be with Roxy going to be foiled before she ever had a chance to try?

CHAPTER SEVEN—ROXY

"What are you doing here?" said Roxy to Mo in a whisper that she hoped dearly no one else would hear.

"You were gone all day. What was I supposed to do? I am hungry and there is no fish at home."

Mo clearly hadn't gotten the message about whispering and answered at full volume.

Roxy looked at her watch.

"Crap. I'm so sorry, Mo. I lost track of time. But I thought we agreed you'd stay in the apartment."

"I'm tired of the apartment," said Mo petulantly. How did she learn to whine in human form, wondered Roxy briefly, before her thoughts were interrupted.

"So, Roxy, you going to introduce us, or what?" said Chayo, giving her a rather stern look that Roxy had no idea how to interpret but which immediately made her nervous.

"Oh! Yes. Sorry, uh…" Roxy had no idea what to say, but she had to offer some kind of explanation. She looked over at Tessa and realized that she was watching her carefully. She had to come up with something for Mo. An identity that made sense but that excluded the possibility of a romantic relationship. "Mo is my…sister. I mean cousin. I mean, my sister-cousin. I mean, not like *that*. Oh God. I mean, we're so close we could be like sisters. But she's my cousin."

The words came out fast and jumbled. It all sounded ridiculous.

"*She's* your cousin?" said Lisa, the incredulity dripping off her tongue.

"By marriage," added Roxy. *Fuck*. That wasn't what she'd wanted to say. "We grew up together. So, you know, we're almost like sisters. Mo is, uh, temporarily homeless. She's staying with me in Ptown for now."

Mo nodded. At least she'd cottoned on enough to play along.

"Roxy is my savior. My protector," added Mo solemnly.

"Wow," said Tessa with admiration now in her voice. She looked at Roxy, and Roxy felt warm from the tips of her toes to the top of her head. She was certain she was blushing. It'd been a long time since anyone had looked at Roxy with such overt admiration. "You're quite the hero."

The heat in Roxy's face intensified.

"Oh, gee, it was nothing—"

Lisa stood up and interrupted with her queenly voice. "I think I'm ready to go to my lodgings now. Tessa, will you escort me?"

Roxy felt a stab of jealousy go through her. Luckily, Chayo saved the day.

"I'd be happy to show you to your lodgings, Ms. Collins," she said with more charm than Roxy was prepared for. Chayo opened the snug door, stepped through, and put her hand out to help Lisa out of the snug all in one swift movement. Lisa, who was apparently not quite as rude as Roxy had initially suspected, accepted the offer, if somewhat reluctantly. Roxy noted the look of longing on Lisa's face that appeared and disappeared just as swiftly. She recognized it from her own romantic misadventures in the past. Was there still something between Lisa and Tessa?

Once Chayo and Lisa were gone, it was much quieter and spacious in the snug. The server came back and cleared away some of the dishes and took an order for a plate of seafood for Mo. Roxy hoped to goodness that she'd be okay eating cooked fish and shrimp as opposed to the raw stuff she'd been wolfing down back at the apartment.

"She is an unpleasant person, is she not?" said Mo matter-of-factly.

"The server?" Roxy was confused.

"No. This…Lisa Collins. She was very rude." Roxy had to hide a smile. Mo's own speech came off as condescending and rude.

"I'm so sorry, Tessa. My cousin is very, uh, forthright," said Roxy.

"It's okay. Lisa is not for everyone. And she likes to be in charge and get her way."

"You see?" said Mo, as if Tessa's affirmation made it all right to say whatever she liked about Lisa.

"Yes, but it's not nice to say stuff like that about people, Mo. Not with human beings. I mean, you know, my friends?" Roxy tried to emphasize the last word, hoping the significance of the word would impress Mo and really hoping Tessa didn't notice her weird remark about human beings.

"It's fine, really, Roxy," said Tessa, and she gave Roxy's arm a squeeze. It was the smallest of gestures, but Roxy felt a spark of connection instantly.

"Thanks," she said, her mind suddenly blank. What had they been talking about?

"What will you be doing here in Provincetown over the winter?" said Tessa.

"I will be helping Roxy. She helped me and I will help her."

"What will you be helping her with?"

"I will help her find her true—"

"My true calling," interrupted Roxy before Mo could finish and say, "true love."

Mo gave her a look of confusion that she answered with a wink. Did mermaids know what a wink meant? It was impossible to know.

The food arrived. Roxy had ordered Mo the grilled catch of the day with garlic sauteed shrimp. Even though she'd just eaten, it all smelled delicious.

Mo wrinkled up her nose at the smell of it though. She picked up a fork, (they'd been practicing at the apartment) awkwardly holding it in her fist, and tried stabbing a piece of shrimp.

"Why is it *hot*?" asked Mo, looking at Roxy with dismay.

"Just try it!" said Roxy encouragingly. "She, uh, normally mostly eats sushi," she said to Tessa by way of explanation.

Mo took a small bite of the sauteed shrimp and made a face.

"Ugh! It's awful."

"Oh no," said Tessa. "Is that not what you wanted?" She sounded genuinely concerned, and Roxy had no idea what to do. She couldn't have Mo eating raw fish right there in the restaurant.

"Maybe try the fish?" said Roxy.

Mo nibbled a bit of the grilled fish. She made a face of disappointment but kept eating.

"This is…better," she said.

"Oh good," said Roxy. "Eat up. Maybe the shrimp was too, uh, garlicky."

"Maybe next time she could try the seared ahi tuna," suggested Tessa helpfully. "That's almost like sushi."

Of course, thought Roxy. Why hadn't she thought of that?

"Great idea," she said, giving Tessa a grateful look. She let her gaze linger on Tessa's face and found that she didn't look away. Finally, Roxy looked back at Mo, whose eating habits were still rather wild.

"Mo, come on," she muttered, elbowing her. How someone so beautiful could eat in such a disgusting fashion was beyond Roxy's comprehension. Bits of fish were all over Mo's face, and she was eating with gusto now, shoveling fish and even shrimp into her mouth with both hands, the fork abandoned on the table. It would have been funny if it weren't so utterly disgusting.

What would Tessa think of her now? She stole a glance at Tessa and was relieved to see that Tessa was holding back laughter on her side of the table.

Roxy felt a bubble of laughter in her chest rise up. Suddenly the whole situation seemed completely absurd. There she was, at a pub, with an incredibly attractive woman who was clearly attracted to her as well, and with a mermaid disguised as a human being with terrible table manners.

Before she could stop, a hoot of laughter escaped her mouth. The more she tried to cover her giggles, the harder she was laughing. Soon both she and Tessa were laughing so hard they were clutching at their stomachs and gasping for air.

Finally, Mo finished eating and surveyed them carefully.

"You are laughing? Why so?"

Roxy had no idea what to say. The last thing she wanted was to insult Mo. Who knew how she'd react?

Tessa came to her rescue.

"I'm sorry. I made a funny face at Roxy. It's my fault. I was… imitating Lisa."

This explanation made sense to Mo, and she nodded. Her serious demeanor was undercut by the sheen of butter and garlic around her mouth, and Roxy had to work not to start laughing again.

"Yes, Lisa is too serious. She needs to…how do you say? Lighten up."

At this pronouncement, Roxy felt sure she'd lose it all over again, but Tessa showed herself to be a consummate performer. She nodded along with Mo and kept her expression neutral.

"Yes, I expect that is absolutely true. She could definitely use some help lightening up." She paused for a moment, as if thinking. "You know, maybe you could help with that, Mo. What do you think? Maybe you could help us out with the play? You could be Lisa's assistant. That is, if you want to. No pressure. It sounds like you are going through some stuff."

Roxy wasn't sure that having Mo at the theater, much less working with someone as clever and discerning as Lisa, was a good idea.

"Wow, that's such a nice offer, Tessa. Mo and I will talk about it at home," said Roxy, elbowing Mo hard.

"Ow!" said Mo, rubbing her side. "Why did you do that?"

Roxy put her head in her hands.

"I'm sorry. I didn't mean to cause problems," said Tessa. "Talk it over and let me know. We can always use more help." She smiled winningly at both of them, and Roxy could feel her heart melt a little more. If only Mo wasn't so socially inept, this would all be a lot easier.

❖

Roxy and Tessa settled up soon after that, and they all left the pub. Tessa went to check on Lisa and how she was settling in, and Roxy frog-marched Mo back to the apartment as quickly as possible.

"What is the rush?" said Mo once they were finally back in the studio apartment. She flopped on the bed in a clumsy way that bespoke the fact she was still struggling with her permanent human form.

Roxy pulled up a chair.

"The thing is, you can't just show up like that when I'm with other people."

"Why?" She sounded genuinely hurt.

"Because you're going to give yourself away."

Mo looked at her blankly.

"As a mer—"

"Don't say it!"

"Ack, sorry. As a non-human."

Mo nodded sagely. "I see. So how do I be more human?"

As if that wasn't the question for the ages.

"Just…try to say *nice* things. Or don't say anything at all. People don't like to hear mean things."

Mo looked skeptical. "But this means not saying the truth. My people always speak the truth."

"Try not to think of it as lying…think of it more as being kind."

Mo mulled this over before finally sitting up and nodding again. "I think I know what you mean. Be nice. Especially to the Lisa Collins. She will be the star of the show, yes?"

Roxy nodded.

"And she is the former lover of Tessa?"

Again, Roxy nodded. Mo narrowed her eyes and studied Roxy carefully. Under her scrutiny, Roxy felt herself blush. She thought in that moment of Tessa, sitting across from her in the snug, eyes sparkling, face flushed with laughter, looking beautiful.

"And *you* are in love with Tessa!"

"What!?"

Mo wore a triumphant grin, pointing at Roxy to emphasize her conclusion.

"Yes, I see it. You love her and she loves you."

"That's not possible, Mo. We barely know each other."

Mo clearly didn't believe her. She sat back on the couch, arms folded across her chest, looking pleased as punch.

"Seriously, Mo, that's not how human love works. Love at first sight—that's just nonsense. Sure, I mean, I *like* Tessa. I'm interested in her. And I *think* she's interested in me. Maybe. I dunno." She threw her hands up in the air in frustration. "Now that her ex-fiancée is here, an actual Broadway star, maybe they will get back together. Isn't that how it always is—the star of the show and the director?"

Mo looked at her blankly.

Of course she had no clue what Roxy was talking about. How could she? She could have no way of knowing what Broadway was or what it meant that Lisa was both beautiful and famous—and probably rich, too.

Comprehension dawned on Mo's features. "I see. You are worried that Tessa loves Lisa." She chuckled in that odd manner that Roxy hadn't yet gotten used to. Her chuckles sounded more like a seal barking than anything remotely human. "You are so silly!" She threw her head back and barked ever more loudly.

Finally, the laughter stopped, and Mo looked again at Roxy with a look of incredulity and humor.

"Can you please explain to me why you're laughing? Am I being unreasonable right now?"

"Yes, of course you are unreasonable. It is so obvious that Tessa loves you, not Lisa."

Hope began to take shape again in Roxy's breast. "Are you sure?"

Mo nodded and smiled warmly. "Yes, clear to me as water. She looks only at you."

Roxy's heart fluttered a bit, and she involuntarily touched her arm where Tessa had squeezed it a mere hour earlier.

"See? You know it. And you love her too."

"Okay but, Mo…you really have to say 'like,' not 'love.' You have to know someone a long time to love them. First like, then love."

Mo gave her a look as though she'd just grown a second head. "That is the most ridiculous thing you've said so far, Roxy."

"Fine, whatever. I thought we were talking about how to make sure you pass for human, anyway."

"Of course, of course," said Mo, her gaze still steady on Roxy, as though trying to make her out, like a puzzle. "Talking to you is already helping me understand the humans."

"Oh yeah?"

"Oh yes. I see. Humans do not want to say their true feelings. They say what is not true to hide what they really feel. I do not yet understand why that is. Why hide feelings? My people do not do this."

"Clearly."

Mo continued as if Roxy hadn't spoken. Maybe mermaids didn't understand sarcasm.

"Maybe humans are scared to say true feelings?"

"You might just be on to something," said Roxy. She paced around the living room, trying to give Mo's question a real answer. "We're scared. All the time. We don't want to be rejected. We don't want to tell people how we really feel because what if they don't feel the same way? Then it hurts even more."

Roxy paused, her mind suddenly miles away from Provincetown and the tiny apartment and Mo. Her mind drifted back to her most recent ex. The one she thought was finally the One. She and Amy had seemed so perfect for one another. They'd met two summers ago doing the kayak tours. It had been a novelty to have a girlfriend who was "outdoorsy" like her. It had all seemed so easy and perfect and wonderful, and Roxy found herself falling in love not long after meeting Amy. All her relationships before that suddenly felt like nothing—mere infatuation. This was the real thing.

She'd let herself say "I love you" to Amy mere weeks after they started dating. After all, it hadn't felt like mere weeks. They'd spent nearly every day together, working together during the day, sleeping in one another's arms at night, spending every waking minute talking together, dreaming together.

But Amy never said "I love you" back. When the summer ended, Amy returned to California and grad school and, after a few phone calls, told Roxy it was better to end things since she "didn't do" long-distance relationships.

It was over a year now since that devastating phone call, and Roxy hadn't dated since. One-night stands? Sure. All the time. She'd overindulged in that kind of behavior quite a bit after Amy. The only way to heal was to inure herself from pain by having these meaningless flings. Finally, Hazel and Jazz staged an intervention. They'd wanted to do it sooner but had also been afraid. Afraid of what Roxy had become. They waited until the accident when it finally seemed inevitable.

Because Roxy hadn't messed up her knee doing something cool like doing tricks on her dirt bike, or something legitimate like loading heavy kayaks onto the truck at work. Nope. She'd screwed up her knee while leaving the apartment of her latest conquest, late on a rainy night that past September, still drunk from the club. She'd stepped badly off a curb that was higher than she'd realized, and because she'd picked up the girl at the club whose number she didn't have, she had no way of contacting her once she was out of her apartment.

She'd lain in the street, barely able to move, dazed from the fall, knee suddenly unable to bend, until, through the haze, she was able to fish out her phone and call Jazz. She'd been too embarrassed to call Hazel.

Jazz drove over in her little electric car, picked her up, took her home, and put her to bed. The next day they came back and, no judgment whatsoever, checked up on her. It was only the next day that Jazz came back with Hazel and they sat her down and told her it had to stop. The cycle of destruction had to end. Not only was it affecting her health (she'd sprained a ligament in her knee that night), but it was affecting their friendship with her. They were concerned. They wanted their friend back.

It was the looks on their faces that mirrored back to her what she already knew—she'd taken her anguish too far. She had to stop acting like a selfish teenager and work on becoming an adult. A functioning person.

"Roxy?"

"Hmm?"

She looked over at Mo, slowly leaving her memories behind, for now. Mo's beautiful face was etched with real concern.

"Your heart has been hurt, yes?"

Roxy nodded.

Unexpectedly, Mo came over to her and folded her into a big hug. It felt wonderful to be held by someone. By a friend, Roxy realized. Hazel was a great hugger, and she missed those best friend hugs. She and Hazel had been texting every day since Hazel and Elizabeth had left for their extended honeymoon, but it wasn't the same.

When they pulled apart, Roxy was startled to realize that Mo had tears in her eyes.

"What's wrong?"

Mo sniffed and wiped away a tear that had slid down her cheek. "I am so scared, Roxy. I am sad that I am not at home in the ocean and with my many sisters. I miss the ocean so much. And my tail. And I am scared. Scared for what keeps me here."

"Oh no, I'm so sorry, Mo. I should have been more sensitive." Roxy put her arms around Mo and gave her another hug. She squeezed her tight—the only reassurance she could provide. "Look, I'll do what I can. But we've got to figure out who or what is keeping you here—and how to break the spell."

Mo looked at her with hope in her eyes. "You would do this—for me? But how? You are just mortal. How can you help?"

Roxy began pacing the room again. Her first thought, of course, was to text Hazel, but something held her back. First of all, she'd promised herself that she wouldn't bother Hazel on her honeymoon with her own problems or negativity. Hazel had let her know they'd arrived in Florence and sent her some pictures of delicious gelato that made Roxy's mouth water, and Roxy had sent pictures of the brewery along with lots of questions about the flight and hotels. But they'd been keeping it all lighthearted. It was Hazel's honeymoon after all. Roxy didn't want her worrying needlessly about magical emergencies an ocean away.

Then there was the second issue, which was that Mo's situation was delicate. Roxy had enough experience with the Otherworldly and magic to know that they had to tread carefully. If they tried to use magical tools to help Mo, they might inadvertently risk exposing her to the very people or creatures who were hunting her. Besides, what could Hazel do from a continent away? Not much. Even magic had its limits.

Roxy paused in her pacing. "What we need is to find someone who knows a lot about magic and spells, but who won't get suspicious about why we need it. Maybe even someone who knows about your kind, but from a nerdy side of things."

"What is 'nerdy'?" Mo looked concerned.

"No, no, it's nothing bad," said Roxy. "I mean, someone who likes to know things just to know them, not necessarily because they need that information to do something. Does that make sense?"

"I think so." Mo did not look convinced one bit.

Roxy stared at the ceiling in concentration. Where could they find a nerd who knew a lot about the ocean, but specifically in terms of magic, myths, legends? She took out her phone and did a quick search. There was a library in town—she supposed they could start there. She was about to check the hours of operation when something else caught her eye on the screen.

But no.

It couldn't be.

She looked again.

"Wow!"

"What?" There was a tremble in Mo's voice.

"This is good. This is one hundred percent amazing, actually," said Roxy. "I had no idea, but apparently Provincetown has a museum all about seafaring history. It looks like they even have an exhibit all about sea monsters and mer—I mean, magical sea creatures."

"Really?" Mo's eyes got wide.

"Yep, totally," said Roxy. "Let's see what we can do."

It was too late to call the museum that day, but it was open the following day. Roxy didn't have to be at the brewery until noon, so she and Mo made a plan to go to the museum right when it opened at ten.

Just as Roxy was putting her phone down to charge, a message came through. Mo was already snuggled up on the couch that was doubling as her bed—she insisted that it was more comfortable than sharing the bed with Roxy—and fell fast asleep. Apparently, mermaids slept twelve hours a day, as Roxy was learning.

Tessa.

Had a great time hanging out today. Any chance you have some free time this weekend? The weather is supposed to be nice, and I was thinking we could grab coffee and go for a walk.

Roxy felt her heart speed up. This weekend would be a bit tricky since she was due to learn some of the front-of-house duties at the brewery, but she would make it work. She wanted to know more about the gleam in Tessa's eye and the warmth of her gaze on her.

No. She needed to get to know Tessa. Rather than just focusing on the attraction between them, they needed to get to know one another. A lot of time had passed since that year of college they'd shared. What was Tessa really like? What was her personality? What kinds of things did she do for fun? And why was she "Tessa" and not "Teri" anymore? There was a lot to talk about, and Roxy couldn't wait.

But first, she had to help Mo.

CHAPTER EIGHT—TESSA

Tessa took the long way around to the bed-and-breakfast where Lisa was staying. The cool evening air was sharp and bracing, the night sky a deep black, sprinkled with stars. Orion was already rising, reminding Tessa of the quiet power of the stars and planets in the sky. The sight of the glimmering orbs in the sky calmed her, as did the distant sounds of the waves in the bay, lapping on the beach. She was reminded of a short incantation for rest and calm at night, and she paused a moment to repeat it to herself, hoping her hedge witch spells would give her strength to face Lisa.

No matter how slowly she walked, though, or how many side streets and alleys she turned down, eventually, she ended up in front of the bed-and-breakfast. No matter how many calming breaths she inhaled and exhaled, how much she told herself that she and Lisa were *finished,* and they were going to have a *professional* relationship now, she felt herself getting nervous, even in spite of her incantation

What if she'd made a mistake casting Lisa in the play?

Before she could steady herself, the door to the bed-and-breakfast flung open and Lisa strode out, as only she could, phone glued to her ear.

"I can't get any fucking reception in that goddamn hotel room, Ramón, and believe me, I want you to hear me very clearly when I say that nobody here had a goddamn clue that I was arriving today. And whose fault was that?"

Her voice, whose timbre could be clear and beautiful like a bell, was pitched low and angry. Her eyes were clouded with frustration, and Tessa was instantly transported back to their breakup. It had been ugly, and Lisa's words to her in their final fight had imprinted themselves on Tessa's brain forever. What had made it all the worse, though, was that Lisa's anger that day hadn't been of the kind she was exhibiting today. No. It had been much worse—the cool, almost cold, emotionless anger that was so calm, it absolutely froze her bones.

"Ramón, I've got to go."

Tessa's thoughts receded and she realized that Lisa had finally noticed her, standing on the sidewalk at the gate that opened onto the walkway to the bed-and-breakfast.

Unexpectedly, Lisa's face broke into a smile, her voice completely different than when she'd been speaking to her assistant. It was warm. Kind, even. Tessa felt off-balance with the sudden switch, the angry, disappointed ice queen in her memories still haunting her.

"Hi," said Lisa. "I didn't think I'd see you again tonight."

"Oh," said Tessa. She was still struggling with how to respond to the about-face. "You're our star. And a friend," she added. "Of course I'm going to come and check on how you're settling in. I feel bad about the fact that we didn't know you'd be arriving today."

Lisa opened the gate and Tessa walked through. The cold was starting to get to her, and she could feel her body tensing as a gust of wind blew through her jacket.

"As you may have heard, I've given my assistant a proper reaming out, and that's all that can be done for now," said Lisa. She smiled at Tessa with what seemed like genuine warmth. "You look cold, though. Let's go inside. The B and B has a fireplace in the parlor, and I think it's empty right now."

Lisa held the door open for Tessa and guided her gently to the parlor, which was indeed quite cozy with two perfectly positioned armchairs in front of a roaring fire. Tessa was reminded of all the reasons why she'd been attracted to Lisa in the first place—and why she'd stayed with her for several years.

Lisa could be attentive, kind, even doting. Of course, as Tessa had realized much later, it was all about control for Lisa. She liked to be in control of everything and everyone; this meant being the boss but also being the caretaker, the planner, the "Mom" in the relationship. Living in New York City and trying to gain a foothold in the thankless world of acting had been alienating for Tessa; having someone to take care of her had been a luxury.

"This is nice," said Tessa, once they were settled in the armchairs. Lisa, true to form, had found a blanket and handed it to Tessa. She had the impression that Lisa would tuck her in if she asked for it.

"Yes, the fireplace is a pleasant bonus," said Lisa. "I'll miss it when I move into my regular apartment for the duration."

"I meant the B and B more generally. But yes, the fireplace is nice. The rental might have one too. I can have Joy check tomorrow. She's our assistant director."

"Oh, it's fine. Don't worry about it, Tessa," said Lisa. "Tell me. How have you been?"

Again, Tessa felt like the rug had been pulled out from underneath her. Lisa's presence was so overwhelming, especially in such close proximity, she hardly knew what to say. It was a relief to realize that whatever attraction she'd had to Lisa was gone. Lisa was beautiful—stunning really. In the firelight, she could be a Renaissance painting of Venus, her features lit up in chiaroscuro against the dark of the room. None of that changed the fact that Tessa had no desire to kiss her or be in her arms.

Lisa's caresses came at too high a price.

Still, there was something about her that was larger than life. She commanded a room, even when she was silent, which wasn't often. Tessa felt sure she would be a major star very soon, and she wouldn't be surprised at all if Lisa were to make the jump from the stage to the screen any day now. She was already winning all sorts of accolades, including a Tony nomination.

By comparison, Tessa's life sounded very small. She lived in a shared rental not far from her folks and where she grew up in south Boston. She commuted to her job. She taught high school kids the basics of acting and dramaturgy. She directed high school plays. It was light years away from the height of her successes in New York.

But unlike her life in New York, she loved her life in Boston. She didn't dread going to work. She didn't agonize over every career choice. And she wasn't stuck in a relationship with a control freak.

She couldn't say any of that to Lisa. She went with something more neutral.

"I'm great! So excited for this play and this opportunity. And grateful that you can be a part of it. Really, I am. I know this is a far cry from Broadway."

"Oh, please. You know I'd do anything for a friend. Besides, this role is so juicy. I doubt I'll ever have the chance to play Leontes ever again."

Lisa sounded genuine, and the smile on her face was too.

"That's great. I'm so happy that we're going to do this. And it's really great for the local community. We have a lot of community outreach built into the grant—it's part of the grant requirements—but of course you already know that."

Lisa nodded. "Yes, I made sure to read through the proposal myself rather than having Ramón skim it for me. I'm aware. Meeting with local high school students. Should be a lot of fun."

Tessa smiled. She knew that Lisa prided herself on her community outreach, another reason why she was a great choice for this project.

"I'm glad you think so. I'm excited for you to meet my students in particular, of course. They'll be coming to one of the dress rehearsals later in February."

"You really like this teaching thing," said Lisa, and it was more a statement than a question.

Tessa couldn't help nodding enthusiastically. "Absolutely."

"And you don't miss the roar of the greasepaint? The smell of the crowd?"

"I get that and more at a high school dress rehearsal, believe me," said Tessa with a chuckle.

"True," said Lisa. "I was just thinking about your career in New York. You know, you didn't have to leave it all just because we broke up."

Actually, I did. Feelings that Tessa had been working through for the last year suddenly rose up again inside her. Disappointment. Anger. Resentment. Exhaustion.

Some of those feelings must have shown up in her expression.

"I'm sorry. Did I say something wrong?" Lisa's tone was cooler now. More guarded.

There were so many things Tessa wished she could say to Lisa, but she knew she wouldn't feel any better afterward, and it would be the end of their working relationship, so she smiled and shook her head instead.

"Nothing. It's fine. I've heard it all before. 'Come back to the theater. Leave teaching high school. You are so talented.' Believe me. Everyone's said it. Well, everyone except my mom. She's very happy that I'm living a few blocks away, and she can bring me soup whenever she wants."

"I'd believe it," said Lisa. Her expression softened again. "I didn't mean it to sound condescending. I was just wondering if you missed it. Because you could definitely go back. If you wanted to. You are a talented director."

"Thanks. But I love my life now. I really do."

There was a lull in the conversation, and Tessa found herself staring comfortably at the fire, wishing that it was Roxy sitting here with her, and not Lisa. She was so lost in her thoughts she didn't realize right away that Lisa was speaking to her again.

"Sorry?"

"I was just wondering if your wonderful new life that you love includes a special someone to love?"

"No," said Tessa warily. "It does not. What about you? Got someone now?" The question came off more aggressively than she'd intended.

"No," said Lisa. Her expression and tone of voice were carefully neutral. "All on my own these days."

Tessa had no idea what to say to that, so she decided she'd wait for Lisa to speak again, which she did and, yet again, managed to take Tessa by surprise.

"Tell me about Roxy. Is she an old friend? Old roommate? The name rings a bell." She paused, giving Tessa a careful look. "And she just happens to be out here on Cape Cod for the winter? That's a fun coincidence."

"Total coincidence," said Tessa. "Yes, she's an old roommate from UMass. Freshman year. We lost touch after that, but I knew she'd be at my colleague's wedding on New Year's Day here. I had no idea she was planning to spend the winter at Cape Cod. So yes...a fun coincidence."

"Nothing else?"

Not that it's any of your business. Tessa tried not to let her growing frustration with Lisa's interrogation show.

She made a big show of yawning and standing up.

"Wow, this fire is making me super tired. I think I'd better head home and get some rest. We've got a lot of stuff to get ready before rehearsals begin next week—as you know."

Lisa stood up as well, the shadow of a pout on her face. Tessa was glad to see that she'd realized she'd overplayed her hand.

"How about dinner tomorrow then? Or sometime this weekend? I'd love to have a proper catch-up when we're not both exhausted."

"I'll have to take a look at my calendar tomorrow with Joy before I commit to anything." Tessa put as much finality as she could into those words.

"Of course," said Lisa. "I'll check in tomorrow, then. I can stop by the theater?"

Tessa would prefer that she didn't, but there wasn't any nice way to say that.

"Sure." Tessa put on her coat and scarf and folding up the blanket again. "But I won't be there all day. You can leave a message with Joy. Or text me. But if I'm not there, then I'm sure Joy can give you a tour of the theater."

Lisa looked disappointed and Tessa couldn't help feeling a small stab of guilt. Was she being too mean?

"But I'll be happy to give you a tour if you like," she added to alleviate that feeling. "Stop by in the morning, before ten, and I'll definitely be there."

"Wonderful," said Lisa. Unexpectedly, she leaned in and gave Tessa a hug. "Thank you, really, for inviting me. I'll see you tomorrow."

Tessa left the B and B feeling completely confused about Lisa and wondering how exactly she was going to direct someone who came with quite so much baggage.

As she walked home, her mind swirled with emotions both past and present. Lisa was a tough nut to crack. Tessa knew that Chayo disagreed. After the breakup, when Tessa was temporarily living on Chayo's living room floor in the Bronx, Chayo had argued the very opposite.

"She's a control freak and she emotionally abused and manipulated you. She made you believe you're weak. What did she say to you at the break-up?"

Tessa had been curled up in a fetal position on the blow-up mattress, huddled under a blanket, still reeling from breaking up with Lisa and calling off their engagement just two days earlier. The words Lisa had said to her, those last words before she'd run out of their apartment, were: "How could you do this to me? And to yourself and your career? *Who are you without me?*"

She could barely get the words out, and when she did, she saw Chayo get angry all over again.

"She's not complicated, Tessa. She's a cold-hearted bitch," Chayo had said, no doubt biting back many a harsher comment in her head. "Forget about her. She didn't know what she had right there in front of her. You're sensitive and smart, talented, beautiful…you're the whole package. Who is *she* without *you?* That's what she should be asking."

Chayo's righteous indignation had helped a little bit in the moment, but it was really her whole-hearted support, her ride-or-die dedication to Tessa and the puddle of emotions that she'd been reduced to in those first few days and weeks post-breakup that made Tessa eternally grateful to her. She knew it was a lot of pride to swallow for Chayo to agree to work on a project with Lisa.

Tessa's mind swirled with these memories, and she wondered again if she'd made a mistake casting Lisa. She'd rationalized it six ways to Sunday, and yet, here she was, wondering one more time.

The logical side of her knew that it was a done deal; there was nothing to do but move on. And Lisa's question had a new poignancy for Tessa: who was she without Lisa? She was an ambitious director, a dedicated teacher, and a person looking for love. Unlike the twenty-three-year-old noob that she'd been when she met Lisa, she was older and wiser now, and she knew what she wanted out of life and love.

And she had a good feeling about Roxy. Roxy was confident but kind, energetic like Tessa, but more chill and less high-strung. That was the energy that she put out, and Tessa felt sure their energies would complement one another.

When she got home, she texted Roxy right away, before she lost her nerve. She wasn't going to make any plans with Lisa until she'd nailed something down with Roxy. It was Roxy she wanted to spend time with and get to know. Her heart beat faster as she clicked "send."

CHAPTER NINE—ROXY

The next morning, after yet another breakfast of cold cereal for Roxy and cold fish for Mo, they set off for the museum.

Tiny snowflakes danced through the air, and the sun was nowhere to be seen, but this was exactly the kind of winter weather Roxy loved. The whole world got quiet when it snowed, the drifting flakes cloaking everything in a plush silence. There was something rather magical about it all.

Mo appeared to be enjoying the experience as well. It was her first real snowfall since arriving on land. Roxy watched as she stuck out her tongue like a kid, catching snowflakes out of the air, and she couldn't help smiling. Mo really was something else.

Now that they'd been living together for going on four days, Roxy had gotten used to her. The raw fish and eating habits aside, Mo wasn't too hard to get along with. She could be intense, of course, and Roxy still wasn't sure what Mo's oath to help her would entail, especially now that she knew Roxy was attracted to Tessa. Overall, though, she was enjoying having a roommate. It was nice to have someone to talk to in the mornings and evenings. That morning she'd taught Mo how to make coffee with the machine, and Mo had been delighted when the fresh coffee began dripping into the carafe, even if she had absolutely no interest in drinking the coffee once it was done.

Everything was new to Mo, from silverware to soap to television and TV dinners. The toilet had been a whole thing. Roxy had shown her how to use it, and Mo had practically screamed when she'd flushed the water. Luckily, she'd grasped the concept fairly quickly, though not before explaining to Roxy how disgusting it was going to the toilet in human form.

"Believe me," Roxy told her. "I know."

Now as they walked through the falling snow, Mo's curiosity and joy in all the new things made her more aware of everything as well. The feel of snowflakes landing in her eyelashes, the many shades of gray and white in the sky, and the crunch of snow and ice beneath her warm winter boots all became unique pleasures to be savored.

Her feelings of loneliness from Hazel's wedding were lessened now. Between the brewery and the theater, Tessa and Mo, Roxy was starting to feel like a part of a larger community again. They were all welcome distractions that helped her refocus away from those feelings of sadness and isolation from earlier in the week.

The entrance to the museum was on one of many adorable streets that ran perpendicular to the bay. Around it were residential homes as well as a café and a couple of shops. Ptown was like that—little hidden gems sprinkled in and around the peninsula, and you never knew what treasure you'd find just around the corner.

If she hadn't been looking for it and known the exact address, Roxy would have missed the museum for sure. The sign outside was off to the side and faded; the building itself looked like a residential home in the classic New England style all around them—wooden shingles and white trim, with slate-colored shutters outside each window.

"This is it," she said to Mo as they mounted the steps to the museum.

Inside, they found themselves in what looked like someone's living room, but with a gift shop and checkout counter inside it. Old photographs of Provincetown's past, as well as even older maps and drawings hung on every inch of available wall space that wasn't covered in shelves with books and knickknacks. It wasn't immediately clear what was for sale and what wasn't, but there was a merry, cluttered look to the place that felt very homey to Roxy.

The room was empty, but on the counter there was a small bell and a sign encouraging visitors to ring the bell if no one was around.

"Go for it," said Roxy to Mo, gesturing at the bell.

Mo approached the bell with unnecessary caution. What on earth did it look like to her, wondered Roxy. Finally, she tapped the bell far too hard, and the bell jangled loudly, startling Mo nearly a foot into the air.

"Hey, it's just a bell," said Roxy. She touched it more softly to demonstrate. "See? No big deal."

"Maybe for you," muttered Mo.

Before she could respond, a short person with a storm of white-blond curls bustled into the room.

"Hallo!" she said. "So sorry! Just puttering around in the back, you know. Hope you haven't been waiting long."

The woman's voice betrayed an accent that Roxy couldn't quite place. It was like an English accent, but not. Australia maybe? New Zealand? Something like that. The museum staff member was quite petite, and her blond hair seemed like it belonged to a much younger person, but Roxy could easily see that she was quite a bit older than she'd originally assumed. Maybe forty or forty-five? She was pale and ruddy, wearing loose-fitting jeans, a wild hot pink and black sweater, and black Converse sneakers that seemed far too spring-y for the wintery weather outside. Her glasses were clearly for a strong prescription as they made her eyes look small and far away.

"No, not at all," said Roxy. "We just got here."

"Welcome!" said the woman. "I'm Clare. Lovely to meet you. Are you wanting to enter the museum? We have a general entrance and then we also have an entrance with a tour. Oh, but our tour guide isn't here today. Of course, I've forgotten. But I can give you a little tour with the general entrance. It's no bother. Nobody's here." She laughed nervously. The whole speech was delivered very quickly, and Roxy wondered how many people came to the museum in the winter. Not many, she surmised.

"Nice to meet you," said Roxy. "I'm Roxy. This here is Mo. We were, uh, actually interested in the exhibits about the…erhm…magical creatures under the sea." She screwed up her face trying to remember what the exhibit had been called on the website. "Oh! Yes. The myths and legends exhibit."

"I see," said Clare with interest. "Is this for a school project?"

Roxy and Mo looked at one another.

"No," they said in unison.

How young does she think we are, thought Roxy.

"Personal interest then?" said Clare pleasantly. "Or is it something more than that?"

"More than that?" Roxy wasn't sure what the woman was getting at.

"It's just that for some folks around here, myths and legends aren't really legends. They're real. We get quite a few people like that. Interested in magic and witches and mer—"

"STOP!" The word flew out of Roxy and Mo at the same time. The unsuspecting museum guide was somewhat stunned.

"Sorry? Something I said?" she sputtered.

"Don't say that word!" Mo was practically glowing with ferocious energy, looking more like an animal than a human. Roxy would have sworn Mo's hair had stood on end, even if just for a second.

"It's just, uh, my cousin here is a bit sensitive to *that word*. The 'm' word if you know what I mean," said Roxy with a big, theatrical wink. "I think she'd prefer, uh…" Roxy looked over at Mo questioningly.

Mo stared back at her blankly.

Clare tried to fill in the silence. "Water nymph? Nereid? Kelpie? Siren?"

At the last word, Mo breathed in sharply. "No. Not siren! Sirens are something else. Something evil."

"Oh?" said Clare pleasantly. "Well, yes, I suppose you're right if you know your Greek myth."

"What? I'm confused." Roxy definitely did not remember anything about Greek myth.

"Well, in the Greek myth, sirens were women with beautiful voices whose singing enchanted sailors to jump off their ships and drown. Only later people began using the word siren to refer to…" Clare's voice trailed off.

"Magical sea creatures," supplied Roxy. "Is that okay, Mo?"

Mo nodded somewhat reluctantly. "It's not exact, but it's fine."

Clare nodded. "Got it."

"Where I am from, the siren is a terrible creature, an evil woman who may live both underwater and on land. She hunts my people, and we fear her."

Roxy looked over at Clare to see how she reacted to Mo's odd statements, but, to her relief, she appeared to be taking it all in as a matter of course—as if people were always coming to the museum and talking about evil magical creatures who were hunting them.

Roxy paid the general admission fee for the two of them, and they began the tour of the museum's myths and legends section. They bypassed the other rooms filled with fishing nets, whaling harpoons, paintings of Cape Cod Bay, and life-size dioramas of fishermen's homes in the nineteenth century. Clare was a veritable font of information, even if it was at times a bit difficult to follow because she often spoke so quickly and often jumped from topic to topic. Her lilting accent kept Roxy guessing, too.

They soon found themselves in front of a display case with some curious objects, and next to it was a diorama of a ship's prow, with a mannequin dressed like a sailor looking down into the water. The "water," or whatever it was, shimmered at their feet, and in the medium they could see an unclear shape, something between a manatee and a mermaid. The placard next to the diorama explained that often sailors would claim to see mermaids when what they'd really seen was some other kind of aquatic animal.

Of course that made sense. The water could distort whatever was under the surface, and if you were a sex-starved, drunk-on-rum sailor, then you were probably thinking about women all the time.

"Here we are," said Clare. "Anything I can tell you about the, ah, magical sea creatures and their link to Cape Cod?"

"Actually, we're a bit more interested in, um, other people who might be looking for these creatures. Or, rather, who want to hunt them and use them for magical purposes…" Roxy's voice trailed off. She was sure Clare would think they were total kooks.

Luckily, Clare took this line of questioning in stride. In fact, she appeared quite excited by these particular questions and knew exactly what Roxy was getting at.

"I see what you mean," she said, giving them both a knowing glance.

Mo had been remarkably quiet in the museum. No doubt seeing all the usual sea objects here on land and inside a house, no less, was a bit of a shock for her.

"Do you?" Mo finally was able to focus on Clare and take her eyes off the diorama, shaking her head with disdain.

Clare nodded wisely. "I've actually been looking up quite a bit of lore around the topic in the last few weeks. Just before the New Year it was, I had a lady here show up asking some very similar questions to you."

Roxy's eyes widened. This *had* to be someone involved in Mo's enchantment. She and Mo exchanged a look, and Roxy saw fear in her eyes.

"Oh yeah?" said Roxy, trying to sound casual. "Who, uh, was she? Maybe we know her."

"Can't remember much," said Clare, brows knitted in the effort to remember. "Goodness. It's like looking through fog in my brain. All I remember is it was a woman. She didn't want the full tour either. Just wanted the stuff about the, er, magical sea creatures. Was asking if we had any books on the subject. I told her we do, but that we don't generally allow the public to enter the back library except by arrangement ahead of time. She was a bit miffed at that."

"I'll bet she was," said Mo darkly. "I doubt it stopped her."

"Oh?" Clare looked confused. "We haven't had any break-ins, if that's what you're getting at."

"But you were saying that you looked at these books yourself?" Roxy tried redirecting the conversation.

"Oh. Yes. Yes, that's right. I did say I'd been reading up on it," said Clare, her thoughts clearly a bit scattered now. "I'm sorry. It's just the strangest thing that I can't remember what this lady looked like. Normally I'm quite good at remembering a face. We don't exactly get lots of crowds here. There was something about her that struck me as particularly memorable."

Clare looked incredibly frustrated that she couldn't remember. Meanwhile, Roxy's mind was working overtime. Was this evil magic at work? Had this other magician or sorceress used some kind of cloaking spell or befuddling enchantment so that Clare wouldn't remember what she looked like? It felt like a distinct possibility. After all, they were dealing with someone who had no problem trying to capture and possibly kill a mermaid. A chill went through Roxy just thinking about it.

"It's all right," said Mo. "Could you tell us about what you read?"

"Sure," said Clare. "You were asking about legends or lore that had to do with why someone might want to capture a mer—I mean, magical sea creature? Or hunt one? Yes?" She looked at them each in turn and they nodded. "I'm sorry to say, it seems there are many reasons. Men who want a beautiful, magical wife. Circus folks who want to display them as freaks. Scientists who want to study them and learn how humans could learn to breathe underwater. Then there's the even crazier people who want them as pets." She ticked off each category on a finger as she spoke.

"Yes, yes, but what about magical reasons? Reasons relating to doing magic or spells or enchantments?" said Mo with some energy. There was an edge to her voice.

Clare nodded. "I did read about that, too. Lots of legends about their tails, in particular. Or was it their scales? I did find a grimoire, if you can believe it, in the library."

Roxy and Mo exchanged another glance. A grimoire was a spellbook and that spelled trouble.

"We believe it," said Roxy. "We're believers, in case you couldn't tell."

"You're not trying to capture one of these creatures and do a spell on it," said Clare with a bit of a twinkle in her eye and a smile that died on her lips when she saw how earnest and dead serious Roxy's and Mo's expressions were.

"No," said Roxy. Either they would sound completely ridiculous or they might just get Clare's sympathy, but she decided to take the plunge. "We're concerned that someone is hunting these creatures in the waters of Cape Cod Bay and putting the population at risk for maiming or worse."

If Clare thought it was a joke, she needed only to glance at Mo to see the pained, drawn expression on her beautiful face to know they were not joking.

Understanding dawned on Clare's face. "And you think that lady who was here before you is this person or part of this group of people? I see. Well, the situation is quite serious then."

"That's why she was asking those questions," said Roxy.

"How do I know you're not one of those people, too?" said Clare, eyeing them suspiciously. She'd clearly gone from taking it all as a joke to being wary of them, too.

"How do we know you're not one of those people?" countered Mo, hands on hips, eyes blazing. "Roxy is trying to help me—I mean, help these creatures, and we are taking a huge risk coming to you."

"Also true," said Clare. She paused at looked them both up and down. "Fair enough. I trust you. I wish I could say that other lady who was here asking around smelled of sulfur or had horns coming out of her head, but I can't. She may be one of these people you're talking about, or she might have been just another tourist. Or someone like you, maybe, who is trying to help."

"Could we see this grimoire?" said Mo.

"I'm afraid I can't do that," said Clare. "I told the other lady that too. Books in the special collection are only by prior arrangement with our archivist, and she's currently on holiday in Greece."

Disappointment filled Roxy. How would they know what was in the grimoire and what enchantment they were fighting if they couldn't look at it?

"Don't look so glum. She'll be back next week. Let's go up front and you can fill out a request card."

Roxy had a thought. "Did the other lady fill out a request card, too?"

"I believe she did," said Clare with renewed energy. "Yes, I'm fairly sure of it. We can take a look at it together."

As they turned to leave the display, Roxy and Mo took one last glance at the display case. The objects in the case all related to mermaids somehow. There were several fragments of figureheads from a ship that had had a mermaid as a figurehead. There were some small mermaid figures whittled by sailors. They were crude but nonetheless fascinating. There was a necklace with a locket that had a painting of a mermaid inside it and next to it—the space was blank.

"Wait," said Roxy. "What was supposed to be here?"

Clare walked back to the display case and her eyes widened. "There's an object missing here," she said.

"It's not out for cleaning or something?" said Roxy.

"No," said Clare, and her voice trembled. "It's *missing*. Oh no oh no oh no," she moaned, clutching her head with hands. She was upset and Roxy felt bad—but she also had a sinking feeling about the missing display object. She was certain that the other person had stolen it. And dollars to donuts, a page was missing from that grimoire too. She didn't say that, though, as she didn't want to agitate the poor guide any more. "Oh dear, I'll have to call up Rhoda and interrupt her holiday and let her know. She's our archivist and the owner of the museum, and she will be *so* upset."

"What was it?" said Roxy.

"It's just a small gold chain, but it was supposedly the bracelet of Gwenhidw, the Welsh queen of the mermaids," said Clare in a rush. She was so agitated that the word mermaid slipped out of her mouth without a second thought, even as Mo clamped her hand on Clare's lips.

"Shhh! Don't say that word!" said Mo.

They all paused and looked all around, as if expecting something or someone to materialize out of thin air. After a couple of beats, the museum was as silent and still as a tomb, and they were alone. Mo took her hand off Clare's mouth and stepped away.

"I am sorry," she said.

"It's all right," said Clare. "You're worried *that word* will do something? Summon someone or something? But we say that word here all the time. We have a whole museum display about it." There was cool logic to her words that soothed Roxy. Clearly, that word couldn't be as powerful here as in other places. On the other hand, if one of Mo's pursuers had already been here, and had even stolen a bracelet, then perhaps the museum wasn't the safest place to be, either.

Mo accepted Clare's explanation, however, and nodded. She was still agitated by the whole experience though and wrapped her arms around herself tightly. Roxy gave her shoulder a squeeze as they followed Clare back to the front room. It took her a while, in her agitation, to find the rarely used museum log for missing and stolen items. They stood there so long that Roxy felt certain Clare had forgotten about them.

"Are you still going to let us fill out a book request? And show us the request from the other person interested in mer—I mean, magical sea creatures?" said Roxy. She didn't want to let her guard down, just in case.

Clare looked up, somewhat wild-eyed. "What? Oh. Yes. Hold on. Let me get that for you."

It took another five minutes to locate the logbook underneath the stacks and stacks of papers on the counter, but it was worth the wait. Clare opened the logbook to the current page, and right there in black and white was one single entry:

Name: Faustina Clerval

Book Requested: *The Moon Tide Grimoire*

There was also an address listed and a telephone number. The address was a local one in Provincetown. At least that would be easy.

"Unique name, eh?" said Clare. "I don't know how I could have forgotten it."

Clare's remark gave Roxy an unsettled feeling. She knew what it was like to be under someone else's spell, to have one's memories messed with. Had this Faustina person done something to Clare's memories so she wouldn't remember anything about her?

Roxy filled out her own request and put down the same book title. Her fingers were itching to page through the grimoire, but she settled for writing down Faustina's address and phone number in the small notebook she carried with her everywhere.

"Sorry I couldn't help more," said Clare. "But I'll let you know as soon as our archivist returns. I'm sure we can accommodate your request. I can prioritize it, if you like." She gave them a wink, and Roxy couldn't help smiling.

"You're a peach, Clare. It was great to meet you, I'm sorry to hear the museum was the victim of a burglary, though, and I hope you catch the perp."

Clare sighed. "What a nightmare. You'll have to excuse me, now, as I've got to get in touch with Rhoda and the police."

Back outside, the weather had turned nasty. The wind was whipping at their hair and scarves, and the gentle snowflakes from earlier had changed to an unpleasant wintry mix.

"What do we do now?" said Mo, looking worried.

"Let's go home and warm up," said Roxy, shivering. She paused to look at the address for Faustina Clerval again. "But you know, I think we've got time to check out this address. Let's walk by it on the way home."

Mo nodded with some energy. Unlike Roxy, the cold did not affect her. She found it invigorating, or so she'd told Roxy.

The address was right off the main drag in Ptown, and it wasn't too hard to find—though the building itself looked nothing short of creepy. To her surprise, Roxy saw the name "Faustina Clerval" painted onto the window. This person wasn't too secretive about their whereabouts. And despite the fake sound of the name, she was an actual person.

The window display said, "Faustina Clerval, Clairvoyant. By appointment only."

It was impossible to see through the thick curtains in the window.

Roxy sighed. "Well, we know where she is, I guess. Let's go home and have a think."

Back at the apartment, Roxy parked herself on the radiator to warm up while Mo took the opportunity to throw back some mackerel filets.

Roxy had been so preoccupied with their morning visit to the museum, that she'd forgotten to write Tessa back. She would be busy with the brewery that afternoon and Saturday evening, but she had most of the day free on Saturday. She had no idea what to do about Faustina and whether to make an appointment with her. The thought made her shiver, to be frank.

The weather was due to clear up the next day. Maybe a daytime date with Tessa was just the thing to distract her—sometimes that was exactly what she needed to clear her thoughts. Plus, it would give her a chance to get to know Tessa. Just the thought of her warm brown eyes made her feel warm in a way completely unrelated to the radiator.

She picked up her phone and replied to her message: *Got some time tomorrow?*

CHAPTER TEN—TESSA

Tessa felt her energy shift when she spied Roxy walking toward her, as if her whole body were straining toward her. She was glad for the warm winter layers in that moment, including the hat and scarf that helped camouflage her excitement and nerves a bit. The blush in her cheeks could easily be attributed to the occasional gust of chill wind. Nothing could stop her smile, though.

She waved. "Hey you!" Roxy smiled, the thoughtful, somewhat grim expression wiped from her face as she recognized Tessa from half a block away.

They were meeting in a part of Provincetown Tessa was less familiar with, on the outskirts of the small hamlet. It was just far enough from where she was staying in town that Tessa had driven to the trailhead. Roxy had evidently walked the whole way, and Tessa felt very stupid for not offering to pick her up that morning. It would have given them extra time together.

"Hey," said Roxy once she was closer. "You ready for this?"

"Absolutely," said Tessa, nodding. She had learned to enjoy hiking and being in nature after the breakup. The breakup had, in a way, launched her into nature and into becoming a hedge witch. The soothing effect of being outside, among trees and fields and the wide-open sky, had reminded her that there was a world outside of the New York-London theater junket. Pursuing hedgecraft had only reinforced to her the power of the natural world, and its ability to impact her life positively.

Still. Hiking in winter was a whole other story. She'd never been much of a winter sports person. She'd done some ice skating as a kid in Boston, but her family had never been the kind to be able to afford ski trips or things like that. Hiking in the snow or snowshoeing was not something her family had done either.

Luckily, she did have some warm winter boots for walking with her in Ptown, plus the requisite "big coat," warm hat, mittens, and scarf for a New England winter. The Cape was generally a bit warmer than the mainland, warmed by the Gulf Stream, and today was a perfect example of that. It was in the forties with only an occasional breeze. The trail they were to walk was very sheltered, though it would eventually lead them to the ocean beach. Just in case, she had cast some hedge witch charms on herself for positive thoughts and openness to new experiences—as well as a charm for her boots to keep them extra warm.

"All right," said Roxy with a big smile. "Let's hit the trail."

They were soon walking through sparse but beautiful woods. The trail was somewhat muddy, but mostly free of ice and snow, and in the shelter of the forest Tessa warmed up quickly, as Roxy kept a fairly brisk pace.

"How was your morning?" said Roxy.

Tessa couldn't help groaning somewhat. "It was kind of crazy, to be honest," she said. "I was supposed to spend the morning organizing the scripts for everyone for Monday's read-through, and instead I had to take Lisa on a tour of the theater, and it sort of ate up my whole morning. Which is fine," she added quickly. She didn't want Roxy to think she was a constant complainer. "I just really wanted to get ready for when the rest of the core cast members arrive and the read-through on Monday, and I felt a bit rushed."

She didn't add, of course, that Lisa had started in right away ordering people around and making suggestions for how to "improve" everything. Chayo had been staring daggers at her by the end of the morning. Tessa had to soothe Chayo's ruffled feathers, as well as those of the props mistress, once she'd figured out how to keep Lisa busy. She'd finally realized that Lisa could organize the scripts by herself in the greenroom while Tessa worked with Joy in the office to double-check all the lodging bookings for the cast and crew arriving on Sunday.

"That sounds pretty hectic," said Roxy. "It was a busy day at the pub yesterday, too. I was learning all the front-of-house duties when a giant family group showed up and kept us busy for a couple of hours. It was a trail by fire."

"A trial by fire?"

"Trail, trial. Potato, po-tah-to," said Roxy with a grin and a chuckle. "Sorry. I'm always mixing up my sayings. I once told a customer not to count their chickens before they're eggs."

Tessa couldn't help hooting with laughter. "What was their reaction?"

"I think they were too nice to say anything," said Roxy. "Though I prefer to think that *they* thought they'd been saying it wrong all along instead of me."

"Completely possible," said Tessa with a grin.

They walked along in companionable silence for a few minutes, and Tessa took the opportunity to take in their surroundings and soak up the peace and quiet of the place, the only sounds the crunching of their boots in the snow and ice and the occasional twitter of a distant bird.

Roxy cleared her throat. "Do you mind if I ask you a, uh, personal question?"

Tessa's heart raced. "Sure." She had no idea what Roxy was going to ask, but if she just happened to tell her right then and there that she was in love with her, Tessa was ready to jump in her arms. After nine years of wondering and crushing, she was ready.

"How come you're Tessa Flowers now?" said Roxy. Tessa felt a pang of disappointment quickly followed by a sense of ridiculousness at her own assumptions.

Of course, Roxy wasn't just going to declare her undying love for her four days after meeting again for the first time in nearly a decade.

"I was thinking about it, and I realized that in college you were Teri. Teri...K..."

"Kwiatkowski," supplied Tessa.

"Yeah! That's it."

Tessa felt slightly embarrassed. Should she tell Roxy the whole truth? Or just part of it? She hesitated long enough that Roxy rushed to fill in the silence.

"I'm sorry. That's probably really personal for you. You don't have to answer that question."

"No," said Tessa with as much kindness as possible in her voice. "It's okay. It's a fair question for someone who knew me as Teri." She paused again, trying to find the right words—words she could say without bitterness. "I changed my name when I got into show business in New York. Lisa was the one who suggested changing my name. Teri and Tessa are both nicknames for Teresa, which is the name on my birth certificate. Kwiatkowski is a Polish last name. *Kwiat* means "flower" so "Flowers" is as close a translation of Kwiatkowski as you can get. And of course it's a lot easier for people in the US to pronounce."

"So the *w* in your last name is actually pronounced like a *v*?" asked Roxy, sounding intrigued. "I had no idea I'd been saying it wrong this whole time." She tried saying it like Tessa, "Kvyat-ko-ski"

"Yep, that's it. Great job," said Tessa, feeling an unexpected rush of emotion. So few people took the time to learn how to pronounce Polish names correctly that to hear Roxy trying, really trying, felt special in a wholly new way.

"So is Teri what your family calls you?" said Roxy, clearly curious to learn more. Tessa felt flattered.

"Actually no, not at all. That was a nickname from grade school," she said. "My folks are both from Poland, and in Polish the nickname for Teresa is Terka or Tereska. My mom always calls me Terunia, which is definitely a pet name. Most of my Polish family calls me Tereska."

"That is *so* cute," said Roxy. "I wish Roxy had more nicknames…I'm not Roxanne, you know. It's just Roxy. I mean, I like that it's so easy and short, but sometimes it would be nice to have some other options. Sometimes friends call me Rox, but that's about it."

"Polish people love nicknames and diminutives. Nobody goes by their given name there."

"That's super interesting," said Roxy. "Did you grow up speaking Polish too? I feel like an idiot asking that, actually. I feel like this is something I should remember." She sounded a little sheepish.

"I did. But it's not something I advertised in college. I kind of went through a phase where I was a bit embarrassed that my family was different, and my parents weren't like other kids' parents."

"Hey, don't feel too bad about that," said Roxy with real warmth in her voice. "We all go through that. Man, I was a *mess* in college. There's a reason I didn't come back after freshmen year."

"What?" Tessa stopped dead in her tracks. All along she'd thought that Roxy had simply put in a room request after their first year to room with someone else on the soccer team. Or that she'd transferred to play for a better team at another school.

"Oh, you didn't know?" Roxy sounded embarrassed. She scratched the back of her head awkwardly. "I lost my scholarship after my GPA tanked."

"Oh no! I'm so sorry, Roxy. I didn't mean to bring up something painful on this beautiful hike."

Roxy met her worried gaze with a big smile. "It's all water under the brink, you know? Er, that ship has been buried a long time. Or whatever the saying is." Her gaze was full of warmth and whatever earlier embarrassment was gone. Tessa basked in her attention before finally looking away just in time to duck under a particularly low-hanging tree branch.

The trail had gotten narrower and they were forced to walk single file. Tessa enjoyed the view from the back as Roxy led the way. As they walked in silence, she let her mind wander, imagining what it might be like to be folded into Roxy's strong arms, to feel her soft, red lips pressing on hers—

"Oof!"

Roxy had stopped at the top of a small rise in the trail, and Tessa hadn't noticed in time. She walked right into Roxy and her backpack, which was surprisingly hard and heavy.

Roxy turned around and put an arm around Tessa to catch her as much as herself. Her arm was every bit as strong and steady as Tessa had just moments ago been imagining.

"You okay?" she said with a wink.

"Yes," managed Tessa, somewhat breathlessly. "Why did you—"

Beyond the small rise in the trail, the trees opened up onto a spectacular view of the ocean beach. After the enclosed trail, it was a stunning contrast to see the wide, empty space of the beach, unbroken except where the land curved, with the cold winter water splashing onto the beach. The sound of the ocean was similarly stunning after the quiet of the trail.

"Oh, it's gorgeous here," breathed Tessa, nearly to herself.

"Isn't it?"

As they walked out onto the beach, separately but together, Tessa could feel the wind pulling at her scarf and locks of hair. It was colder here than in the sheltered forest, and she instinctively ran up to Roxy and grabbed her arm to create a bit of a wind block.

"A bit nippy out here, huh?" said Roxy with a smile. "Good thing I've got a plan."

Tessa raised her eyebrows. "Oh yeah?"

Roxy nodded and, keeping Tessa's arm securely through her own, guided them toward the dunes, to a sheltered spot that still had a great view of the ocean but was miraculously much warmer.

From her backpack, Roxy pulled out two packable down blankets, one of which she folded in half for them to sit on with their backs to the dune. She sat down on half of it and motioned for Tessa to join her. She threw the second blanket over their backs before, to Tessa's great pleasure and surprise, she pulled out a big, heavy green thermos and two small plastic mugs.

"How do you feel about hot chocolate?"

"Yes, please," said Tessa.

Roxy poured them each a cup of steaming hot chocolate and they sat there in companionable silence.

Sitting next to Roxy, the warmth of her body against hers, the coziness of the blankets, and the view of the ocean and dunes with a warm mug of chocolate goodness overwhelmed Tessa with a sense of calm and relaxation she hadn't felt all week. It was this moment, here, where she could finally feel completely at ease. It was almost as though she'd managed to convince herself that all her concerns and worries about the show, the grant, Lisa, and even her reunion with Roxy were minor things that could be ignored.

Basking in the winter sunshine of a brand-new year, enjoying a perfect moment with a very attractive woman, Tessa breathed deeply and felt some of those stresses melt away.

"Is it okay?"

"It's perfect," breathed Tessa.

"It's just a mix," said Roxy, "but I'm glad you like it."

"I meant…everything," said Tessa, gesturing at the beach vaguely. "Thanks for thinking up this whole thing. I was a little hesitant when you suggested a hike. I was worried it might be too cold."

"We got lucky with the weather, that's for sure," said Roxy. "But I always bring backup just in case," she added, tapping the top of the thermos with a gloved finger. "Anyway, I'm glad it worked out. I love being outside whenever I can. I just feel sort of…trapped if I'm inside too long. Does that make sense?"

"Sure," said Tessa. "I didn't used to appreciate being outside as much. When you work in theater, you are inside a lot, for sure. There would be some weeks I wouldn't be outside for more than five or ten minutes a day during shows. I didn't realize how bad it was for my mental health until I left New York and went back to Amherst for a while and—"

Tessa stopped short, realizing that she'd been on the brink of blurting out that she had begun the life of a hedge witch in Amherst. She had no idea how Roxy would react to that news, and she wasn't ready to find out. Perhaps she would think Tessa was completely nuts or delusional? Something about Roxy and her practical outdoorsy-ness made Tessa doubt how she'd react to the idea of magic and charms and hedgecraft. Best to wait on that revelation.

"Oh yeah?" said Roxy. "How was it being back there? Sometimes I wonder if I should go back and visit. But then I don't because I think it would be too hard. I still regret that I didn't go back and finish my degree."

"It's not too late," said Tessa. "If you still want to, I mean."

Roxy was silent for a beat, and Tessa wondered if she'd said something wrong.

"Yeah. I don't know about that," said Roxy. Her mind was clearly elsewhere at that moment, and Tessa regretted what she'd said.

"Hey, college isn't the end-all be-all," said Tessa, trying to regain some ground in the conversation. "No one else in my family went to college. My sisters give me a hard time sometimes, calling me Miss Fancy Degree."

Roxy turned to look at her. Sitting this closely, her face wasn't that far away and just for a moment, Tessa wondered if Roxy would lean in and kiss her.

"I'm sorry," she said, her face marked with concern. "That's gotta kind of suck. I mean, you obviously worked real hard for that."

"That's true," said Tessa. "And I don't want you to think badly of them. They are really proud of my career. They like to brag about me to their friends and neighbors. But they also like to give me a hard time about some of it, both going into showbiz and then leaving it. I think my mom still feels I owe her a trip to the Tonys or something."

"*Did* you ever get invited to the Tonys?"

Tessa laughed. "Only as Lisa's plus-one."

"Ah, okay," said Roxy. "And you two…"

She let the sentence drag out, unfinished.

"Done. Over. Nada. It took me a long time to realize, but she was not the one for me. Luckily, I had good friends like Chayo to make me realize I deserved someone better."

"And you still cast her for the play? Even with all that history? I don't know if I could have let big ones be bygones like that."

Tessa had to laugh at Roxy's malapropism.

"Oh no. I did it again, didn't I?" said Roxy with good humor. "What is it supposed to be?"

"Let bygones be bygones," said Tessa through giggles. "Which, now that I think of it, doesn't make any sense at all."

Soon they were both laughing, the words somehow meaningless the more they said them. Tessa was glad to bring some levity back to their conversation. The laughter was just as soothing and relaxing as the view of the ocean and the hot chocolate in their cups—and reminded her of how infrequently she and Lisa had laughed in their relationship.

"Done with the hot cholate?"

Tessa nodded, handing Roxy her empty mug. Roxy packed up the gear and slung the backpack back on.

"Ready?" she said, raising her eyebrows and giving Tessa a mischievous grin.

"For what?"

"Race you!"

Before Tessa knew what was happening, Roxy had taken off like a shot, running down the beach at a sprint. Moments later, Tessa found herself running too, the wind in her hair, the sunshine on her face, her eyes full of Roxy.

When she caught up, she felt warmed from the tip of her head down to her toes. Roxy had brought bread for the seagulls, or "beach pigeons" as she liked to call them, and they threw bread to the birds for a while before turning to go back to the trail. Roxy insisted they try hopping, skipping, jumping, and even turning cartwheels on the way back.

At first Tessa felt a bit silly doing all that, but soon enough she found herself exhilarated. This was completely different to all the managerial work she had to do at the theater, and it was a literal and figurative breath of fresh air. This was not the day she'd expected with Roxy at all. She hadn't known what exactly to expect, but this wasn't it. And she loved it.

Back on the trail, she felt winded and full of her own thoughts; it seemed Roxy was the same. They walked for a while in silence until Roxy interrupted.

"This is totally random, but I was wondering if you'd ever noticed that place on Standish Street, Madame Faustina Clerval? Clairvoyant?"

"Hmm?" Tessa had just been thinking about how she could incorporate the dunes and historic beach shacks they'd just seen on the beach into their production of *A Winter's Tale*.

"It's that weird little purple building, just a few doors down from where the gay bookstore used to be."

"I guess I haven't noticed it before," said Tessa. She racked her brain but couldn't bring the storefront to mind. She turned the name over in her mind. "Faustina Clerval. Ha!"

"What do you mean, ha?"

"Obviously a fake name. But a pretty good one for a clairvoyant."

"Why is it obviously fake?"

"Faustina can't be her real name, or at least, it doesn't sound like one. It's based on Faust—the man who made a deal with the devil? Christopher Marlowe, a contemporary of Shakespeare's, even wrote a whole play about it called *Dr. Faustus*. And 'Clerval' is the last name of Victor Frankenstein's best friend in Mary Shelley's *Frankenstein*."

"What?" said Roxy, evidently surprised. "That is great to know. Thanks for the tips." Tessa felt a surge of joy that she could be helpful to Roxy, even as a part of her was intrigued, wanting to know more.

Roxy pulled out her small notepad and pen and stopped on the trail briefly to make a note, piquing Tessa's curiosity further.

"Are you interested in going to learn about your future? From Faustina?"

They had started walking along the trail again; it was broad enough this close to the trailhead that they could walk side by side again, and Tessa was enjoying being next to Roxy yet again.

"No, nothing like that," said Roxy. "Not that I'm against it. It's just…"

Here Roxy hesitated, and when she spoke again, she pitched her voice much lower, even though they were clearly alone. The trail that day was deserted.

"I think she might be involved in a crime."

"What?"

Roxy nodded. "Mo and I went to the local museum yesterday, and it turns out there was an artifact missing in one of the cases. Faustina Clerval was one of the most recent visitors to the museum, and apparently, she'd been interested in the exact same display at the museum."

Tessa couldn't decide if Roxy was pulling her leg or being serious.

"Surely the museum gets all sorts of visitors, though," said Tessa. "You can't be sure either way. It could have been some bored local kids."

Roxy shook her head. "I've been thinking about it ever since we left the museum. The guide there had no idea anything was missing until we went to the display. The case was intact. I think it was even locked. No signs of forced entry. The guide, Clare, was a little scatterbrained, but I think she would have noticed a broken door or window in the museum or the display case."

"I guess that's true," said Tessa. "But people are often not very observant. Maybe there is a broken window in the museum's basement that just hasn't been discovered?"

"Maybe," conceded Roxy. "But there's more to it." Again, Roxy hesitated, and Tessa felt bad for critiquing her ideas so quickly. She should have been more supportive. After all, she wanted Roxy to trust her, and that meant putting the cool, logical Tessa, the theater manager and director, away for a moment and focusing on being supportive and open. One of the hardest things she'd had to learn in her hedgecraft study was precisely that—being supportive and open, and loving, even, for herself and for others. It wasn't something she'd mastered yet.

"Go ahead," said Tessa as encouragingly as possible. She touched Roxy's arm gently. "What else made it suspicious?"

Roxy sighed. "Mo is, uh, interested in myths about the ocean and, um, magical sea creatures and things, and there's a book in the museum's library that talks specifically about those things. You have to fill out a special form to request to see a library book in the special collection, and when we went to fill it out, Faustina Clerval had requested the same book."

"Interesting," said Tessa. "How does that connect to the missing artifact?"

"The artifact is a bracelet that supposedly belonged to this mythical ocean creature. A magical bracelet. And, well, Mo is convinced that there is a negative force in Provincetown right now. I know, I know, it sounds completely bananas. But anyway, this Faustina Clerval, with her weird name and the weird coincidences…it's too much of a coincidence for both of us. Feels like she's involved in it somehow."

"Or she might know something. Have more information?" offered Tessa.

"Yes," said Roxy. "But I don't know how to go to her without sounding suspicious."

"Or accusatory."

"Absolutely," said Roxy. "If she is involved, we don't want her to know that we suspect her."

Tessa nodded, absently stroking a beautiful red leaf she'd picked up, the single remnant of autumn that had somehow not turned brown on the forest floor. She had to remember her connections to nature. It was so calming here and energizing. Her work in hedgecraft had made her more aware of the natural world and how much healing there could be in nature. Her mentor Freya had always emphasized to her that the most magical healing qualities in hedgecraft were all centered on nature and the natural world, and she tucked the leaf away into her coat pocket to include in her calming evening rituals. The emphasis on nature, but also on finding the magical within daily ritual and routine, had been some of the most healing aspects of hedgecraft for Tessa.

She wanted desperately to help Roxy somehow with this mystery, even if it didn't make sense or lead to anything except extra closeness with Roxy. She wished there was something in her hedgecraft that could be helpful, and she decided she would look into it when she got home. For now, though, she let her theater director brain take over.

"What if I engaged Madame Clerval's services?" said Tessa. "I could make an appointment with her and see what she's like? I could ask her some questions about potential evil on Cape Cod relating to the theater? That wouldn't be too suspicious, would it?"

"I don't know," said Roxy. "That still sounds a bit too risky." She paused, thinking it over. "Do you have someone working on the show who you trust, but who is really into things like fortune telling or tarot or magic? Someone who wouldn't seem suspicious asking about it."

Tessa slapped her forehead with her mittened hand. "Of course! I don't know why I didn't think of this before. Our office manager and assistant director, Joy, is exactly the perfect person for this. She is super into crystals and tarot and chakras. She will be really excited to meet Madame Faustina and have an appointment with her."

"Excellent," said Roxy. "That's perfect."

On the drive home, they made a plan to get Joy involved without telling her too much of why they wanted her to visit Madame Faustina. Tessa marveled at how natural it felt to be making plans with Roxy. There was an ease to their interactions now, as if they were old friends rather than former roommates who'd been out of touch for nine years.

"We could pick up Mo and go out for a late lunch," said Tessa as she pulled up to Roxy's building, wanting nothing more than to spend another hour in Roxy's company. Every minute in her company felt precious.

Roxy smiled sadly. "I wish, but I have another shift at the brewery today. But hey, I have all of Tuesday off. Why don't I spend the afternoon at the theater?"

"Sure," said Tessa, brightening. "Would you like to bring Mo, too? She doesn't have to be Lisa's assistant. We can find plenty of stuff for her to do. I bet she'd love working with Joy, actually."

"Great!"

Tessa waved and drove away, a piece of her heart staying behind with Roxy. She marveled inwardly at how, in these moments, nothing, not even Lisa or the whole grant and the theater production, were as important to her as this one beautiful, wonderful, funny human being, and she couldn't help feeling that she'd wasted too much of her life on other things and not enough on finding this feeling now. This happiness was everything

She decided to stop at a local deli and pick up a lobster roll for lunch. While she waited in line, she checked her phone, and her heart sank.

Three missed calls and several texts from Joy. Two missed calls and several texts from Lisa. Several texts from Chayo and other cast members who'd already arrived. Some others whose flights were delayed. She sighed. The memories of her beach day with Roxy were fading fast in the face of all her other obligations, and she felt tired suddenly. Tuesday couldn't come soon enough.

CHAPTER ELEVEN—ROXY

After the excitement of their discoveries on Friday morning at the museum and the solid game plan she'd agreed on with Tessa to get to Madame Clerval, Roxy had almost expected additional new developments to follow fast on their heels. The whole thing had been making her jumpy, and she'd half expected to find Mo in another mermaid trap at any second all weekend. She'd almost called in sick to the brewery that Saturday, she'd been such a ball of nerves. Simply sharing part of their discoveries and suspicions with Tessa that morning had made her nervous.

She wished she could tell Tessa the whole story, but she knew that would be a betrayal of Mo's trust. Plus, she really had no idea how Tessa would react to the knowledge that Mo was a mermaid. While it was true that theater people tended to be fairly open-minded, it was one thing to put on plays about magical creatures, and quite another to actually come face to face with a real live mermaid.

Then there was the issue of the play. She still hadn't read it. Or even tried. She hadn't even looked up a decent summary of the play. She shook her head at her own anxieties as she let herself into the apartment after her date with Tessa.

Inside, she'd found Mo lounging on the couch in the studio apartment, watching a reality show on television, her brows knitted in intense concentration. The complete normality and banality of the situation was a bit hard to square with the intensity of Mo's earlier concerns for her own safety.

Nothing of interest had happened since their visit to the museum. Roxy wasn't even sure exactly what she'd been expecting, but it hadn't been this complete *lack* of action or developments.

Luckily, the brewery had been keeping her busy. Not that babysitting Mo didn't come with its own set of challenges. Mo was clearly getting bored and not a little restless now that there wasn't any immediate danger. On Monday afternoon, she showed up again, unannounced, at the brewery, demanding to see Roxy and then complaining loudly that she was bored and had nothing to do. Roxy, who was assigned to helping the master brewer that day with some of the brewery duties, had no idea what to do. She finally managed to convince Mo to go back to the apartment, but only very reluctantly.

Now it was Tuesday and she had been looking forward to seeing Tessa again, but it was evident that she could not leave Mo alone again all day.

"Okay, Mo, let's go. You're coming with me to the theater today," said Roxy that morning over breakfast.

Mo looked up from her bowl of raw shrimp with a giant smile.

"Really? You mean it?" A piece of glossy, translucent shrimp slid down her face and Roxy tried not to gag. It was really beyond her ken as to how someone so graceful and beautiful could be such a disgusting eater.

Roxy smiled as warmly as she could and nodded. "Absolutely. It'll be better for you to be near me. And maybe we can find you something to do over there to keep you busy. And safe, of course. I can't imagine anyone would try to use evil magic in a place that is full of humans." A part of her was still worried about letting Mo mingle with regular humans at the theater, especially since they'd inevitably have to spend time apart. Another part of her was frankly bored with babysitting Mo, especially since Mo was having a harder and harder time coping with staying in the apartment. Roxy couldn't blame her either; she'd be crawling the walls after four days of doing nothing, too.

Mo nodded. "You are very smart, Roxy. That is a good idea. And I am very bored."

Roxy sighed. This had been a constant refrain for the last few days. "Yes, I get it. And I'm sorry you're bored. I wish you could go home, too."

"You are tired of me?" Mo sounded genuinely hurt.

"No, of course not," said Roxy, mustering up as much sincerity as possible. She felt bad for Mo, who was strange but in general very nice and obviously in an unusual predicament. The complaining left something to be desired, though. "I meant that I'm sorry you're stuck here since it's making you unhappy."

"I am happy to help you, though," said Mo. She winked at Roxy. "I will help you today with Tessa and getting your true love."

"Oh no," said Roxy quickly. "Really, that's okay. I've got it handled."
Mo gave her a look as though she didn't quite believe it.

"Don't worry about it," continued Roxy. "Just try to act normal—
human—at the theater. Don't criticize people. Just agree with them and
help them. I'm sure Tessa can find you something to do to be helpful."

Mo looked the tiniest bit hurt but finally smiled and nodded before
slurping down the rest of her chilly breakfast.

❖

The theater was oddly quiet when they arrived at nine, even though
that was the time Tessa had instructed them to show up.

They walked round and round the back areas of the theater, Roxy
retracing her steps with Tessa the week before when she'd given her a tour,
but there was no sign of anyone. The theater felt empty and so quiet, it
unsettled Roxy. The goose bumps she'd been waiting to feel ever since Mo
showed up were finally rising on her skin, and the back of her neck pricked
in anticipation.

"Are we too early? Too late?" asked Mo, the expression of concern on
her face mirroring Roxy's own.

"I don't know. I thought she said nine," she said. She started to pull
out her phone to check their latest exchange.

Before she could figure out which pocket she'd slid it into, a door
behind them burst open and in strode Lisa with a gust of cold winter air
behind her.

When she saw Roxy, she smirked a bit. Roxy didn't like that jagged
smile, more like a threat than a greeting.

"You," said Lisa, without any preamble or greeting. "Come back to
help out today?" Roxy felt Lisa's gaze sizing her up in a way that she didn't
understand at all.

"That is the plan," announced Mo, her voice meeting Lisa's iciness.
Roxy looked at Mo, impressed. She'd drawn herself up to her full height,
somewhere around six feet, and with her shoulders squared and arms folded
across her chest, she looked like a formidable foe. "Why are *you* here?"

"*I'm* the star of the show," said Lisa. It didn't come off as vain or
boastful. She was simply stating a fact. She took a step toward Mo, taking
off her beautiful gray cashmere coat and matching beret as she approached
and shaking out her stunningly long, platinum blonde hair. "Are you going
to be my assistant?"

Mo looked a bit uncertain, and she glanced over at Roxy. Roxy shrugged. It wouldn't be her first choice, but if there was anyone who would be too self-centered to notice Mo's quirks, it was Lisa.

"You did say you wanted to help out," Roxy reminded her.

Mo thought it over. "You are not very nice," she said finally, meeting Lisa's gaze. "But you are the star of the show. So even though I am the daughter of a prince, I will be your assistant. For now."

Roxy's eyes got big and her jaw dropped. Mo had *clearly* forgotten their agreement to keep a low profile and try to "act human."

Lisa's eyebrows had shot up at this announcement. "I didn't know I was in the presence of royalty."

"She means, um, the prince of...um, Prince of the Sea! It's a restaurant. Back home." Roxy stammered as she spoke, trying to think on her feet. "Seafood, you know."

"Yes, I seem to recall how much you enjoy sushi," said Lisa, irony tingeing her words, but her expression was, unusually, one of amusement.

Mo glared at Roxy. She was not a fan of Roxy's explanation, but Roxy simply shrugged again. She couldn't have Mo mouthing off about being a princess. People would start thinking she was delusional.

"I think it would be *great* if you would give Mo a trial run as your assistant," said Roxy loudly, patting Mo on the shoulder. "Weren't you *just* telling me how bored you've been at home?"

"You won't have that problem with me," said Lisa.

Mo sighed and nodded. "A trial run?"

"Yes," said Roxy. "You can do it this week and see if you like it."

"Okay," said Mo, nodding.

"We can start with today, tomorrow, and Thursday, if you like," said Lisa. "Nine a.m. sharp here at the theater until at least three, maybe four or five, depending on the schedule. Deal?"

She put out a hand to shake.

Mo stared at it. She glanced at Roxy. They hadn't covered handshakes. Who shook hands anymore?

Mo put out her own hand and let it hover in the air next to Lisa's like a dead fish, then sort of...gently slapped Lisa's hand with her own. It looked completely bizarre.

Lisa rolled her eyes. "Wow. She's a little rough around the edges for a princess." She chuckled at her own joke. "I see I've got a lot of work ahead of me if I'm going to train you to be my assistant." She shoved her coat and beret at Mo and added her cream-and-blue scarf to the pile in Mo's arms. "Come along then. Tessa showed me my private dressing room yesterday."

The two of them started to walk down the winding hallway, away from Roxy.

"Hey!"

Lisa looked back, eyebrows raised. "Yes?"

"What about me? Where's Tessa? Where's everyone else?"

Lisa cocked an eyebrow. "That's interesting. Didn't Tessa tell you? She's got a morning meeting with Joy and Chayo and the theater manager. Rehearsal doesn't start until after lunch. I'm here early to work on lines and set up my dressing room."

"Tessa told me to come at nine." Roxy felt rather deflated. She'd been counting on seeing Tessa that morning, and she felt a bit forgotten. Tessa had seemed so keen to spend time with her on Saturday, but maybe she'd misread her?

"She's in charge of a lot of people and money," said Lisa as she began walking away again, Mo trailing behind. "I'm sure you can keep yourself busy in the wood shop."

The last words were hard to hear, as Lisa had already turned the corner, but Roxy recognized the nasty implications in her voice. Lisa clearly didn't think of her as anything but a measly little stagehand.

She now found herself alone in the dim hallway, wondering what to do. She felt small pinpricks of disappointment behind her eyes; she could hardly believe it. She wasn't going to cry over a small misunderstanding, was she? Of course not. She would simply go to the wood shop and get busy until Tessa and Chayo were free.

She had a good sense of direction, so finding the wood shop where she'd spent the day the previous week wasn't hard. But the door was locked. She pulled and pulled on the knob, but it wouldn't budge.

She walked back down the hallway and into the theater. She shivered. The house was cold, the heating clearly turned down while not in use. Theaters were often kept on the cool side since the performers had to perform beneath such hot lights on stage. Remembering that small detail made Roxy feel better, a little less lost. She wasn't a complete theater noob. And Tessa had definitely invited her. She just had to find her.

She walked across the stage and toward the other set of wings, when something up in the rafters caught her eye. Several somethings, in fact. She squinted and counted no less than seven small, lavender-colored sachets hung up in the rafters. Having grown up with a witch for a best friend, she recognized them as magical objects and her heart began to race.

Was there a magical presence in the theater? Was it dangerous? Was it related to Mo, Madame Clerval, and the missing bracelet from the museum?

She wished she knew how to get up to the catwalk, but that hadn't been part of her tour the other day. Should she mention them to Tessa when she saw her? Then again, maybe they were part of the show. Tessa had mentioned something about magic being part of *The Winter's Tale*. Or had she? She tried to remember what she'd heard Tessa discussing with Jack at the brewery when they'd been talking about the play, but honestly, she'd tuned them out.

She decided she'd play it by ear, somewhat, and later that day she'd see if there was a way to draw Tessa's attention to the mysterious sachets in the rafters.

Unless…was it possible Tessa was involved in the plot to catch Mo? The thought hadn't occurred to Roxy, but now it hit her full force. She hated the idea, but she had to consider it. If she was, then Roxy had already revealed too much about Mo and Madame Clerval and the museum. *Crap.* She would have to be more careful until she knew exactly what was going on—even if the idea that beautiful, talented, sparkling-eyed Tessa could be a mermaid killer felt so very, very wrong. Roxy hoped to goodness she was overreacting.

She continued her search for signs of life in the theater once she'd regained her composure, deciding that she'd go to the front of the house and see if anything was going on in the lobby of the theater. As she walked into the theater, the temperature rose significantly, and she enjoyed the sudden warmth.

There were also voices. Suddenly, a door near the box office window swung open, and a short, squat woman strode out and brushed past Roxy without a second glance. She was older—probably over sixty, Roxy would guess, with an old-fashioned hairdo popular among women of that generation, cut into short layers that looked a bit like a helmet, sprayed together with heavy-duty hairspray, dyed an unflattering and completely unnatural shade of dark blond. Her face was scrunched up with a sour expression that put Roxy in mind of a toad.

What was perhaps most noticeable, however, was not this woman's appearance. She looked like any number of women in their early sixties. There was really nothing remarkable in her appearance at all. Instead, what was remarkable was the immediate and almost overwhelming chill that radiated off her. Roxy felt it physically, as though a wave of cold water rushed over her and was gone again. She'd never felt anything like it—nor did she wish to feel it again.

She shuddered and rubbed her arms to warm herself up again and was surprised to find that her hands and arms were warm. Had she imagined that feeling of icy cold water passing over her?

Roxy approached the door the woman had just exited, and saw that it was marked "Office." She felt sure she'd heard Tessa's voice inside. She knocked gently on the door.

The door swung open violently.

"Yes?" There was an edge of frustration to Tessa's voice, her expression stormy. Clearly, this was not a good time to interrupt and Roxy felt her hackles rise. Why had she been invited to come that day if she wasn't wanted? She and Tessa had been texting just the night before and it had all seemed so simple. Tessa had sounded enthusiastic and encouraging, but it was all too easy to misread a text. Roxy began to doubt herself even more.

"Hey, um—"

Before she could apologize for interrupting, Tessa cut her off, her expression changing immediately to one of warmth, a big smile chasing away the clouds of worry. "Roxy!" She enveloped her in a spontaneous hug, and Roxy felt her concerns ebbing away. Tessa was warm and soft and fit perfectly against her body. She felt something deep within her surge with anticipation and something else, more tender. "I'm so glad you're here. I'm sorry I was so rude just now. I thought you were Lisa."

Tessa rolled her eyes at Chayo at the mention of Lisa, and Roxy couldn't help smirking a bit. Lisa thought she was a hotshot, and she liked dressing down Roxy, but Tessa and Chayo were not in on it as Lisa had implied.

"Nope, definitely not Lisa," said Roxy with a grin. "At least, not last I checked."

She was rewarded with a giant smile from Tessa and a chuckle from Chayo.

Tessa was wearing a bottle green sweater dress that hit just above the knee and hugged her slim yet curvy frame in all sorts of delicious ways that made Roxy wonder how long she could hold out on her promise to herself to "take things slow." Especially if Tessa kept giving her hugs like that last one.

Tessa was wearing a bit more makeup than the last time they'd hung out, and she looked beautiful, professional, and sexy all at once. The color of her dress brought out the deep aqua and green streaks in her hair as well as the green stones in her earrings.

For once, Roxy was grateful to Jazz and Hazel for taking her shopping last fall. They'd insisted she get rid of all her ripped-up work pants and jeans, the faded old flannels that had seen better days, and replace them with new, spiffier versions of the same. It had been a birthday present, they said, and while it felt awkward to accept their money in this way, she was now happy she had. Her brand-new maroon work pants and slate gray button-down looked sharp and not at all out of place next to Tessa and Chayo, who was dressed in all black with a dapper gray plaid newsboy type cap, but it was clear that the button-down shirt and black jeans were of good quality. The two of them were evidently dressed a bit nicer than usual, probably due to whatever meetings they had that day.

Tessa sighed and dropped into an office chair next to Chayo, indicating a third one for Roxy. The theater office was small and cramped, with an inner door on one wall that led directly into the box office. There were filing cabinets serving as supports for the desks, two computers, a printer/fax machine, and several shelves, all covered in stacks of paper as well as folders and binders with even more papers. The rest of the wall space was jam-packed with framed posters, playbills, and signed celebrity photos. Rather than feeling homey, though, the space was cluttered and ugly.

"I'm sorry I wasn't able to meet you at the door," said Tessa. "Glad you found us."

"Lisa said you had a meeting with the theater manager?"

Tessa and Chayo nodded. "The main cast is all here and a good portion of the crew, so we had to meet with the theater manager, Barb, to discuss schedules. The meeting was supposed to be yesterday, but somehow they forgot to tell me that the theater manager had yesterday off."

"Oh. How frustrating," said Roxy. "Did Barb just leave here? I saw a woman leaving the office right before I got here. She looked…"

"Like she'd swallowed a bug?" said Chayo.

"That was exactly how she looked." Roxy couldn't help grinning even as she suppressed another shudder. Even the memory of that person and her aura, or whatever you would call it, was enough to strike ice in her heart.

Tessa smiled momentarily before her expression changed back to one of concern.

"She's a real pain in the neck right now."

"You can say that again," Chayo, grimaced. "Everything about this woman is annoying."

"Sorry to hear that," said Roxy. "Everything okay for the play?"

Tessa nodded slightly, her expression back to one of tension and concern. She shrugged. "Honestly, I don't know. During the grant application process, the theater owner had been so supportive and wonderful. I thought I'd be working primarily with him. But it turns out that for day-to-day operations, he has nothing to do with it. Instead, it's Barb who handles it."

"And Barb is…a barbarian?" said Roxy.

Tessa chuckled a little before heaving another deep sigh. "Kind of the opposite, actually. She has so many rules about everything. Some of them seem reasonable, but others are nitpicky and annoying. She's already had an unpleasant run-in with Lisa, too, and that didn't make things any better."

"The worst part of it is that she treats us like kids." Chayo shook her head in disgust or frustration, Roxy couldn't quite tell. "Like she's doing us a giant favor and just expecting us to screw it up."

"That's horrible," said Roxy. "Is there anything you can do? Can you complain to the owner?"

"I don't want to do that just yet," said Tessa. "I'm hoping we can figure it out on our own." She shook back the tendrils of hair that had fallen onto her face, as though shaking away the concerns about the theater manager. "Let's talk about something more fun," she said. She directed a big smile at Roxy that made Roxy feel warm all over.

Chayo and Tessa filled Roxy in on some of the schedule for the rest of January before walking together to the wood shop, where Tessa left them for a while. Chayo and Roxy fell into the easy rhythm of working together. They were working on the throne again, sanding the wood and preparing it for painting. Roxy felt a pleasant sense of calm come over her during which she could forget about Lisa, Mo, Madame Clerval, Barb and her chilling vibes, her anxieties about the future, and everything else.

The only thing she couldn't forget about, no matter how hard she worked, was Tessa. As she sanded some rough corners of the wood, focusing with all her intensity, she found her mind wandering back to Tessa, her smile, the way she crinkled up her nose when Roxy made a joke, the happiness in her eyes when she saw Roxy at the door. There was a kind of serene happiness that came over Roxy when she was with Tessa. Of course, there was attraction, too, but there was something more. She wanted to make Tessa happy, to please her.

"That's looking great," came a voice from behind Roxy, just as she was standing up from sanding part of the bottom of the throne.

She turned around, and there was Tessa, as though her own thoughts had manifested her out of thin air. Chayo had stepped out for a minute, and Roxy hadn't even noticed because she'd been so focused on her task—and her thoughts.

"It's wonderful," said Tessa. "It almost feels like a shame to paint it."

"You really like it?" said Roxy. Pride filled her from within.

Tessa nodded. "It looks more regal and elegant than I could have imagined."

"I'm glad I can help."

"I meant to tell you, I really enjoyed Saturday," said Tessa. She stepped a bit closer to Roxy—so close that Roxy could smell her lotion and breath mints and something else. Just Tessa, she supposed. It was a heady mix. Her gaze met Roxy's, and Roxy was pleasantly surprised to see desire there. Her stomach dropped and she felt hot all over. Instinctively, she stepped back, away from Tessa.

"Me too," she said, her voice wavering a little bit.

Tessa looked a little disappointed that Roxy had stepped away, making her feel that she was sending the wrong message. Because she was attracted to her, wasn't she?

Remember your resolution. She couldn't break her resolution just one week into the New Year? Could she?

Resolutions were dumb. Wasn't that what Jazz always said?

On impulse, she took a step back toward Tessa and, taking her smaller hand in her larger one, she guided their hands together over the smoothened edges of the armrests on the throne, the wood sanded down so there wasn't a single rough patch on it.

"Wow, and it's so smooth," marveled Tessa, her body now dangerously close to Roxy's.

"Hard to believe it just takes some sandpaper and elbow grease, huh?" Roxy's voice was low and husky, her body thrumming with the electricity of their joined hands.

Tessa lifted her head to meet Roxy's gaze, lips parted.

The door banged open and in walked Chayo with a large box that had just been delivered.

Roxy and Tessa jumped apart, Tessa's cheeks reddening visibly. Roxy's heart was pounding so hard she could barely manage a smile.

"Hi, guys." Chayo gave them a look. Like she knew exactly what was going on and she didn't quite like it.

Tessa coughed to clear her throat. "Hi, um, again." She pulled self-consciously on her dress and smoothened an invisible wrinkle on it. "Oh, did the stains arrive all right?" She gestured to the box that Chayo had just brought in and set on a worktable.

Chayo nodded. "Yep. And it all looks in order so we can start staining the throne this afternoon."

"Great," said Roxy weakly.

"Bad news, though," Chayo gave Roxy a funny look. "There's a police officer out there looking for you." She cocked an eyebrow. "Anything we should know about?"

Roxy's eyes widened. A police officer? Could they be looking for Mo? Was that possible? Then she remembered the break-in at the museum.

"It's probably to do with the break-in at the museum, right?" Tessa gave Roxy an encouraging smile.

"Yep, that's probably it. Can't be anything else." Roxy nodded.

It was with mixed emotions that Roxy left Tessa and Chayo behind to go find the police officer in the lobby of the theater. She didn't trust police overly, having had some unpleasant run-ins with police when she was a teenager pulling pranks, but on the other hand, if they could find the thief, then maybe Mo's problems would be solved as well.

She wasn't sure if she was disappointed or relieved that Chayo had interrupted her and Tessa, either. As she walked up to the lobby through the theater, though, one thing she felt certain of—there was something between Roxy and Tessa, something good. Even if her mind and her heart were at war on how fast to proceed, there was a thrill just knowing that Tessa was definitely, absolutely, one hundred percent into her.

CHAPTER TWELVE—TESSA

What exactly did I just walk in on?"
Tessa swallowed hard. Her throat went dry, and she couldn't help playing with one of the rings she was wearing, twirling it round and round her finger in a nervous habit she'd never been able to break.

"Well?" said Chayo. She closed the door of the wood shop and sat down comfortably on a folding chair. She crossed one leg over the other, took a sip from her coffee cup, and gave Tessa a meaningful look. "Spill it."

Tessa's mind was a swirl of emotion. Her body hadn't yet recovered from being so close to Roxy's, from their hands touching, from their lips *almost* touching. A hunger deep inside her had surged to the surface and now she was fighting to keep it down again. She began pacing nervously between the throne and one of the saws.

Finally, she stopped and looked at Chayo again. She was her best friend, the one who got her through the whole ordeal with Lisa. The one who knew everything about her. Why was she afraid to tell Chayo the truth?

Because she does know everything.

Tessa pinched the top of her nose with her fingers and closed her eyes, her thoughts racing to the past, to the very day that she and Lisa had returned from London after Lisa's successful West End debut, an engaged couple, no less. Lisa had proposed to her on the night of her final performance at a bustling crowded restaurant, where they'd been sitting with a crowd of people from the show. How could Tessa say no to Lisa in that moment? The thought didn't even cross Tessa's mind. She'd said yes and put the ring on her finger, a rising sense of panic and claustrophobia in her chest that she quashed by telling herself it was nerves. Being in a foreign country. Being far from friends and family. Being in a crowded restaurant.

But she couldn't shake the sense of having the world closing in on her.

After a transatlantic flight next to Lisa, the feeling of claustrophobia was even more intense, and Tessa felt keenly the need for a stretch. She'd walked all the way from their Meat Packing District apartment to Central Park, to one of her favorite spots in the Ramble. It was the perfect June day, sunny, warm, but not hot, with a little breeze on her face. There was one spot in particular where she liked to sit and think and look out through the branches onto the Upper West Side but, as she neared it, she realized there was someone already there.

Two women, more or less her age, had been sitting there, chatting animatedly. One of the voices actually sounded familiar to Tessa, and she'd been about to approach the women and say hello, as she felt sure that at least one of them was a friend, when that woman turned her face enough that Tessa could see who it was.

And that's when she realized it was her old college roommate, her old crush, Roxy.

Tessa had done something that day that she always felt embarrassed by later, but it had been automatic, something she did without thinking.

She'd hidden herself nearby and eavesdropped on their conversation.

Even in the Ramble, which was meant to mimic a wilder, more forest-like landscape than a manicured park, it wasn't exactly easy to be inconspicuous, but she did it anyway. And she'd been lucky, she realized later, that no other park visitors had walked by her that day in that small, tucked away corner of the Ramble.

She didn't remember what Roxy and her friend—Hazel, she realized now—had been talking about. She simply couldn't take her eyes off Roxy.

Things had already started falling apart with Lisa by then. Their relationship had suffered from their London trip, rather than bringing them together as she'd hoped. She'd felt lonely in London, like a mere addition to Lisa, her "plus-one." She'd given up a major career opportunity in New York in order to accompany Lisa to London, at Lisa's insistence of course. Being in a foreign city hadn't helped, even if Tessa had, eventually, found a way to network in London's theater scene in a way that was good for her too.

The unplanned, unexpected run-in with Roxy had been the true beginning of the end of her and Lisa. Not that she had talked to Roxy then. She'd been far too nervous to do anything like that. But Tessa had gone home that day feeling completely changed. Lisa had already gone to bed by the time she got back to the apartment they shared, but Tessa was amped up, unable to sleep. Instead, she'd arranged to meet up with Chayo that night in the West Village, at their favorite little hole-in-the-wall that always had Charlie Chaplin movies playing on a screen next to the bar.

She'd poured her heart out to her best friend, about how truly lonely she'd been in London. About how much she'd missed New York while over there. About how distant she'd been feeling with Lisa for a long time.

And she'd told Chayo about Roxy. About how she'd seen her old crush. And a flame of desire that she'd thought she'd forgotten had been fanned that day.

Chayo had listened and been there for her, reassuring her about her career and validating her feelings about Lisa.

"Hey, if seeing an old crush is making you have doubts about your relationship, then yeah, maybe your relationship needs reconsidering," Chayo had said at the time. "Maybe you should talk to Lisa about how you feel?"

But Tessa had been too chicken to do that. Instead, she'd done everything wrong. She'd let her crush on Roxy and her unhappiness in her relationship with Lisa take her down a dark road.

She became obsessed with Roxy. She started looking her up on social media. She downloaded her pictures online to her phone to look at, surreptitiously, at work or when Lisa had a late rehearsal in the evenings. She started fantasizing about Roxy.

The unhappier she got with Lisa, the more time she spent thinking about Roxy, writing about her in her journal, looking for more and more photos of her, even going home for a weekend to see if she could find any prints of pictures taken in college, back when she'd still been using a cute little silver digital camera and ordering prints at the pharmacy off campus.

There had been one picture of her and Roxy, from the start of their time in the dorm. Someone had snapped a photo of them in front of their dorm room door with their names on it. They were arm in arm, cheesing it up, looking like babies, for crying out loud, but Tessa hadn't cared. She'd tucked the photo carefully into the pocket of her purse, like a talisman.

Then, one day, she got an offer to direct an off-off-Broadway play with a script by a friend she admired. Chayo would also be working on the production. It was going to be the Three Musketeers, they'd joked. And even as Tessa was slowly realizing that she had to end it with Lisa, she put it off. She let herself fall into the wild and relentless pace of working on a show.

And it was easy enough to have long hours when directing a show. She avoided Lisa by making her schedule exactly opposite to hers while still making sure to spend a few hours together each week so Lisa wouldn't get suspicious.

The show helped Tessa forget her obsession with Roxy as well. She was too busy with rehearsals, meetings with producers, costumers, the tech director, the theater manager and the box office, reading and rereading the script until she knew everyone's parts by heart, and on and on. It was what she loved, even as she felt herself teetering on the brink of burnout.

Some days she was so tired, she was stammering by the end of the day. She would go home and fall into bed, bone-tired, and then find herself unable to fall asleep, her body still humming with the nervous energy and strain of working sixteen-hour days in order to avoid her girlfriend. Fiancée. She started having migraines, which she'd never had before.

The show was a success, in the end, but Tessa was a wreck by the end of opening weekend. Lisa insisted that she take a day off once the Monday after rolled around, and for once, she put her foot down when Tessa tried to beg off.

They'd actually had a really nice day together. Lisa had treated them to a morning at her favorite and very pricey spa, with a couples massage and a champagne brunch afterward. In the afternoon, they went down to the Strand bookstore and browsed before heading back to their apartment.

It was on the steps to their building that Tessa, still exhausted from the build-up to the show and opening weekend, tripped going up the stairs, and, losing her balance, grabbed onto Lisa's arm, in the process dropping her bulging bag of books from the Strand and her pocketbook. The wallet hadn't been closed correctly after paying at the bookstore and its contents spilled all over the stairs.

The two of them gathered up everything just as the rain started. Tessa hadn't noticed in the hubbub that Lisa had picked up the picture of her and Roxy from college.

Instead, they went upstairs and Lisa cooked an early dinner for them. She insisted that Tessa take one of her sleeping pills that night and go to bed early. For once, Tessa fell asleep quickly and slept long and sound.

She went to bed so early that night that the next day, she was wide awake at six in the morning. Oddly enough, Lisa was not next to her in bed. Instead, she found her sitting at their breakfast bar, still wearing the clothes from the day before.

Lisa was holding something in her hands, knuckles white with tension.

Tessa felt, then and there, that it was all over.

After Lisa found the photo, her suspicions had been raised. She'd gotten Tessa's phone while she slept and, horrified, had looked through her photos and found the stash of social media pictures Tessa had downloaded of Roxy. There were only fifteen or twenty, but it was enough. She even found an old text thread between Tessa and Chayo where Tessa mentioned her crush on Roxy—and she didn't have even a shred of humility for violating Tessa's privacy in such a way.

Instead, all Lisa could focus on was Roxy. It didn't matter that there was no communication between Tessa and Roxy. It didn't matter that she'd stopped mooning over Roxy when she started working on the show.

To Lisa, it was as good as cheating.

"When you're not cheating on me with her, then you're cheating on me with the show," said Lisa, her words like arrows. They hit Tessa right in the heart. Because she wasn't wrong. Tessa had simply been too scared to tell Lisa the truth.

But then, Lisa turned nasty. And she said those words: "Who are you without me?"

The implication being: nobody.

When Tessa finally stumbled into Chayo's apartment a few hours later, early enough still that Chayo was in her pajamas sipping her café con leche, Tessa told her everything. *Everything.* Including her short-lived but highly embarrassing online stalking of Roxy.

Finally, Tessa's eyes refocused into the present. Chayo was still sitting there, in the folding chair, but her gaze was softer now. She got up and gave Tessa a big hug.

"Hey, it's okay. You don't have to relive the past all the time. It's in the past."

Tessa nodded, her eyes pooled with tears. She wasn't sure why she was crying. No, she did know. Her relationship with Lisa had meant something to her. And when it came time to end it, she'd done it in the most passive of ways. She'd been a coward. And she wasn't proud of what she'd done to Roxy either.

Chayo squeezed her hands gently. "Let's make you a tea, all right?"

Tessa nodded and mutely followed her to the greenroom, where there was a small kitchenette area set up with an electric kettle. Chayo knew her well enough to know that in times of difficulty, Tessa needed hot tea. She'd often joked that for Polish people it was a cure-all for all hurts, whether physical or emotional.

Hands wrapped around a mug of lemon green tea, sitting on one of the comfy couches in the greenroom, Tessa felt better already, even if she also felt a little silly for getting so emotional.

"I'm sorry," said Tessa. She took a sip of tea that immediately soothed some of her frayed nerves.

"No, I'm sorry." Chayo made herself another coffee with the pour-over funnel she'd contributed to the kitchenette. She wasn't much of a tea drinker. "I didn't mean to make you feel like I was judging you. That's not what this is about." She sat down opposite Tessa while the coffee dripped through. "I'm just worried about you. First you tell me you're gonna see your old crush at a wedding here in Ptown. Then you invite her to work on the show. Now I walk in on the two of you and see you making googly eyes at each other. It all seems, I dunno, kind of fast."

Tessa couldn't help smiling at Chayo's characterization. "You're absolutely right," said Tessa, nodding. "It does seem fast."

"I don't want to see you get your heart broken." Chayo paused, looking down at the floor before meeting Tessa's gaze again, her eyes full of sadness and concern. "I've already seen that once. And once was enough."

Tessa felt a stab of guilt. She'd leaned on Chayo so much in their friendship already. She didn't want her to feel like she had to be her emotional support animal.

"It's not like that," she said finally. "I really do want to have a relationship with Roxy. And I'm willing to take the risk of getting hurt."

"Okay," said Chayo, nodding. "Will you tell her about the internet stalking? About how it ended your relationship with Lisa?"

"It's way too early for that." Tessa felt a bubble of panic rising in her chest.

"Is it? Are you sure? Cuz that sounds like something Roxy should know. Up front."

"No, that's all wrong," said Tessa. "I don't want to scare her off. Not before I know if she's into me."

Chayo gave Tessa a knowing smile. "Chica, given what I just saw, she's into you. She looked like she wanted to eat you up with a spoon just now."

Tessa laughed. "Really?"

"Really," said Chayo.

Tessa's heart fluttered at the word. Chayo was absolutely certain that Roxy was into her. And that closeness, that almost kiss in the wood shop. Something inside Tessa agreed, on an instinctive level.

"We've only been around each other for a week," said Tessa tentatively. "Isn't it a bit soon to start talking about the past?"

"Is it?" said Chayo again. "I dunno, Tessa. It can take a lot less than a week for some people to fall in love. What kind of Shakespeare fangirl are you anyway if you don't know your *Romeo and Juliet*?" She grinned and Tessa couldn't help laughing again.

"You know, they ended up dead," she pointed out, the levity of the conversation making her less stressed, calmer.

"Because of secrets and bad communication," countered Chayo, a note of seriousness entering the joke. "Look, just promise me you won't wait until your wedding day to tell her you kind of, sort of stalked her and it ended your previous relationship."

"OMG, now you're talking weddings," said Tessa with a nervous laugh. "I just can't."

"More to the point," continued Chayo, undeterred, "don't wait so long that Lisa decides to tell her instead."

"Okay, okay," said Tessa. "Agree to agree."

"Don't wait so long that I decide to tell who what?"

Tessa and Chayo looked at each other before their necks swiveled in unison to see Lisa walking into the greenroom.

Tessa felt hot all over. How much had Lisa heard? Had she been eavesdropping on their conversation?

"I was just saying that Tessa needed to talk to the theater owner about Barb's rules before you did it yourself," said Chayo smoothly, and Tessa breathed a sigh of relief.

"Is the water still hot?" said Lisa, indicating the kettle, and Tessa nodded. Lisa fixed herself a cup of the same green tea as Tessa and seated herself on the couch near Tessa and opposite Chayo. "Ah yes, Barb. What a pill," she said, rather unironically, thought Tessa. The thought made Tessa smile a bit. "For once I agree with Chayo. I think you're absolutely within your rights to talk to the owners about her Draconian rules. Honestly. No guests backstage? Or in the dressing room? No food deliveries of any kind? How am I supposed to eat? And what do I do when my *real* assistant finally shows up?"

"I'm sure we can put Ramón on the crew list," said Tessa. She was pleased her voice wasn't as shaky as just a few minutes ago. The last thing she wanted was Lisa suspecting she was still hurt by their breakup, or that she ever thought about it at all. "But yes, the food deliveries issue is a problem. I'm going to have to clarify with Barb what that means exactly. She can't expect everyone to be working here all day without food."

"And no scents or perfumes or even scented lotions?" continued Lisa, on cue taking out a small tube of very fancy scented hand cream from her oversized purse, then squeezing a small dollop of it on her hand and gently massaging it into her skin. She always did have very dry hands, Tessa remembered. Not like Roxy, whose hand had been warm and soft and perfectly smooth against her own.

She found herself getting warm at the thought of Roxy's touch, and she hoped her warm feelings were not showing themselves on her face as well. The *last* thing she wanted was for Lisa to know about her feelings for Roxy. At least, not before she was absolutely sure that Roxy reciprocated them.

"A lot of places are going in that direction," said Chayo in answer to Lisa's complaint. "Allergies, chemical sensitivities…there's a lot of folks who can't be around scents."

"I don't have a problem with that, in general," said Lisa, putting away the lotion. "But it's the hypocrisy. That woman stank to high heaven of some old lady perfume. I could barely stand being next to her."

Tessa couldn't help a smile, no matter how unprofessional Lisa's characterization was. It was true. Barb smelled awful, as if she'd bathed with an old bottle of cheap perfume.

She shrugged. "We'll just have to make do until I can figure out a way to negotiate with her. Or like you said, Joy and I will have to set up a meeting with Barb and the theater owner to hash this all out."

Chayo nodded. "Her list of dos and don'ts goes on for pages. I've never seen anything like it."

"Maybe Barb is her own kind of Leontes," said Lisa, raising an eyebrow. It was the closest Lisa ever got to making a joke. Given that Leontes of *A Winter's Tale* was a major tyrant, that suggestion wasn't too far off.

"Sure. You could shadow Barb for a bit. You know, get Method for the part," said Tessa.

Lisa generally was not a fan of any kind of teasing, so Tessa was relieved to see her smile at the mock suggestion, and Chayo chuckled too. It felt good to be here, all three of them, just making little theater jokes and hanging out in the greenroom with hot beverages.

The door opened, and Joy popped her head in, bright dyed-red curls and red cat's eyeglasses frames drawing their attention immediately.

"Sorry to interrupt, gals. Phone call for Tessa in the office and," she looked over at Lisa, "I think your new assistant is looking for you?"

All three of them got up, and Lisa groaned.

"You have a new assistant?" said Tessa, surprised. She racked her brain to think who it could be.

"Yes. Roxy's sister or cousin or whoever? That gorgeous but utterly brainless girl who calls herself Mo," said Lisa, rolling her eyes. "It's going to take a lot of work to train this one. I sent her out to get us lunch just to see how she'd do. It hasn't even been fifteen minutes, so I can't imagine she's brought back anything."

"Oh! Well, think of it as a favor to me," said Tessa, glad that she could, however indirectly, be a help to Roxy. "She sounded eager enough."

"She's a weird one," said Lisa.

They parted ways in the corridor, Chayo heading back to the wood shop, Lisa going in the direction indicated by Joy, and Tessa following Joy to the office.

After a brief phone call with one of the nearby costume shops where they'd requested some costumes for the smaller parts in the play, Tessa hung up and looked through her planner to see what else was on the docket for the day. She saw the little reminder to herself to ask Joy about Madame Clerval.

"Were you able to make an appointment with that clairvoyant here in town?" asked Tessa, looking over at Joy, who was perched on the edge of her desk, her bright purple and red chunky heels swinging. Joy loved "living out loud," as she called it, and everything about her was colorful. Tessa appreciated her energy and positive outlook.

"I did," said Joy, sliding off the desk and riffling through the papers on her desk, then her purse, before pulling out her day planner and flipping back a few pages where she'd taken some notes. She gave Tessa a curious look, eyebrow raised. "She's quite the character, even for someone in the trade."

Tessa nodded. Joy was one of the only people who knew that Tessa dabbled in the magical. Nobody really needed to know she was a hedge witch. It was something she did for herself. She'd been attracted to the lifestyle precisely because it was a solitary practice: no ceremonies or rituals with others, no covens, nothing like that. But Joy's interests in astrology, healing crystals, chakras, inner balance, and other New Age practices made her a natural confidant. Tessa appreciated having someone to confide in on this topic. Despite the stereotypes about theater people, they weren't all accepting of such practices—Lisa least of all.

"Oh?"

Joy nodded. "That number on the store front isn't for a cell. It's a landline. No answering machine either. I tried calling all times of day and evening until finally last night, just on a hunch, I called late. Ten thirty."

"And?" Tessa was dying of curiosity. What kind of business kept such strange hours?

"She answered. Very interesting voice," said Joy, whose "voice readings" were something of a legend among her friends. She had a knack for knowing all sorts of things about a person simply based on the tone and timbre of someone's voice, or so she claimed. Tessa had found her insights to be correct on several occasions, so she never doubted Joy.

"Oh, come on. Tell me already," said Tessa, giving Joy a playful and rather tame shove on the arm. "Don't leave me hanging."

Joy relished her momentary power and cackled at Tessa's impatience before turning somber. She gave Tessa a meaningful look. "She's powerful, Tessa. She's the real thing."

"Shit." Could this mean that Roxy was on to something?

"Oh yeah. She knew exactly who I was—even though I was calling from the office phone—she knew my name, what I was wearing, even my birthday."

"Wow."

Joy nodded seriously. "She told me Patty-cakes was doing well, too." Patty-cakes, also known as Princess Pancake, was Joy's pet cat that had passed away a few months ago.

Tessa's jaw dropped. "What? How could she possibly know that?"

Joy shrugged. "I have no idea. But her aura was strong, even over the phone."

"What was her aura like?"

"It was hard to read. I felt strength and power and knowledge, but I couldn't tell if it tended positive or negative. Which makes me think negative. I mean, why would someone hide positivity from their aura?"

"Maybe to cultivate a sense of mystery? She makes a living off it after all." Tessa wanted to keep an open mind, but it was getting harder. Madame Clerval could be incredibly dangerous if she really was as powerful as Joy was suggesting—and if she was involved somehow in the robbery at the museum, as Roxy believed.

"Anyway, I made an appointment for her first availability." Joy paused.

"When is it?"

"In *two weeks*." Joy gave her a look of consternation. "She said that was the soonest I could get in because she doesn't have regular hours in the winter. She also said she needed to wait for Venus to 'move into the correct quadrant' before she could help me." Joy paused dramatically. "And I didn't even tell her what I needed help with."

"Two weeks?" Roxy wasn't going to like that. "Still. I guess it's better than nothing. Are you sure you want to go through with this?"

Joy smiled and waved the question away. "Are you kidding? Now I *have to* go. I'm dying of curiosity to know what she'll tell me."

Tessa smiled, trying to hide her concern. "Great."

"Is there anything you want to know about specifically? Anything I should ask?"

Obviously, she couldn't tell Joy to ask Madame Clerval about the museum specifically, so what could Joy ask her instead?

"Let me think about it and I'll let you know. Now that we know we have two weeks, we can really consider it." Tessa paused. "Off the top of my head, I'd say, ask her about the play. You could say you've felt some evil vibrations at the theater and around Provincetown, and you're worried about the success of the project."

"Have you really felt some evil vibrations here?" True concern entered Joy's voice and she studied Tessa's face carefully.

Tessa shrugged. "Some twinges, I guess. Something feels out of balance. It could just be Lisa. Or Barb."

"Got it."

Tessa put a note in her planner for the date and time of Joy's appointment, and their conversation turned to the first rehearsal that afternoon.

They heard a commotion of voices, Lisa's loudest among them.

Tessa and Joy shared a glance before leaving the office and running down the corridor toward the greenroom.

When they arrived in the greenroom, Lisa was yelling at Mo, Mo was crying, and Roxy was attempting to calm both of them down.

A strong salty, fishy smell assaulted Tessa's nose.

On the floor of the greenroom lay a large fish, fresh from a fisherman's boat or market. Tessa had no clue about fish, but this one was fairly large, still completely intact.

"It was a mistake! Come on, Lisa. Give her a break," Roxy was saying to Lisa, before putting an arm around Mo and trying to move her away from Lisa and her wrath. "Let's go, Mo. Let's take a breather."

"But the fish. I must save it. It cannot stay on the floor," Mo was saying between sobs.

"This is some ridiculous joke, isn't it?" said Lisa. She saw Tessa had arrived and she glared at her now. "Are you in on this too? You suggest Mo be my assistant, and then give her a dead fish to bring me for lunch?"

Tessa and Joy worked like a well-oiled machine in that moment. While Joy took care of Roxy and Mo, Tessa managed to convince Lisa that it wasn't a joke. It was some kind of misunderstanding. She pulled Lisa into the corridor and walked her down to her own dressing room. Some of the crew had arrived in the meantime, and one of them, Sam, had heard the noise and come to find her. She gave him a twenty and sent him out to get Lisa a lobster roll and a latte, before leaving to check on the greenroom scene.

While she'd been gone with Lisa, Joy had calmed down Mo and Roxy and corralled some more crew members to bring cleaning supplies to the room. The fish was now in a plastic bag and Mo's tears had subsided.

"Is everything okay?" said Tessa to Roxy. She patted Mo on the shoulder gently. "I'm sorry Lisa yelled at you." Tessa decided not to ask why Mo had brought a fish to the theater; it felt a little soon for that. "She'll get over it."

Mo looked at her with a tear-streaked face that was still impossibly beautiful, her liquid green eyes glowing with concern, before turning to look at Roxy.

"I am sorry. I let you down. I said I would act normal, but I cannot."

"Hey, it's okay," said Roxy, rubbing her back a bit. "Do you want to go home? We can take the fish home, too. I'm sure you'll appreciate it more than Lisa."

Mo nodded, and the three of them arranged for Roxy and Mo to go home for lunch, and to remove the offending fish from the theater. Tessa thanked her lucky stars Barb wasn't around to berate them for having a dead fish inside her hallowed theater walls.

They were about to leave when they bumped into Sam from the crew, returning with Lisa's food and coffee.

"Hey, Sam," said Tessa. "Wait."

She took the food from Sam and handed it to Mo.

"Do you still want to work here as Lisa's assistant?"

Mo nodded somewhat reluctantly.

"Then here. Take this to Lisa. Apologize," she said gently. "Tell her you'll be back in an hour for whatever she needs this afternoon."

"Okay."

Roxy and Tessa stood outside Lisa's dressing room just far enough down the hallway that Lisa couldn't see them, but they could still hear her and Mo's conversation. Tessa tried not to obsess over how close they were standing to one another while eavesdropping, their hands sharing the same air space. She wanted to grab Roxy's hand, but she resisted. Chayo was right. She needed to slow down a little and get to know Roxy better.

Lisa had calmed down a bit and the lobster roll and latte were helping patch things up between them. When Mo left the dressing room, she was smiling again.

"She said I was very pretty and very stupid," said Mo with a grin. "So that is compliment, yes?"

Tessa and Roxy exchanged a look.

"Sure, of course," said Roxy. "You're definitely very pretty. And we'll work on the other thing." She gave Tessa a wink that sent a spark of desire shooting through her. Was there a way to take things slow—but not too slow?

She walked Roxy and Mo to the door of the theater.

"I'll be in rehearsal all afternoon," said Tessa as Roxy put on her coat and hat. "But maybe we could have dinner tonight? At my place? I'd love to cook for you."

Roxy looked at Mo with concern. "Would that be okay? Will you be okay on your own tonight in the apartment?"

"Oh, of course Mo can come, too," said Tessa with a smile, but hoping against hope that Mo would say no.

Mo looked from Roxy to Tessa and back to Roxy, a funny little smile on her lips, like she knew a secret and was bursting to share it. "Thank you very much, Tessa. But I am sure Roxy would like to eat your food without me."

Tessa saw Roxy redden, and her heart swelled. Maybe Roxy had mentioned to Mo that she was interested in Tessa? She felt like she was getting back on the roller coaster of emotions, just as she'd calmed down and assured herself that she was ready to be responsible and get to know Roxy.

"Okay then," said Tessa, finally breaking the awkward silence. Mo looked like the proverbial cat that ate the canary, she was so pleased. She promised to text Roxy the address and time later that afternoon, once she was sure that rehearsal would be over in a timely fashion—and since she was the director, she would see to it that it was. No burning the midnight oil tonight, not unless it was at the side of Roxy Bright.

She waved them off and was just about to pull the door closed, as it had an annoying tendency not to close all the way, letting in chilly winter air, when she felt someone on the other side pull the door open sharply.

It was Barb.

Tessa felt her heartbeat speed up.

"Oh, hello, Barb," she managed to choke out. "Great to see you again."

Barb gave her a dark look that clearly said she would not be engaging in any pleasantries.

"Did I just see someone leaving the theater with a raw fish in a bag?" There was an edge to her harsh, raspy voice that immediately grated on Tessa's nerves.

"A raw fish? That's ridiculous. Why would we have a raw fish at the theater?" The lie slipped out, Tessa's voice firm. She was not going to let this troll of a woman bully her.

"I don't know. You tell me," said Barb, pulling off her coat and dusting the snow on it directly onto Tessa's feet. The flowery, cloying smell of her perfume expanded into the hallway. "I just told you, no food or messes at the theater. This is Provincetown's most historic entertainment venue, and I am in charge of keeping it—"

Tessa cut her off. "No one cares more for this theater than I do. In fact, I care for it so much, that I think it would be good for us to go over your list of rules with Ted in a meeting with all three of us, as well as Joy and Chayo." Ted was the theater owner. Tessa knew he was currently at his vacation home in Florida, but she didn't care. She would put him on a video call if it meant shutting Barb down.

Barb's eyes narrowed at Tessa. Tessa was on the short side, but Barb was even shorter. In spite of her stature, though, she seemed somehow bigger than Tessa. As if she was taking up more space than necessary. A shiver ran down Tessa's spine that had nothing to do with the winter weather.

"Fine. You want to play it that way? That's fine by me." She strode off without another word, leaving Tessa wondering what on earth her words meant.

CHAPTER THIRTEEN—ROXY

Promptly at eight, Roxy found herself outside the door of Tessa's duplex. At Mo's urging, she'd stopped to pick up a small bouquet of flowers at one of the little local grocery stores and a growler of beer from the brewery bought on heavy employee discount—as much as she could afford on her still somewhat limited budget. Her knee was twinging a little bit from the dampness in the air, and she bent and stretched it a bit before straightening up, running her free hand through her hair, and finally knocking on the door.

The door swung open immediately, and there was Tessa.

She looked beautiful. Roxy felt her palms start to sweat again, and she was glad to come inside and shrug off her coat, even if it meant standing dangerously close to Tessa, who was still in her body-hugging sweater dress. She'd exchanged her boots for adorable, embroidered slippers that looked vaguely ethnic, but very pretty and colorful. She was currently wearing an apron with a colorful flower pattern on it that also looked ethnic, but again, Roxy couldn't put her finger on what it was right away, though it seemed a little familiar.

"I hope you like pierogi," said Tessa as they walked into the kitchen. A big pot of water was burbling away on the stove with the stuffed dumplings bouncing around; more dumplings were browning in a skillet with some onion next to the pot.

"Gosh, I hope you haven't been making all this just for me," said Roxy, remembering now their earlier conversations about Tessa's family being from Poland. The embroidered slippers, the flower pattern on her apron, they must all be Polish, thought Roxy with a smile. Of course. Never having had a strong sense of her own ancestry growing up, Roxy was always excited to learn about—and eat the food of—those who did.

And she loved pierogi.

Tessa chuckled. "Oh no. This is all from my mother who worries I'll starve out here if she doesn't send me home with a week's worth of food every time I see her."

"Wow. That's so nice." Roxy's mother was not much of a cook and had often declared proudly that she cooked at no one's request.

"I guess," said Tessa with a little bit of an eye roll. "She's a real Polish mama, and that comes with good things, like delicious food, and some distinctly less good things, like Polish mom guilt."

Roxy chuckled. "Well, at least the food is good." She offered the flowers and beer to Tessa once she was done checking on the food.

"Awww, you didn't have to," said Tessa, but the glow in her eyes made it clear that she was completely delighted. "Please sit, and I'll pour us some beer and put the flowers in water."

Soon enough they were sitting at the small dining table in the living area of the condo, which adjoined the kitchen. It was a small but newly updated apartment, made for renting out to people visiting Ptown. Everything was white, silver, black, and gray, generic to the extreme, though Roxy noted that Tessa had tried to make the place her own.

There was what Roxy assumed to be a Polish folk scarf draped over the couch, its bright pinks, greens, and blues instantly warming up the space. There was a scented candle on one of the side tables, a crocheted blanket that was a vintage piece, done all in hues of orange and brown, and a piece of Polish pottery with some chocolates in it on the coffee table.

The pierogi were delicious, much better than any Roxy had ever had at a deli or market in either Salem or Boston.

"These are incredible," she said, stuffing another bite of sauerkraut and mushroom dumpling, followed by a bite of cheese and potato.

Tessa flushed with pleasure. "I'm so glad you like them. My mom really is an amazing cook. I can't believe how lucky I was growing up with all those homemade dinners. I never appreciated them fully until I went to college."

They paused to reminisce about some of the terrible food at the UMass student cafeteria. Normally, Roxy didn't much enjoy reminiscing about her one year of college, but with Tessa, it felt easier. There was a lightness to their exchange. Tessa was also a very funny storyteller, and Roxy could see why she'd been drawn to theater and drama. As a professional storyteller herself, in her guise as ghost tour guide in Salem, Roxy appreciated Tessa's talents. She felt oddly proud of her.

"Of course, nowadays the university's dining halls are beautiful. They look like restaurants in Disney World and serve gourmet food practically," said Tessa once they'd both stopped giggling over her description of the tasteless, overcooked burgers in the dining hall. "It figures it's much nicer now. Kids these days, eh?"

"Don't know how lucky they are," said Roxy with a chuckle.

Tessa cleared their plates away and brought out a small plate with homemade chocolate chip cookies. "Now *these*," she said proudly, "I did make."

"What? When did you even have time?" Roxy took a bite and savored the sweet and salty flavors of the cookie.

"I like to stress-bake," said Tessa. She grabbed a cookie for herself and took a big bite. "Mmm."

"How does that work?" It would never in a million years occur to Roxy to bake when feeling stressed. Wasn't baking a stressful activity?

"It's like, when I'm working on a big project, and it's going to be several months before I have the results, it's nice to bake something fast and easy that I've done a million times and I know will turn out perfectly. Like these cookies. It's very satisfying," she added with a smile that made Roxy's insides go flip-flop.

"Whatever the reason, they are delicious," said Roxy. "Clearly, you've inherited some of your mom's talents in the kitchen."

"Someday hopefully I can cook for you myself," she said, her expression even warmer than before, and if it weren't for the fact that Roxy's hands and lips were covered in greasy cookie crumbs, she would have leaned in for a kiss right then.

"I'd love that," said Roxy. "I'm afraid I can't reciprocate. Unless we go camping. In that case, you should see me with a Dutch oven. I can work some magic there."

"I just bet," said Tessa, and the words came out with something more than flirtatious banter. Something hotter, full of desire. She leaned in toward Roxy, and Roxy's breath caught in her throat.

RIIIIIING!

The sound of an old-timey telephone jarred them apart before their lips could touch, and Tessa, flustered, jumped up to see to her phone that was so loudly ringing.

"I'm so sorry," she said to Roxy. "I have to answer. I'll just be a minute."

Roxy nodded her understanding. Her heart was pounding and she couldn't speak. Had they really almost kissed? Yes. There was no denying it. Did she still want to kiss Tessa? Yes. Of course. And there was nothing wrong with that. They could kiss *and* take it slow—right?

Tessa went into the bedroom with the phone, and before she closed the door behind her, Roxy could hear Joy's distinctive voice on the line, discussing something technical about the theater production. She breathed a sigh of relief. She was glad it wasn't Lisa. That woman made her nervous as hell.

She believed Tessa when she said she wasn't interested in Lisa. That much was clear, especially given their almost-kiss. But that only made Roxy more worried about Lisa. What if Lisa realized that they were involved? Would she make Roxy's life miserable? Or Mo's? She didn't know Lisa well enough to know how vengeful she was, and she didn't want to find out.

To keep herself busy, Roxy cleared the dishes off the table and started cleaning up around the kitchen. Growing up she'd been a total slob, constantly getting in trouble for the mess in her room, leaving stuff all over the floor when she got home from school, and shirking her duties around the house. She'd often used the various sports she'd participated in as a teen as an excuse for not having time for chores. It was her best friend Hazel and her small business that had made her understand the value and importance of keeping spaces tidy—and pitching in to help others with chores too. Over the years she'd helped Hazel mop the floors of the shop, dust the shelves, and wash the windows when Hazel was falling behind on those things. Running a small business was a lot of work, and Roxy was proud now that she was the kind of person who didn't think twice about helping out.

By the time Tessa emerged from the bedroom, their dishes were done, the remaining pierogi were in a container in the fridge, and the pots and pans were drying in the rack. Tessa found Roxy wiping down the countertops and table with a sponge. When she saw Tessa, she threw the sponge in the sink and dried her hands on a kitchen towel.

"Wow," said Tessa, taking it all in. "Thanks so much. You didn't have to do that."

Roxy smiled. "I wanted to."

Tessa took a step toward Roxy and, as though they'd planned it, as though it was the most natural thing in the world, as though they did this all the time—they were wrapped in each other's arms, kissing.

The kiss was both hot and tender, and Roxy felt as though her feet were no longer on the ground. Tessa's lips were soft but passionate, eager to explore Roxy's. Pleasure coursed through her like hot honey, making her entire body heavy with desire. She reveled in the feeling of Tessa's body on hers, pushing together, Tessa's hands on Roxy's back, holding her close. Roxy marveled at how a new kiss could feel, and yet, how completely natural. She felt warm from inside out, and when Tessa deepened the kiss, she felt her whole body go into overdrive, her heart in her throat, her whole body on fire.

After what felt like an eternity, but also far too short a time, they broke apart.

"Wow," said Tessa again, this time her voice quieter, breathier.

"Wow is right," said Roxy, and they both laughed. Tessa hugged her again and let her head rest on Roxy's chest.

"This feels so right," murmured Tessa into Roxy's flannel shirt, her breath warming Roxy's skin through her shirt. Roxy gave her a squeeze and kissed the top of her head. It all felt so natural with Tessa, even as Roxy was suddenly terrified. She had to get things right this time around. The responsibility of not fucking this up settled onto her with an unexpected weight. This person in her arms was trusting her with her heart, and she felt fragile, like a bird, in Roxy's arms.

This was not some fling or one-night stand. This wasn't some stranger. She had to make things work, and to do that, she couldn't do what she'd always done.

Roxy pulled away slightly so she could meet Tessa's gaze. She saw pleasure, happiness, and longing, her deep brown eyes warm and inviting, but also a tiny bit scared.

Tessa was terrified too. It wasn't just Roxy.

They were both there, in each other's arms, wanting each other, but scared that they would mess this up. It was comforting to Roxy to know that.

"Is it okay if we take things a little...slow?"

Tessa's face broke into a wide smile and there was relief in her expression. "Oh gee, I thought you were going to say you didn't feel *that way* about me."

Roxy laughed in surprise and wonder. "What? No. Not at all. I just... I've messed stuff up before. Going too fast, if you know what I mean. And you're too special for that." She leaned down to plant a very soft but chaste kiss on Tessa's lips before pulling away again—even though every single part of her wanted to take Tessa to the bedroom right then and there, strip off that body-hugging dress, and throw her on the bed beneath her.

Roxy pushed that R-rated image out of her mind with difficulty, and instead focused on Tessa—the Tessa who was in front of her, smiling still a little shyly, but nodding with understanding.

Tessa planted a similarly chaste kiss on Roxy's lips—like a butterfly landing, barely there but full of potential. "That's completely fine," said Tessa. "I'd like that. I don't want to rush anything with you. I want to savor every moment."

It was nearly midnight before Roxy walked home very reluctantly, her heart singing with joy but also sad to leave Tessa behind. In the spirit of taking it slow, they'd spent the evening playing cards. Tessa taught her how to play a two-person version of solitaire called "Garibaldka" in Polish, which, upon internet searching, turned up the delightful factoid that the game was known in French as "crapette." They'd laughed over that probably longer than it warranted. Roxy smiled at the memory of Tessa's head thrown back in laughter, her beautiful neck just waiting to be kissed, as she trudged to her apartment in the cold. Tessa had beat her the first time, but then she'd gotten her revenge—partly because she'd managed to distract Tessa with a little bit of footsie—something else that made Roxy smile and barely notice the cutting winter wind and wild snowflakes falling across Ptown.

She found Mo still awake, reading *The Winter's Tale*, of all things. Lisa had given her a copy of the script to read so she could help her run lines. Roxy wasn't sure what the mechanics of learning to read a human script were for a mermaid, but Mo appeared rapt when Roxy plopped down next to her on the couch.

"Any good?"

"Mmm?" Mo didn't look over at Roxy until she'd finished the scene she was reading. Finally, she stopped and set the script on the table. "You know this play?"

Roxy waffled a bit. She'd downloaded an ebook version of the play to read on her phone, but somehow, she couldn't make herself do it. Every time she went to open it, memories of high school English classes cropped up in her mind, words swimming on the page, her whole body hot and cold with anxiety that she'd be called on to read, haltingly, like a child, in front of the whole class. She'd always much preferred the contemporary plays and musicals her high school had put on to Shakespeare. The words of

Shakespeare plays felt heavy as she tried to read them, slowing her down like running up a steep hill. Better to simply avoid them.

"It is very interesting," said Mo, sounding a bit like a teacher. Roxy was impressed. Here was Mo, learning a new language in a week—albeit she did have some magic to help her with that—and then reading Shakespeare. And apprenticing with Lisa Collins no less. "Lisa will play Leontes, and he is…terrible."

Mo looked very concerned about this, and her concern made Roxy want to laugh, but she didn't. She'd explained to Mo what a play was and what acting was, but it was still a concept that Mo struggled with.

"Just remember, it's not real."

"But, Roxy, how can I think this? He orders his own daughter to be thrown away. And he is so mean to his wife, to his friends, to everyone, until it is too late." Mo had tears in her eyes as she talked about the play, and Roxy began to feel worse and worse about not having read the play, leaving Mo alone all evening, making her be the assistant to Lisa. "And what about me? Am I not exiled here? Alone, away from family? Will I have my happy reunion?" she said, looking at Roxy plaintively, tears streaming down her face now.

Roxy hugged her tight. "I'm so sorry, Mo. I shouldn't have left you here alone all evening. Especially not after the tough day you had with Lisa."

Mo pulled away and sat upright, less upset and more curious. "You spent all evening with your One True Love?"

"Her name is Tessa, Mo. And we barely know each other."

Mo barely registered Roxy's protestations. "And you kissed, yes?"

"Mo, come on, that's personal—"

"Yes, I see it. You kissed!" Mo clapped her hands with delight. "This is good. Very good." She paused, her eyebrows knitting together, a look of confusion on her face. "But why are you here and not with her? Go and spend all night with your beloved. You cannot be here."

"We want to take it slow," explained Roxy. "I really like her."

Mo looked possibly even more confused than before. "What is 'taking it slow'?"

Roxy crinkled up her nose and rubbed her chin, trying to think of an easy way to explain the concept. She had no clue what mermaid courtship, or sex, was like, so she decided to tread as carefully as possible.

"It means…um…it means…"

Mo's rapt gaze was locked on Roxy now, and it felt like all the words in her head were gone. "Yes?"

"It means we don't sleep over at the beginning," said Roxy finally, settling on what felt like the simplest explanation. She looked at her watch—nearly one in the morning. "Okay, we'd better get off to bed. Don't you have to be at the theater tomorrow at nine?"

Mo nodded, her look of concern returning.

"Hey, you don't have to do this." Roxy patted her gently on the arm. "I can try to get you a little job at the brewery."

Mo wrinkled up her nose.

"What?"

"I cannot be around the smell of cooking fish all the time." Mo made a face like she'd just smelled a fart.

"Okay, then," said Roxy. "What *do* you want to do?"

Mo sighed. "It's fine. I will try to remember what you said—it's not real. And maybe Lisa will like me someday." She sounded rather unconvincing.

"Oh! I just remembered. I talked to Tessa about Madame Clerval."

Mo grabbed her by the shoulders and squeezed so hard in her excitement that Roxy yelped in pain.

"Sorry!" Mo let go of Roxy. "What did she say? Will she go talk to her?"

"Yes," said Roxy. "Though, wait. Not her. She's going to have Joy go. You know, the lady with the reddish hair? And red glasses? Loud voice?"

"Oh yes," said Mo, nodding. "Why her?"

Roxy shrugged. "Tessa says it might be too obvious if she goes. If this Madame Clerval is the real deal, I mean, if she's really evil and magical, then she might know why Tessa is there. She could sense it, you know? But Joy doesn't know that *I* asked her to go, so in theory, it should be safer."

"Okay. That sounds good. When will she see her?"

"Not for two weeks. I'm sorry. That's the soonest she could see her."

Mo flopped back on the pillows with a sigh of frustration.

"I know. It's disappointing."

Mo sat up again, flicking her bright neon green curls away from her face. "What is the next step? What else can we do? We must do something."

"There's still the museum library. We can check it out on Friday again. Maybe we can take a look at that grimoire?"

Mo sighed again, and Roxy felt bad she didn't have any other ideas. It was an impossible task—find the people keeping Mo on land without actually dealing with them face-to-face. But what if there was another way to break the spell keeping Mo there?

"We could also go to the public library. Do some research? Or we could search online? If only Hazel and Elizabeth were here. We could talk to them about how to do the research." Hazel had recently texted Roxy to let her know she would have little to no internet access for the next two weeks as they were renting a cottage in the Apennines for the last part of their honeymoon, and they'd purposefully chosen a place with no Wi-Fi. They wanted to completely disconnect and relax after a week of touring Rome, Florence, Venice, and Milan.

Roxy was happy for Hazel, who rarely got to take extended vacations as the proprietor of her own small business, but her heart squeezed a bit. She was in over her head, and she could really use her best friend there to guide her through what was increasingly feeling like a dangerous situation. Evil sorcerers or magicians, a stranded mermaid, and a chance at true love? It was a lot to deal with.

Unexpectedly, Mo hugged Roxy. "Thank you for trying. Yes. Let's try to do the research, like you suggest. But you're also right; we should get some sleep."

"We'll figure this out," said Roxy. "I promise." She hugged Mo back, grateful for the hug. She'd been trying to reassure Mo, but in the end, it felt like they were reassuring one another.

CHAPTER FOURTEEN—TESSA

Tessa was walking on clouds and rainbows for the rest of the week, and nothing, not Lisa and her constant blowups, or Barb with her sudden arrivals and departures and Byzantine ways of running the theater, or any other number of hiccups could derail her mood.

Roxy liked her.

This thought thrummed through Tessa with every heartbeat, with every step down the labyrinthine corridors of backstage. It was a refrain that sang along with the spoon that stirred the honey into her hot tea and the song that she sang to herself in the shower: Roxy likes me. It was a solemn tattoo and a soaring pop song in her head.

"You are alarmingly bouncy this morning," remarked Lisa as their paths crossed in the hallway near her dressing room the next morning after kissing Roxy. Tessa was determined not to let anything bring down her mood, though, so she simply smiled at Lisa and kept on humming her own made-up tune.

She was already several steps past Lisa when she heard Lisa call her.

"Yes?" Tessa turned around to see Lisa approaching her with a warmer expression on her face.

"Sorry, I didn't mean for that to sound so aggressive. Just getting into character, I guess." Lisa cocked an eyebrow and smiled sheepishly.

"Sure, no problem. Thanks for starting us off yesterday with such a great first rehearsal. I appreciate you," added Tessa. It was never a bad thing to compliment a diva, especially if she was the star of the show.

"I'm glad to hear it," said Lisa. She was clearly still a little thrown by Tessa's bursting energy and positivity. It wasn't that Tessa was a negative person—it was more that in their relationship, Tessa had never shown this side of her. "I don't suppose there's time today to grab lunch together? I rather don't trust my assistant to get it, if you know what I mean."

"I hope you'll give Mo a fair shake, Lisa. She's clearly working through some issues, but it means a lot to me that you'll help her out like this. This grant is all about creating opportunities for community outreach."

"Of course, of course," said Lisa, arms raised in the sign of surrender. "So how about it? Lunch?"

"Sorry, not today, unfortunately," said Tessa. "I've got a working lunch with Joy and Chayo. But I'm actually off to meet with a local business owner to discuss some PR events in a few minutes. It's very close by. Would you like to come with? I was thinking we could even discuss a meet and greet event focused on you." Tessa turned on the charm and ended with a purr of admiration for effect; she knew better than most how much Lisa's vanity controlled her decisions. She hoped Lisa wouldn't figure out her little white lie, either. She wasn't having lunch with Chayo and Joy, but she didn't want Lisa to spoil her plan of surprising Roxy at work.

"That sounds good," said Lisa. "We don't have rehearsal until the afternoon, correct?"

"Right," said Tessa. "I'll meet you at the front of the theater in fifteen."

Not much later, Tessa found herself in Lisa's company, walking through the center of Ptown. The sun was shining brightly in that way that it does in winter, a shard of bright ice in the sky, its cold luster in harmony with the little warmth they felt from it this time of year. Just a few days earlier, it would have made Tessa wild with anxiety to think about walking around Ptown with Lisa. Today it didn't matter at all. All that mattered was that she was going to go to the brewery at lunch and surprise Roxy—the beautiful woman who liked her.

All of Ptown was wrapped up in rainbows in Tessa's rose-colored vision. It was winter, so there were fewer Pride flags than usual, but here and there she could spy them. She enjoyed the many colorful houses on the Cape, painted in pastel yellows and lilacs next to more traditional wood shingled homes in brown and shades of gray and white. On a sunny day in winter, they all looked stunning and joyful.

She was so wrapped up in her thoughts, admiring the town and thinking about Roxy and *that kiss* that she just about forgot where they were going—and she definitely hadn't been listening to Lisa talking about the different inflections for part of Leontes's speech in Act I. Oops.

"Wait! I think we were supposed to turn back there," said Tessa just as Lisa had been about to say something else.

They doubled back and turned onto Standish Street, one of the larger thoroughfares in town, and before long, they were standing in front of a well-known bookshop in town—Recovering Hearts.

"That's weird." Tessa looked at the address on the scrap of paper where Joy had scribbled it down for her, comparing it to the numbers on the building. Sure enough, they were the same. "I thought this place closed."

"Closed? That would be a tragedy," said Lisa. She was already halfway through the door, excited about something that didn't center around herself, Tessa noted with surprise.

Tessa waited on the sidewalk for a moment before following her. There was something odd about the whole situation. She could have sworn she'd read an article about how the shop was closing. The shop had been there for twenty-eight years and the owner was ready to retire. She was sure a friend had sent her the clipping when she'd announced her grant and how she was going to use it. She'd only been to Ptown twice before, but each time she'd loved hanging out at the bookshop. It was Lisa, in fact, who had introduced her, as Lisa's biggest not-so-guilty pleasure was sapphic romance, and this bookstore sold it. In large quantities.

That's why it'd been a big deal to everyone in the sapphic community around Boston and the Cape—and beyond—when it was announced the shop was closing. It was the end of an era, truly.

Except it wasn't, apparently.

Why was the shop still here? There were natural explanations, of course—the closing was delayed or the owner had found a buyer who shared her vision and wanted to continue her legacy. But something didn't sit right with Tessa.

She took a moment to steady herself, right there on the sidewalk, and reached out with her magic to sense the aura of the place. Strangely, she could find no aura at all. It was like a black hole had sucked up any traces—and that *was* suspicious. A place like Recovering Hearts *should* have an aura and yet, inexplicably, it didn't.

She pulled back the threads of magic to herself and fingered the moonstone necklace she'd been wearing for protection ever since Roxy had warned her that something wasn't right. More than ever, she was glad she'd hung up those wards in the theater. Perhaps she needed to use additional protections. Something was off.

Gingerly, she entered the shop and found Lisa already with a stack of books in her hands. Her favorites were always the ones about doctors and nurses and paramedics saving lives and falling in love.

"God, I love this place," said Lisa. "I'm so glad it didn't close."

"Oh no, we could not let that happen, now could we?"

Lisa and Tessa turned toward this new voice that seemingly came out of nowhere, coming face-to-face with a woman who was, evidently, the new proprietor.

She was a tall woman of indeterminate age, very elegantly dressed in a white blouse, white slacks, and long white duster, her blond, nearly white hair pulled away from her face in a delicate if somewhat dated chignon. Her eyes sparkled brightly, almost unnaturally, in the light, though Tessa couldn't tell what color they were. She was an imposing figure and very beautiful if somewhat unearthly.

She was also a witch or magician of some sort—that much was obvious to Tessa. The fact that she didn't bother to hide it was more confounding.

"Hello, I'm Isidora." The woman reached out a hand. The last thing Tessa wanted to do was shake this woman's hand, but there didn't appear a way around it that wouldn't be hopelessly rude.

"I'm Tessa. From the theater," she said, finally grasping Isidora's hand and suppressing a shudder. There was something in her handshake that made her skin crawl.

"Yes, I've been expecting you." Her smile lacked any warmth, and her words sounded less inviting and more like a threat. Tessa had to work not to touch her talisman in front of her.

She glanced over at Lisa, but Lisa appeared completely unconcerned. She smiled back at Isidora and was already following her to one of the displays in the store. Reluctantly, Tessa followed them.

Isidora gestured to a particular display, and for a moment, Tessa's misgivings fell away. Here were copies of *A Winter's Tale*, tastefully displayed, in the edition Tessa had recommended, with just enough glosses for an interested reader to understand the play and its contexts, but not too many so as to make it overwhelming. As she took in the display, she noticed that there were also several modern rewrites and adaptations of the play on the shelves below, as well as a small selection of other Shakespeare plays. It was eye-catching and attractive, and Tessa couldn't help gushing.

"Wow, this looks great," she said, smiling genuinely at Isidora.

"I'm so glad you approve," said Isidora. "I thought it would be a nice addition to the display to have some related books."

"I agree completely." Tessa glanced around the space, noting that this part of the bookshop was a little less cluttered and more open than the rest. "Would this be the event space, if we did any events here?"

Isidora nodded. "Yes. There is room here, I think, for a small, intimate sort of meet and greet type of event that Joy described to me over the phone."

"It's very small," said Lisa, looking a bit worried. "Don't you think it would get crowded?"

"Not at all," said Isidora. "We would keep it very exclusive." The emphasis on the word "exclusive" achieved the desired effect. Lisa was both reassured and flattered.

They spent the rest of their short appointment there discussing some details for the event, which would take place closer to the play's opening in March. As they went into logistics and event planning, Tessa let go of some of her misgivings and let her theater director and producer brain take over. She was also pleasantly surprised at how easy it was to have Lisa there. Lisa could be a professional when she wanted to, and she was perfectly suited to this situation, asking pertinent questions and making suggestions.

Before they left, Lisa purchased her stack of books, and they were off, heading back to the theater. As they walked away, Tessa took one last look back at the shop, and she felt her heart stop for a beat. Isidora was in the window of the shop, her eyes locked on Tessa's. It was an odd sort of look in her eyes that gave Tessa the creeps, before turning into a smile and a friendly wave.

"I can't wait to dive into these," said Lisa. "I'm glad I could come with you today."

Tessa was barely listening. Once they'd rounded the corner from the shop, she asked, "Don't you think she was a little, I don't know, creepy?"

"What?"

"Creepy. Isidora. She gave me the willies."

"Really? Seemed normal to me." Lisa gave her a sidelong glance. "She seems very competent and ready to help us out."

Tessa began to doubt herself. Maybe she'd simply gone looking for oddities and weird feelings after what Roxy had told her about Madame Clerval. Maybe the stress from the show was already starting to drive her a little batty. "Sure," she said finally with a smile. "I'm probably imagining things."

"Of course you are," said Lisa. "It's your signature style—overthinking every little thing. It's what makes you a fabulous director. But I promise, Isidora is just a bookshop owner with an old-fashioned name. And what really matters is that she's keeping Recovering Hearts alive."

Tessa nodded. That was true. She'd been devastated when she'd heard the shop was going to close. It was a Ptown institution. And it was doubly good luck that the new owner was dedicated to stocking so much sapphic literature like the owner before her.

They walked the rest of the short way to the theater together making small talk about the show and the weather. There was snow in the forecast, and everyone was starting to get excited about it. Tessa hoped it wouldn't snow too much as she didn't want the travel plans of the remaining cast members to get thrown out of whack. There were a lot of moving parts to the show, even at this early stage.

When they returned to the theater, they parted ways, and as Tessa walked back to her office, she marveled at what a normal interaction she'd had with Lisa. She hadn't said as much to Roxy, but part of the reason she'd agreed to "take things slow" with her was because she wasn't quite ready to tell Lisa they were dating. Lisa didn't miss much, and if Tessa and Roxy were sleeping together, she'd nose it out right away. She'd already noticed Tessa's good mood earlier that morning. And Tessa wanted to keep things with Roxy a secret. She didn't want to examine her feelings too closely as to why that was; for now, she told herself it was because it was more special that way. And they'd only just reconnected a week ago—even if it was a whirlwind of a week. Best to take things slow, get to know one another, and enjoy their early relationship intimacy away from the prying eyes of others.

She was glad Roxy was working at the brewery today because she doubted she could hide how she felt with their kiss still fresh in her mind. She couldn't wait to see Roxy for lunch in just a few short hours. In the meantime, she had a bunch of payroll stuff to go over with Joy, and she hoped that by throwing herself in the work, the hours would go by all the faster.

A few hours later, she found herself sitting at the bar at the Pride of Ptown. She was enjoying a very small pour of the coconut porter, trying not to drink too quickly since she had a whole afternoon of rehearsals and meetings still ahead of her. She'd only caught a glimpse of Roxy so far, and her whole body fluttered with anticipation at the sight of her, tall and ruddy, bringing in boxes of supplies from the delivery truck into the backrooms. Roxy's face lit up at the sight of her, making Tessa's heart beat hard in her throat. She couldn't remember the last time she'd felt so much nervous anticipation centered around a single person—except when she'd roomed with Roxy in college and realized she was totally crushing on her.

Finally, her food came out, along with Roxy, who placed the plate of blackened drum po' boy with a side of fries and coleslaw in front of her with a flourish.

"Madam, your fish," she said with a smile. "Oh, I almost forgot the pickle." Roxy dashed back to the kitchen before Tessa could tell her it really didn't matter; no pickle was as important as an extra few seconds in her company.

Roxy returned with a small plate and two pickle spears.

"Mm, pickles," said Tessa appreciatively. She was suddenly starving, but she also wanted to talk to Roxy. "Do you have some time to hang out?"

Roxy checked the large, masculine watch on her left wrist. "Yes. I do. Not a lot but enough to chat." She smiled at Tessa a little shyly. "I had a great time yesterday."

Tessa flushed with pleasure. "Me too."

"Did you have a good morning?" Roxy picked up a towel and slowly began drying off some glassware behind the bar. It was a slow day without many customers, which Tessa was glad of. She didn't want to be interrupted.

She began eating her food and chatting with Roxy between bites, all the while admiring her practiced movements, picking up the various glasses—tulip-shaped, snifter-style, pint glasses and others that Tessa didn't know the names of—and drying them deliberately and carefully, checking in the light to make sure they had no spots, and then placing them carefully in their places. Her sleeves were rolled up halfway, exposing the hands and forearms that Tessa so longed to have around her body.

She quickly pushed that thought aside as she felt her whole body getting hot immediately.

"Yes. Pretty good. Though…"

"What?"

"We went to the bookshop in town where we are going to have some promotional events, and I got kind of a weird vibe from the new owner, Isidora."

Roxy paused in her work. "Oh really? Like a Barb bad vibe?"

Tessa nodded.

"Tell me more."

"I don't know. I just got a bad feeling at the shop, like something was off. And then I got the major creeps when I shook Isidora's hand. Lisa said I'm making too much of it, but it just felt weird."

"Lisa was there too?"

"Yes. But she said I was overreacting. Which I guess is possible. Sometimes I overthink things."

"You seem pretty intuitive to me," said Roxy with a warm smile. "I always say, follow your gut."

Tessa smiled back. "Right now, my gut is pretty darn happy. This fish is amazing."

"I'm always glad to hear we have a happy customer," said Roxy, her tone of voice flirtatious, sending Tessa's mind into a whirl of emotion.

"You seem pretty happy here too," said Tessa.

Roxy was thoughtful for a moment. "Yeah. I am."

"It's a nice gig?"

"Definitely," said Roxy. "And who knows? Maybe it'll be more than a gig. I could see myself working here, you know, full-time. I never thought I'd want to leave Salem, but with a job like this, I think I would consider it."

"Oh really?" said Tessa, her heart unexpectedly dropping into her shoes. Roxy's staying in Ptown to work at a brewery was not the fantasy she'd been building in her mind. "Would you really want to work in a restaurant?"

"Why not?" Roxy lay down the rag now that she'd finished with the glasses. "Free food and booze, great coworkers, fun vibe. Plus, learning about how to brew beer has been really interesting, even if I'm still just learning the basics."

"Sure," said Tessa. She took another bite of her sandwich to cover her consternation. Why would Roxy want to work in the service industry when she was clearly so good at so many other things? It didn't make sense. "But it's not really a career, is it? I just mean, you are so talented and smart— you could do anything with your skills."

An odd look crossed Roxy's face that Tessa wasn't sure how to interpret. Roxy opened her mouth to respond just as they both heard someone call her name.

"Roxy, we're ready to get started." Jack waved to her from the staff entrance. "Hi," he said to Tessa politely, but it was clear that he was in the middle of things, impatient to get back to it.

"Duty calls." Roxy smiled and doffed an imaginary hat at Tessa.

"Have fun," said Tessa.

"I'll text you later," said Roxy before disappearing into the back.

Tessa finished off the last few French fries on her plate before flagging down the bartender at the other end of the bar and asking for her ticket. She couldn't help feeling that their interaction hadn't quite gone the way she'd hoped, and she wished she could call Roxy back and have a do-over.

Back in the theater office, she only had a few minutes to get ready for rehearsals. A look at her schedule only made her heart sink—she wouldn't have any free time, day or evening, until the weekend to see Roxy. But Saturday was only two days away. She messaged Roxy and proposed they do something together, with Mo, if necessary. She didn't want Mo to feel left out either. Being Lisa's assistant was no walk in the park.

At the last minute as she was about to head to the theater, she added one more line to her text: *I'm sorry if I said something that made you uncomfortable earlier. I didn't mean to.* But she immediately deleted it. It was too soon for misunderstandings, wasn't it? Instead, she wrote, *It was great seeing you today. Can't wait to hang out again soon!!!*

Hopefully that message would be enough to communicate to Roxy how much she meant to her and how interested she was in her. Because she was. Very interested.

CHAPTER FIFTEEN—ROXY

Roxy woke up on Friday morning feeling more confused than ever—about Tessa, their kiss, and her weird comment at the brewery.

She knew there was a spark of *something* between them, that much was clear. But was it really any different than all the other sparks she'd had with other women? Was it any different from what she'd had with Amy? Everything had felt completely real and amazing at the start with Amy, too. How was she to know that things would be different with Tessa, especially if she rushed into things with her?

They had chemistry, sure. But what about their lives and futures? Roxy couldn't help bristling at the thought that Tessa had so easily shrugged off the idea of working full time in a brewery. Perhaps it was a sign that things weren't meant to be.

Full of doubts, Roxy had retreated to her signature style—she'd avoided interactions with Tessa, even ignoring her last text after their interaction at the brewery. She had no idea where things were leading, but she was reminded of her vow to herself to take things slow as well as her promise to Mo to help her find her way home. There were things that needed prioritizing, she reminded herself, and running after a woman like Tessa, used to intellectual conversations about Shakespeare and dating famous stars, felt suddenly rather silly. Chemistry was one thing; a relationship was quite something else.

Roxy made a conscious effort to focus on Mo that day, and her issues. They had breakfast together and then made their way over to the museum. Although they were there only a week earlier, it felt like a completely different place.

The door to the museum had a bright shiny new lock on it, and inside, instead of the friendly if slightly dotty curator, Clare, there was a very serious woman with a very tight bun and dark-rimmed, square-style glasses. Roxy guessed she wasn't that much older than her, but her entire vibe was that of someone much older. She looked the very caricature of a strict librarian, thought Roxy, who did not, strictly speaking, have the best relationship with librarians in general.

The woman was completely absorbed in some kind of account book she was working on at the counter, and after a few moments, Mo nudged Roxy, who then, very quietly, cleared her throat.

"Uh, hello," said Roxy, as the woman looked up at them. Roxy felt as though she were being sized up.

"May I help you?" said the woman, whose nametag said "Rhoda." She was the curator that Clare had mentioned. "I'm afraid the museum is currently closed to visitors, though the shop is open."

"The museum is closed?" said Roxy. A look toward the entrance of the display area confirmed that there was black-and-yellow police tape across it. That was a bit surprising, given that the theft had happened over a week earlier. She gave Mo a worried look.

"Yes, unfortunately, we've had our second theft in a month," said Rhoda, sounding less hostile now and more despondent. She sighed before standing up from the stool she'd been perching on as she worked. "Were you hoping to see something specific in the exhibits?"

"Actually, we were hoping to see something specific in the library," explained Roxy. "Wait. You've had a second theft?"

She nodded sadly. "A book from the library, actually."

Roxy looked at Mo again, whose eyes had widened visibly.

"We were here last week. We, um, kind of noticed that there was something missing from one of the displays. That woman Clare was really worried about it, and later I had to talk to the police about it too."

The woman's demeanor changed. She was friendlier and less guarded. "Oh, I see! Yes. Clare did mention that there were some guests of the museum who had noticed the missing artifact. Thank you so much for noticing that. We have so many artifacts here that sometimes, with just the two of us, it can be hard to keep track."

Roxy felt herself flush with pleasure. She always loved being able to help with something.

The woman picked up a different book on the counter and flipped through it.

"Oh yes, I see," she said. Her voice tightened, the warmth drained out of it once more. "You're Roxy?"

Roxy nodded. "And this is my, uh, cousin, Mo." She still hadn't gotten used to introducing Mo. It always felt wrong to lie like that, even if there wasn't a better option.

"You had signed up to look at the grimoire. You and Madame Clerval both signed for that book." She looked suspiciously at her and Mo, an accusation clearly forming itself in her mind. "Was that some kind of a joke or prank?"

"What?" Roxy was stunned. Was there something about her that screamed she wasn't a regular museum visitor? Or was there something else that just made people assume she was a prankster? Either way, it wasn't flattering.

"You are very rude," said Mo, who had been standing next to Roxy quietly until then. "We are the ones who alerted you to the missing bracelet, and we signed up to see the book that we wanted to see, and you are assuming bad things about us." Her voice was strong and full of righteous indignation, eyes blazing with fire.

Rather than be offended at Mo's tone of voice, the woman's expression softened. "I'm sorry. I don't know what came over me. It's just been so disheartening to deal with the theft of two of our prized artifacts in our collections."

"Was the grimoire the book that was stolen?" Roxy asked, putting two and two together.

Rhoda nodded. "The grimoire was one of the most unusual books in our entire collection. Not the oldest or most valuable—simply the most unusual."

"Why is that?" said Mo, prodding her to go on.

"First off, it's the only grimoire in our collection, and it looks to be quite old—early nineteenth century. All handwritten, too. We have no idea who the author is as it's not signed by anyone. And, finally, the most unusual thing about it is, perhaps, that we have no idea of how it came into our collection here at the museum. It simply…appeared one day." Rhoda ticked off each oddity on a finger before sitting back down on her stool and shrugging helplessly. "Of course once we found it, we logged it into our collections. We even had it out for an exhibit for a while, but too many people wanted to take photos of it with their flash on, and a book that old and fragile simply cannot be exposed to that much intense light."

"Wow, what an interesting book," said Roxy. "Now I really wish we could take a look at it."

"Why did *you* want to see it?" said Rhoda. "It does seem awfully suspicious that two patrons request to see the same book—and that book is then stolen."

"Are you sure it was stolen?" said Mo.

"What?"

"Are you sure it was stolen? You just said the book appeared in the collection, and you didn't know how it got there. But what if it simply… disappeared, also?"

"That's a good point," said Roxy.

Rhoda looked a bit put out. "The book was most likely an oversight in one of our larger donation drives. I misspoke earlier when I said it 'appeared one day.' That makes it sound more mysterious than necessary."

"It *is* a grimoire," pointed out Roxy.

"Exactly," said Rhoda, clearly frustrated. "Spell books attract all sorts of people, and not always the ones who should have access to one. Gives them ideas." She paused and looked carefully at Mo and Roxy again. "You still haven't told me why *you* wanted to see the grimoire."

This, at least, Roxy had prepared an answer to. She knew she might need a legitimate sounding reason for looking at an old spell book in the museum's collection. Not everyone was a kindred spirit like Clare. It was, honestly, a bit disappointing that Clare wasn't there that day. Roxy had been looking forward to seeing her again.

"Mo here is doing a class project on magic and legends relating to magical creatures in and around Cape Code. For her community college class," Roxy said. "When we came last week to see the exhibits, Clare mentioned that there might be some books relating to that topic in the collection. *She* suggested the grimoire."

"Is that true, Clare? Did you suggest they take a look at the grimoire?" asked Rhoda just as Clare walked past the crime scene tape and into the shop. She was carrying two large cups of coffee, which explained why she'd been out when they'd arrived.

"Oh hello," she said, her expression brightening as she recognized Roxy and Mo. "For a second there I was worried we had the coppers in again."

"Nope, just us," said Roxy with a smile. "Great to see you. Sorry to hear about the second missing item."

"Not our month, is it?" said Clare with a tight smile before setting down the carryout cups on the counter. "Yes, Rhoda, I do think I suggested that they look at the grimoire. But honestly, I don't think I would have even thought about it except for that Clerval lady coming in and asking about it just the week before."

"I see," said Rhoda. She was disappointed that Clare's explanation was so reasonable.

"You don't think they're mixed up in all of this?" Understanding dawned on Clare's face. "No, these two are just doing a project. Didn't they tell you they were researching the merfolk?"

"Something like that," said Rhoda. "Well, they won't get to look at that grimoire today—if ever. And to answer your previous question, yes, we know there was a break-in to steal the book. Other objects were disturbed, and our security system went off."

"Who would break into a museum?" said Mo. "Only a monster." Her tone of voice was dark, her expression cloudy.

Rhoda nodded, her expression exactly the same. "I agree."

Roxy wasn't sure if it was only a monster. She could think of any number of magical individuals who might like to get their hands on an enchanted bracelet or spellbook. But she kept her thoughts to herself.

"Oh well," she said finally. "I guess we'll go and see what the public library has on the topic."

"Wait," said Clare as they turned to leave. "We might have some other books on myths and legends of Cape Cod. Plenty of stuff about the merpeople around here, don't we, Rhoda?"

Rhoda took a moment to think about it before nodding. "That's true. We do have a small collection on those topics. Most of it is bunk of course, but if you're specifically interested in *legends*, then you've probably come to the right place."

The change in topic galvanized Rhoda, and after taking down Roxy's information, she allowed her and Mo to enter the museum's library and archive. They left Clare to staff the shop, and Rhoda pulled down several books for them to look through. Soon enough, she left them to parse through it all while she busied herself with some other work at the back of the room.

Roxy and Mo spent an hour flipping through the books Rhoda had provided them with, but there didn't seem to be anything about mermaid hunters or mermaid parts for spells or anything like that. Roxy was just about to give up in frustration as she skimmed the last book when a paragraph caught her eye on the topic of mermaids and their magical powers: *Some even believed that the merfolk could turn other creatures into mermaids by cutting their legs with a scale from a mermaid tail in salt water under a full moon. This was how the merfolk kidnapped human children and kept them for themselves.*

"Hey, look at this," said Roxy, pushing the book over to Mo and pointing at the relevant passage.

Mo wrinkled her nose. "This is nonsense. We do not want your stinky children."

Roxy chuckled. "Okay, so this is mostly legend. But what about this part? About turning humans into sea folk with the scale from a tail?"

She read the rest of the passage to Mo out loud, "*There are some who believe that a scale from a mermaid tail can be used in magical spells or enchantments to endow practitioners of the dark arts the ability to change from human form to siren form at will.*"

"I have never heard of such a thing. But this must be it. The reason why I am stuck here, hunted and in danger," said Mo. Her voice trembled with fear. "Roxy, to cut a scale from my tail is death."

Mo's fear was palpable. Roxy's breath caught in her throat. She swallowed hard. "Yep. I bet this is it." She paused. "So what is a siren, again, exactly?"

"It is evil creature. They may live under water and above; but their changing comes at a terrible price. They will lose their sense of self the longer they keep their siren form. Eventually they will be nothing left but monster." Mo's voice was full of bitterness.

"Why would anyone want that?" It sounded horrible.

"Sirens have their own special magic powers. Perhaps that is why. The powerful always want more power."

There was a beat of silence as they contemplated what Mo had just said before being interrupted, loudly, by Mo's growling stomach.

"Oh dear," said Mo. "That was me." She looked at Roxy and giggled.

"Sounds like you need some lunch," said Roxy with a chuckle. "We got what we came for. Let's get some grub."

"Grubs sound good."

Roxy wrinkled her nose. "You eat grubs too!?"

Mo shrugged. "They are like delicacy for us."

They stacked the books and let Rhoda know they were done. On their way out of the shop, they stopped to chat with Clare before stepping out into the sunshine. It had turned into a beautiful, if breezy, winter day, and

Roxy was glad to be outside again in the fresh air. Dusty libraries and archives were not her favorite places to be, even if they had their uses occasionally.

Roxy had finally gotten her first paycheck from the brewery, so they decided to splurge on a meal at a restaurant that served both cooked food and poke bowls with raw tuna for Mo. In the afternoon, they went to the library, Roxy registered for a card, and they picked out a bunch of books to peruse at home. Roxy was working an evening shift at the brewery, so after taking the books back to the apartment, she had just enough time to change her clothes and run a comb through her windblown tangles before heading out the door again.

Mo already had her nose stuck in a book, reading about mermaids. Who would have thought a mermaid would want to read more about mermaids?

As Roxy entered the brewery, the sweet-sharp smell of brewer's yeast hit her nose in a way that was comforting and familiar. She'd fallen into the rhythm of the brewery effortlessly. Everyone was easy to work with, and she appreciated having to start from the bottom up. She'd done everything so far from cleaning floors to pouring beers for patrons to wiping down tables in the dining room to unloading trucks full of brewing supplies. The day before when Tessa had stopped by was her first time getting a more hands-on lesson in the brewing process, and it'd been fascinating.

She hadn't been kidding when she'd told Tessa that she was really enjoying herself here—and starting to wonder if this might be the beginning of a new chapter for herself. It felt simple, even natural to her, even though she really hadn't ever seen herself working in the food industry or hospitality.

As she hung up her jacket and hat in the staff area, though, she was reminded yet again of Tessa's reaction to their conversation on that topic two days earlier. As if working in a brewery was beneath her or somehow a bad job. She hadn't had a chance to ask her to clarify, and she wasn't sure if she wanted to. She'd been enjoying getting to know Tessa, and in some ways, it was fun to hear her talk about herself and ask her questions—but she was realizing now that she hadn't really had a chance to tell Tessa much about herself. Maybe Tessa didn't want to date someone who worked in a brewery?

All the more reason to focus on other things and take it slow. It all might still come to nothing, and if Roxy could protect her heart in the midst of everything else going on, all the better.

It was a Friday night at the brewery, and it was busy. Even in winter, people liked to come out to Ptown for a quick getaway, and the work kept her mind off Tessa and her own concerns about what, if any, future they had together. The rest of the evening passed in a blur, for which Roxy was grateful. It was nice not to worry about Mo, or mermaid hunters, or even cute but complicated women like Tessa.

CHAPTER SIXTEEN—TESSA

Tessa was on pins and needles all weekend. She could feel herself getting jumpy and irritable in meetings; everyone seemed bent on annoying her. She found herself snapping at Chayo and Joy for no good reason, except that she hadn't heard from Roxy in four days.

Four long days.

She should have been enjoying being in the middle of working on a show. This was her baby after all. Costumes were arriving, sets were getting built, and the actors were working with her in rehearsals on blocking, character development, and line delivery. In some ways, it was the most creative part of putting on a play. Nothing was set in stone yet. The relationships between the actors and their characters were still in process, and usually Tessa would have been laser-focused on her role as director.

But her unsatisfying interaction with Roxy at the brewery coupled with the lack of communication following on the heels of that absolutely perfect kiss in her apartment were making it impossible for Tessa to concentrate on anything. She kept replaying the conversation in her head and berating herself for making assumptions. Other times she'd find herself annoyed that Roxy was so sensitive. If she was so upset, couldn't she simply tell Tessa what the issue was?

Tessa thought she'd been doing a pretty good job of hiding her inner turmoil from everyone else, but when Sunday rehearsals wrapped up around two in the afternoon, Chayo and Joy practically frog-marched Tessa to the box office.

Chayo closed the door behind her, and she and Joy stood in front of Tessa, identical looks of concern on their faces.

"It's that obvious?" said Tessa. She felt her annoyance and frustration drain away, replaced quickly by a feeling of overwhelming sadness.

"Hey, no need to get all dramatic," said Chayo. "We're worried about you. You haven't been yourself since last Wednesday."

"Your aura has been completely off." Joy rubbed her arm. Tessa sighed.

"I've been preoccupied with personal stuff." Tessa sniffed. She was a complete and total crier, and anything even slightly emotional made her immediately turn on the waterworks. She could feel the tears gathering in her eyes, her throat closing up with emotion. Her voice shook. "I'm sorry."

Chayo hugged her, and Joy did too. Tessa felt their warmth and goodness surround her; she was so lucky to have good friends and colleagues like Joy and Chayo.

"Don't be sorry." Chayo took a step back and pushed away a tear of her own from the corner of her eye. "Ay, chica, you're going to make me cry. I just want to make sure you're okay."

Joy nodded. "Me, too. It's not like you to be so snappish. Is there anything we can do to help?"

Tessa blushed. "I don't think so. It's…"

"It's about a woman, isn't it?" Chayo winked at Tessa, and Tessa couldn't help smiling.

"Ohhhh," said Joy. "Now I understand. It's Roxy, isn't it?"

Tessa hadn't said anything to Joy before about being interested in Roxy, but Joy's intuition coupled with Tessa's inability to be subtle to save her life made her love life an open book, apparently. She nodded.

"We kissed on Tuesday night at my place. Nothing else! Promise." Chayo gave her a disbelieving look. "We both want to take it slow. But I think I might have messed up."

She filled in Chayo and Joy on her conversation with Roxy at the brewery.

"I think I might have offended her," said Tessa at the end of the short recap.

Chayo sighed. "It's possible. You don't know her that well. It's been what? 10 years since you last saw each other?"

"Nine."

Chayo rolled her eyes. "Whatever. It's a long time. People change. Look at yourself."

"True." Tessa nodded.

"How well did you know her in college?" said Joy.

"I guess…not that well?" Tessa felt more and more uncertain. She thought she knew Roxy. They'd lived together in the dorm for a year, after all. But the more she thought about it, the more she realized maybe she hadn't known her that well back then either. "She always seemed so confident in college. Like she had the world at her feet. But maybe that's how I saw her because my self-confidence was so low." Roxy had dropped out of college after that year, and Tessa never would have guessed that except she'd told her.

"Maybe you need to get to know each other better before you start weighing in on each other's careers?" said Chayo. She always cut to the chase.

"Ouch. Rude," said Tessa. "But okay. Agree. That makes sense."

"And don't jump to conclusions," said Joy. "Maybe she got spooked by the kiss. Sometimes strong emotions can be scary, especially if someone has been hurt in the past."

Tessa nodded. It was all solid advice. She knew she was prone to overthinking things and acting impulsively sometimes. She could be overly emotional. She knew that. She took a deep breath and let it out.

"Thanks, pals." She gave each of them a hug in turn. "That helped."

"Now, go and do something healing," said Joy. "Do something for yourself to get centered again."

"And then go after your girl," said Chayo. "Really get to know her—and let *her* get to know *you*." Tessa felt certain that last remark was in reference to her short stint as an online stalker.

She nodded. "Okay. I can do that."

Tessa decided to go home and take a bath to take her mind off Roxy and try to center herself. She added her favorite mix of relaxing herbs and spices to the bath: lavender, lemongrass, cinnamon, dried orange peel, and green tea. She'd found the recipe in one of her hedge witch grimoires, passed down to her from her mentor Freya. She kept the mixture of dried aromatics in a small silk sachet that infused the bathwater, and she'd had just one left for her time in Ptown. She would need to make some more soon. For now, though, she let herself relax in the bath, reciting the words of a calming incantation, letting her mind drift away.

After a long soak, there was still a tiny bit of daylight left, and Tessa decided to face the situation with Roxy head on. She dressed herself warmly and walked over to Roxy's apartment. She hoped it wasn't too bold of her. She'd gotten Roxy's address off the tax paperwork she'd filled out so they could pay her out of the grant. Although most of the paperwork asked for a permanent address, she'd had Roxy list a local address as well, since the grant was supposed to be benefiting people on Cape Cod in particular.

"Don't overthink it," she said to herself as she arrived at the door of Roxy's apartment and pressed the buzzer.

There was significant shuffling and muffled voices on the other side of the door, and for a moment, Tessa doubted whether she'd made the right decision. Maybe it was presumptuous of her to show up unannounced on a Sunday afternoon?

Finally the door opened and there stood Roxy. Tessa's breath caught in her throat. Something about being in her presence immediately made Tessa hot all over.

"Hey! Didn't expect to see you today," said Roxy. Her voice betrayed confusion, but her expression was warm and welcoming. Tessa had no idea how to interpret that combination of reactions, but she decided to stick to her plan.

"I hope it's okay that I stopped by. I was at home and just thought about how much I would love to go for a quick walk before sunset. Maybe you'd like to join me?"

The words hung in the air between them, and for a second, Tessa was sure Roxy would say no. It was impossible to read her expression.

"Sure, that sounds nice," said Roxy after a moment. "Let me just let Mo know. Come on in."

Tessa stepped inside and waited on the doormat while Roxy disappeared down the hallway into another room and behind a closed door. She could hear the sounds of water splashing and Mo's distinctive low tones mixed with Roxy's more moderate ones. After a moment, Roxy returned, grabbing her black and red buffalo plaid coat along the way and stepping into her winter boots.

"Sorry about that. Mo's taking a long bath tonight, so I wanted to let her know I was going out," said Roxy. She wrapped a warm scarf around her neck and pulled on a ski cap. "All right. I'm ready."

She made no move to kiss Tessa, so Tessa said nothing on the topic even though her mind was full of their kiss from Tuesday night. Would they kiss again? Ever?

Soon they were outside again, and they decided to walk down Commercial Street towards the farthest end of the Cape. The wind was cold, but not so strong that they couldn't talk. Tessa decided to start with some small talk to ease them into conversation, starting with an update on what was going on at the theater and asking Roxy some questions about Mo and how she was faring as Lisa's assistant.

Once they had exhausted those topics, Tessa paused, hoping Roxy would fill in the silence. Instead, they walked without speaking until Tessa couldn't stand the tension any longer.

"So, uh, is everything okay? Between us?" The question came out inelegantly, but at last, it was out there. "I haven't heard from you since Wednesday, and I thought maybe you were mad at me. For what I said at the brewery." She paused to take a breath before continuing. "I'm sorry—"

Roxy interrupted her. "I'm not mad. But I needed some time to think. About what you said. About us. About kissing you." She smiled at Tessa, and Tessa could feel her heartbeat speed up. Perhaps all was not lost.

"Did you come to any conclusions?" Tessa's natural impatience was getting the better of her.

"I did," said Roxy. "I was thinking, maybe we need to get to know one another better. Before we go any further." She was stilling smiling, but there was a more serious undertone to Roxy's words.

"Absolutely," said Tessa, nodding enthusiastically. "I agree. I really wish I could take back what I said at the brewery. I didn't mean to make it sound like brewing beer or working in a restaurant is somehow worse than any other job."

"Sure," said Roxy. "But I'm kind of glad you did say it. Because I think it's important we get some stuff out in the open."

They had been walking briskly in the cold early evening air, and they now arrived at the Pilgrim's First Landing Park. After crossing the parking lot, they were now at the edge of the beach, overlooking the harbor as well as the causeway. In the distance, they could see Long Point Light Station, backlit by the setting sun. Tessa felt like none of the beauty of the moment could reach her, though. Roxy's words chilled her, even as she knew that she too had things to share. Heavy, awkward things.

"Okay," said Tessa. "That sounds like a good idea. I have something I have to tell you, too."

"Is it okay if I go first?" said Roxy. She was nervous, Tessa realized. "I don't want to lose my train of thought."

Tessa nodded.

"I mentioned last week, when we kissed, that I wanted to take things slow, and I meant it. Maybe you heard some stuff about me from Elizabeth, about how I played the field a lot, dated a lot, how I wasn't serious. The truth is, I've always been looking for something serious, something special. And I can't seem to find it. My last relationship, with Amy...I thought it was the real deal. We fell in love so fast, we had chemistry and everything." Roxy's voice shook, and Tessa's heart ached for her. "And she ended it like it was nothing. She broke my heart." Roxy paused again. "Or maybe I broke my own heart. Going too fast. Getting caught up in the moment. And I don't want to do that again."

"Okay, I understand," said Tessa.

"I'm not sure you do," said Roxy. "I feel like we come from two different worlds, Tessa. You've lived this exciting, fast-paced life, traveling to Europe, hanging out with celebrities, living in New York. I'm not from that world. I didn't finish college. I probably never will. I don't have a bright shiny future, and there's nothing right now that says things are going to change. Maybe you see something in me that isn't the real me, is what I'm saying." Roxy paused and sighed. "I haven't even read your play. I'm too scared to because…it'll be too hard. I'm dyslexic and reading stuff like Shakespeare brings me right back to all my worst moments in school."

It took all of Tessa's self-control not to launch herself at Roxy and hug her tightly and whisper it would all be fine. This wasn't the moment for easy platitudes. Part of her was disappointed that Roxy hadn't read *The Winter's Tale* yet, and she would have to examine more closely why that was. She forced herself to focus on everything else Roxy shared with her. She was too prone to speaking quickly, off the top of her head—it was her improv training no doubt. Now was the moment for deep reflection, and after a few minutes of silence, Tessa came to a realization.

"Thank you for sharing all that, Roxy," she said. "I can't change the past or how you think about yourself and your abilities. I'm realizing that we don't know each other as well as we should. I remembered what you were like in college. You seemed successful, confident, cocky, even—" Tessa was delighted to hear Roxy chuckle at that description of herself. "Yes, cocky. And I had zero self-esteem back then. You were…impressive. And hot."

"Wow," said Roxy. "That is not at all how I thought of myself back then. But still, nice to hear."

"Exactly. We weren't the closest of roommates and…I sort of made up a version of you in my head. I had a crush on you." Tessa swallowed, her mouth suddenly very dry. She looked Roxy in the eyes. "Still do."

"That's very flattering," said Roxy. She smiled. "But the real me is a ball of nerves, feeling like I don't belong in your theater world."

"You belong wherever you want to be," said Tessa. "And if you don't feel up to reading *The Winter's Tale*, that's fine. We can watch a recording together. I can read you my favorite parts. I love this play and

I'm an educator. Making Shakespeare accessible to everyone is kind of my jam. And I want to share it with you." She paused, recalling Roxy's other concerns. "As for living an international celebrity lifestyle, I want to point out that I left that behind on purpose. Not just because of Lisa. I left it behind me because it was toxic. I was burned out. I truly love being a teacher. And none of that makes me better than you."

Roxy smiled sheepishly. "Thanks. That makes me feel better."

"Good," said Tessa. She took a long breath to steady herself. "I'm sorry for making assumptions about what you want to do with your future. Or what job is or isn't good enough for you."

"Thanks for saying that," said Roxy. "I appreciate it."

There was a natural pause in the conversation as they both turned to watch the sun dipping beneath the horizon, spreading its blazing pink-orange glory onto the water and clouds.

"Wow," said Tessa under her breath.

Roxy put an arm around her and she enjoyed the warmth emanating from Roxy as they blocked the wind together.

It didn't take long, and the sun was completely gone beneath the waves. Tessa turned to face Roxy, Roxy's arm dropping back to her side.

"There's something you should know about me," said Tessa.

"Uh-oh," said Roxy in mock concern. "You're not actually ten rats in a winter coat pretending to be a theater director?"

Tessa chuckled nervously. "Honestly, if only." She took a deep breath to steady herself and plunged ahead. Best to get things over with, even if she couldn't look Roxy in the eye while she admitted it all. "I wasn't lying when I said I had a crush on you in college, but also now. And most of the time in between. When my relationship with Lisa was getting really bad, I internet stalked you, and when Lisa found out, it ended our engagement."

Tessa found the courage to look at Roxy, finally. Her expression surprised Tessa. She was smiling.

"I'm sorry, I know I should be somehow shocked by all that," said Roxy, "but I can't be. Honestly, in every relationship I've ever had, *I've* been the one doing the chasing. I was the one going after the other woman. It is incredibly satisfying to hear that for once in my life, I'm the one being pursued." Her smile wavered a bit. "Is that okay?"

Tessa felt relief crash over her like a wave. "Of course," she said. She chuckled nervously. "I was so worried that I would sound like a freak." She filled in Roxy on the details of what actually happened with Lisa and the social media stalking.

"It doesn't sound *too* stalker-y," said Roxy when Tessa had finished. "I'm not scared for my life just yet."

They began walking back up Commercial Street, and Tessa felt grateful for Roxy's warm arm around her shoulders as they walked side by side, the wind blowing right through her wool coat.

"I wanted you to know before Lisa could tell you. I wanted to get it out in the open because I'm realizing that I *am* serious about you. About us," said Tessa. "My comment about working on the brewery was partly snobbery, I'll admit it, but it was also partly panic. If I'm teaching in Boston and you're out here on the Cape, I won't get to see you as much as I'd like." Tessa's heart sped up again and she felt hot. Admitting to Roxy that she wanted something long term, when they'd only just been talking about taking it slow, felt like she was putting her heart on the line yet again.

It took Roxy a moment to respond, a moment that felt like an hour to Tessa.

"It means a lot to me that you'd say that," said Roxy, her voice low and full of emotion. "No one has ever said to me that they were already making long term relationship plans with me—even if it was in their head."

Tessa's heart squeezed. How could no one else have seen the beauty and generosity and creativity that she so clearly saw in Roxy now? Tessa was starting to see past the idealized version she'd had of Roxy for nine long years to see who she really was. Not some perfect hot butch soccer player, but rather a human being who needed to be seen and loved for all her qualities, both her good ones and her bad ones.

"I know it feels soon to be talking about long term plans," said Tessa. "But I'm also okay taking it slow—really, I am. And if that means less kissing and more talking, I'll be okay with that."

Roxy stopped and turned to face Tessa. "I mean, we don't have to *not* kiss at all." A mischievous grin painted itself across Roxy's face before she leaned in and planted a soft kiss on Tessa's lips.

"That was nice," said Tessa. Her whole body was fit to burst with happiness right there in the middle of Ptown.

"Agree," said Roxy.

They were now nearing the corner where they would have to go their separate ways to get home. The temperature was rapidly dropping in the darkening evening air. Tessa couldn't help shivering a little.

"I'm really glad we talked," said Roxy. "I'm sorry I ghosted you. I needed some time to think."

"It's okay. I mean, I was going just a little crazy worrying that you'd never want to talk to me again but you know, nothing major." Tessa laughed nervously.

Roxy chuckled. "I'll try not to do that again. I feel much better now having talked than before when I was avoiding you. Sorry. Old habit."

"I think we're both going to have to find ways to chuck our old habits. But I know it'll be worth it." She looked deeply into Roxy's eyes and kissed her, letting her lips linger on Roxy's while she wrapped her arms around Roxy's waist and hugged her tight. She'd never felt safer with anyone than in that moment with Roxy, even after baring their deepest fears to one another. "Please tell me you'll always call me on my shit when I say things that aren't cool."

Roxy's hands lingered on her shoulders, and she met Tessa's gaze without hesitation. "Agree. Promise me that you'll always call me on *my* shit when I go into lockdown mode."

Tessa smiled. It was hard to imaging calling Roxy anything other than *cutie*, *hottie*, or *babe*, but she nodded. "Yes, I'll try."

Reluctantly Tessa parted from Roxy and walked home to her little apartment. She had a lot to think about, a lot to consider, mostly about herself and how she was going to make sure that going forward, she stopped making assumptions about Roxy and focused on really getting to know her. Because it was hard to be logical when Roxy's mere presence made her forget about everything else in her life.

Case in point: as soon as Tessa walked into the apartment, she saw her grimoire, candles, and travel herb set that she'd left out on the table. It hadn't even occurred to her, when she and Roxy were "coming clean" to one another, to bring up the fact that she was a hedge witch. She'd gotten used to keeping it a secret, but if she was going to be serious about Roxy, then shouldn't she tell her? On the other hand, she had only just begun to develop her magical abilities. Perhaps it was too soon to bring up something so deeply personal, not to mention unusual, before she knew what the future held for them? Either way, she was home now, and Roxy was in her own apartment, and she would have to wait for another good moment to share that information.

Truly the course of true love never did run smooth, she reflected.

CHAPTER SEVENTEEN—ROXY

R oxy spent the next few days feeling as though she were walking on air.

The conversation with Tessa had dispelled many of her fears about what was going on between them. Something about spilling her guts made her feel like a new person—and those kisses weren't bad either.

Beyond all that though, she relished in the rather new to her sensation of being the pursued rather than the pursuer. Whether it was her most recent relationship with Amy or her earlier, misguided pursuit of Hazel's now-wife Elizabeth, or any number of previous failed relationships and hookups, inevitably it was Roxy who had always done the chasing. Tessa's confession to her about how she'd had a crush on Roxy for, well, *years*, didn't freak her out at all. Instead, Roxy was enjoying knowing that for once *she* was being pursued by someone else.

"Ah! She is woo-ing you," said Mo, once Roxy had relayed to her the gist of their conversation.

"You sound like you've been reading more Shakespeare," said Roxy. She flopped onto the couch and picked up the books Mo had left half open around her. *Romeo and Juliet, Twelfth Night, A Midsummer Night's Dream.* Roxy had heard of *Romeo and Juliet*, but the rest were a mystery to her. "Anything good?"

Mo nodded enthusiastically. "Oh yes. I am enjoying the comedies much more. I asked Lisa what else to read when I finished *The Winter's Tale*. She suggested these. They are all about love. Strange love, but love."

"And you like it?"

"Roxy, they are very strange to me, these stories, but very interesting. I am learning so much about what it means to be human!"

"I guess that's good then." Roxy paused and looked carefully at Mo. A thought occurred to her. "They help fill the time, too."

"Yes, it's true. They take my thoughts away from my home, my family." Mo's tone was upbeat, but her expression was, to Roxy, less certain. She leaned over and gave Mo a hug.

"That's great, pal. Keep at it, if it helps."

"Roxy, what really helps me is to know you are on the path to find your true love. Maybe the books of Mr. Shakespeare can help us on this quest. You say he is the favorite author of your true love, no?"

"Okay, let's not get ahead of ourselves. I like Tessa. She likes me. But we're still getting to know one another. Calling her my true love feels a little weird." As she said the words, Roxy wondered if she really believed them. There was a part of her that felt like she and Tessa really did click, especially after that afternoon's conversation. But she'd been hurt so many times before, her denial was an automatic defense mechanism.

Mo rolled her eyes, and Roxy was reminded instantly of Lisa. Mo was picking up her tics after just a week of being her assistant.

"Please, Roxy. Listen to me. You must do some of the Shakespeare." Mo picked up one of the books and started flipping through the pages. Roxy got the distinct impression she wanted to read her part of *Romeo and Juliet*.

"Can we watch a movie version to start?" That would be a good way to ease into things.

Mo looked slightly disappointed but agreed, and soon enough they were watching Claire Danes and Leonardo di Caprio making googly eyes at one another. Since Mo had no concept of when Shakespeare was alive, she didn't seem bothered by the fact that the action was in 1990s Brazil and the characters used guns instead of swords. Roxy found herself absorbed by the film and its story, and she even cried when Romeo killed himself, thinking his Juliet was really dead. This was worlds away from the older, more traditional version their ninth-grade teacher had screened for them in school, and she was really digging it.

Maybe there was a part of Shakespeare Roxy could like, after all.

The following weekend, the weather was miserable, so Tessa and Roxy made plans to cook and watch a movie together. The work week had been a busy one for both of them; by Friday Roxy felt like she'd hardly seen Tessa, even though they'd both been working at the theater all day Tuesday and Thursday. In between Roxy had taken Mo twice more to the library to get additional books out about mermaids and Shakespeare; she'd worked several shifts at the brewery; and she'd had to go to the grocery to stock up on salt for Mo's nightly saltwater baths. It was the only way Mo could return safely, however briefly, to her usual form, though Roxy had started to notice that Mo needed more salt with each passing day for the bath to activate her tail.

She was glad to have her date night in with Tessa to distract her from Mo's situation, even if part of her was terrified about what they were planning to watch. Tessa said she wanted to watch her favorite performance of *The Winter's Tale* together, and Roxy was already sweating bullets over it. What if she couldn't understand it? What if it was so boring she fell asleep watching it? What if it was just *awful*?

Mo had been coaching Roxy on all things Shakespeare, and the two of them had watched movie versions of several more plays: *Much Ado About Nothing* with Emma Thompson, which Roxy had rather enjoyed; *Hamlet* with Mel Gibson in the main role, which Roxy had enjoyed less so; and *Twelfth Night* with Helena Bonham Carter which was by far her favorite thus far. They had also talked over *The Winter's Tale* and the action of the play, but it didn't much help. Roxy couldn't keep all the names in her head, and she ended up feeling less prepared and more nervous than before.

Still, she was there, in front of Tessa's door, with a growler of her favorite coconut porter from the Pride of Ptown and a plate of brownies that she'd managed to whip up, with some help from Betty Crocker and Mo. Although she had no interest in actually eating the brownies, Mo had turned out to be rather adept at baking.

"Come on in," said Tessa. She opened the door and Roxy felt a lot of her concerns melt away. This was Tessa, after all. Fancy New York theater director, sure, but also a smiling, beautiful woman who was clearly happy to see her—and whose apron was currently splattered with tomato sauce.

"Everything okay?"

"What? Oh." Tessa looked down at the mess of sauce on her apron and smiled. "I'm a messy cook. But I firmly believe that means the food will be delicious."

Roxy followed Tessa into the kitchen and set about pouring them each some beer while Tessa found a vase for the flowers. The aforementioned tomato sauce was burbling quietly on the stove next to a pot of water that had started to boil.

"Perfect timing," said Tessa. "I've made my world famous puttanesca sauce—just kidding about the world famous part of course. I'll put the pasta in to boil and it'll all be ready in a few minutes."

"Great," said Roxy, whose mouth was watering. She was finding it harder and harder to eat around Mo, whose appetite for raw fish only seemed to be increasing lately. Her table manners were terrible, and Roxy was relishing the thought of eating home cooked food without having to watch or, more to the point, *listen* to Mo's enthusiastic chewing.

Soon enough they were digging into spaghetti alla puttanesca, which was delightfully salty and completely new to Roxy, who usually ordered Bolognese at an Italian place. There was homemade garlic bread and a big tossed salad, and they spent dinner talking about Mo and Lisa, discussing Roxy's progress in the woodshop, and griping about Barb.

Roxy pushed back from the table when her plate was clean. It had all been delicious.

"You still haven't gotten a meeting set up with the theater owner?"

Tessa wiped her mouth with a napkin and shook her head. "Uh-uh. He's apparently on vacation down in Florida, on a boat no less, and it's been impossible to get a message down to him. Hopefully next week we can figure it out." Tessa looked at Roxy with sparkling brown eyes. "But thanks for your concern. Let's not talk about Barb any more though. I don't want her to spoil our whole evening."

Roxy hadn't minded at all. The longer they chatted about their own production of *The Winter's Tale*, the more they put off watching whatever Tessa had planned for them. Roxy was well aware there wasn't any recent movie version of the play. She and Mo had looked and looked. It didn't seem like a very popular play at all, and that had Roxy worried.

"Oh sure," said Roxy. She had an idea. "I'll help you clean up before we dig into the brownies."

Before Tessa could protest, Roxy cleared the table and began doing the dishes.

"We can put it all in the dishwasher," said Tessa.

"It's okay," said Roxy. "I like doing dishes." Hopefully, Tessa wouldn't notice her little white lie.

Tessa began drying the dishes, and the conversation turned toward chores, growing up, and who was more of a slob. Roxy never would have thought Tessa could be a slob judging by her pristine apartment.

"That's because you've never seen my office at school," said Tessa. She winked at Roxy as she put away the last of the dishes. "Let's save the pots for later."

There was no easy way to get out of the film screening at this point, though Roxy did, for a second, entertain the notion of leaving early on the pretense that she was tired from working at the brewery that day.

Already Tessa was queuing up the recording of *The Winter's Tale* and getting cozy on the couch. She'd placed Roxy's plate of brownies on the coffee table along with their beers. There was nothing to do but join Tessa on the couch—not *too* close—and steel herself for the experience.

And it was…awful. Just as Roxy had feared. The performance featured a couple of famous actors, sure, including Kenneth Branagh who Roxy remembered from *Much Ado About Nothing*, and Dame Judi Dench, who was one of Tessa's all-time favorite actors. But the play itself was nigh on unwatchable. After an hour of it, Roxy could feel her eyelids growing heavy.

This particular performance was a recording of a staged version of the play, and it was all heavy drama. Lots of long speeches. It was hard for Roxy to pay attention or even want to pay attention.

"Roxy?"

Her eyes fluttered open. Oh, crap. Had she really fallen asleep? Judging by Tessa's expression, she had definitely fallen asleep. Was the movie at least over? She glanced at the TV and saw it was paused on a scene in the play. Not the credits. She suppressed a groan.

"Sorry, I must have nodded off. Long day at work and all."

"It's okay," said Tessa. "We can turn it off." Her voice betrayed disappointment, and Roxy felt awful, even as she was also filled with relief that she wouldn't have to sit through the rest of it.

"No, no," said Roxy. She tried to sound convincing. "I want to finish it."

"It's late. We can finish it another time," said Tessa. She smiled at Roxy, but the smile didn't reach her eyes.

"I'm sorry." Roxy decided it would be better to be truthful. "I was having a hard time getting into it. Maybe if it was more like a movie, you know?"

"Sure," said Tessa. "Excuse me." She left the room and Roxy heard the bathroom door close. Oh God. She'd really offended her.

Roxy checked her watch. It was just past ten in the evening and getting rather late for both of them. It was probably best to simply get going. She was already back in her boots and coat when Tessa emerged from the bathroom.

"You're not leaving? Already?"

"Erm, yeah, I was thinking it was getting late. We both have work tomorrow so...you know," said Roxy. "We can finish *The Winter's Tale* some other night." She hoped Tessa didn't notice her lack of enthusiasm for the idea.

"Oh," said Tessa, clearly at a loss for words. "I just thought..." Her voice trailed off and Roxy felt stupid and awkward.

"I'll see you at the theater!" Roxy tried to keep her voice upbeat as she let herself out of the apartment. She was halfway home before she realized they hadn't even kissed. Then again, maybe Tessa had finally realized that they weren't really suited to one another if Roxy couldn't enjoy the very play that she was putting on?

Not that Roxy had ever really had a chance with Tessa. Who had she been fooling? Only herself, apparently. As the biting winter wind blew through her, all she could think was that she deserved to be alone and cold on a gusty night.

CHAPTER EIGHTEEN—TESSA

The next morning, Tessa woke up feeling groggy and tired. She had already snoozed her alarm twice, and she knew she should get up, but something was off.

At all once, she remembered. The nice dinner with Roxy, deciding to watch the play, Roxy's dozing off and then leaving so suddenly they didn't even say a proper good-bye.

Her heart squeezed uncomfortably and tears came to her eyes. She'd cried herself to sleep the night before, too, and her eyes felt raw and sandy.

Why oh why had she insisted on watching that stupid recording? Why hadn't she simply read some short parts of the play to Roxy? Or just talked to her about the play? Anything to avoid having Roxy actually fall asleep during the recording. Her face burned with the memory. She hardly knew who she was more annoyed with: Roxy, for falling asleep, or herself, for putting them into this situation.

The Winter's Tale was not an easy play, nor was it one of Shakespeare's more well-known and well-loved plays. That was precisely why she'd chosen it—she'd wanted a challenge. It wasn't called a "problem play" for nothing, and there was a reason why there weren't any popular film adaptations of it. It was a weird play.

But that was also why she loved it. She absolutely adored the passion of the first half, and the tender love and redemption of the second half. She could have simply told Roxy about that—what she loved about the play and left it at that. But no, she *had* to try to force the issue.

At the same time as her heart hurt for what she'd done, another part of her was also wounded. Could she really fall in love, and more to the point, *stay* in love with someone who didn't share her passion for Shakespeare?

Who didn't read or watch the plays she was passionate about? Couldn't Roxy have made a better effort, for crying out loud!? She knew how important the play was to her. A petulant, whiny voice inside Tessa's head kept asking her, *why couldn't she have done it for me?*

Tessa groaned out loud and rubbed her face with her hands, pushing away the tears, before blowing her nose loudly. In the quiet of the apartment, she felt pathetic and disheartened.

A glance at the clock confirmed that she had to get out of bed and shower or she'd be late for yet another irritating meeting with Barb, and she couldn't risk that. She dragged herself to the shower and let the hot water sluice over her, trying to clear her head. Afterward, she made a cup of strong coffee in the pour over coffee maker. Her stomach rumbled, and she realized she was hungry. She'd been so preoccupied in her thoughts, she'd started pulling on her boots and coat without even having breakfast. She still had time for that.

Tessa made herself some eggs over easy and toast, grateful for a hot meal to start the day. As she sat and ate, the simple ritual of breakfast revived her, and her thoughts turned toward her grimoire. She'd put it away in advance of Roxy's visit, and now she couldn't help thinking that perhaps she'd never have the chance to tell Roxy she was a hedge witch since it seemed like it might all come to nothing.

She paged through the grimoire until she landed on a page in Freya's handwriting, "Incantations and Salves for Clarity and Concentration." Perfect. The incantation was simple, more of a mantra or chant than a spell, and the salves were likewise uncomplicated—which made sense, given that if you needed clarity and concentration, you probably didn't have the patience to do much. Lavender, spearmint, and rosemary were all easy enough to source from the kitchen cabinets and her own stores. The recipe suggested making an aromatic steam bath for the face to breathe in, or to make a simple tea. At this point, Tessa didn't have time for facial steaming, but she packed the herbs into her favorite thermos for looseleaf tea and decided to make a kind of chai for herself. A little bit of steamed milk, black tea, some cinnamon and cardamom, plus the herbs, and she was ready to go.

Already the small rituals of her hedgecraft were beginning to kick in, and Tessa was pleasantly surprised to feel a stirring within her of magic, a kind of golden warmth in her chest that was radiating outward to her hands and face. She felt calmer now, less stressed.

Tessa still didn't know what to do about Roxy, but one thing she knew for certain: while her feelings might have been hurt, she wasn't ready to give up on them.

With that thought, and the strength of the magic within her, she strode toward the theater, hardly noticing the cold winter drizzle settling on her hair and face.

❖

Tessa was hardly in her office five minutes when the door flung open violently.

It was Mo, looking and sounding as though she'd run all the way there. Her hair was a windblown mess, with strands pointing in all directions.

Before Tessa could say or do anything, Mo flung herself at Tessa's feet.

"Please accept my sincerest apologies!" Her arms wrapped themselves awkwardly around Tessa's legs.

"Hey, Mo, it's okay. Really. Whatever it is, I'm sure it's fine. We can work it out with Lisa or assign you to a different job—" Tessa tried to extricate her legs from Mo's grasp to no avail.

"No," moaned Mo. "It's not Lisa. The Lisa is fine. It is Roxy. I apologize for Roxy!" Her voice was strained, almost as though she were in pain.

Tessa could feel her face grow hot. Did Roxy send Mo to apologize for her? The thought rankled. "Did Roxy send you?"

Mo interrupted again. "No, she does not know I am here. Please to not think badly of her. She is so sad. She told me about yesterday and I yelled at her and told her she was not right to sleep through the Shakespeare. He is the greatest living man, after all."

"Mo, actually, Shakespeare is not alive—"

"He *died*. Oh my goodness. How awful," said Mo. She had finally stopped hugging Tessa's legs and was, instead, sitting back on her knees, hands cupping her face, an expression of horror that would have been comical if it weren't for the fact that she seemed genuinely sad.

"He died a long time ago," said Tessa. "He is one of our greatest poets, it's true, but he lived and died a long time ago, and he had a very fulfilling and successful life, as far as we know."

Mo looked relieved. "Oh. Yes. Good." After a moment, though, her expression of worry returned. "But Roxy. And you. You have fought. And it is Roxy's fault. She knows it. But she says she is not good enough for you, not smart enough. And maybe this is true?"

"No!" The word came out almost involuntarily. Was that what Roxy was telling Mo? That she wasn't smart enough to be with Tessa? The thought made Tessa's heart hurt. "No, that's not true. Mo, there are lots of ways of being smart."

"But Lisa says that appreciating Shakespeare is a sign of being more evolved."

Tessa sighed. That did sound like something Lisa would say.

"Look, Mo, Lisa isn't always right. Don't tell her I said that, of course, but there are lots of ways of being smart. And the whole point of my project is to make everyone learn to appreciate Shakespeare's plays."

"Not everyone appreciates his plays?" Mo sounded incredulous, and Tessa wondered what kind of a rock Mo had been living under for the majority of her life.

"Surprising, I know," said Tessa dryly. "Anyway, it's not really your business to get involved in what's happening between Roxy and me."

Mo shook her head violently. "No, you see, it *is*. I am pledged—" Mo paused, as if thinking better of what she had been going to say. "I promised Roxy that if she helped me, I would help her. In any way I can."

"Help her with what?"

Before Mo could answer, the door to the office swung open yet again, nearly as violently, and in strode Lisa.

"There you are," she said. She gave Mo a trademark Lisa glare. "You're late. You were supposed to be in my dressing room ten minutes ago."

Mo gave Tessa one last pleading glance before getting up. "I am sorry, Ms. Lisa. I was just talking to Ms. Tessa on a matter of grave urgency." To Tessa she said, "Please, talk to her yourself. Give her another chance."

Lisa's expression turned quizzical, and an eyebrow lifted in such a way that made Tessa feel she was reading her mind.

Eventually, the two of them left together, and Tessa had the office to herself. She locked the door and flung herself into her chair again, hoping to have some peace and quiet before her meeting with Barb. The theater owner had finally gotten in touch with her and they were going to have a conference call to hash out some of the rules and regulations that Barb claimed to be "standard" at the theater, but which to most of them sounded absurd. While Tessa hated the idea of being in that small room with the troll of a woman, she was glad they were going to have this conversation and get some answers.

❖

The conversation had gone well, to Tessa's relief. She'd managed to negotiate quite a few perks for herself and the rest of the cast and crew, much to Barb's evident dismay. Tessa couldn't help smirking a few times when the theater owner sided with Tessa. He'd apparently had no idea that Barb had such a long list of Byzantine rules.

Unfortunately, Tessa was sure that now she was definitely on Barb's blacklist, and the dark look she'd given Tessa as she left the theater office didn't bode well.

Tessa distracted herself from Barb, and the drama with Roxy and Mo, by plunging into her work at the theater. She didn't have time to dwell on the dark aura coming off Barb, or the weird interaction with Mo that morning, or even her disappointing experience with Roxy the night before as there was so much to do with the show. They had decided to cut back some of the longer speeches to cut down on the total run time, so new scripts needed to be printed and distributed. They had local actors joining them that day for the smaller roles and they all had to be fitted for costumes. Then there were the meetings with Joy about the budget and the grant, Chayo about the colors of stains for the banquet table, as well as the costumer, props mistress, and set designers.

Rehearsals would go into the evening that day to accommodate local actors' schedules, but at the dinner break, Tessa had a chance to check her phone.

Her heart sped up when she saw that Roxy had texted. She could hardly breathe as she clicked to read the message, all her mixed emotions filling her up again from that morning.

I'm sorry about last night. I promised not to ghost you again, so here I am texting you. If you're not interested in dating any more, I completely understand, but I'm still interested.

Tessa swallowed hard, and she could feel tears rising up again. She couldn't imagine not being with Roxy, or at least giving it a shot, Shakespeare be damned. She typed back to Roxy:

Of course I'm still interested! I was disappointed last night, but I'm hoping you'll give me another chance to show you why I love the play so much. I really want to give "us" a shot.

Tessa's hand trembled as she pressed "send." Roxy's message had been from several hours earlier, so there wasn't necessarily any reason to believe there would be an immediate response, and yet, she waited, phone in hand, her whole body as though on pause.

A moment later, the phone screen flashed with a message notice. Roxy!

Great!!! I'm scheduled to come to work in the woodshop tomorrow and work with Chayo. See you tomorrow?

They texted a bit more to set a time when they could chat the next day, and Tessa's heart fluttered in anticipation. She had to find a way to show Roxy what was so special about the play. In a way, her whole project and her whole love life depended on it.

CHAPTER NINETEEN—ROXY

Roxy felt both anticipation and trepidation as she entered the theater that Friday, pulling the door closed behind her and Mo. The weather had warmed up significantly, and the sun was out for the first time in days. A part of Roxy wanted nothing more than to go for a hike and stretch her legs, but the rest of her needed to figure out what was going on with her and Tessa.

Somehow, things felt different with her—and it wasn't only because Tessa was so clearly, obviously into her, no matter what sabotaging thoughts she had occasionally on her own worthiness. It felt like there was so much more on the line this time. Roxy's vow to herself to stop playing around and get serious, Mo's magical promise to help her find true love, and Tessa's own confession to her about her feelings made it all more serious, but maybe in a good way. Roxy knew, deep in her heart, she had to give them a shot—even if it meant learning to like Shakespeare.

As they hung up their coats and hats on the hooks by the door, Roxy reminded herself that plenty of couples disagreed on things and still found a way to be together. She remembered how anti-magic Elizabeth had been when she and Hazel first met her. Elizabeth had been loudly and proudly anti-magic, a non-believer, and yet, eventually, she came around. Even if she wasn't a huge fan of Halloween, she and Hazel had made it work. You made things work when it came to true love.

Roxy and Mo walked down the winding hallway backstage. It was now filling up with all sorts of paraphernalia for the show, and they often had to walk around boxes and carts set up along the hallway for lack of space. At the woodshop door, Roxy paused and put her arm on Mo's.

"Now, remember," she said. "Don't talk about me and Tessa to anyone. Not to Tessa. Not to Lisa. Nobody, okay? We have to figure out things for ourselves." She tried to be as gentle but insistent as possible. She'd blown up at Mo the day before once Mo confessed to her meddling. Mo had cried, Roxy had felt horrible, and they'd made up soon after, both of them in tears.

Mo nodded. "Yes, of course, Roxy. Anything for you." They hugged, and Roxy felt reassured. Mo's intentions were pure, but honestly, she was making a mess of things just as much as Roxy—and Roxy really didn't need any help on that front.

They parted ways and Roxy was glad to enter the now-familiar, calming space of the woodshop. Chayo was already there, waiting for Roxy with stains and brushes, as well as a coffee for herself and a hot chocolate for Roxy.

"Thanks, man," said Roxy, sipping the sweet, soothing concoction from a local coffee shop.

"Anytime," said Chayo. "It's expensed of course."

"Awesome."

"We're gonna have to stain the table out on the stage today. I've got tarps set up for it. It's just too big to do in here. Rehearsals were moved to the lobby and greenroom, but we really have to do as much as we can today so they don't have to keep doing that."

Roxy nodded. "Can't wait to start." She started picking up the brushes and cans of stain.

"Hold on," said Chayo.

Roxy paused and put everything back on the table. "What's up?"

"I just wanted to say that, you know, I really want Tessa to be happy."

"Oh yeah, me too. Is she okay with how the banquet table came out?" Roxy wasn't sure what Chayo was getting at, but she had an inkling.

Chayo smiled. "I mean, romantically. I know she's into you. And I'm pretty sure you're into her. And I don't want to interfere. But as her best friend, I'm looking out for her."

"Oh yeah," said Roxy. Her heartbeat sped up. She didn't know how to handle this situation. She'd never had someone talk to her like this about someone she was dating. Maybe because most of the time she never got far enough into a relationship to meet friends and family.

"Look, don't freak out, okay. Tessa talks to me sometimes, and this— you and her—means a lot to her."

"Sure, of course," said Roxy. She cleared her throat. "It means a lot to me too. But—"

"But what?"

Roxy felt her throat go dry and she sipped more hot chocolate. She felt hot under the collar and wished she could peel off another layer. Chayo's serious expression was giving her the sweats.

"It's just…I'm not sure I'm into Shakespeare like she is. I don't know if she told you but…I kind of fell asleep while we were watching a version of *The Winter's Tale,* and I feel terrible that I did that but…honestly, it was so boring. What does that say about me?" The words came out in a rush, but afterward, Roxy felt better for saying them. She'd articulated her greatest fear to Tessa's best pal. Now it was all out in the open.

"Oh my God. Did she try to show you that Kenneth Branagh version?" Chayo was grinning.

"Yes. And I just couldn't get into it. I really tried—"

Chayo started laughing. Roxy didn't get it. What was funny about that? Hadn't Chayo just said she was looking out for Tessa? Making sure she wasn't making a mistake?

"Girl, even I can't watch that version without falling asleep," said Chayo finally.

"What?"

"Dude, that version would put anyone to sleep except a hardcore Bard fan like Tessa."

Roxy felt relief wash through her. She even felt emboldened to make a joke. "I think you mean 'Bardcore.'"

Chayo started laughing even harder. "So. True!"

Roxy chuckled. "Oh my God, I'm so glad you talked to me about this. I was really hating myself for falling asleep when it's like Tessa's all-time favorite. I was really trying!"

"I'm sure you were," said Chayo. "But remember, not all Shakespeare is created equal. Especially when it comes to the performances."

"Whew," said Roxy. She wiped imaginary sweat off her forehead. "So you think I still have a chance with Tessa?"

Chayo nodded. "Absolutely. And while we stain, I can tell you what I like about this play. And what I don't like. And how we're going to manage to make it the best performance of *The Winter's Tale* ever put on. Did Tessa mention to you that it's all going to take place in space?"

"In space?" said Roxy.

Chayo smiled mischievously and nodded. "Oh yeah. Let's go. I'll show you."

They picked up their materials and headed out to the stage, Roxy's mind full of wonder. *The Winter's Tale* in space? Maybe this play would be pretty cool after all.

❖

The time passed quickly while they worked to stain the banquet table. After a while, Tessa joined them as well, and even picked up a brush to do some of the work herself.

While they worked, Tessa and Chayo filled Roxy in on how the play would be staged, and what Tessa had thought up for it. It all sounded pretty rad to Roxy, and working together, all three of them, made it easier to be with Tessa, even though they hadn't had a chance to really talk one-on-one since Wednesday's debacle.

Finally, it was time for lunch, and Chayo discreetly excused herself so they could chat. Tessa invited Roxy to join her for lunch in the greenroom, where they ordered delivery from a local deli.

"I made sure to negotiate that we can order food to the theater," said Tessa as she filled in Roxy on her conversation that morning with the theater owner and Barb. "She was *not* happy about that. But I promised we would clean up and take out our garbage every evening."

"That's something," said Roxy. Suddenly, she was very hungry.

The food arrived quickly, however, and soon enough they were chowing down on delicious subs.

"I had no idea that you were going to put on the play in space," said Roxy when she no longer felt ravenous.

Tessa nodded. "I had this idea of making it a space opera. It's so hard to have a character like Leontes, who is so evil and awful, but then later you kind of feel bad for him and he's redeemed. I started to think, what genres do we see such melodrama? Science fiction is what I landed on. You know, stuff like *Star Wars* is all quite melodramatic."

Roxy nodded. She was an avid *Star Wars* fan. "Oh yeah. Like the story of Darth Vader. First we hate him and then later we feel bad for him."

"Exactly. It's very Shakespearean."

"I never would have thought of it that way," said Roxy truthfully. "If only my high school English teacher had used that example."

"That's what I'm here for," said Tessa. She grinned at Roxy. "The Bard's number one fangirl."

"You're the hype guy for old Bill," said Roxy. They both laughed. Most of the tension she'd felt ever since she'd left Tessa's apartment after the film was gone. It felt natural to joke around and have lunch together like old friends—except you didn't want to kiss your friends while hanging out. And Roxy most certainly wanted that.

Tessa was adorable, even in the old overalls and gray turtleneck she'd been wearing for working on the banquet table. Her hair was a mess from the drizzle and wind, and Roxy loved it even more. The streaks of teal and blue in Tessa's hair looked like electricity, and that's exactly how Roxy thought of Tessa—electric, pure energy, with high voltage sexiness, if that was a thing.

She must have been staring because Tessa blushed and looked away.

"Sorry," said Roxy.

"Are you still hungry?" asked Tessa. "Because you looked like you were about to eat me up." She giggled nervously.

"I guess I'm that obvious," said Roxy. Best to steer them back to safer territory. "I'm really digging your idea of having the play in space. Will you have to change a lot of the original play to fit the theme? Or is it going to be more like the *Romeo + Juliet* movie from the nineties?"

Tessa looked suitably impressed. "Actually no, we won't be changing much of the original language at all. We have switched some lines and scenes and shortened some stuff to make sure the play's run time sticks to a tight two hours, but otherwise it'll be all Bard. Just in space." She paused and looked a little uncertain. "Would you like to watch a rehearsal today? Just to see what it's like in person?" The words came out in a rush.

"Absolutely," said Roxy. Now that she knew more about how the play would be staged, her curiosity was piqued.

They had to part after lunch since Tessa would be working one-on-one with Lisa on some character building before the larger rehearsal, so Roxy returned to the woodshop. She was relieved to hear that Mo would be sitting in on the one-on-one, taking notes for Lisa so she wouldn't have to.

Not that she was worried Tessa was still into Lisa. She was much more concerned that Lisa was still into Tessa. But she filed away that thought for later. Maybe she could even ask Mo for her opinion about Lisa's love interests?

A few hours later, Roxy went to the greenroom to watch some of the rehearsal, as Tessa had suggested. The greenroom was small and intimate, and Roxy felt a little awkward at first. She worried someone would ask why she was there, but no one did. The actors all seemed used to having random people sitting in on rehearsals, and soon enough Roxy's attention was pulled into the scene in front of her. Tessa had provided her with a binder with the script, so she could follow along, but it wasn't really necessary. They were working on a single scene, often going over specific elements and trying different reactions or line deliveries, and Roxy found it fascinating to learn how a small change in inflection, a tiny adjustment in blocking or facial expression of the actors could instantly change the feeling of the scene.

In high school when she'd helped with sets and things, Roxy had never really watched a rehearsal. Dress rehearsals, sure, but not the earlier stuff. It was more interesting than she would have originally considered, and having the framing idea of *Star Wars* and other sci-fi dramas in her mind helped her enjoy the drama between the characters even more.

All that aside, something about listening to the lines being delivered by actors right in front of her, rather than on a screen, made it that much more exciting.

"So, what'd you think?" said Tessa as they walked out of the greenroom a couple of hours later. She sounded anxious and hopeful at the same time.

"That was incredible," said Roxy. She meant it, too. There was no need to feign enthusiasm. "Something about seeing it in person and watching you and the other actors in action right in front of me was awesome. Totally different than watching it on TV. And it was so cool seeing you directing. Your suggestions made everyone do better, and they all totally respect you. You can tell right away."

Tessa blushed. "Thanks, that means a lot. I'm really glad you liked what you saw. I can't wait to put it all together." Her voice was a blend of pride and modesty, and Roxy couldn't help but put an arm around Tessa's shoulders and give her a squeeze.

"Me, too," said Roxy.

As they rounded the corner of the hallway, they came face-to-face with none other than Barb.

"Oh," said Barb, her expression cloudy as always. "I was looking for you."

It sounded ominous.

"Everything okay?" Tessa's voice broke on the second word, and a surge of annoyance went through Roxy. No one should have the power to make Tessa feel so nervous. She deserved better than that.

A strange sensation came over Roxy, as though her veins were filled with electricity. Her breath caught in her throat. What was that sensation?

Before she could figure it out, it passed. How odd.

"You have a phone call," said Barb. She stepped forward, forcing Roxy and Tessa to break apart, but not before Barb gave them a knowing look. One Roxy didn't like one bit. She felt something like an aftershock of the earlier electric sensation pass through her. If she ever had a chance to talk mano a mano with Barb, she'd have plenty to say about how she treated others.

"Whew, that was a close one." Tessa was clearly shaken by the interaction. She shivered. "I'd better go to the office. We've got rehearsals again tonight, on the stage. The banquet table should be dry enough to be moved to the side. Will you join us again?" There was pleading in Tessa's voice, and Roxy wanted nothing more than to say yes.

"I'll have to check with Mo," she said. She squeezed Tessa's arm. "She's been having a tough time, and I want to be there for her."

"Why don't you bring Mo, too? Maybe Lisa will need her there anyway."

Roxy admired her persistence. It would all depend on Mo's energy levels after her salt bath. Lately, she'd been going to bed right after and sleeping for twelve hours straight. Roxy's instinct was that something was not right.

"I'll check with her," said Roxy. She kissed Tessa gently on the cheek and inhaled her mingled scents that day: lavender, vanilla, and something citrusy.

They parted ways, but the scents lingered in Roxy's nose, like a memory she couldn't quite remember. Later, she recalled the strange little sachets she'd seen hanging up above the stage, and she cursed herself for not remembering sooner. Her feeling of foreboding at Barb's approach made it even more pressing to ask Tessa whether she knew about those odd bags up there.

CHAPTER TWENTY—TESSA

The next several days passed quickly, and before she knew it, Tessa found herself walking Joy to her appointment with Madame Clerval. They walked briskly, the winter wind coming off the ocean and whipping their hair and scarves, stronger gusts pushing against their whole bodies. During the day was bad enough, but now, at nearly ten at night, it was wretchedly cold. Tessa couldn't help feeling annoyed with Madame Clerval and the weird hours she kept. Not that Ptown ever really felt unsafe, per se, but still. It was dark and cold, and Tessa couldn't help feeling that the whole situation was slightly menacing at this hour.

"You'll be okay?" said Tessa at the corner where they'd decided to part ways.

Joy smiled. "Are you kidding? This is an adventure."

"If anything feels off at all, you let me know," said Tessa, perhaps a little too seriously.

Joy rolled her eyes. "Honestly, it'll be fine, Tessa. I go to people like this all the time. Ten at night is nothing. I once went to a séance that didn't even let people in the room until after midnight."

Tessa laughed nervously and gave Joy a quick hug. Joy turned and walked in the direction of Madame Clerval's, and Tessa walked across the street to the pub nearest to it. She managed to even find a table next to a window where she could see down the street in that direction.

Roxy and Mo were supposed to meet her there any time now. She checked her watch and her phone. She was on time; no messages. She tried not to let herself obsess about why they were late. The whole thing was making her nervous, though she wasn't really sure why except that it was dark and later than she was used to being out in bars anymore. She'd never really been a going out kind of person, even in college. In bed by eleven was her usual MO.

Things had been going swimmingly for her, both personally and professionally. There really was nothing out of the ordinary that had happened since her chilly handshake with Isidora and the occasional creepy vibe from Barb. The show was going full steam ahead. Rehearsals had been going smoothly. Lisa had been behaving herself, and even Mo had shown herself to be a quick learner. She still talked back to Lisa, but somehow, Lisa was tolerating it. It was almost as though Lisa was enjoying Mo's spunk. Few people ever stood up to Lisa's overwhelming personality, so perhaps it was a welcome if surprising change of pace for her.

The sets were also shaping up well. Chayo, and the set designer, Amanda, were honest-to-goodness geniuses, and they'd taken Tessa's crazy ideas about staging the show and turned them into something truly amazing. It had taken Tessa ages to come up with a concept that she was happy with. She'd wanted to do something truly unique and interesting, something that would really speak to younger people and make the story somehow both modern and classic—hence the outer space setting, with a midcentury modern slash space-age aesthetic. The two main families of the play were visually separated by style—1950s classic looks versus 1970s disco style, and they were meant to represent the royalty of two different moons orbiting the same planet. For a while, Tessa had worried that she should have chosen a theme and aesthetic more connected to Ptown, but everyone working on the show was super enthusiastic about her ideas, and of course, the grant committee had been as well.

Now that some of the major set pieces were coming together and more of the costumes were arriving, she could see how it was all going to come together and be truly visually spectacular. *The Winter's Tale* was a romance with magic, drama, and comedy—it was ripe for a space opera adaptation, she reminded herself.

There was no reason to worry about it. Just like there was no reason to worry about how things were going with Roxy. Things were going very well—if a little slower than she would have liked—but there hadn't been any more awkwardness between them. In fact, when they spent time together, it all seemed very natural and easy. Roxy was easy and fun to talk to, and Tessa was enjoying getting to know Roxy, even if part of her was impatient to get to the next level with her.

In part, they *had* to take things slow because they were both busy. There were lots of days when Tessa had to get to the theater by eight, and she didn't leave until eight or nine at night. People were constantly wanting to talk to her and meet with her; she had to keep track of her grant money and how it was being spent; and, of course, she was running rehearsals as the director of the show. It was a dizzying amount of work, and she was grateful that they didn't have to work the weekends—yet. It wouldn't be long, though, before they'd be working every day.

Unfortunately, Roxy often *did* have to work on the weekends, so the weekend had passed without a longer outing like their hike to the beach.

The weather had been obligingly awful, so at least she didn't have to feel guilty about being inside all the time. If it wasn't cold and rainy, it was cold and snowy, or cold and windy. She and Roxy had to grab time together when they could, which lately meant eating takeout together in the greenroom or stealing a quick kiss in the hallway. That past Sunday they'd managed another quick walk around Ptown and dinner together at a slightly nicer place—Tessa's treat. That was really their only "date" since they'd eaten dinner together at her apartment. They spent a lot of time together with other people, of course, but Tessa didn't really count that as dates—especially when Mo was very interested in everything Tessa said and did. Sometimes they'd be chatting, and she'd notice that Mo's face was getting closer and closer to hers, so as to be right up in her personal space. Roxy had explained that she had a hard time reading social cues, and if that wasn't an understatement.

Tessa chuckled a bit and shook her head. She checked her watch again—five after ten. She picked up her phone, and this time there was a message from Roxy, saying they were on their way, but they'd had to go back to the house because Roxy had forgotten her wallet.

She was glad they were on their way. The bar was rather empty, and she was getting the willies sitting there all by herself at a table in the corner. She wasn't quite sure why. Nothing of note had happened in the last two weeks that would count for the "weird auras and evil magic" category of things. She hadn't had much time to work on her hedgecraft in the last week, and that was weighing on her. The pool of magic within her that had risen up so beautifully the week before was ebbing again. Freya had warned her of that, and yet she'd let herself get caught up in the show and Roxy and had forgotten to sharpen her most important tool.

The next day, she vowed, she'd make sure to work on some small castings around the apartment, just to remind herself she could.

"Hey, cutie. Why so serious?"

Tessa looked up and smiled. There were Roxy and Mo, bringing the cold air with them as they sat down across from her at the table. Roxy leaned over and kissed her quickly on the lips. Her lips were cold and yet the kiss made Tessa feel warm all over, chasing away the chill.

"Just worried about Joy, is all," said Tessa, choosing the simplest truth to share with them.

Mo nodded. "I am worried also." Her voice conveyed an even greater sense of concern than Tessa's.

Roxy sighed. "Maybe we're all wrong?" She shrugged. "Maybe Madame Clerval is just a hack who makes good guesses?"

"We can only hope," said Tessa.

"Hey, we're out on a Wednesday night," said Roxy brightly. "Let's get some drinks and celebrate getting out of the house," she added with a wink at Tessa that made Tessa blush.

She looked over at Mo who, as usual, was sizing her up. Well, at least she was smiling at her this time, though with a somewhat crazed look in her eyes.

"Sure," said Tessa. "I'll have a glass of white wine."

"Perfect," said Roxy. "Mo—your usual, I assume?"

Mo nodded, still staring at Tessa.

Roxy left the two of them to go get their drinks at the bar. Tessa cleared her throat. "So, uh, things are going well working for Lisa?"

Mo blinked a few times, as if not understanding the question. "Oh, yes," she said, finally. "It is all fine. What about you and Roxy? Is it all *going well*?" She put a strange emphasis on the last two words that Tessa couldn't quite figure out. Was she trying to ask if they were sleeping together? That was personal, to Tessa's mind, but she supposed that since Roxy and Mo were cousins and roommates, there probably weren't a whole lot of secrets. Still, she wasn't about to spill her guts to Mo.

"I think so," said Tessa.

"You are okay *taking it slow*?" Again, that weird emphasis. Tessa could hardly believe that Mo was asking about her sex life, but there really wasn't any other way to interpret the question. She reminded herself what Roxy had told her about Mo not understanding social cues and decided to ignore whatever innuendos might be present in Mo's words.

"Of course," said Tessa. "Whatever Roxy wants."

Roxy came back with their drinks, and Tessa was saved from having to make any more awkward conversation with Mo. The three of them enjoyed their beverages and whiled away the hour. Finally, Tessa spied

Joy walking back down the street. A moment later, she joined them in the booth, sliding in next to Tessa.

"Brr, you're bringing in the cold with you." Tessa rubbed her arms. It really was frigid out.

She tried to get a good read on Joy from the side. She seemed…fine.

"Sorry! I guess the cold air just clings to you," said Joy with a smile. She shivered a bit in her jacket and blew on her hands. "I can't believe I forgot my gloves."

"So, how was it?" said Roxy. "We're all dying to know."

Joy sat back in the booth and shrugged. "It was fine. A little spooky. She's good, you know. Knew a lot about me and the theater and the show. But again, it's a small town. We've been here nearly a month. She could get a lot of information from anyone or just from keeping her eyes open."

"Nothing out of the ordinary?" asked Tessa. "What did you talk about for an hour?"

"We talked a lot about Princess Pancake, to be honest," said Joy. Her eyes teared up a bit. She sniffed. "That was nice."

Roxy and Mo were clearly confused. "Who is Princess Pancake?" said Mo, sounding intrigued.

"That was Joy's pet cat who passed away recently," explained Tessa. "Joy had had her for over fifteen years."

Roxy and Mo looked disappointed.

"So that was it? Just stuff about your cat?" said Roxy.

Joy wiped her nose with a tissue before stuffing it back in her purse. "We talked about the show. I asked her if she thought the show would be a success."

Tessa's heart started to hammer. Not that she put much stock into the words of a for-hire clairvoyant, but the show was her baby. She wasn't sure she could stand to hear anything bad or concerning about it.

"And?" Tessa prompted her, trying to read Joy's expression, which was suddenly a blank.

Joy cleared her throat. "This is where it got kind of weird, honestly. She said the show would be a success, but not in the way that I expect."

"What on earth does *that* mean?" said Roxy.

Tessa could feel her throat go dry.

"I don't know," said Joy. "I tried to press her on it, but all she would say is that there are too many factors at work in the theater and the future was too foggy to know. Or maybe she said vectors?"

"Or actors?" suggested Roxy.

"I don't know," said Joy, looking concerned. "I mean, she did say it would be a success. I guess that's good. And I asked if we should be concerned about any kind of sabotage. And she just said that thing about too many factors or vectors or whatever it was."

Tessa sighed. This was getting ridiculous. "Joy, what was your feeling about *her*? Is she the real thing? Or just a hack?"

"The stuff about Princess seemed awfully real, but it's still such an emotional topic for me. Maybe she's just a really good fake."

Tessa nodded. "That's what I think. We can't take her words at face value."

"Really?" Roxy sounded deflated, as if she'd been hoping for a more exciting explanation. Next to her, Mo looked unconvinced.

"What does this Madame Clerval look like?" said Mo. "Can you describe her?"

"Sure," said Joy. "She was very ordinary. I mean, anywhere from forty to sixty years old, long brown hair pulled up and back, no makeup, but she looked pretty good. Not stunning but not ugly either. She looked like a librarian or a schoolteacher. Just…ordinary."

Roxy and Mo looked disappointed.

"Were you expecting a turban and gold chains?" said Tessa teasingly.

Roxy smiled. "I guess. I mean, what's the point of being a clairvoyant if you're not going to wear the part, right?"

Joy nodded. "She was wearing very practical winter boots and some rather basic black pants and a sweater. The place was kind of dingy. Hardly any decorations or anything. Like she was in a temporary space except that her name was painted on the window."

Somewhere in Tessa's mind, a faint alarm bell was going off, though she couldn't quite figure out why.

"Maybe she knows she doesn't have to invest in that stuff if people already want her services," said Tessa. "How much did it end up costing?"

"A hundred dollars for the hour," said Joy.

"What?" said Roxy, clearly startled by the cost.

"That's pretty normal," said Joy. "Which, by the way, Tessa, you still owe me your half."

Tessa had a fifty ready and passed it over to her.

"Thanks for doing that," said Tessa, "even if we didn't get a whole lot out of it. At least we know sort of what she looks like now. Oh, did you ask her about coming to the theater to see if she could detect any evil spells?"

They'd concocted this idea as a way of getting Madame Clerval to come to the theater so Mo, Roxy, and Tessa could get a sense of her vibe.

"I did, but she said absolutely not. She was very adamant that she wouldn't go there. Sorry."

"Did she say why?" said Roxy.

Joy shook her head. "It was kind of weird. She was pretty even keel the whole time I was there, but when I mentioned the possibility of her going to the theater, she got kind of harsh. Like I'd offended her. She did say the theater was completely safe, though, but that she wouldn't go there. She made it sound like I was asking her to go there like a freak show, which I guess, under the circumstances, it kind of would be."

Roxy sighed. "That's too bad. Huh." She thought for a moment. "You said she was ordinary looking. So how would I recognize her if I saw her?"

Joy paused to think about it before smiling. "She *was* ordinary, *but...* she was wearing a ring that was not. Ordinary I mean. It was a large green stone, but not an emerald, and to be honest, it kind of looked like an eye."

"Wow, that is pretty unusual." Tessa tried to keep her voice neutral, even as the alarm bells were going off in her head. An eye ring. That *had* to be a magic object—and not good magic, either. It was still possible it was a fake, like the rest of Madame Clerval. But Tessa's intuition said otherwise.

They chatted a bit more about more general topics before Tessa started yawning. Soon they were all yawning, and they decided to call it a night. They walked Joy home first, as she was staying right in the center of town with a friend, then they walked to Tessa's apartment, since Roxy didn't want Tessa walking home that late by herself.

They left Mo at the gate, and Roxy walked Tessa all the way to the door before cupping her face gently in her hands and kissing her deeply. Instinctively, Tessa pressed her body against Roxy's and put her arms around her. Even through the layers of winter wear, she could feel Roxy's hard body. Her own body lit up with desire. Her worries and concerns about everything else were momentarily forgotten.

They pulled apart, and Tessa could see the hunger in Roxy's eyes, mirroring her own. She wanted to keep on kissing her forever, but another giant yawn came over her.

"Sexy," said Roxy with a laugh before catching the yawn too.

"Ha." Tessa snuggled up against Roxy. "I miss you. I know I get to see you almost every day, but somehow, I still miss you."

"I know the feeling." Roxy kissed the top of Tessa's head through her hat. "I have this Saturday off, though, so maybe we can spend the day together?"

"Mm, sounds good," said Tessa before planting another kiss on Roxy. She couldn't help herself. This time, Roxy's arms went around her tightly and squeezed, and Tessa felt herself melting inside, even as the wind cut through all her warmest layers. She sighed into Roxy's mouth, and she felt rather than heard Roxy's breath hitch.

They broke apart, both of them breathless.

"Roxy! Is everything okay?" shouted Mo from the sidewalk, and Roxy and Tessa laughed.

"I'm going, I'm going," said Roxy. She gave Tessa a chaste peck on the cheek. "See you at the theater tomorrow, right?"

Tessa nodded, still too wound up to speak. She waved at Roxy before letting herself into the apartment. Her whole body was thrumming with desire.

CHAPTER TWENTY-ONE—ROXY

That Saturday, Roxy picked up Tessa at her apartment, and they drove to a location picked out by Roxy. It'd snowed the day before, turning all of Cape Cod into a picture-perfect New England holiday village. The snow had stopped early enough that the plows finally came through and the roads were relatively clear. With the help of Jack and Hunter, Roxy had planned the perfect winter weekend date, and she couldn't wait to surprise Tessa.

"Am I dressed warmly enough for today's adventures?" asked Tessa as she got into the car.

Roxy took in her fleece-lined pants, snow boots, ski coat, warm hat and mittens, and shook her head with a laugh. "Absolutely. Also, you are the cutest snow bunny."

Tessa smiled with pleasure before leaning over and giving Roxy a kiss on the lips. The kiss was electric, soft, and yet also full of passion and things unsaid. Roxy marveled yet again at the fact that this beautiful, smart, adorable person wanted to be with her, kiss her, and generally, spend time with her. It was a novel sensation—being wanted so unabashedly.

"Okay, that's enough of that," said Roxy with a grin. "We might never get out of this parking lot if we keep going like this."

"Would that be so bad?" said Tessa, and Roxy felt desire deep inside her flare up, heating her through. Her resolution to take things slow was pretty much gone. Three weeks *was* taking it slow, and if their date went well, Roxy had a feeling that it might be time to pick up the pace.

"Now, now," said Roxy. She flashed a grin at Tessa as she backed out of the parking lot and pulled into the road. "I've got the perfect winter date planned for today and your sexy eyes are not going to distract me."

They giggled as Roxy drove and continued the flirtatious banter while admiring the snowy landscape.

It didn't take them long to get to their first stop—the Wellfleet Bay Wildlife Sanctuary. Roxy had the supreme pleasure of surprising Tessa with snowshoes that Jack and Hunter had lent them for the day. Tessa had never snowshoed before, and Roxy could tell from her excitement that it was a pleasant novelty. Roxy felt the glow of pride in being able to bring Tessa so much joy, even if she'd had some help with the idea for the date. In fact, in some ways, she was absolutely delighted to have had help—her employers and new friends were showing themselves to be truly generous and genuine people, and she loved both working for them and having them as friends. It was amazing how much her perspective on life had changed since the night of Hazel's wedding.

They had the trails to themselves, and aside from the quiet crunch of their snowshoes in the fresh snow, it was blissfully peaceful and quiet. After about half an hour, they made it to the spot Jack had told her about. Roxy stopped and pulled out some binoculars he'd lent her for the outing.

Tessa looked at her with a smile of surprise. "Binoculars?"

Roxy nodded with a grin. She lifted them to her eyes and began scanning the trees, looking for the spot Jack had described to her. Just as she was about to give up, she saw it. She couldn't help gasping quietly—it was more majestic than she'd expected.

She moved the binoculars away from her face and gestured to Tessa to come closer.

Tessa lifted the binoculars and then paused. She looked up at Roxy, who was standing slightly behind her now. "What am I looking for?"

"Hold on," said Roxy. "I'll show you where to look."

Tessa looked intrigued. She put the binoculars up to her eyes, and Roxy bent her knees slightly to approximate her height. She could see the bird now with the naked eye, and she directed Tessa's binoculars in that direction.

"Right there, that tree with the big branch next to a bulge in the bark," said Roxy.

"Oh my God," said Tessa quietly, her voice hushed in awe. "It's beautiful. Majestic."

When Roxy had asked Jack about what kind of wildlife they might go out and see in the wintertime on Cape Cod, he mentioned this wildlife sanctuary and a specific spot where you could often glimpse a snowy owl. Roxy had worried it would be hard to find one out in nature, but Jack had assured her that there was one particular owl that everyone in that area knew about. It showed up regularly in the preserve, and the community had jokingly named it "Bob."

"So cool, right?" said Roxy, pleased that the bird had impressed Tessa.

Tessa gazed at it a little longer before turning toward Roxy and handing her the binoculars. "You should look again. He's really something."

They took turns looking at the owl, and Roxy marveled at it again and again. It was really something to behold in its natural habitat. They also managed to spot a few other birds—some sparrows, a dark-eyed junco, and even a brilliantly colored purple finch that Tessa spotted.

As they stood there, Roxy felt herself getting cold again, and she figured Tessa must be too. They snuggled together as they bird-watched in the snow, and Roxy felt a deep sense of calm. She loved that Tessa enjoyed being outdoors, and she also loved that it was a place where she had some expertise over Tessa. At the theater, she often felt like a fish out of water, but here, in nature, this was her domain. And she was glad to be able to share it with Tessa.

Tessa handed back the binoculars one last time, and Roxy placed them in her backpack after taking one last look at the finch. She turned back to Tessa and kissed her gently on the lips.

"Wow, you are *cold*," said Roxy, pulling away. Tessa's lips were like ice.

"Gosh, I hardly noticed until you said that just now. I guess I am pretty cold." Tessa shivered right on cue.

"Let's go back to the car and warm up."

The walk back in the deep snow certainly helped them warm up, though by the end, Roxy's fingers and toes were numb from the cold. The temperatures were dropping over the course of the day, so their next stop was all about getting warm—a tea shop.

It didn't take long to drive over to one of the little towns halfway down the Cape where there was a tiny little tea shop Hunter had told Roxy about. Roxy had called on Friday to reserve a table, just in case, and they were right on time.

Adeline, the proprietor, was a tiny little old lady with gray hair in a bun, bejeweled chains on her tiny reading glasses, and a fluffy pink sweater with a teacup and saucer embroidered onto it. The tea shop was cluttered and homey, with every inch of wall decorated with tea-themed décor. She escorted Tessa and Roxy to a table that was already brimming with tiny sandwiches and cookies, slices of decadent cakes, plates, silverware, and embroidered napkins. Two teapots sat on the table, steaming with hot water.

"Here is our tea list," said Adeline, handing them each a menu printed on light pink cardstock. "Take a moment, have a think, and I'll come back in a jiffy with the teas."

After she left, Tessa looked over at her with a big smile. "This place is amazing. How on earth did you find out about it?" She sounded genuinely pleased, and again, Roxy felt herself beaming with pleasure. Working at the theater several days a week for the last two weeks, it was impossible not to notice how much hot tea Tessa drank all day long. Just in case, she'd double-checked with Chayo, too, and she'd enthusiastically agreed that an afternoon tea would be just the ticket for Tessa. Apparently, she'd grown fond of them during her time in London.

"A girl never shares her dating secrets," said Roxy with a wink. "So, you like it?"

"I love it." Tessa studied the extensive tea list. "So many options, I hardly know how to choose. I kind of want them all."

"I'm no tea expert, so feel free to choose for both of us and we can share," said Roxy. "I'm pretty sure we each get two flavors as part of the booking."

Tessa was excited and impressed. When Adeline returned, Tessa ordered a black breakfast tea and a black currant hibiscus fruit tea to start. Rather than pull out little baggies as Roxy expected, Adeline brought out tiny tins of whole leaf and whole fruit tea mixes, expertly filling up small silver balls with them on a chain and placing the whole ball into each of their teapots. She left and returned almost immediately with tiny pitchers of cream, an adorably miniature pot of honey with a little honey stick in it (just like in a cartoon), and a sugar bowl with an elaborately decorated spoon in it.

"Now then, would either of you like anything else to eat? Today's hot lunch specials include clam chowder or tomato bisque, quiche Lorraine served hot or cold, or a warm croissant sandwich—ham and brie with cranberry sauce or roasted vegetables and avocado."

Tessa decided on a bowl of the bisque and Roxy ordered the ham and brie croissant. It was the perfect way to warm up after their snowy hike. There were also plenty of little finger sandwiches. Roxy had to stop herself from eating too many to leave room for the desserts, which were plentiful—raspberry swirl pound cake, lemon poppyseed muffins, Linzer tart cookies, carrot cake mini muffins with cream cheese frosting, and tiny scones with raisins and jam.

At the end of their meal, Adeline showed up again with a decorative cardboard box that she loaded up with their leftovers.

"Do you think Mo would like to try some of these?" asked Tessa as they got into the car, and she placed the box with leftovers onto the back seat. Roxy let the engine idle for a few minutes as the car warmed up. Her old truck did not like the winter cold, but Roxy was in no position to buy a new one. Besides, she loved the beat-up old thing, even if it did take nearly ten minutes for the heat to kick in.

"Oh no," said Roxy. "Not nearly fishy enough. I mean…she's not really into sweets," she amended, realizing that she'd almost given away Mo's secret. She'd need to be more careful.

Tessa laughed out loud with a hoot. "Oh, that Mo. She's one of a kind, huh?"

Roxy bristled at that. "She's unique." The words came out with a touch of defensiveness she couldn't help coming into her voice.

"I'm sorry. I didn't mean it as an insult." Tessa sounded genuinely apologetic. She put a hand on Roxy's knee, and Roxy felt her entire body light up with electric desire. She put her own hand atop Tessa's and gave her a squeeze.

They were on the road back to Ptown now, as the final part of their winter date was on the way home.

They didn't have far to drive, and soon Roxy was turning off the main road down a side street. Finally, they parked, and Tessa looked around.

"Ice skating?" Her voice was full of wonder, once she saw the sign down the street from their parking spot. They were in one of the many small towns sprinkled up and down the Cape, so picturesque Roxy could hardly believe it. It was even more adorable than the town where they'd had their tea, and the rink looked like something right out of a postcard for New England.

They rented skates from the warming hut, and soon they were both toddling around on the ice with varying levels of ability. It was a small rink, but they had it nearly to themselves, the low temperatures keeping many at home.

After a few minutes, Roxy felt quite at ease on the ice. She'd done a fair amount of pickup ice hockey with her brothers growing up, and muscle memory did wonders for things like ice skating. She hadn't been ice skating in several years, but it all came back to her quickly.

Tessa was much more wobbly, and after a few minutes, Roxy circled back to keep her company.

"It's been so long since I ice skated." Tessa grabbed onto Roxy's hands for dear life as Roxy skated backward in front of her. She smiled up at Roxy, and Roxy felt her heart melt a little.

"When was the last time?"

"Gosh, I have no idea. At least ten years ago. Maybe more. I think it was in high school."

"Anything coming back yet?"

"Not yet," said Tessa, though Roxy could tell already that in the ten minutes they'd been on the ice, Tessa was already much steadier on her feet.

"You're doing great." Roxy released one of Tessa's hands and turned around to skate next to her. She took in their surroundings—the kids laughing and screaming on the rink, a few other couples equally wrapped up in one another, the tall pine trees on the north edge of the pond, the sun peeking out occasionally from behind the clouds, dazzling her eyes with its wintertime brightness. It really was a picture-perfect moment, and she gave Tessa's hand a quick squeeze.

"I feel like I'm holding you back, though." Tessa gave her hand a squeeze back.

"Never. I'm exactly where I want to be. I hope *you're* having a good time."

"The best." Tessa smiled up at her before promptly starting to lose her balance and grabbing onto Roxy.

Roxy felt herself losing her balance for a moment with Tessa's weight on her, but her feet reacted quickly, and she managed to catch them both before falling. She pulled Tessa close into a hug.

"You okay?"

"Uh-huh," said Tessa, and they kissed.

In that moment, with the kiss on her lips, Roxy felt she was on cloud nine. She felt her mouth melting into Tessa's, deepening the kiss and tightening her arms around her, holding her as close as possible in spite of all their layers of winter wear. That flame of desire deep inside her roared up, and she wanted nothing more than to peel off all their clothes as quickly as possible and feel their skin on skin—

Roxy forgot where she was for a moment, and she felt the two of them starting to move across the ice.

Roxy pulled away and caught her balance. "Whew, that was a close one."

She looked at Tessa and saw desire blazing in her eyes as well. "Maybe we should get off the ice and somewhere warmer." She glanced over to where some teenagers were goofing off and howling with raucous laughter. "And maybe more private?" she added, with a raised eyebrow that made her intentions clear.

"You read my mind," said Roxy, surprised at how husky her own voice sounded. It was time, she thought, to stop taking it slow.

CHAPTER TWENTY-TWO—TESSA

Tessa's heart was beating so hard with anticipation, she hardly noticed the landscape passing by them as Roxy sped back to Provincetown as quickly as she dared. The one distinct advantage of being on Cape Cod in the winter was that they had the roads to themselves and could drive along Route 6 with hardly any traffic on the roads.

There was a tension between them in the car—a good tension. Roxy turned on the radio and they listened in silence, hands intertwined on Tessa's thigh. It was so strange to feel so hot under her clothes and yet, her face and hands and feet were freezing. Love in the wintertime was complicated.

"What're you smiling at?" said Roxy, taking her eyes off the road for a glance at Tessa.

"Just wondering how I'm going to undress you when I can't feel my fingers."

Roxy squeezed her hand. "Oh, that's no problem," she assured her.

"Oh?"

"You've got a shower, right?"

Tessa's hands shook with cold and desire as she unlocked the door to the apartment and let them inside. They kicked off their shoes and hats, gloves, coats, and scarves on the floor and couches before Tessa grabbed Roxy's hand and pulled her into the bedroom.

Roxy tore off her flannel, revealing a black underlayer that made Tessa feel even more turned on, if that was possible. She could feel herself getting wet in the car and now, it felt like a waterfall between her legs. She was desperate to feel Roxy's hands there, touching her, caressing her most tender folds, but she was also on the verge of shivering. Her hands were like ice.

Clumsily, she helped pull the long-sleeve under layer off Roxy, revealing a cotton undershirt.

"You've got to be kidding me," said Tessa with a laugh that mixed with an involuntary groan of frustration.

"It's cold out there, sweetheart." Roxy peeled the sweater and turtleneck off Tessa before pausing to admire Tessa's bra.

She'd worn it on purpose, hoping, wishing she would be able to show it off today. It was black lace with a low v-cut and mesh and lace across her nipples, which were visible through the mesh.

"Damn," said Roxy, her voice low and full of desire. "That's gorgeous. But…I'm still gonna take it off." There was sauciness in her voice that made Tessa shiver with pleasure—or was that the cold air of the room? She could hardly tell.

"Do it." She put her arms around Roxy's neck and nibbled the skin there as she felt Roxy's bare arms encircle her nearly naked torso. Roxy unhooked the back of the bra and then, her hands, which were, miraculously, completely warm, unlike her own, traced along her back and arms gently, almost lazily, to pull the straps off her. She felt Roxy's hands cup her breasts and she kissed Roxy's neck harder, sucking, nibbling, not caring if there was a mark there the next day.

Roxy shifted and moved so that her lips found Tessa's, her tongue found hers, and Tessa's entire body lit up with pure sensation. Roxy continued massaging her breasts and now, occasionally, pinched and twisted her nipples until they stood erect and hard. Tessa groaned into Roxy's mouth. She wanted more. She pushed her body against Roxy's, twisting her hips against hers, and tangling her hands in Roxy's curls.

Roxy pushed her away gently and pulled off her undershirt, revealing small, tight breasts and large pink nipples that Tessa moved to put her mouth on, but Roxy shook her head.

"Hold on there, baby," she said quietly before unzipping her winter pants and kicking them off, along with her socks, then hooking her thumbs into the band of Tessa's fleece-lined pants and slowly pulling them down her legs. Tessa lifted her feet, marveling at the sensation of having someone undress her; it felt like ages since she'd been undressed. The cool air of the room hit her legs, and she felt goose bumps rise even as her body also felt hot, glowing like an ember with desire.

"Let's get wet," said Roxy with a smile that could only be described as dirty—in the best possible way. Tessa felt a gush of wetness at those words, and she felt like she could hardly move her legs, they were so heavy with desire. Roxy took her by the hand and led her to the bathroom, turning on the shower and letting the water warm up. It only took a moment, but it felt like agony to wait as Tessa's entire body trembled with need.

Finally, the water was warm and Roxy slipped two fingers into Tessa's underwear, cupping her buttocks and kissing her again deeply before sliding the lacy thong off her and then taking off her own boy shorts. Tessa wanted to drop to her knees right there and worship at the altar of dark brown, nearly black curls between Roxy's legs, but her cold hands and feet finally won out and she let Roxy lead her into the shower.

The hot water sluiced over the two of them. Their bodies were now flush against one another, naked and wet, one body not two. Roxy held her tight as her mouth melted with hers, their tongues entwined, desire and need racing through Tessa's veins.

She slid a hand between Roxy's legs and felt the wetness—that *other* wetness—and she rubbed and caressed, feeling Roxy's body stiffen next to her and hearing her gasp into her mouth before moving her hand aside and putting her own between Tessa's legs.

Now it was Tessa's turn to sigh and groan with desire. Roxy's fingers slid between the many folds of tender flesh, finding her center and teasing her there before sliding the finger up to her clit and circling it over and over until Tessa's breath grew ragged and her hips began grinding rhythmically against Roxy's hand.

"Mmm, you like that," murmured Roxy, bending her head to suck on Tessa's neck before stopping what she was doing and using both hands to cup and squeeze her buttocks, fingers ever so close to her sex, and yet not quite touching it in an agony of pleasure.

"You tease." Tessa was enjoying the sensation of being teased even as her body cried out for satisfaction.

"Don't worry, I'll take care of you." Roxy's voice was low and tender and yet also full of passion.

"Is that a threat or a promise?" Tessa's voice was barely above a whisper. Her entire being was focused on the sensations both surrounding her clit and elsewhere, deep inside of her, where something was slowly clenching, curling up, building with want.

Roxy responded by massaging Tessa's breasts again and rolling her nipples in her fingers so they stood erect, even as Tessa's body was now heated through from the shower. She was no longer cold from being outdoors, but the hot water still felt delicious. She pushed her body against Roxy's yet again, begging wordlessly for her hands to return to that sweet spot below.

Roxy cupped her sex, again, fingers sliding inside her, in and out, over and over again in an inexorable rhythm, occasionally sliding them all the way out and encircling her clit several times, sometimes pressing it gently with her thumb, before entering her again and again and again until Tessa could feel something shift inside her.

Her breath was ragged, and she was moaning and sighing, inarticulate, in the very throes of desire, the deep coiling sensation within her wound up to a fever pitch until finally, Roxy slid her fingers deep into Tessa and touched her clit with her thumb; the multiple sensations overwhelmed Tessa and she felt her hips bucking and the orgasm cresting within her, sending spasms of pleasure through her body. She was grateful for Roxy's steady strength, helping her stay upright as everything else seemed to be falling around her. Tessa saw stars and fireworks as her body continued to orgasm for longer than she thought possible, and she felt Roxy continue to pump her, her body clenching around those fingers, until she finally had to put a hand on Roxy's chest to signal she was spent.

Roxy pulled her into a hug, and she laid her head on Roxy's chest as the water continued to pour over them, though now it was somewhat cooler. Even so, the water felt good on Tessa as she caught her breath. Roxy leaned against the side of the shower stall and Tessa leaned on her, feeling deliciously spent and yet, at the same time, desperate to make Roxy feel the same sensations that were now coursing inside her.

The water in the shower cooled off noticeably.

"Time to get out," said Roxy. "Brr!"

"Mmm," murmured Tessa through her haze of pleasure, forcing herself to turn off the shower and reach for the towels.

Getting out of the shower and toweling off took much longer than necessary, of course, because Tessa couldn't help falling into a long, blissful kiss, or else caressing Roxy's arms, or stopping to admire her seriously fit bottom.

"Like the view?" Roxy smiled as she caught Tessa staring.

"Oh yeah," said Tessa quietly. "Bedroom. Now."

Roxy raised an eyebrow but followed directions obediently. Still naked and mostly dry, they climbed into the luxurious king-size bed. Tessa found herself under Roxy and, with just a little bit of nudging, managed to get Roxy to flip onto her back—just where she wanted her. She climbed on top of her and began grinding her very wet pussy into Roxy.

"Oh my. What a dirty girl you are."

"The dirtiest," said Tessa, her eyelids low, her gaze still full of liquid desire. She pushed herself back between Roxy's splayed out legs and gently touched Roxy, trailing her fingers lazily between her legs, all the way to her buttocks and then back up, ever so lightly, up to her clit, which was already stiff, an erect nub of pulsing heat. "I see," she said, her voice low and husky. "You're all ready."

Roxy moaned with desire rather than answer her, and Tessa, thus encouraged, lowered her head and began to stroke across the length of Roxy's sex with her tongue in long, slow, luxurious licks, tasting the salty sweet liquor of desire, before focusing on the clit, flicking it, playing with it, sucking on it, and then circling it. She could feel Roxy's body stiffening around her, feeling her arch rather than seeing it, and she couldn't resist slipping a finger deep inside her as she continued to suck her erect clit.

It didn't take long for Roxy to come, and it was a quieter kind of climax than Tessa's loud, unrestrained cries. Still, she felt Roxy's muscles clenching around her fingers, still inside her, and felt the bucking of her hips, and a deep sense of satisfaction filled Tessa. She noticed with pleasure that she had grown wetter again, her body responding to Roxy's, and she felt a deep sense of connection between them. Her college freshman crush felt long gone; this was something else, something both more tender and more passionate. She wanted to know everything about Roxy, know her to her very cells and mitochondria, but she also wanted to simply be with her and hold her close, their breath and skin as one.

She pushed herself up so her body was next to Roxy's, her head next to hers on the pillow, and she traced a finger along Roxy's torso, now glowing with sweat and heat. Roxy was breathing hard, but she turned to face Tessa, and they lay like that, simply taking each other in, tracing invisible lines of desire across each other's bodies.

Tessa didn't want this afternoon to end. Or was it evening? She realized, with a start, that it was already getting dark outside, which meant it must be after four. Or maybe even five? Was it possible that the whole day had flown by in Roxy's company?

Roxy noticed the elapsed time as well as her gaze fell on the bedside clock. Her head lifted off the pillow as she looked more carefully at the time on the display, and her eyes grew large with surprise.

"Is that the right time? Is it really after five?"

Tessa got up and found her phone. "Yes. That's the right time. Crazy, huh?"

"Oh my gosh," said Roxy, jumping up with a look of guilt and concern. "Mo's been alone in the apartment all day, and we're all out of fish. I mean food. I told her I'd be back by three."

"She's a grown person," said Tessa reasonably. "If she wants to eat, I'm sure she can go get something—right?"

Roxy rubbed her face with her hands before gathering up her scattered clothes. "You don't understand, she can't be left alone like that for a whole day," said Roxy, clearly distracted and rushed. Tessa felt her heart sinking. She thought for sure Roxy would stay for dinner and spend the night. Suddenly, she felt like crying.

Roxy paused and looked over at her, recognition painting itself across her face, and her expression softened. She was only wearing one shoe, her socks, and pants, but she stopped what she was doing and limped over to Tessa, folding her into her arms with a soft squeeze. Tessa felt the dread rising up in her recede as Roxy's strong arms encircled her with steady, gentle pressure.

"I'm coming *right back*," said Roxy. "Don't you think for one minute that this is a one-night stand or something. I don't want to leave, I just have to. I'm sorry." She paused and sighed. "Mo is my responsibility, and let's face it, she *is* pretty clueless. Please don't feel bad. I promise I will be right back. I just need an hour to check on her, make sure she's okay and has something to eat."

"Okay," said Tessa quietly. Wrapped in Roxy's solid embrace, it was easier to hear those words, even if they were not at all what she wanted to hear. She tried and almost succeeded in keeping the sob out of her voice.

"Hey, hey," said Roxy soothingly, rubbing Tessa's back. "I promise, I don't want to go. I…I really like you, Tessa. More than just about anyone I've ever met. I want this to be the start of something, not the ending."

Tessa snuggled against Roxy and held her even tighter. "I never want to let you go. I want to hold onto you all night."

"And you will," said Roxy, gentleness mixed with firmness in her soft alto. She kissed the top of Tessa's head and moved away from her. "The sooner I go, the sooner I'll be back." She gave Tessa a quick kiss on the lips and began getting dressed again.

All too soon she was at the door, coat on, gloves and hat in her hand. Tessa felt her heart sinking as Roxy fished the car keys out of her large plaid coat. She'd wrapped herself in a bathrobe, and she had her Polish folk slippers on to keep the chill off her feet, but still, she felt cold.

"Come here," said Roxy gently, opening her arms.

Tessa just about ran to her and enjoyed one more embrace and one more hot, passionate kiss before Roxy left. No longer cold, her body felt hot, feverish, as Roxy's mouth moved against hers, tongues entwined, the fire of desire flaming up inside her again—it hadn't had time to go out.

"Mmm," Roxy murmured, pulling away reluctantly.

"Can't tempt you to stay, can I?" Tessa ground her hips against Roxy, keeping the one place of connection between them for another moment.

"I wish," said Roxy. "Honestly, who knew a m—my *cousin*—could be so much work. My cousin, I mean." Roxy coughed and cleared her throat.

"Cousins can be that way," said Tessa knowingly. "Hopefully, someday I can take you to Poland to meet my extended family, and then you'll really see what cousin drama can be." It was true; her family in Poland was quite extensive, and there was drama in every branch. Honestly, it made sense she'd made drama her life's work, in a way. Human drama was a huge part of her life. She was glad, though, that it was never so much a part of her closest family.

"I'd like that," said Roxy, her eyes shining with an emotion Tessa couldn't readily identify. "Okay, I'm off. I'll see you soon."

"You better."

She could have stayed there bantering with Roxy and kissing her in the foyer forever, but finally she simply stood back and let Roxy go. It was true what Roxy said—the sooner she left, the sooner she'd be back.

Tessa fought the urge to sit around feeling sorry for herself. Instead, she decided to use her time wisely. She hopped in the shower again and found it necessary to take care of herself. She felt deliciously dirty, touching herself, finding herself so incredibly wet. She came quickly, with a shudder and a sigh, letting the hot water rush around her. She turned it up as hot as she could stand, and it was cleansing in a whole other way. The first time having sex with someone was stressful in its own way, even if with Roxy it was clear that they were in sync. The heat of the shower erased whatever lingering tension was in her body, and she felt much less worried about Roxy's sudden departure afterward as she got dressed.

She put on her favorite purple oversized sweater and black leggings and made herself a quick dinner, her stomach complaining that afternoon tea was now long gone, especially in light of her recent activities. She reheated the last of the stuffed cabbage that she had in the freezer from home and enjoyed the contrast of earthy rice, meat, and cabbage with bright, acidic sour cream and tomato sauce. She washed up and made a hot tea with lemon and honey before it even occurred to her to take a look at the messages on her phone.

There had been a flash of a message preview on the screen when she'd first picked it up, but she'd been distracted by Roxy and hadn't noticed who it was from. She was tempted to look at the messages right then, but she'd felt cold in just the bathrobe and had decided to get dressed first.

Tessa went back to the bedroom now to check the phone, and realizing how much it smelled like fresh sex, decided to pull back the sheets and crack open a window. Not that sex was a *bad* smell, but it was, she realized, a *strong* one. It made her smile even as her nose wrinkled a bit. The fresh air of an early winter's evening was just the thing. She lit a vanilla-scented candle as well. Might as well set the scene for more debauchery.

She hadn't brought much in terms of sexy clothing, but she enjoyed lacy underclothes, so went through and pulled out what she did have in the dresser and was happy to find a cream-colored underwear and bra set she'd forgotten about. She laid it out and was about to change into it when she saw her phone screen turn on again with a phone call coming through.

It was Joy.

"Hey, what's up?"

"*Tessa*! My goodness I thought I'd never get through to you. Woman, where have you been?" Her voice was strained, and she spoke at a million miles a minute.

"I had the day off with Roxy. Slow down. What's up?" Her hackles went up. "Is Lisa causing problems again? I told her—"

"It's not Lisa. It's the *theater*. Oh God. You have to get down here." Joy's voice cracked on the word "theater," and the words tumbled out of her faster than she could contain them. "You have to come here. You have to see this. I don't know who did this. I just don't know—oh God. Now Barb is here."

Fuck. What on earth is going on at the theater? Tessa felt fear go through her. What had happened at the theater? *Who* had done *what?*

"I'm on my way."

Tessa moved as fast as possible, grateful that she'd already gotten dressed and eaten. Fear was coursing through her veins. This project was so important to her—the most important thing she'd ever done. Her entire reputation was on the line with this grant and this production, and nothing could get in the way.

She just hoped whatever it was that had happened, that Joy was exaggerating. It couldn't be *that* bad…could it?

With her heart in her throat, she rushed around the apartment to pick up her work stuff, threw on a coat and boots, and ran out the door, before remembering it was after dark and definitely below freezing. She went back inside and grabbed her car keys. She didn't care if she was a wimp about the cold; she was not going to walk ten minutes in this. Judging from Joy's tone of voice on the phone, there wasn't a moment to lose.

Chapter Twenty-three—Roxy

The cold air was refreshing on Roxy's overheated skin. It wasn't a long drive to the apartment she was sharing with Mo, so she took it nice and slow. She needed the time to cool off.

Being around Tessa was like standing next to a campfire. It was cozy and warm in a dark, cold world, but stand too close for too long, and you'd start to sweat. It was a nice metaphor. Tonight their passion had been a roaring fire, nearly out of control, the spark that had been kindled between them leaping into something larger that put off heat in all directions. Luckily, it felt like a good kind of fire, not a forest fire that ate up everything in its path. Roxy had had relationships like that before, that flared up seemingly out of nowhere, burning a path through her heart, only to go out completely when the other person effectively threw water over their relationship.

No, this was something else entirely. Having sex with Tessa was like coming home. There was not a single part of her that felt awkward about it, either during or after. She'd felt terrible about leaving her like that, but there was something—a sixth sense almost—that was calling her home to Mo.

What she'd told Tessa was absolutely true, after all. Mo was *not* human, and even four weeks on land wasn't enough to change that or to teach Mo how to pretend to be human. Mo was simply wearing a human skin, but underneath, or simultaneously, she was something completely different, something alien and not of the human world. Roxy had enough experience with the magical world or the Otherworldly, as Hazel called them, to know that it was not safe to assume they would follow the rules of humanity. How could they? They weren't human. Roxy tried not to hold this against Mo as she left the arms of the woman she had so suddenly and completely fallen for.

She pulled into her parking space and checked her watch. Only five minutes had passed since she left Tessa's. Hopefully, everything at home was one hundred percent *fine* and it was just a matter of taking Mo to the convenience store and getting her some bait. Roxy had had her doubts about that idea when Mo had first found the bucket of minnows at the shop, but apparently, they were quite the delicacy. Who knew?

As soon as Roxy stepped into the apartment, however, she knew something was wrong.

There was no sign of Mo anywhere, but the apartment was a mess, particularly the kitchen. It looked like they'd been robbed by someone who was desperate for the proverbial cup of sugar.

"Mo?" said Roxy a bit tentatively as she took off her shoes and coat. "Are you here?"

Maybe Tessa had been right. Maybe Mo took some of the cash Roxy had left for her on the kitchen table earlier that week and went to the convenience store herself. It was only two blocks away, after all.

She heard splashing—water gently plashing and plopping onto the floor before becoming what sounded like waves of water, an entire *tub* of water, gushing onto the floor.

"Roxy!" Mo's voice was weak and upset. It shook over the vowels in her name, followed by an unearthly sound that was, to Roxy's ear, a mixture of a groan of frustration, a cry of fear, and words in another language.

Roxy dashed to the bathroom. It took a few moments for her to process what she was seeing.

Mo was in the tub, which was not, in and of itself, unusual. Her evening salt bath was a matter of ritual at this point. There were three rather empty-looking containers of salt on the floor, half soaked with the water that had splashed out of the tub. This was a bit more unusual. Even with needing progressively more and more salt, she'd never needed more than two cups' worth to get the magic to work.

Roxy's train of thought was distracted from the salt by the sight of Mo's tail—or rather, her *lack* of tail. Instead, what she saw was something between a tail and two legs, a weird, unnatural fusion of leg and tail in which both were visible and yet neither was complete. It was as though Mo had gotten stuck in the middle of the transition from one form to another.

And, clearly, she could not get unstuck.

"Crap," said Roxy. "Are you all right?"

"Of course I am not all right, Roxy. I am stuck. I am *stuck*." Mo's face was a mask of fear and desperation, her voice half human, half something else entirely that chilled Roxy to the bone.

"What, what, what…" Roxy felt herself stutter with confusion. What on earth could they do, should they do? Her mind was an utter blank, even as she felt herself covered with the sweat of anxiety. It occurred to her then that maybe Mo could die in such a state.

She racked her brains trying to think of all the mermaid lore they'd been reading for the past couple of weeks, even as Mo was groaning and moaning, clearly in pain, mumbling in her native tongue, her hands clawing uselessly at her leg-tail.

The selkie. The story of the selkies came to Roxy—how they would hide their fish skin so they could go on land, and if someone found it and hid it, they couldn't go back to their fish form. Maybe this was a similar situation? Maybe Mo needed to, *had to*, go back into her native waters? Perhaps salt water in a bathtub wasn't strong enough? She'd evidently tried to do something like this herself by adding additional salt to the water.

"Mo. *Mo*." It took Roxy a moment to get Mo's attention, even after she crouched down so their faces were level. She put her hand on one of Mo's arms, and Mo stilled for a moment. She looked at Roxy, tears silently pouring down her face, her bright green hair darker than usual from the water, her amber-yellow-green eyes full of fear.

"I tried, Roxy, I tried to…I tried using more salt, but it's not working," she said, each word a trill of terror, her breathing labored, and Roxy felt that same terror enter her heart. Was she about to witness Mo *die* right here in her rented apartment?

Unexpected courage filled her. She had to help Mo. She pushed away the guilty thoughts that were nagging her at the back of her head, reminding her that she'd been off gallivanting and seducing Tessa the whole day while Mo was alone in the apartment, apparently on the verge of mermaid death. There was no time for those kinds of recriminations. She had to do something and *now*.

"I'm going to take you back to the ocean."

"But, Roxy, it's not safe—" Mo's eyes widened with fear. "How can we—I can't—"

"Mo, we *have to*. You're stuck. What other option do we have?"

Mo looked at her, suddenly paler than before. "They will find me. Surely they will."

"What else can we do? Is there something else? Something I haven't thought of?" It was hard keeping her voice calm when every second felt like a step closer to Mo's untimely demise.

"I don't know, I don't know." Mo shook her head helplessly. "If I don't go, I die. If I do go, I might also die."

"That settles it," said Roxy. "We have to take you to the ocean. Maybe just a few minutes will be enough, you know?" She tried to make her voice encouraging. It was clear to her now that Mo was not capable of thinking for herself. She was too in the moment, fearful and panicked, incapable of logic and reason—not that she had ever really had that good a grasp on human logic, anyway. "Are you completely stuck? Or can you get your legs back do you think?"

"I...don't know," said Mo. "I hadn't thought of that." She closed her eyes and screwed up her face, and Roxy had to stop herself from laughing a little. Mo looked like a little kid whose parents had asked them to try a little harder. After a moment, she opened her eyes and sighed. "No. I cannot."

"Okay, let's try to get you out of the tub, out of the salt water. Maybe that'll help."

Roxy helped Mo leverage herself out of the tub by putting her arms on the floor and pulling her fused legs out behind her. Roxy grabbed her leg-tail so the transition would be less sudden and potentially harmful. Once Mo was out of the water, Roxy grabbed a towel and began rubbing the bottom half of her body dry.

They both breathed a sigh of relief when the tail and scales receded and Mo's human legs were back—though a blue-greenish opalescent cast remained to her skin, as though the tail was not completely forgotten. Still, her legs were back, and she could walk to the car and into the water herself rather than needing Roxy to carry her again—for which Roxy was immensely grateful.

Mo began to cry.

Great big heaving sobs wracked her body, and she leaned her head onto her arms, folded on the side of the tub. Her shoulders shook, and the sounds that came from her were some of the saddest sobs Roxy had ever heard.

Fuck. Of course she was concerned about Mo, but it was also dawning on her now that there was no fucking way she was going to be able to get back to Tessa's in—she checked her watch—thirty minutes. Somehow half an hour had passed since she'd left Tessa's warm embrace and promised her, no less, that she'd be back in an hour. *Fuck.*

She found a fresh, dry towel and wrapped it around Mo as best she could, giving her a squeeze on the shoulders.

"It's gonna be okay," she said with as much conviction as she could muster. "Cry it out. Take a minute. I'll be right back."

Roxy went to the kitchenette where she'd left her phone, charging. She tried calling Tessa first, but no one answered and eventually it went to voice mail. Roxy hated voice mail, but she didn't have time to send a text, and, in some ways, it was perhaps easier to leave a voice message.

"Hey, baby it's me. Mo's having an, er, emergency, so I'm going to take her to…uh…urgent care. I'm *so sorry*. I didn't mean for this to happen. My feelings for you are…completely sincere. Please call me back when you get this." She paused, not wanting to hang up. "I miss you."

Reluctantly, she ended the call and sighed. What a night this was turning out to be.

CHAPTER TWENTY-FOUR—TESSA

The scene of wreckage that met Tessa at the theater was beyond her comprehension.

She'd tried to steel herself for whatever had happened, but if she was truly honest with herself, she'd assumed Joy had been exaggerating. She was prone to that. She once overheard Joy telling someone that she'd worked on twenty shows with Tessa, when Tessa knew that it was actually seven. But Joy liked to tell a good yarn, and she loved holding her audience captive, so Tessa figured this was something similar.

Maybe one of the sets had fallen over and cracked? Maybe some paint had spilled onto something valuable? Maybe Barb had found some of the cast and crew eating cheesesteaks in the greenroom? None of those things were good, but they were fixable. They had another four weeks until opening weekend—plenty of time to right even a fairly major wrong.

Everything and everyone was in disarray when she arrived. Crew members were running around, panicked looks in their eyes, and it took a while of walking around the backstage corridors to find Joy and Barb, who was with her.

Barb was in what Tessa had come to think of as her uniform—a white polo shirt and black work pants. She was always in short sleeves, regardless of the temperature outside or inside. Her small, dark eyes normally looked full of suspicion, and it was therefore disconcerting to see something akin to glee in her expression that evening.

Joy was next to her, running her hands almost ceaselessly through her ever more disheveled red curls, her eyes rimmed red. Had she been crying?

And when the two of them took her over to the costume room, Tessa understood Barb's glee, Joy's red eyes.

The entire room was filled with scraps of ripped up costumes.

The space-age, silver and white costumes of the Planet Sicilia and the gold and yellow costumes of the Planet Bohemia lay mixed together on the floor into a horrifying confetti of unsalvageable fabric scraps. Everything was ripped and ruined. Some costumes had been ripped nearly to shreds, while others had been haphazardly ripped in half, but in such a way as to render them unusable even with the help of the handiest seamstress.

Tessa's heart sunk, and her skin was instantly covered in a cold sweat. The piles of ruined costumes represented a good chunk of the grant budget for the play. There was no way they could order these costumes again—they couldn't afford it, aside from the fact that she doubted they could even get them made again in time.

How would she explain this to the grant committee? To her cast and crew? Her mind swirled, and just for a moment, she felt as though the world was spinning. Little dots began to appear in front of her eyes, and she felt a darkening around the edges of her sight. She was going to faint, she realized, but she was too out of it to respond. Perhaps it was better to simply embrace that darkness—

"What on earth is going on here?" Lisa's patrician tones pierced through Tessa's lightheadedness, and the darkness at the edges of her vision receded.

She twirled around to see Lisa, in her signature cream-colored pants and silk top, gold chain, and large cream-colored jacket standing in the doorway, taking in the sight of the ruined costumes before looking over at Tessa.

Her expression softened, and she took a step toward Tessa. Wordlessly, Tessa stepped into her arms and let Lisa hug her, holding her steady as her knees threatened to buckle beneath her. The tears were now streaming down her face, and she worried that they would stain Lisa's shirt, before she remembered that she wasn't wearing any makeup. She hadn't had any time to do that after her shower with Roxy.

It was weird to be held by Lisa, and especially so after being in Roxy's embrace for most of the afternoon, but Tessa realized, with a jolt, that it was nice, too. Comforting. Not that she wanted Lisa romantically or sexually. Not at all. But she was realizing that maybe, just maybe, she and Lisa could be friends.

It was true that Lisa had been…changing…since Mo had become her assistant. She seemed happier, more balanced, less diva-ish. She heard Lisa laughing more, and it seemed that she and Mo were developing a genuine actor-assistant relationship. Aside from that, there hadn't been any taunts or impertinent questions from Lisa about Tessa and Roxy. Of course, they'd been trying to hide their relationship on set, keep it private and so forth, but even so. They were obviously friendly with one another, and Lisa, well, she didn't seem to mind. Or care. And she'd been polite and courteous to Roxy the few times they'd had to share a space in the last week. Even Chayo had remarked to Tessa recently that Lisa seemed different. She'd bought the crew members lunch last week—something that she'd never done before.

"Tessa, I don't know what happened. Joy called me just now as I was talking to Ramón, and I rushed over to see what I could do."

"Clearly, someone from the cast or crew can't be trusted," interjected Barb, her voice as true to her name, her tone barbed as ever.

Tessa pulled away from Lisa slowly, pushing her tears away with the back of her hand and trying to calm herself. She saw that Joy was still upset, and even more upset at Barb's words. She gave her a quick hug too before turning to Barb.

"Just what are you implying?"

"Either someone on the cast and crew committed sabotage, or they were negligent and left a door unlocked over the weekend," said Barb, her eyes hooded and unreadable, her expression grim. Her tone of voice seemed to suggest that really, the fault was Tessa's, for not being at the theater all the time to supervise everything.

"Everyone on this project is a professional," said Tessa tartly, glad to feel an emotion other than utter despair. "Both of those options seem highly unlikely."

Barb raised an eyebrow. "Then what do you suggest?"

Tessa leaned over and picked up one of the ripped up costumes nearest to her. It was a beautiful dress meant to have been worn by the character Perdita on her wedding day. It was one of the few items that hadn't been ripped into tiny bits of fabric confetti. She examined it, holding it up to the light, turning it around from all angles.

"Lord, it looks like it was ripped up by a *beast*," said Joy, her voice trembling. "Tessa, honey, I have no idea how this could have happened. I'm *so sorry*—"

Tessa realized with a jolt that Joy was worried Tessa would blame *her*, since she was second in command and meant to be at the theater all day that day.

"When did you get here today?" said Tessa.

"Please don't be mad…I…I know I was supposed to be here at nine, but Bobby"—the head of the crew—"called me this morning that he had a family emergency back in Boston and he had to go see to it, so he said the crew could take the day off. I took care of some of my own errands today. I haven't been here all day. Nobody has. I thought…" Joy's voice trailed off.

"So you didn't get to the theater until just before you called me?" Tessa was trying to reconstruct the events of the last twenty-four hours in her head, but it felt like walking through deep mud. Her mind felt clouded and yet…something about this whole situation felt wrong. "Joy. I'm not mad. I'm just trying to figure out what happened."

"Yes. Indeed. You'd better figure it out fast. I'll have to report this to the police. And the theater owner," said Barb, poison dripping from every word. She sounded gleeful.

"Don't speak like that to her," interjected Lisa.

"It's okay, Lisa. Barb is right. The owner needs to know. And there will have to be a police report since I will have to report this to the grant committee." Tessa looked pleadingly at Barb. "But we need to know *what* exactly to report. Can you give us half an hour to think this through?"

Barb clearly didn't want to grant even that much grace, but her phone buzzed and, after glancing at the screen, her entire demeanor changed.

"Fine. I've got to go right now anyway." She glared at them all one more time. "I'll be back in half an hour and I want an explanation."

When she left, they all breathed a sigh of relief.

"She is a *pill*," said Lisa.

"I think you mean she's a certified *bitch*," said Tessa.

Joy laughed. "Oh God." She rubbed her face with her hands for the umpteenth time that evening. "What are we going to do? Tell the grant committee and everyone else that a werewolf destroyed all the costumes and sets?"

"The sets?" Lisa and Tessa spoke in unison, and Tessa felt her heart sink all over again. The sets too? What had happened to the sets? What would they do? Her entire vision for an interplanetary space opera *Winter's Tale* was disappearing from possibility before her very eyes.

Wordlessly, Joy gestured for them to follow her to the wood shop, where, like in the costume shop, everything was a mess. Two-by-fours were, quite literally, broken in half, large splinters of wood all over the place. It did not look like something that was humanly possible. Had a giant or ogre from a fairy tale broken into the theater?

On stage, where Chayo and Bobby had already been working on putting up the main flats for the backdrop, there was a similar mess, similar destruction. It was no longer shocking to Tessa—only heart-wrenching. The flats were all lying on the floor, similarly destroyed, ripped, and shattered in ways that made absolutely no sense.

As they surveyed the sets, Chayo showed up.

She looked as distraught as Joy, as angry as Lisa, and as disappointed as Tessa felt. They hugged for a long time, before breaking apart.

"This is my fault," said Chayo, her voice choking up. "I think I might have left the side door unlocked last night."

"What?" said Joy.

Chayo nodded. "I was leaving with Bobby and Sam, and we were talking, and I just...I don't remember...I can't remember if I locked up or not." Her voice cracked with shame and despair, tears welling up in her eyes. Tessa's heart squeezed. Seeing one of her oldest, toughest friends lose her cool like this made it all seem that much worse.

"It's okay," said Tessa. "This is not your fault. Even if you didn't lock up."

"Of course not," said Lisa with some impatience.

They all looked at Lisa questioningly.

"Chayo most certainly locked up, because the theater was locked tight when I was here last night."

They all looked at Lisa in surprise, but Lisa explained calmly that she hadn't been able to sleep the other night because the people in the room next to hers had been, ahem, extremely noisy in their evening activities. She'd come to the theater, hoping someone was still there to let her in, but when she'd arrived, just after eleven, it was dark and locked tight. She'd gone to a nearby bar for a nightcap before going home to bed.

"See? It isn't your fault," said Tessa encouragingly.

Chayo heaved a sigh of relief. "That's good to know. I got worried because the theater was already unlocked this morning."

"You were here in the morning today?" said Joy, sounding confused.

"Yeah. Barb was here. Everything was normal. I had my key, but I didn't need to use it. I thought it was a little weird that she'd unlocked the front of the theater and the side door when no one else was there—"

"What time was that, more or less?" asked Tessa.

"Probably around nine. I wanted to get ahead on the statue of Hermione. I stayed until about lunchtime and then called it a day. I asked Barb if I should lock the side door when I left but she said no. She said she was having a training with the crew."

Tessa's eyebrows knitted together in consternation. Clearly, there was no training with the crew since Bobby had told everyone to stay home that day. *Clearly*, Barb was doing shit behind her back, but was she also somehow connected with this sabotage?

"Why would Barb lead a training for the crew? Everything relating to the show is the purview of Tessa and Joy, and you and Bobby," said Lisa reasonably, giving voice to Tessa's own confused thoughts. She had her hands on her hips, looking like she was about to Sherlock Holmes the shit out of the situation, and Tessa couldn't help but smile. Lisa did like to be in charge, after all. "It sounds like Barb owes *us* an explanation, not the other way around."

Lisa looked like she was about to march out to find Barb right then and there.

"Wait," said Tessa. "Let's take a closer look at the sets and the wood shop first and see if we can get Sam here." She wanted to talk to her stage manager to verify Barb's story. Had there been a crew training planned without Bobby's knowledge?

"I'll text him," volunteered Joy.

Chayo and Tessa examined the broken sets together.

"I don't get it," said Chayo, confused by what she was looking at. "This doesn't make any sense. Some of this stuff looks like it was…I dunno…*ripped* apart. But how is that possible?"

"I don't get it either," said Tessa. She leaned over and touched one of the places where the wood looked as though the Hulk had ripped it.

A current of magic shocked her hand, like static discharges she'd been dodging from her car all winter.

"Ow!"

"Careful there," said Chayo. "There's lots of splinters."

"Yeah," said Tessa, massaging her hand, but knowing that this was no splinter that had stung her hand. It was *magic*. Magic had done this. "Why don't you go to the wood shop and see what's salvageable in there, okay?" She needed to be alone with this destruction to investigate further.

"Absolutely," said Chayo.

When Tessa was alone on the stage, she got down on her knees next to the broken sets and closed her eyes. It felt wrong to call on her magic in such an open, unguarded place where anyone might come in and interrupt her and see what she was doing, but she had to confirm that there was magic here.

She felt the familiar glow of it pooling deep within her, and she urged it to spool out into her hands and fingers, welcoming the warmth of it, like gold, heated up to liquid, slowly filling her. It took all her concentration to call it up at a moment's notice like this—she was out of practice.

Tessa held her hands close, palms facing one another, just inches apart, until she felt a concentration of magic between them, before holding her hands out, palms down, next to one another, over the broken pieces of the sets.

She had a vision of the sets breaking before her eyes. Magic always left its traces, and even though this sorcery was of a different quality and type than what Tessa summoned in her hedgecraft, it was still somehow legible to her. She marveled at the watery vision in her mind of the wood and canvas ripping apart—but she could not see who was behind it. She tried concentrating harder, focusing on what was behind the set, zoning in on the gray background of the vision.

For a moment, she was able to see past the destruction of the sets, and she saw not one but three vague shapes in the background. It was fuzzy at best, and she couldn't tell if they were women or men, or even see their faces at all, but they were the magicians who had wreaked this destruction. Their magic felt *wrong* to Tessa, aside from it being used to destroy her sets and props and costumes…it was dark and somehow *slimy*. She shuddered, and the vision crackled and frayed at the edges.

"No, not yet," she said under her breath, breathing deeply to steady the vision. If she concentrated just a tiny bit more, she would be able to see their faces, she just knew it.

Just like that, the vision disappeared.

"No!" cried Tessa, louder than she meant to. Luckily, she was still alone in the theater, and her cry disappeared into the ether. She groaned in frustration. She'd been *this close* to seeing the faces of one of the sorcerers or magicians behind this. She was sure of it. If only she was more powerful.

She went to stand up, only then realizing just how much energy she'd used to conjure up the vision. The world tilted around her and spun for a moment.

Tessa sat back down on the stage, clutching her head. Why oh why, hadn't she kept up with her magic practice? She'd been taking it for granted for far too long.

She closed her eyes and steadied herself until the dizziness passed. She would have to be careful with how she expended her energy for the rest of the evening.

Energy. Of course. Her *wards*. She'd hung her wards in the theater to catch negative energy, and they hadn't gone off. Was that another mistake she'd made because she wasn't practicing magic regularly?

Tessa glanced upward to the catwalks and her heart jumped into her throat.

All her wards were gone.

What did this mean?

Her mind raced, but really, there was only one conclusion—something she should have realized sooner. Bells had been going off in her mind as soon as she'd stepped into the theater.

Someone had done this purposefully, to sabotage the play—and they'd gone to the trouble of removing the wards first.

And what was her hedge witch's instinct telling her?

This had something to do with Madame Clerval. With Mo's and Roxy's suspicions. With whatever evil was lurking on Cape Cod that winter. And maybe with Barb, too. There'd been three people in her vision. Could it be Madame Clerval, Barb, and…someone else? There was a name at the edge of her consciousness, but she couldn't think of it. She groaned in frustration again. Why couldn't she think of the third person…a third person who would make up a powerful triumvirate—so powerful they could remove her wards and her senses didn't pick it up. So powerful they could destroy her sets and costumes and turn them into unsalvageable shreds.

Tessa realized with a lurch that she hadn't checked her phone since she'd left the house and, according to her watch, it was well over an hour since Roxy had gone home to check on Mo.

Oh God. Roxy would be shivering outside her apartment by now, or maybe she'd even gone back home, thinking that Tessa was a complete flake.

She'd left her phone in her bag by the side entrance, which meant passing by the wood shop and the costume areas, checking in with Joy and Chayo again, and trying to listen politely as they reported that literally *nothing* could be salvaged. Finally, she excused herself and ran to her phone, where she found a message from Roxy—a voice message no less, which was weird, because honestly, who left voice messages anymore?

When she heard Roxy's message that Mo was unwell, her mind began to race again. Her instincts were in tune now and she realized that Mo had to be somehow connected to everything that was happening. This couldn't be a coincidence….could it?

She began getting dressed to go out, only to realize that she literally had no way of knowing where Roxy and Mo were at that moment. How on earth would she find them?

Tessa called Roxy—but it rang and rang and finally went to voice mail.

"Roxy, it's Tessa. I got your message. Something bad happened at the theater. I'm worried it's related to…a mutual acquaintance. Where are you? I need to find you."

She hung up, not sure what to do next.

Breathe. Take a minute.

Tessa tried to calm herself, calling to mind all that she'd learned not just as a hedge witch, but also in therapy. Deep breaths. Reminding herself that her thoughts were hers to control. That panic was not useful and not necessary.

The photo. Roxy's photo. She had a photo of Roxy in her wallet that she took out and held in her hand—she'd never discarded it after all, and even though it was old, she could use it to locate Roxy. She smiled at the image of her and Roxy as college freshmen, momentarily lost in nostalgic reflection, before remembering about the task at hand.

She had to find Roxy and Mo. This was not the time for reminiscing.

And yet, Tessa hesitated. She was still tired from the magic she'd called up to use in the theater; using still more deep, powerful magic to try to locate Roxy could be dangerous.

She took another deep breath and closed her eyes. She tried to imagine the magic within her not like a well of water that could run dry, but rather like a river flowing through her, drawing energy from around her, or the ocean, whose waves crested and receded in an endless cycle.

That helped. The magic within her rose up, not as strong as earlier, but fuller than she expected. She concentrated her energy on the image of Roxy in the photo, and as the magic began unspooling beneath her fingers, the sounds of waves on shore filled her ears, the smell of the bay in her nose, and in her mind's eye she glimpsed the moon and a lighthouse.

There were no images of a medical clinic, no sounds of medical equipment beeping or the familiar creaking of plastic chairs and shifting of bodies Tessa would normally associate with an urgent care clinic on a Saturday evening.

Somehow, Tessa wasn't surprised. At this point, nothing could surprise her.

She concentrated her energy onto the lighthouse. It was familiar to her, and she urged her magic to bring the image into focus.

The lighthouse shimmered into focus just for a moment before the entire image disappeared. It looked like any number of lighthouses in the area, none of which were in a place where she would imagine Roxy going in the dark on a cold winter's evening with Mo. Maybe the lighthouse was a symbol in her mind? She groaned. Tessa felt powerless for a moment, in spite of the magic that had so recently been flowing through her.

She tried to concentrate on the other things she'd seen and heard in her vision. The sound of waves. The moonlight. The rush of saltwater smell, sharp and brackish. Tessa felt sure that Mo and Roxy were on the beach in Provincetown, on the bay side. What they were doing there, she had no idea, and she didn't have the wherewithal to make a guess, but she felt very certain that they were there, and that they were in trouble.

Just as she was about to leave to go find them, Chayo showed up. Tessa had been so focused on her vision, she hadn't seen her best friend coming down the hallway toward her.

"What's wrong? Where are you going?" Chayo didn't waste time with pleasantries.

"I have to find Roxy," said Tessa. "I think she and Mo are in trouble."

"Is it connected to what happened here?" Chayo was always quick on the uptake.

Tessa nodded. "I think so. I don't know how but I…feel it. Instinct."

"I'm coming with you."

Before Tessa could protest, Joy showed up. She took one look at Tessa in her coat and hat, and Chayo, who was putting hers on as well and said, "Wherever you're going, take me too. I can't stay in this place. I've changed my mind, Tessa. I think it's definitely, one hundred percent haunted."

"Fine," said Tessa. She would need Joy's help if there were three magicians to contend with. "Chayo, I need you to stay here in case they show up looking for us. Please."

Tessa thrust the car keys at Joy, who knew Ptown the best of the three of them, and told her to drive them to the marina beach. Her hands were shaking, and she was filled with a sudden fear that they were too late—that Roxy and Mo were in the clutches of whatever power had destroyed fabric and wood like it was nothing. Her heart ached.

She couldn't lose Roxy—not when she'd finally gotten her.

CHAPTER TWENTY-FIVE—ROXY

The beach was unimaginably cold. The wind was whipped up to a frenzy, with gusts that took Roxy's breath away. Even Mo, who usually didn't show signs of feeling the cold very much, was shivering. Was this another sign that her mermaid state was somehow…wearing off? Was that possible?

Again, the legends of the selkies sprung to Roxy's mind. Those stories, though, seemed to suggest that as long as the selkie could get her "skin" back, she would return to her selkie state and leave behind her human form, so it wasn't quite the same thing. Without their skin, they were mostly human—except in their mind, where they always remembered their former selves. Could that be similar to Mo's situation?

The moon was huge in the sky, a giant glowing yellow-silver orb that lit up the whole bay, albeit unevenly. They were at the dog beach, since Roxy had figured that part of the beach would be safest from prying eyes, but still close enough to get to quickly and had twenty-four-hour access. It wouldn't be suspicious for them to be there, even in the evening after dark.

Still, the place was creeping Roxy out. She'd brought the flashlight out of her car that she always kept there, but in the light of the moon, it didn't do much. The moonlight was bright, but, as she always found with moonlight, it didn't quite do the job she needed. It created strange shadows on the beach, especially here where the beach was wide and full of small tidal pools that were all too easy to step into.

The entire scene was all too reminiscent of the night when Roxy had saved Mo from the water—that had been a full moon too. Hazel, she remembered, had been so excited that their wedding would be New Year's Day *and* a full moon to boot. It occurred to Roxy that perhaps Mo's fading mermaid abilities had to do with the moon and the fact that she'd been out of the ocean for an entire moon cycle. Roxy had learned from Hazel the importance of the moon cycles to all magical beings, so the idea wasn't so unlikely.

Finally, they made it to the edge of the water. A gust of wind blew off the bay like a knife through Roxy's outer layers.

Mo looked at Roxy, her expression a mixture of fear and desperation. Roxy gave her a giant hug, squeezing her as hard as she could, even though she was also full of dread.

What would happen when Mo got into the water? Would thunder and lightning fill the air? Would a magical net catch Mo again—and what would that even look like?

She gave Mo some hearty pats on the back and shouted to her over the wind. "You've got this. Just be quick, okay?"

Mo nodded and began to undress, throwing her human clothes into a pile by their feet. Roxy picked them up so they wouldn't get too wet and placed them a bit farther away from the shoreline.

When Mo was completely undressed, Roxy kept her eyes carefully on Mo's face.

"It's time. Get in fast, but stay close to shore so I can get you out if anything happens." She looked around the beach, but it was quiet and empty except for the wind. Up in the sky, the moon was temporarily obscured by dark clouds that flitted across it and then disappeared again.

The wind settled for a moment, and Mo spoke, her voice strong, but with a slight tremor. "Wait, Roxy. This could be dangerous for me and for you."

Roxy met Mo's gaze. There was determination there now and something else almost like joy. Of course, thought Roxy, she was glad to get back into the water. It was her home after all.

Mo pulled at Roxy's hands and pulled the gloves off awkwardly. She threw those on the ground too, and Roxy had to stop herself from protesting. Those were her *best* gloves—but never mind. This was clearly not the time.

Mo arranged their hands so they were pressed against each other, like little girls on the playground playing "Miss Mary Mack" or some other hand slapping game that, frankly, Roxy had never had the patience or interest to play as a kid. There was an intensity to the pressure Mo was using to press into her palms, and Roxy pressed back.

A jolt that passed between their hands, and Roxy had no idea if the jolt had come from Mo and into Roxy's hands, of if it had come from Roxy's hands into Mo's. The second possibility was impossible, though, wasn't it?

A look of satisfaction painted itself over Mo's face. "I knew it," she breathed, and she said something else in her own language.

"What?"

"You *do* have magic," said Mo in English again. "I always knew it from the day we met."

Roxy sputtered. "That's…that's not possible. I'm human. Just human."

Mo shook her head slowly. "I can feel it inside you. Close your eyes."

"Mo, you're *naked*. Aren't you cold? Shouldn't you get in the water?"

"I'm fine. I can feel the water in the sand on my feet and it is already helping. I feel better. But I cannot go in that water unless I know you are ready. You must have your weapon ready."

"My *weapon*?" Roxy's mind was full of protest, but somewhere deep inside her, she felt rather than knew the truth of what Mo was saying. Something inside her had been sleeping until she met Mo.

Part of her could not accept it. She had to protest it—almost as if this was the only way she could accept the truth of Mo's words.

"How do you know this isn't just *your* magic, Mo?" said Roxy. "Mer—I mean, your people have their own magic. Like how you learned to speak English. And your tail and legs changing. Maybe you're just *giving me* some of your magic?"

"Search your feelings, Roxy," said Mo quietly but with intensity. She put a hand over Roxy's heart and one on her forehead in a gesture that felt both strange but also strangely familiar. "Close your eyes. Feel the truth. Feel your power."

"Mo, we're wasting time. We're out here, exposed—"

"Until I get into the water, we have as much time as we need," said Mo reasonably. "Now. Please, concentrate. Don't think. Simply feel."

Roxy heaved a sigh and closed her eyes. Perhaps it was simpler to do what Mo asked of her. She'd been Mo's guide to the human world; the least she could do was let Mo guide her where she was the expert.

At first, there was nothing, only darkness and the sound of the waves crashing around them, whipped up to larger than usual by the wind. She heard a lone bird in the distance and the sound of a car engine.

She was about to open her eyes and complain to Mo that they were wasting time, when she felt it. Whatever it was, she wasn't sure, but something shifted inside her—a strange but familiar sensation, something that had always been a part of her, but which she'd never known about or considered. At first, it was just a quick flutter, as of excitement, but soon it felt like the crackle of electricity, radiating from just behind her heart out through her fingers.

It was the same feeling she'd had when she'd seen Barb—a snap of power within her like lightning.

She opened her eyes wide and saw that Mo was still watching her carefully. Mo removed her hands from Roxy and instead extended an open palm to Roxy.

Gingerly, Roxy touched the palm with the index finger of her right hand.

A small discharge came off her fingers with a flash of bright light.

"What on earth…" Roxy was amazed. This was crazy. This was a dream. It had to be. She was *just a human woman.* She wasn't magic. She couldn't be. Could she?

The discharge was small and yet it made Mo's hand clench into a fist, as if struck by a small bolt of lightning.

"Are you okay?"

Mo nodded. "Yes, it was a small one."

"A small one what?"

"A small bit of your magical power," said Mo. She said it as if it was the most logical thing in the world.

Roxy shook her head, still unable to grasp the meaning of this. "It's winter. It must be static electricity."

Mo smiled at her. "Please, Roxy. Consider. Did it feel like 'static electricity'?"

Damn if she isn't grasping sarcasm like a regular human now.

Roxy shook her head and tried to clear her mind. She closed her eyes, and this time, she felt the crackle of hot lightning in her hands immediately. The power was growing within her, as if it couldn't be contained once she'd activated it. This was definitely *not* static electricity. This was not winter discharge of electrons. This was something else, something exciting and thrilling that Roxy did not at all have the wherewithal to make sense of at the moment.

"No, it doesn't," she said. "But what—?"

"Shh," said Mo. "We don't have time."

"Oh, so *now* we don't have time to discuss it?"

Mo shot her a look.

"Okay, okay," said Roxy. "Fine. What now?"

"I'm going to get into the water. You are going to protect me. If any of the hunters come here, you must use your power."

"What if you start to drown again?" said Roxy, suddenly filled with fear. Protecting Mo as a human woman was one thing…protecting her with magic against someone else's super powerful magic was quite another. She felt panic rising up inside her like bitter bile. "How can I protect you with this power? I don't even know how to use it. And what if I hurt *you* with it?"

This time, it was Mo's turn to give Roxy a hug. Roxy was so distracted that she barely noticed that she was hugging a very naked and very beautiful mermaid on an empty beach at night in the wintertime.

Mo pulled away finally. "Use your heart. Your instinct. You know how to do that. Keep your eyes open and you will know what to do."

Before Roxy could protest any more, Mo threw herself into the surf.

Roxy looked up and down the beach, toward the parking lot and then out at the water again. There was no one and nothing. She was alone on the beach, and Mo was, at the moment, nothing more than sea foam and spray.

Panic rose in Roxy yet again. Where was Mo? Was she hurt? Had she been pulled under by a strong current?

Before her thoughts could spiral out of control, Roxy spotted a bright blue-green tail in the water, larger than that of any fish Roxy had ever seen. A second later, Mo rose in the water, farther out in the Bay, and she smiled and waved at Roxy. She looked happy and relieved, like her old self again, full of confidence and joy, right before diving into the water again.

Roxy breathed a sigh of relief. Mo was back to her mermaid self. It *was* possible.

Moments passed, and Roxy scanned the beach again. She wasn't sure what she'd been expecting. The sizzle of electricity? A thunderclap? The smell of sulphur and ashes?

Instead, there was nothing but the beach and sand and Roxy, alone with a pile of Mo's clothing.

A few more moments passed, and Roxy felt tension mounting again. She scanned the water over and over, but the moon was covered in clouds again, the water impossibly dark, and there was no sign of Mo.

Roxy realized with a start that they hadn't really made a plan beyond taking Mo to the water. Fuck. What the hell was she supposed to do now?

Mo had tasked her with protecting her, but what if all their fears had been unfounded and Mo was simply free to go home? Maybe she was already halfway there. Roxy's breath caught in her throat as she realized she'd been counting on seeing Mo again. She'd gotten used to having a roommate, even a weirdo like Mo who ate nothing but raw fish.

Roxy hadn't thought about life after Mo, and she was surprised to realize she was genuinely going to *miss* having her around. But she supposed it was for the best. Mo was from another world, and she'd never really fit in with the human world, always missing her life in the water.

Disappointment rushed through Roxy, and she felt tears welling up in her eyes. Mo had become a friend, and now she was gone without so much as a good-bye. Maybe their friendship had never truly been real; perhaps Mo had used her so she could get home.

Roxy picked up the pile of clothing off the beach and raised her hand to give one last wave. The wind had dropped, though the water was still in turmoil, but the moon was visible yet again, though higher and smaller than earlier.

"Good-bye," said Roxy quietly, almost to herself, as she gave a wave to the spot in the water where she'd last seen a flash of Mo's tail.

"Oh, don't worry, my dear, I doubt this is good-bye," said a voice behind Roxy.

Roxy whirled around, her throat gone completely dry with surprise and dread.

Only a few feet away on the beach, between herself and her car, stood three figures in black cloaks. One of the figures—the speaker, she had no doubt—had her hood pulled back somewhat so she could see her.

She was a beautiful woman of indeterminate age, hair so fiery red it looked dyed and yet, somehow Roxy knew immediately it was colored by magic. The woman's features were sharp and well-defined, with dark black eyebrows and eyelashes so thick and black that they looked fake, but instinctively, Roxy knew that they weren't. Or rather, they were magically enhanced.

The woman fixed her bright green eyes on Roxy, and her smile held no joy.

"Who the fu—" Roxy started to speak but was distracted when the woman held out her hand and on it, clearly lit up in the moonlight, was a rather large green ring in the shape of an eye. "Faustina Clerval?"

"At your service," said the woman with an unpleasant cackle—high and grating. "So you've figured it out, have you? A bit too late for your friend, I'm afraid."

Roxy's mind raced. This woman didn't look anything at all like the nondescript person described by Joy at the bar where they'd hung out just a few days ago. A few days ago—was that all it was? It felt like weeks.

Faustina was clearly a powerful magician who could perform a glamour. Maybe she was a vampire? Vampires could put on glamours as well. But Mo had been caught in a spell here on Cape Cod, and that didn't sound like vampires at all. It was beyond the kind of magic Hazel would have usually done as well. But perhaps that was the benefit of working as a team?

Before she could speak, a sound behind her distracted her.

Roxy whirled back to the water and horror filled her as she saw Mo swimming to the shore—no, she was being *dragged* by an unseen power to the shoreline. Mo's beautiful face was etched with pain even as she struggled with all her might to free herself of this invisible hand, but it was no use.

All too soon, Mo was thrashing on the sand near Roxy's feet, her tail still intact. Roxy dropped to her knees but realized she wasn't able to touch Mo. It was as though she were behind a piece of glass.

Mo's eyes were wide with horror and fear; Roxy couldn't tear her gaze away. Mo tried to say something to her, but Roxy couldn't hear anything. She was terrible at lip reading, and the adrenaline pumping through her veins wasn't helping. She couldn't concentrate on anything except Mo. She had to help her….had to get to her. But how?

Something prickled at the ends of her fingers, like an itch she'd forgotten to scratch. Of course. That's what Mo was trying to tell her: *Use your powers.*

But how?

The wind in her face, the sand flying, Mo writhing in pain, three shadow figures on the sand—three of them! How could she even get close enough to them to do anything?

Roxy looked over at Madame Clerval and the figures on either side of her, one, slightly shorter, and oddly familiar…They were raising their hands, palms clasped together, and Roxy felt something like a shiver in the air. An immense amount of power was surrounding their small group of five on the sand. Roxy felt as though the wind had removed her voice; she was speechless, whether actually from the wind or from magic or base fear she had no idea.

If only she knew what to do...how to help...she felt helpless... Instead, her head was filled with the chanting of evil spells from the three figures holding her and Mo hostage. She couldn't understand the words, but she could feel the intent behind them, and she felt weak with fear.

A shout from behind the figures distracted her from her thoughts.

"STOP!"

Roxy squinted into the darkness and saw two people running toward them at top speed. Madame Clerval and her accomplices turned around, likewise distracted from their spellwork. Their hoods fell back, and in the light of the moon, Roxy saw the three sorcerers and their attackers clearly.

Madame Clerval, Barb, and a tall blond woman reached out their hands toward the two running figures and Roxy finally found her voice.

"Tessa! No! Run away!"

CHAPTER TWENTY-SIX—TESSA

For once, Tessa's powers were ready to go as she needed them—even as she knew, deep down, they were not at full capacity. Her spellwork in the theater had drained her, she knew that. She had no emergency herbal draughts for renewing her power; she hoped adrenaline and luck were on her side.

She ran toward Roxy and the other figure on the beach. Her eyes barely understood what she was looking at, but she recognized evil at work.

Her legs and arms pumped to get her within range. With her powers so depleted, she would have to get dangerously close to them to have any chance of saving Roxy and...Mo? *Mo was a mermaid!?* The blue-green tail glowed on the shadowy beach like sunshine through a piece of sea glass.

Tessa's mind had no time to process the new piece of information, though.

She had the element of surprise on her side—for now. She had to make the best of it.

Joy seemed to be taking a cue from her and was running full tilt by her side. If the sight of Roxy and a mermaid on the beach surprised her, she wasn't showing it. But that was Joy—always ready for whatever came her way. Tessa was grateful for her all over again.

Once they were in earshot, Tessa started to yell stop as loud as she could; Joy joined her after a moment.

Their cries did exactly what Tessa hoped. The figures turned around, arms faltering, spells pausing momentarily as their hands broke apart.

As they turned around, the hoods of all three figures flew back and there, in the light of the moon, wearing black cloaks, were Barb, Madame Clerval, and Isidora.

Recognition blazed through Tessa. She should have known it was those three, she thought as she plowed into Madame Clerval with all her might. Joy was hot on her heels before launching herself at Barb.

"Ha! I've been wanting to do that ever since we met," said Joy through uneven breaths.

"Tessa! No! Run away!" Roxy's voice was weak and small, even though she was only a few yards away.

Tessa didn't have time to respond. She needed to focus her powers on Madame Clerval. She was clearly the ringleader of the three. Her powers at the ready, she thrust her hands to Madame Clerval's chest and used all her magic to siphon off Madame Clerval's magic. Ideally, this would have the double advantage of effectively disarming Madame Clerval, while giving Tessa more power to fight all three sorcerers.

A sharp crack like a whip hit Tessa full in the torso, and a power indescribably strong wrapped itself around her even as her entire body shuddered with an influx of foreign magic. It felt like ice water in her veins, immobilizing her momentarily and squeezing the breath out of her lungs.

For a second, she lay back on the sand, uncertain whether her spell had worked. After a moment, though, she felt the strange sensation of someone else's magic coursing through her, alternating hot and cold. An image flickered through her head—Mo, bleeding, as someone or something removed scales from her tail.

Tessa cried out. The image shuddered and faded, and Tessa was thankful for that. That had been the ultimately purpose of the plan, to capture Mo and maim her precious mermaid's tail. Roxy was an innocent bystander in all this, but Mo—they had to save her.

The scene in front of her was utter chaos.

Madame Clerval was lying on the sand, knocked out, though Tessa knew it wouldn't last long. Joy was sitting astride Barb and punching her—or slapping her? It was hard to tell—as Isidora grabbed at Joy and tried to pull her off. Roxy was holding Mo in her arms, but Mo appeared unconscious.

"Tessa!" Roxy's voice was all anguish, and Tessa could not ignore it, even as her instincts were shouting at her that Madame Clerval was not defeated and their time to strike was limited. But maybe, just maybe, they could get Mo back into the water and out to sea before Madame Clerval attacked her again?

Tessa ran to Roxy, her legs shaking beneath her. Deep down she knew that even with the magic she'd stolen from Madame Clerval, there wasn't much else left to work with. Her magic was at an ebb.

She ignored the warnings. Roxy needed her. Mo needed her.

"Keep at it, Joy," she shouted as she ran over.

"With pleasure," said Joy, who was now throwing salt at Barb and Isidora. *Where did she get that from?*

Tessa didn't have time to consider how Joy knew to bring salt with her. She kneeled next to Roxy and put an arm around her.

"Is she okay?"

Roxy's eyes were streaming with tears as she cradled Mo's head in her arms. "I don't know, I don't know. When you arrived and they turned around, the glass that was between us—I mean, whatever spell was guarding her—just disappeared. She was still thrashing around, but I guess the spell was keeping her alive? I touched her and she lost consciousness. Or...or..." Or maybe she was dead, Tessa finished in her mind. She didn't want to say those words either.

She put her fingers to Mo's throat, but she wasn't even sure that there would be a pulse there even if Mo *was* alive. After all, she was in her mermaid form. Who knows what that means?

Still, she had to try, and after a moment, Tessa detected a very slight pulse.

"We have to take her to the water," said Tessa. That was the only solution. As long as Mo was in her mermaid form, life on land was impossible, or at least that was what her hedge witch instincts were telling her. Always go with your natural instincts, her mentor Freya had told her, and her advice had always been spot-on.

They stood and heaved Mo toward the surf. The water was freezing, but between adrenaline and fear, neither of them thought to stop or complain. In fact, something odd was happening once Mo's body was in the water—she became warm.

On the shore, her body had been freezing cold and clammy, but here in the winter waters of the Bay, Mo was warm, and the warmth from her radiated outward, encompassing Tessa and Roxy like an embrace.

"I think it's working," said Roxy. She looked at Tessa, tears of joy now in her eyes. "She's alive."

Tessa nodded. "Let's push her farther out. Maybe we can get her beyond the power of the Three." Something in her mind automatically capitalized the phrase "the Three." They had no way of knowing what these women called themselves, so the Three was as good as anything.

As they held onto Mo and pulled her farther into the waters, Tessa was thankful for the warmth of Mo's body. Mermaids had their own magic, she guessed, and this had to be some element of that power. It was keeping her and Roxy from freezing, and that was the important thing.

Once the water was up to their hips, Tessa squeezed Roxy's arm to stop.

"This is far enough."

"She's not awake yet," said Roxy. "She'll drift back to shore. We're not far enough."

"We can't go any farther," said Tessa as gently as she could over the crash of waves and wind. She felt Mo's pulse again. It was stronger, more regular. "Her pulse is better now. She's going to be okay."

Just as Mo opened her eyes and took a big gulp of air, all three of them were smashed together by an unseen force.

"No!" shouted Roxy.

Before Tessa could say anything in response, before any of them could do anything, they were being pulled back to shore, like a big hook in an old-fashioned theater that pulled an act off the stage when it was over.

Tessa could still feel Madame Clerval's power within her, and she tried to sense a place where she could direct that power to free them, but it was impossible in that moment to concentrate enough to find a place to latch onto, caught in a magical net, water in her face, Mo's arms and tail, and Roxy's arms and legs all flailing and intertwining with hers.

Mere moments later, they were all lying on the beach again, wet, covered in sand and seaweed, freezing cold. Tessa had to work not to let her entire body start shivering uncontrollably. She called up some of the power within her to warm herself, and it worked for now.

There was still some magic left over. How much, she wasn't certain.

Looming over them were the Three. Where was Joy? Tessa couldn't see beyond them, but she hoped desperately Joy was all right. They wouldn't dare kill any of them, would they?

Before anyone could react, Tessa funneled her remaining power into a shield protection spell—one of the only spells she'd consistently practiced since her days learning with Freya. Despite that practice, she could feel the power leaching out of her. It was too much to keep up.

It occurred to Tessa belatedly that she should have tried to attack them again rather than use her remaining power for a spell of protection. It would run out and then what?

The brash laughter of Faustina Clerval reached her, somewhat distorted, through the pulse of magic between them.

"You dare to use my own powers to fight off my powers?" Madame Clerval shook her head with another cackle of amused derision. "You silly girl."

The Three began to chant again, directing their spell at Tessa's, and Tessa felt it begin to weaken and melt away, like snow in the spring. As her spell weakened, it siphoned off all the remaining power within her. A heaviness entered her limbs, and she could only watch helplessly as her spell faded away and Madame Clerval took hold of her hand.

Her hand was frigid: cold and powerful. She gripped Tessa's wrist and, with one simple motion, aided by magic, threw Tessa into the air, far up the beach. It happened so fast, Tessa had no time to think or react or even scream.

Tessa landed with a thump, and everything went black.

CHAPTER TWENTY-SEVEN—ROXY

Roxy watched with horror as Tessa's limp body flew through the air. Roxy's mouth went dry and pain ripped at her heart like claws. Tears were streaming down her face, mingling with the salt water, and she wanted to scream but she couldn't.

She couldn't see where Tessa was, but Mo was still lying next to her, her eyes fluttering a bit, but she was not completely conscious. Roxy was desperate to find out if Tessa was okay—could anyone survive such a thrashing? Roxy didn't want to contemplate it, but she also needed to protect Mo.

Protection! Of course. Everything had happened so quickly, so horribly, she hadn't tried to use whatever power it was within her that Mo had awoken.

But how to summon it? Roxy wasn't a magician or witch, a wizard or sorcerer. She had no practice in these arts. She barely knew she had it in her, and yet that crackling of energy was back in her palms and the tip of her fingers. Deep within her, she felt a warmth growing, reaching out through her arms, rising and rising, and yet—how to use it?

"Isidora! Tie her up." Madame Clerval's commanding voice broke through Roxy's hurried thoughts.

Roxy looked up just in time to see the tall blond woman approaching her, arms extended as she chanted in high tones and a magical rope materialized between her hands.

Instinctively, as soon as Isidora was within reach, Roxy put her left hand out and willed the power there to leap out toward her. She screamed with all her might and felt a strange sensation, as if her hand had fallen asleep, a thrill or buzz across her palm, and then a great outpouring of lightning energy in her fingertips.

The magical rope disappeared and Isidora flew back several feet away from Roxy, landing on her butt at Barb's feet.

Roxy's eyes widened and she stared at her own hand. Had she really done that? Had she really just used *magic* to stun a foe?

She didn't have time to consider the implications. Barb was advancing on her now, even as Roxy saw, to her horror, that Madame Clerval was slowly approaching behind her holding a strange tool that was both beautiful and terrifying at the same time. It looked like a wrench or pliers made out of mother-of-pearl, and Roxy had no desire to know how Madame Clerval planned to use this torture device on Mo.

Barb looked nothing but delighted to be coming at Roxy to tie her up or otherwise incapacitate her. And Roxy, feeling the surge of power again within her, smiled. Barb had caused enough problems for her and Tessa and the theater.

This time, Roxy found the wherewithal to stand up as Barb approached, and she raised both arms above her before bringing them down onto Barb's outstretched palms.

There was lighting, actual lightning, that discharged from Roxy's hands, as though all her rage, and all her anger for those evil enough to want to harm Mo and Tessa were concentrated into a single packet of light and energy.

Barb screamed, immobilized, before a slight flick of Roxy's wrists made her fly up and over Isidora, past Tessa even.

"Shit," said Roxy under her breath. She had done that? She had done that.

She had no time to consider this either, as now Madame Clerval was nearly upon them. She set aside her terrifying pincers, but she looked no less terrifying than before.

Roxy felt her stomach drop into her shoes. Madame Clerval's face was distorted with anger and disgust.

"*You.* Who are you that you even *dare* to attack the Three Sisters of Provincetown? You will pay for your stupidity." She practically spat the words at Roxy before lifting an arm to throw a spell at Roxy.

Simultaneously, Roxy also lifted both hands, feeling the energy bubbling inside her, as though it was alive and eager to get out. She didn't care about herself at this point; she didn't matter. But Tessa and Mo— they needed saving. They were both alive, she just knew it, but how alive? Mo lying beside her was hanging on by a thread. How long could she survive on land in her mermaid form? Roxy didn't want to know. She was responsible for Mo. She had to do what she could to save her.

And then there was Tessa. Beautiful, smart, caring, kind, and sexy as hell. Roxy didn't want to think about life without Tessa. It was too much to consider for even a second.

Instead, she focused on her friendship with Mo, her feelings for Tessa, and she realized, with a jolt, that she loved both of them.

She loved Mo like the sister she'd never had—the sister who was her responsibility. Not like with Hazel, where she'd always felt like Hazel was in charge, the "smart one," the capable one, the one with her life together. With Mo, Roxy had been the one who knew how the world worked and how to survive in it. She couldn't let Mo down.

And she loved Tessa. She'd been scared to admit it to herself. Roxy had always been the kind to have strong feelings for other women quickly, and it had often come back to bite her. She'd fixated in the past on women who were not interested in her, the thrill of the chase being irresistible to Roxy. With Tessa, it'd been different. Tessa had *wanted* her, and that had made Roxy pause. In part, she wasn't used to being pursued. In part, she'd been afraid it wasn't real—Tessa was going to leave like everyone else, and Roxy had pushed down her feelings, telling herself she wasn't going to be impulsive or get too far in too fast.

They were past that now. Tessa was lying somewhere in the dark on the sand, and Roxy loved her. She loved her, pure and simple.

There was a rush of wind in her ears and Roxy pushed all her energy at the sorceress just as she sent her own spell barreling at Roxy.

The air was filled with the smell of something burning, and Roxy watched with amazement as Madame Clerval stumbled back, her entire body stiff as a board, her eyes full of fear before they closed, and she fell back on the sand.

Roxy was still standing there, staring at Madame Clerval's lifeless form, when she heard a voice.

"Stop! Stop whatever you're doing."

The figure was approaching faster than humanly possible. Within seconds, the woman was next to her.

It was Rhoda, from the museum.

She looked Roxy over and recognition dawned on her. She looked down at Mo before surveying the scene.

"Damn it," she said under her breath. "Not those three. Again."

"Again?" said Roxy.

Rhoda nodded grimly. "Never mind. We'll deal with them in a minute. We have to get the mermaid back in the water. I have some spells that will help revive her, but only once she's in the water. She'll be too weak here on land."

Roxy and Rhoda managed to get Mo into the waters of the Bay again. Once she was floating in a few feet of water, Rhoda lifted a hand over Mo's body and began to recite an incantation.

Oddly enough, Roxy recognized it

"You're a witch," she said quietly. "A hereditary witch. Like Hazel."

Rhoda looked at her, the incantation finished. "I don't know who Hazel is, and I've never heard of a hereditary witch. But yes. I'm *a* witch. And apparently you are too."

"No. I'm not—" Roxy began to protest just as Mo opened her eyes and took a big gulp of air. "Oh my God, Mo, you're okay!"

Mo heaved herself up using her tail to keep the upper part of her body upright. She threw herself on Roxy in a giant hug, and Roxy, full of relief, hugged back.

"Roxy. I know it. You save me." Her speech was accented again and stilted, as though her spells that had made her able to speak in a human language had faded somewhat. Roxy didn't care. Nothing mattered except that Mo was okay.

"I can't believe it. Honestly," she said through chattering teeth. Roxy's body had started to realize that she was standing thigh-deep in icy winter ocean water.

Rhoda muttered a quiet incantation, and she tapped Roxy on the shoulder. Warmth suffused Roxy's body.

"Thanks, Rhoda," she said.

"My pleasure. Now can we please get out of the water? My spells work a lot better when I'm not taking a polar bear plunge at night in January."

Roxy wanted nothing more than to get back on solid land, but she also didn't want to leave Mo.

"What if those magic nets are still out there. For her?" She gestured to Mo.

"Is okay, Roxy," said Mo, squeezing her hand reassuringly. "I can feel…something different now. Their magic net is gone. They are too weak to cast it once more."

"But what about you? Where will you go?" Roxy's eyes filled with tears. Was this really good-bye?

"I will go and see my people. But I will be back. I promise, Roxy."

Roxy looked at her, tears streaming down her face yet again. She pushed them away with a hand salty with ocean water.

"I'm going to miss you, Mo. You were a great friend," said Roxy, throwing herself on Mo in another bear hug. She tried to suppress the sobs that were rising inside her. She hated crying, hating being vulnerable like this, but the thought of never seeing Mo again was mingling with her fear of what she would find when she returned to the beach. She needed to get back to Tessa, but she was also scared of what she'd find. What if Tessa was…what if she wasn't…

"I promise. I will be back soon. Few days. I promise," whispered Mo. "You must do something for me."

"Anything."

"You must get the bracelet of Gwenhidw from these sorcerers. That is the only way to break their spell forever and drive them away from here."

With that, Mo pulled away from Roxy.

"Thank you, friend," said Mo to Rhoda. She extended her hand to Rhoda as if to shake, and Rhoda, to Roxy's great surprise, put her hand out and flapped it against Mo's like a dead fish. Mo reciprocated, completely unsurprised that Rhoda knew this greeting, before waving to Roxy and disappearing beneath the waves.

Roxy looked at Rhoda questioningly, and Rhoda shrugged.

"My mother was a mermaid."

CHAPTER TWENTY-EIGHT—TESSA

In her dream, she was running on the beach with Roxy, racing to the lighthouse in the distance. The sun was shining, glinting off the waves, before the scene changed to night, and Roxy was gone. Tessa was alone on the beach, running from something that was chasing her. Just as she was about to reach the lighthouse and safety, she stepped into a giant hole and felt herself falling—

"Tessa!"

She opened her eyes.

Roxy.

Tessa's mouth felt dry and full of sand. She wanted to say how glad she was that Roxy was there, that she was okay, but she was too weak to even speak. Her body felt heavy, stiff, and lifeless, as though her life energy were a mere flicker of candlelight in the middle of a storm.

"It's okay. Don't try to talk," said Roxy. She kissed Tessa gently on the lips, and Tessa felt strangely as though the kiss was something more than a kiss.

Instantly, she felt warmer, less stiff. Her lips and tongue responded, and she kissed Roxy back.

Roxy's hands on her arms added even more warmth and…was that energy she was feeling? Magical energy flowed from Roxy's hands into Tessa. She felt the stiffness and cold receding. Her body felt light…normal.

She pulled away from Roxy and pushed herself up onto her elbows and then into a sitting position.

"Oh, Roxy," she breathed, pulling Roxy into an awkward hug right there on the sand. "I thought I was going to lose you."

"I thought I was going to lose *you*," said Roxy, her voice wavering slightly. "Are you okay?"

"I feel…better. I don't know what you're doing, but…it feels like magic." Earlier, when they were trying to save Mo, Tessa had acted on instinct, without thought. As she reviewed in her mind all the most recent events on the beach, she was stunned. "Wait. Are you a witch? And what about Joy? Is she okay?"

Panic rose inside her and she made to stand up, but Roxy's hands stilled her, wrapped around her as they were.

"Don't try to get up yet," said Roxy. "You're still getting your strength back. I need to give you more energy. Rhoda says it's the only way we can defeat the Three Sisters."

"What—"

Roxy lifted each of Tessa's hands and placed her hands, palm to palm, with Tessa's.

"Tessa," said Roxy quietly, looking at Tessa with intensity in her beautiful, dark brown eyes, like pools of melted dark chocolate that Tessa could swim in for days, "I love you."

Tessa's heart fluttered.

"I love you, too, Roxy."

Heat began to form where their palms were joined, and Tessa knew that neither she nor Roxy could move their hands apart even if they wanted to.

And she didn't. She felt Roxy's energy pass through Roxy's hands into hers, as though she were pouring crystal clear mountain water into a bucket that Tessa was holding. *Was* Roxy a witch? How had she missed that?

With each passing second, Tessa felt herself reviving. She no longer felt hungry or thirsty; her legs no longer felt like leaden stumps, incapable of movement. After another minute, she felt the magic within her start to fill again, mixing with whatever it was that Roxy was giving her.

She felt the power within her rising, a cool, sparkling river of magical energy. Tessa could almost picture it in her mind's eye, and it was like crystals or rhinestones, full of light, beautiful—and powerful.

The magical connection between Roxy and Tessa ended, and they stood up.

"How do you feel?" said Roxy, her eyes full of concern.

"Wonderful," said Tessa. She grabbed Roxy's face and pulled it toward her own, kissing her with the fierceness of all her fears from earlier that evening. Fearing she would lose Roxy before she ever really had her.

Roxy's lips moved against her own, as if Roxy was feeling the same thing that Tessa was—fear, relief, and endless desire.

"Sorry to break things up, ladies," broke in a stranger's voice. "We're going to have company soon."

Tessa and Roxy broke apart. The stranger next to them was a dark-haired woman with boxy glasses, who looked like a cross between Bettie Page and a stern librarian. In her hand, she held a wand.

"Just how many witches are here tonight?" said Tessa, unable to hold in her surprise.

The woman laughed. "I've been wondering the same thing myself. I'm Rhoda, by the way."

"I'm Tessa."

"Okay. That's all the time we have for pleasantries. Your friend over there is okay. I warmed her up with a little spell, and she's comfortable enough. Best if she stays out of what's about to go down, though." Rhoda paused. "Unless she's a witch too?"

"I don't think so," said Tessa. "Though I didn't think Roxy was either."

"For the last time," said Roxy, sounding a bit exasperated. "I'm not a witch. I just have some…magic, I guess. I don't know what's going on."

"Save the existential crisis for later," Rhoda cut her off. "There's movement over there. Look, you two take the sidekicks. I'll handle Faustina. I've been looking forward to this moment."

"Don't forget the bracelet," said Roxy. "She's gotta have it on her."

Rhoda nodded grimly. "I brought extras just in case. Take one. Maybe it'll help." She pulled out two additional wands, similar to the one she was holding. Tessa wasn't even sure exactly where she'd been keeping them on her person, but Rhoda was wearing a large black trench coat, and she supposed there might be a voluminous pocket somewhere inside.

Tessa waved the wand a bit, testing it out, even as Rhoda was already marching with determination toward the beach where Madame Clerval was starting to stand up and dust the sand off her cloak.

The other two Sisters were also beginning to show signs of movement.

As Tessa moved the wand gingerly, she felt something like sparks flying off it from the slightest movement, paired with a small discharge of her magic.

The wand appeared to be amplifying her magic. Well, thought Tessa, *this* was a game changer.

"Is it okay if I take Barb?" said Tessa, looking at Roxy.

Roxy smiled. "Of course. I think you have a score to settle with her."

Tessa nodded. "Damn right I do."

"I'll take the blonde." Roxy waved the wand a bit too vehemently and a shower of sparks flew out and set a small piece of driftwood on fire by her feet. "Shit." She stomped out the fire with her boots. "These things are wicked, huh?"

She lifted a rakish eyebrow and Tessa felt a bubble of laughter inside her. Even here, on the beach, nearing midnight—the time when the Three would most likely be at the height of their powers, as they'd clearly planned it this way—when things should be the most dire for them, here was Roxy making her smile. Making her laugh. How she wanted to tell her—

But no. There was no time for that.

Tessa squared her shoulders. "Let's finish them and get their evil asses out of our town."

Roxy nodded.

Roxy gave her hand a squeeze and let go, walking off into the dark toward the parking lot where Isidora was just starting to stand up. Tessa hated leaving her to fight alone, but Rhoda was right. They had to make sure that this evil magic was banished from the Cape.

Tessa wasn't sure how to do that, exactly, but a plan formed itself in her mind.

"Get Isidora's ring," she shouted to Roxy. Roxy turned back, already looking small in the distance, but she nodded to show she'd heard.

Isidora had her ring. Madame Clerval had one. It stood to reason that Barb had one too. She would have to immobilize her again, somehow, and get close enough to get the ring off her finger.

Rhoda was already engaging Madame Clerval in a magical duel by the time Tessa was close enough to Barb to throw a spell at her. She used the wand to direct a blinding spell at her, but it missed.

"You'll have to work a lot more carefully to hit me with that blunt instrument of a wand," said Barb, her rough, low tones grating on Tessa's ears with their taunting.

Barb shot a spell at Tessa, and Tessa dodged it—but only just. Tessa was pleased, though, to see that Barb was pissed at that.

She took the opportunity to send an immobilizing spell at one of Barb's arms, and it hit! Tessa tried not to jump with glee and instead focus. Before Barb could send another spell, she waved the wand and, remembering her training with Freya, always focused on nature and using what nature provided, she made some seaweed lying nearby fly to Barb's legs and start to wind itself around her.

The more Barb struggled, the tighter the seaweed laced itself around her.

Tessa approached her cautiously.

Barb was struggling like mad to get free, sending spells right and left. Something flew right by Tessa's left ear, and she jumped back.

A glance over at Rhoda gave her the shivers. She was losing the fight with the extremely powerful force that was Madame Clerval. Tessa needed to finish things up with Barb and get over there to help Rhoda.

She used the wand to create a shield of salt, drawn from the ocean water, to keep her safe from the crazy spells Barb was setting off as she tried to get out of the seaweed vines.

In the moonlight, just for a second, light glinted off a ring on Barb's finger. Yes! There it was.

Tessa's arm would have to extend past the salt shield for a moment to grab it. She pushed her hand through the shield, creating a small hole, but still letting some of the salt coat her hand as she got close enough to Barb to reach for her hand.

But Barb was strong. She started rolling away from Tessa, and Tessa couldn't hold the wand and the spell, *and* keep Barb still enough to pull the ring off at the same time.

The salt shield melted away, leaving behind a shower of salt over Barb and Tessa. Luckily for Tessa, some of the salt fell onto Barb's face and one eye as she was rolling away. She screamed in pain, and Tessa made for the ring, glimmering eerily on Barb's finger—a big green eye, just like Madame Faustina's.

Barb's fingers were surprisingly slim for her squat persona, and the ring was loose on her index finger. Tessa grabbed it and pulled with all her might—rather unnecessarily, since the ring simply slid off and Tessa fell back on her butt with the momentum.

She jumped up again quickly, anticipating that Barb would press her advantage and come after her, but she was still writhing on the ground, clutching her bare hand where the ring had been.

What kind of power had the ring bestowed upon the Three Sisters? Tessa glanced down at the ring in her hand and nearly dropped it. The pupil of the eye was dilating and constricting of its own accord, the eye moving from side to side.

"Ugh!" Tessa groaned, filled with horror at the sight of it. She closed her hand over it into a fist so she wouldn't have to look at it, even as she was filled with a strange desire to put the ring on.

After all, wouldn't she then have the power that Barb had had? She could fight Madame Clerval more effectively…

No. That was not the way—she knew that. The ring was already trying to sway her to evil and she had to resist it.

She left Barb still tangled up in the seaweed and spluttering from the salt on her face and began running as fast as she could toward Rhoda and Madame Clerval. Something was wrong with Rhoda's arm; it hung limply at her side, and her wand was nowhere in sight.

"Too late for you," said Faustina with a growl as she pointed a finger of magic toward Rhoda one more time.

Tessa sent a stream of magic from the wand, without a specific spell in mind, simply willing Madame Clerval to stop and to protect Rhoda.

One second, Madame Clerval was there, the next, she wasn't.

She'd disappeared into thin air.

Tessa ran to Rhoda, who looked just as confused as Tessa felt. Roxy was there by her side as well, putting an arm around each of them, out of breath from running.

"Where'd she go? She was right here. Are you both okay?" The words came in spurts, between gulps of air as Roxy caught her breath.

Tessa looked around the beach. It was completely deserted—except for Joy. "What about Joy?"

"She's okay," said Roxy. "I saw her. She looked like she was asleep."

"She should be," said Rhoda. "As long as no one disturbed the spell I used to keep her warm and cozy."

Tessa nodded. "Thank you for doing that."

"Where did Clerval go? And the others?" Roxy looked ready to fight again if necessary.

Tessa felt tired. The adrenaline of the evening was ebbing quickly out of her, and she felt unimaginably tired. She stifled a yawn.

Rhoda looked down at the ground and, after a moment, crouched down in the sand and picked something up.

It was another ring. Tessa opened her palm to show Roxy and Rhoda Barb's ring. It was identical to Madame Clerval's—as was the one Roxy proffered from Isidora.

"Gross," said Roxy, disgusted painted across her features.

"I'll take them," said Rhoda.

Roxy went to hand the ring to Rhoda, but a stab of suspicion stopped Tessa from extending her ring.

"How do we know you won't use it? Like they did?"

"Tessa, Rhoda is a friend. She helped me save Mo. She hates the Three as much as we do."

"Okay, but why should she have all three? That seems dangerous." Tessa couldn't shake the feeling that she didn't want to give up the ring. The ring wanted to stay with her.

"You want to keep the ring, don't you?" said Rhoda, giving her a searing look.

Tessa gasped. How had Rhoda known?

"It's a ring of power. Not the only of its kind in the history of the world either. Evil rings want to be worn, they want to be used."

"Shit," said Roxy quietly.

"It's not even three rings. It's just one ring," added Rhoda. "Please, Tessa, let me have it."

Something inside Tessa protested. She didn't want power. She didn't want to wear the ring—did she? But she didn't know Rhoda either. What if she *was* evil? She didn't know who she was. What if she had helped them defeat the Three so she could get the rings?

"Look. I know you don't know me. And a lot went down tonight. But here. Take this—I'm giving it to you of my own free will even though it belongs in the museum. It's a token of my good intentions," said Rhoda, and she pulled from her pocket a beautiful, intricately woven gold bracelet with designs and markings on it that Tessa knew, on instinct, must be imbued with magic. Tessa took it from her with her left hand, since her right was still clutching the ring.

The bracelet felt warm in her palm and comforting.

"Is that the bracelet of Gwenhidw?" said Roxy, her voice low and hushed in awe.

"Yes," said Rhoda. "Roxy, put out your hand."

Roxy did as she was told, and Rhoda placed Madame Clerval's ring and Isidora's on Roxy's outstretched palms. Roxy shivered and made a face.

"Yuck. They feel terrible. How could anyone hold them in their hands?"

Rhoda didn't respond or look at Roxy. She kept her gaze trained on Tessa. "You see? I gave the rings to Roxy. She has only pure intentions. Give your ring to her as well."

There was no reason not to do as Rhoda said. In her heart of hearts, Tessa knew that she did not want the rings or what they represented.

She placed the ring into Roxy's outstretched hand, and immediately she felt better, as though a fog had lifted off her. She felt lighter, more energetic, happier.

Tessa barely had time to enjoy this sensation of lightness and joy before the three of them gasped in horror as the three rings rolled together and merged into one large glowing green eye in Roxy's palm.

"Yuck!" said Roxy, instinctively dropping the eye into the sand at their feet.

Before any of them could react, the eye disappeared into the sand, like a crab burrowing into the beach. Quick as a flash, it was gone.

"Crap," said Roxy. "I'm sorry!"

"Oh no!" said Tessa.

Only Rhoda remained silent. After a moment, she shrugged. "Maybe that's for the best."

CHAPTER TWENTY-NINE—ROXY

The next morning, Roxy woke up in Tessa's bed.

She stretched and yawned and looked over at Tessa. She was still fast asleep, and she looked peaceful. A lock of hair had fallen onto her face, and Roxy pushed it gently back over her ear.

Tessa wrinkled her nose in her sleep, sighed, and resettled herself.

Roxy wanted nothing more than for Tessa to wake up so they could discuss everything from the night before properly, but more than that, she wanted Tessa to get some rest. Images of Tessa, lying unconscious on the beach, continued to haunt Roxy, and she'd woken up several times in the night with that image in front of her eyes as if she were reliving it over again.

She decided she'd take the opportunity to shower. They'd been so tired the night before that they'd barely had the wherewithal to change into pj's and brush their teeth.

First, they'd had to wake up Joy and make up some explanation for what had happened before taking her home, then they'd gone back to the theater, where they'd found Lisa and Chayo enjoying some Jameson and chatting away like old friends as they cleaned up and organized the dressing room and wood shop. They'd been relieved and distressed when they saw Roxy and Tessa—relieved to see them, in general, but distressed at the fact that they'd been in the waters of the Bay that night.

By the time they'd assured them they were okay, and fed them the same story, it'd been well after two in the morning, and they were asleep on their feet.

Roxy turned on the shower and enjoyed how the hot water slowly revived her, bit by bit. What was the story they'd settled on? She tried to recall.

Ah, yes. Rhoda had helped them craft something that was akin to the truth—that Mo had wanted to go for an evening walk on the beach, and Roxy had gone with her. There they overheard some people boasting about the vandalism at the theater, and Mo had impulsively tried to confront them. There had been a fight and some of them had gotten in the water in the heat of the moment. When Joy and Tessa arrived, they called the police and then tried to break up the fight. Eventually, the vandals ran away before the police could get there.

Roxy had worried that Lisa and Chayo wouldn't believe their story— it sounded completely ridiculous after all. Maybe it was the Jameson or maybe it was the general chaos of the evening, but Lisa and Chayo didn't bat an eye, even when Roxy shared that Mo had decided to go to Boston and stay with their cousins for a few days because she was so upset by the events of the evening.

It was the most ridiculous set of lies Roxy had ever tried to pass off as the truth, but the actual truth was even less believable.

Roxy combed her hair and dressed. She thanked her lucky stars that she always kept a spare set of clothes in the trunk of her car. It was a habit she'd developed as a kayaking instructor. You just never knew when you'd need a spare pair of trousers or underwear.

Before she left the bathroom, she looked at herself again in the mirror.

It was her same old self, wasn't it? Same dark, curly hair, cut short— needed a trim at this point. Same dark brown eyes and short stubby lashes, same sparse freckles that dotted her nose and cheeks. She looked at her hands—wide, strong, capable of handling a kayak or ski poles, wielding a hammer or screwdriver.

And yet. The night before, there had been something else there in her hands—in *her*.

She had wielded magic.

Roxy smiled. She'd never given much thought to the fact that her best friend, Hazel, was a witch and she was not. It was simply a fact of life. Yet, when Mo had first told her, insisted on it, in fact, that she had magic within her, a flame of jealousy had flared up within her.

She'd always *wanted* to have magical powers, always envied Hazel for that. She hated to acknowledge that, but it was true. And lying to herself about it wouldn't help anyone. She'd envied Hazel's good grades, happy family, and even her marriage to the beautiful and talented Elizabeth—but those were things Roxy was aware of.

Roxy had never fully considered that she might be jealous of Hazel's magic. She'd always thought it was awesome to have a friend who was a witch. Hazel had, for a while, even given her some magic love potions to help Roxy's love life, a habit that had, at one point, not ended well for Roxy. But still, Hazel had always been willing to involve Roxy with her magic and use magic for Roxy's benefit.

This was totally different, though. That sizzle of power in her fingers, the feel of the magic rising inside her like a stream whose banks disappeared during a rainstorm, was like nothing she'd ever experienced. It'd been scary—but also *really freaking awesome*.

She flexed her fingers. They felt completely normal now. Roxy wasn't sure if the magic she'd wielded so easily the night before would always be there when she wanted it, or if it had been the result of something Mo had done to her to activate it. Or maybe it was something else completely? Maybe it had been the panic of the moment, like when a person was able to lift an entire car in an emergency situation? She'd heard of things like that.

Roxy tried to summon the magic again, right there in Tessa's bathroom.

Nothing happened.

Oddly, Roxy wasn't disappointed. Somewhere within her, she could feel a small flame of magic. It was still there, but she didn't need it. It was enough to know that she had used it once—and she could again, if the necessity arose.

Back in the bedroom, she found Tessa awake and smiling. She pouted when she saw Roxy.

"Already dressed? I thought we were going to snuggle this morning."

Roxy hopped on the bed next to her and put her arms around her. "We can snuggle any way we want to, baby." She kissed Tessa gently on the cheek.

"Mmm, you know what I mean," said Tessa, pushing her body flush with Roxy's, and Roxy felt desire stir within her, like a shiver from the inside. Tessa's lips on hers were flaming hot, and Roxy found herself breathing hard in an instant.

"Oh, I see how it is," said Roxy. They kissed a while longer before Roxy pulled away. She wanted so much to strip them both naked and have her way with her, but to be honest, she was *starving*.

Roxy's stomach rumbled loudly, and Tessa pulled away with a laugh. "Hungry are we?"

"Mmm," said Roxy, nuzzling her neck. "I love you. But I also love breakfast." It felt wonderful saying those three little words.

"I love you, too, Roxy Bright," said Tessa, her warm brown eyes full of happiness as she gazed at Roxy. "Come on, I'll make you breakfast."

When Tessa slid out of bed, it was clear to Roxy just how drained and tired she still was from the night before. She looked pale and faded, faintly unsteady on her feet.

"Honeybuns, let me make *you* breakfast today," said Roxy, wrapping her hands around Tessa in a hug. She felt tears well up in her eyes for a moment as she considered, yet again, how close they'd come the night before to losing one another. "You need to rest."

Tessa wrapped her hands around Roxy and rested her head on Roxy's chest. "Maybe you're right. I still feel so tired."

Roxy made her signature scrambled eggs. Not that there were any special ingredients or anything. She joked that they were her "signature" eggs because they were one of the only things she knew how to make from scratch really well. "Low and slow," her grandfather had always taught her, and her eggs were always fluffy and moist.

Roxy relished watching Tessa eat and enjoy the food—and she enjoyed it too. She was ravenous.

When they were finished, they sat for a while at the table sipping their coffee.

"So," said Tessa. "I guess there are some things we need to discuss, huh?"

"Uh, yes," said Roxy with a smile. Now that she was well-rested and well-fed, she found herself wondering about what had happened the night before. She was also relieved that she could finally tell Tessa all about Mo. It had been a secret weighing on her ever since that first kiss at Tessa's apartment. At least, Roxy reminded herself, Tessa also had some secrets she'd been keeping.

"Who first?" said Tessa with a smile over her steaming cup of coffee.

"Oh, I don't mind," said Roxy. She launched into the story, from the beginning—finding Mo on the beach, taking her home, learning she was a mermaid, going to the museum and the whole story with the missing bracelet, the stolen grimoire…it took a long time to recount all the details.

Tessa was utterly rapt by Roxy's story and frequently asked follow-up questions, gasping at the right moments and shaking her head in surprise or amazement as appropriate.

"Wow, that is incredible," said Tessa. "I hadn't ever considered the possibility of mermaids."

"Me neither," said Roxy. "I always knew there was magic in the world, and witches—"

"You did?"

Roxy nodded. At this point, she felt it was pretty safe disclosing Hazel's secret. After all, Tessa was no stranger to the magical world. "Hazel is a witch. From a magical family. She even dated a vampire for a while."

Tessa's eyes widened in surprise. "What? Really?" She paused. "I *knew* that dress was something special."

Roxy chuckled. "Yep. Enchanted by her mom. We put out that it was done with LEDs, but nope. It was one hundred percent magic."

"And you…?"

"A mere mortal," said Roxy. "I can't really explain what happened last night. That night I saved Mo, she seemed to think I was magical somehow. She even thought that I had set the trap in the Bay that night."

"But you'd never…"

"No," said Roxy, lifting her hands in a gesture of helplessness. "I had no idea even that non-witches or magical folk could do magic."

"Then let me be the first to tell you that there are plenty of us who don't come from magical families or long lines of witches and wizards who do magic," said Tessa, putting her hands over Roxy's on the table between them.

"How is that possible?"

"When I went back to Amherst, I rented a cottage from a woman who lived there, Freya. She saw that I was depressed and unhappy, and she sort of…took me under her wing," explained Tessa. "At first, she was just showing me how to do stuff in the garden. We'd clip herbs and she'd show me how to hang them up to dry, explain what they did and how to use them. Eventually, though, she told me that all of us have magic within us, it just takes someone or something to bring it to the surface."

"She taught you how to do that?" Roxy was intrigued, and part of her was a little angry too. How had Hazel or her parents never thought to tell Roxy that? That she could learn magic, too?

Tessa nodded and sipped again at her coffee. "She showed me how to do spells—how to gather energy from the natural world, to create wards for protection, and to cast spells for things like balance, happiness, and new beginnings. None of it is nearly as exciting as what we were doing out there last night. What Freya taught me is called hedgecraft. I'm a hedge witch—though after last night, I'm wondering if that's still even true."

"What does that mean? Hedge witch?"

"Freya always taught me that it means you're self-taught," said Tessa. "Hedge witches focus on magic drawn from the natural world for the betterment of their own peace of mind and those around them. They seek balance, and they use nature as their inspiration. It's not about fancy spells or glamours. Hedge witches take their inspiration from the healing women of the past who tended gardens and gleaned things in the forests and meadows for their salves and medicaments."

"Does everyone know about them? Among the Otherworldly, I mean?" Roxy was still trying to understand how this magic was different from Hazel's. Or maybe it wasn't? Was it the same magic after all?

"I don't think so," said Tessa. "But I'm not sure. Hedge witches tend to keep to themselves. They don't have covens or anything like that."

There was a pause in the conversation. Roxy soon found herself lost in thought, wondering how she could know so much about magic and still be so ignorant of all its forms. Part of her wanted to leave the room so she could send Hazel a text and ask her why on earth she'd never told her about this possibility? She found herself consumed with the idea that Hazel had kept this back from her, even as another part of her refused to believe that. Her best friend knew how important magic was to her.

"What are you thinking right now?" Tessa's voice broke into her thoughts. She sounded worried, and when Roxy looked at her again, she saw real concern in Tessa's gaze.

Roxy smiled. "I'm sorry. I just…I don't understand how Hazel could have kept this a secret from me. I mean, I could have been doing magic for years at this point."

"Is it possible she didn't know that any other magic existed? Maybe she didn't know about hedgemagic at all? Freya mentioned that some magic folk think rather poorly of it. Like it's illegitimate or not real magic or something."

"I guess."

"You said you were really good friends. I'm sure she didn't know about it. Otherwise, she would have told you—right?"

"Right," said Roxy, though without much conviction.

"So that was really your first time doing magic?" said Tessa. She sounded impressed, and Roxy felt her sense of pride push away her feelings of jealousy.

Roxy nodded and smiled. "Yep. First time. Maybe it was beginner's luck? It was…incredible." She let herself relive the feeling of the buzzing, crackling, white-hot power in her hands—the sensation of it under her skin, right there at the surface, ready to burst out at her command. "Is it wrong that I liked it?"

Tessa laughed. "I don't think so. And I'll tell you what, it was damn sexy."

Roxy felt a different kind of power uncoil itself beneath her skin that had nothing to do with the magic she'd used to fight the Three Sisters.

Fleetingly, she wondered if she and Tessa should discuss what had happened to Madame Clerval, Barb, and Isidora, but rested and fed, with a gorgeous woman in a bathrobe next to her, it didn't feel like a pressing concern.

Roxy set her cup on the table and reached out to Tessa; as if on cue, Tessa came over and straddled her, hands reaching up to tousle Roxy's still-damp curls. Their lips met and Roxy felt red-hot desire flow through her. She marveled for a second how different this could feel than the cool, rushing sensation of magic, before her mind turned off and desire directed her arms to enfold Tessa and hold her close, and her lips to connect with Tessa's in a dance of passion and need.

This moment, of lips on lips, tongues mingling, bodies pressed together was a magic all its own.

CHAPTER THIRTY—TESSA

In the afternoon, once they'd had their fill of one another again, Tessa and Roxy went for a walk to the beach before heading to the theater.

Tessa had texted Chayo, Joy, and Lisa separately around lunchtime to check on them, and so far, only Lisa had written back. That woman had a schedule that no late-night brouhaha could change.

The temperature had swung up again. It was nearly fifty degrees out, and the wind from the previous night had died down significantly. There was a soft drizzle coming down, but it didn't last long. By the time they'd walked to the beach, the fog was lifting, and there were small patches of blue sky visible between the clouds.

There was no sign of the struggle from the night before. The tide had risen and receded since they'd been there last night.

Tessa felt strangely disappointed. It was as though the whole night before was a dream.

"Weird," said Roxy, kicking a broken piece of shell into the water with the tip of her black Converse Chucks. "It's so *peaceful* here."

Tessa nodded. "What if we dreamed it all last night?"

Roxy had her arm around Tessa's shoulders, and she gave her a reassuring squeeze. "I know I'll never forget that night. The first time I said *I love you* and really meant it."

Tessa looked up at her, searching out those beautiful brown eyes. "I know the feeling."

"Sorry to interrupt. Again," came a now-familiar voice behind them.

Tessa and Roxy turned to see Rhoda approaching. She was wearing the same black trench from the night before, and she looked as put together as ever.

Rhoda joined them at the surf's edge, looking out at the water.

"Any sign of your friend?" she said. Her hands were in her pockets, and she jiggled one of them. "I have something to give back to her. Or her people, rather."

"The bracelet?" said Roxy quietly.

Rhoda nodded.

"Doesn't it belong to the museum?" said Tessa.

"No," said Rhoda. "It never belonged to the museum. Not really. Artifacts like these don't belong in museums. They belong with the people or creatures who created them."

"So how did it end up in the museum in the first place?"

Rhoda sighed. "My father wanted it. He knew all the mermaid lore. He managed to trap my mother on land, and he took the bracelet from her. She was a direct descendant of Gwenhidw."

"What?" Roxy sounded incredulous. "But that means you're a direct descendant too! You're a princess."

Rhoda smiled. "Not exactly. When mermaids mate with humans, their children don't have the ability to change into the merbody. We inherit some magic, but that's it. And since I can't live underwater, there's really no way to claim a crown or position down there."

"Wow," said Roxy. "You could still keep the bracelet though. For yourself."

Rhoda's voice became tinged with sadness. "I've held onto it too long already. I thought putting it into the museum would keep it safe, but I was wrong. It's not safe until it's back with Mo and her people."

The three of them gazed out at the gray-green waters of the Bay, Long Point and the Long Point Light Station mere specks in the distance.

"Do you think she'll return here?" said Tessa finally.

"She said she would," said Roxy. "She promised me."

"Mermaids always keep a promise," said Rhoda, but her voice lacked confidence.

It was true, thought Tessa. Why would Mo come back to a place that had held her hostage there for a month?

"Why did Mo lose her ability to change to her tail in the tub?" asked Roxy.

"When did she show up here?" said Rhoda.

"New Year's Day."

Rhoda paused a moment, thinking. "A full moon cycle," she said finally. "Mo arrived at the full moon, and yesterday was the full moon.

Merfolk need consistent access to their home waters to keep their ability to shapeshift. If she was staying out of the Bay for fear of the Sisters, then her human form would start to ossify after a twenty-eight-day cycle without that access."

"How do you know that?" asked Tessa, feeling as though she already knew the answer.

"My mother found out the hard way," said Rhoda quietly.

"I'm sorry," said Roxy.

Tessa felt her heart squeeze. She wanted to say something comforting to Rhoda, but she had no idea what on earth she could say in such a situation.

"It's fine," said Rhoda. "I'm glad I could help you yesterday. After the break-ins at the museum, I'd been scanning the area with my crystal ball more frequently, and I could hardly believe my eyes last night."

"We are so grateful for your help," said Tessa. "I don't suppose…"

Rhoda looked at her carefully.

"I don't suppose you could come to the theater and see if there's any way to salvage what the Sisters destroyed there?"

Rhoda smiled. "Of course," she said warmly. "I'd be happy to. Though I'm not sure how much I can do. The Three Sisters were incredibly powerful, especially with the Eye of Power."

"Oh yuck," said Roxy with a grin. "Don't remind me about that creepy eyeball." She looked down at the sand as if expecting it to jump out at her suddenly.

"Do you have any idea how the Sisters got that?" said Tessa, as they walked back up the beach toward the theater. "Or where they came from?"

"Madame Clerval has been here on the Cape forever," said Rhoda, "though it's possible that the real Madame Clerval is gone, and this sorceress was simply masquerading as her as part of a disguise. It's hard to say. I was in Greece for a vacation trip at the start of the year, and when I got back, the bracelet had already been stolen. I think I would have sensed a dark presence here in town beforehand. My mother would have too."

"Your mother is still here? On land?" Roxy sounded surprised.

"She cannot turn back to her usual form," said Rhoda simply.

"What about that Eye?" said Tessa.

"I don't know," said Rhoda. "Dangerous magical artifacts turn up all the time. My guess would be that it turned up in an archaeological dig somewhere around the world, and one of the Three was there to nab it."

"Sounds very Indiana Jones," said Roxy.

Rhoda chuckled. "Yes, I suppose it does."

❖

At the theater, they showed Rhoda what was left of the costumes, the props, and the scenery. Chayo and Lisa had organized some of it, so at least the scraps of fabric weren't littering the floor of the costume shop, but none of it changed the fact that it was an utter mess—and completely unsalvageable.

Rhoda touched a couple of the fabric scraps, rubbing the fabric and holding up some of the bigger pieces up to the light, as if examining an X-ray.

Tessa knew her own body was still healing from all the excitement and energy expenditure the night before, and she didn't dare try to use any of her small pool of magic on anything today. She would let Rhoda use her magic instead. Tessa tried not to feel disappointed by her own lack of magical power; not only was she out of practice, but she had come to understand that she had been under a spell of some kind herself. When she'd handed that ring to Roxy, she'd felt the lightness return. She knew, right then, that the Three Sisters—Barb most likely—had been affecting her ability to use magic, tampering with it and dampening it. She must have been the one who noticed her wards in the theater and had taken them down.

"I'm sorry," said Rhoda finally. "The magic that destroyed this has made it completely unusable. In fact, I'd get rid of it as soon as possible. The residue of the magic on this might still have evil attached to it."

Tessa's heart squeezed in her chest. She felt dizzy and sat down heavily in a chair in the costume room.

Roxy kneeled down next to her. "Hey, babe, are you okay?" Her voice was full of care and kindness, and yet, it made what Tessa was feeling all the worse.

How was it that just as she got the most amazing girlfriend, her career was in the tank? How would she ever explain this to anyone and, moreover, how would they put on a show with no sets and no props and no costumes?

Tessa began to cry. She was overwhelmed with anxiety and anger.

Roxy pulled her into a hug, kneeling at her side. Rhoda stepped into the hallway to give them some privacy.

"How will I explain this to the grant board?" said Tessa between sobs. She put her face into her hands. "All that money…"

"We'll figure it out. If not you, then Joy or Chayo or Lisa or *someone*. We're all here to support you, and we all want the show to succeed," said

Roxy. She was the voice of reason, and Tessa knew that she was right. They would figure this out somehow.

"I'm going to get going," said Rhoda, who had returned to the room. "There's nothing for me to do here, and at home, I'm going to keep an eye on the ball, as it were."

"Ha," said Roxy dryly. "Good pun."

Rhoda winked. "I try." She paused and her expression grew more serious but also more concerned. "If you need help with anything else, though, do let me know. I know just about everyone around here and, well, *you know*." She winked again and handed Tessa a card with the address of the museum and two phone numbers. "My mobile is the best bet. Feel free to call or text as needed, especially if Mo shows up."

Just like that, she was gone, and it was Tessa and Roxy again. Roxy slid into the seat next to her, and they squashed together in the uncomfortable old office chair.

"Mm," said Roxy jokingly. "Cozy."

Tessa managed to slide out from between the armrest and Roxy and settled herself on Roxy's lap instead. It wasn't the most comfortable position, but it was comforting, and that was what mattered. Tessa could hear Roxy's heart beating steadily beneath her ear, and she allowed herself to be calmed by that steady thum-thump. She heaved a big sigh.

"I just want to stay like this forever," she said.

"Mmm-hmm," murmured Roxy.

They sat like that for a while, time passing unwatched and uncounted, until footsteps echoed in the hallway, growing louder and louder and then Joy's face appeared in the doorway.

She took in the scene before her without batting an eyelash. Tessa knew she always had a sixth sense about these things, and especially about relationships during a show.

"Police are here again," she said. "Ready to give a statement?"

Tessa groaned. "I guess," she said. She pushed herself upright and then paused to give Roxy a kiss before standing up completely. Roxy stood up too.

"Let's go together."

CHAPTER THIRTY-ONE—ROXY

Two days passed in a whirlwind of cleaning up the theater, being interviewed and re-interviewed by the police, reassuring the cast and crew that everything was fine, and making a new budget for the grant committee. Roxy was getting tired of having to tell the same story over and over, especially since it wasn't technically the truth. But who would believe the truth?

The police report cleared Tessa of any wrongdoing, along with everyone else officially associated with the show. Barb became suspect number one, though it didn't matter much since she was nowhere to be found in the theater or Provincetown.

Roxy was relieved that Tessa was officially not to blame, but she saw how hard Tessa was taking the whole situation regardless. They'd been spending every night together since the night of the battle on the beach, and Roxy could see the situation was taking a toll on her.

She wished there was something she could do for Tessa to cheer her up—or to help solve the situation at the theater.

Things had only gotten more complicated when the actor playing Perdita in *The Winter's Tale* announced she was quitting. She was, apparently, very superstitious, and the events at the theater were too much for her.

Tessa had cried and cried after that—at home of course. At the theater, she was keeping up the facade that everything was okay. She told Roxy that she had to. She couldn't let the cast and crew know how close everything was to collapsing.

Roxy wished she would be honest with everyone about how difficult a situation they were in. Surely they could handle it—and maybe everyone could pitch in and come up with some solutions together?

But Roxy didn't feel she could make such a suggestion. After all, she knew next to nothing about theater, and Tessa was the expert.

Aside from that, there was still no sign of Mo, and Roxy was starting to wonder if she would keep her promise to come back after all. Roxy was beginning to feel a bit disheartened, and she was glad to have her shifts at the pub on Monday and Tuesday to distract her.

At the pub, it was a whole different world. It was February, and everything was covered in rainbow-colored hearts. The Valentine's special beer that Roxy had helped put into kegs was now on tap at the bar, and it was delicious—a raspberry chocolate porter.

Everyone over at the pub was festive and jolly, and all Hunter and Jack could talk about at weekly staff meetings was starting to plan their summer beer flavors. Pride of Ptown always had at least three summer beers, and this year they were contemplating adding a Gose along with their two fruited sours and their fruited IPA.

Roxy had Wednesday off from the pub, though, so she made her way to the theater instead. She'd had to go to her apartment to get clean clothes, and she was surprised to see what a mess it was in there. Staying with Tessa, she'd gotten used to everything being neat and tidy, and she'd forgotten that her own cleanliness rituals were seriously lacking.

If only she had a magic wand to wave and put everything into its place. But Rhoda had taken back the wands that night on the beach—aside from the fact that Roxy wasn't even really sure if her powers, powerful though they were, could be harnessed for such a mundane task.

Today, the theater was full of life. Opening night was only three weeks away.

Roxy found Tessa with Joy and Lisa in the greenroom, along with the actors who were playing Hermione and Polixenes—or, as Roxy thought of them, the statue-woman and her lover. Or maybe lover? Roxy wasn't sure. She still hadn't cracked open the book with the play in it.

"Tessa, you *have* to cast someone for Perdita. It's a small part, but an important one…you can't put it off," said Roger, the man playing Polixenes.

"Do you have any suggestions?" said Tessa, her voice full of exasperation. She saw Roxy in the doorway and flashed a quick smile at her before continuing. "Perdita doesn't have an understudy."

"Why is that?" demanded Roger.

Tessa shrugged. "To be honest, I kind of figured I could be Perdita's understudy if necessary, but clearly I don't have time to learn the part now. There is too much other stuff to take care of," she said, her voice steadier now. Roxy admired her ability to stay calm under pressure. "Lisa, suggestions?"

Lisa looked over at Roxy and gave her a look that spelled trouble. Now that her and Tessa's relationship was out in the open, Lisa's demeanor had changed again toward her, and she had no idea where she stood with the icy blond celebrity.

"How about Roxy?"

"You're joking, right?" said Roxy with a weak chuckle. She could think of nothing worse than trying to learn a part in a Shakespeare play. It was literally her nightmare.

"Not at all," said Lisa with a grin like the cat that ate the cream. She looked over at Tessa. "Roxy's been around the theater for a month now. And she said she's had theater experience in the past...so why not? As you said, Roger, it's a small part, so it should be pretty easy to learn."

"Lisa, be serious," said Roger, his face softening a bit. "Roxy isn't a trained actor. We are all professionals—"

"Not all," interjected Lisa. She ticked off the names of several people in the play who were local amateurs. This had been done on purpose, as Tessa's grant had several educational objectives, and giving amateur actors the opportunity to learn from professionals was one aspect of the grant. "See? Not *all* professionals." She paused and looked Roxy up and down. "Roxy has that fresh, young, androgynous look—perfect for our Perdita."

Roxy looked over at Tessa, hoping she would take Roxy's side. The whole idea was ridiculous and made Roxy's insides turn to jelly.

But here she was wrong. Tessa was taking the suggestion seriously.

"I mean, it's not the worst idea," said Tessa slowly. She looked over at Roxy. "Won't you think about it, at least? I would love to direct you. It would be a lot of fun." Tessa smiled at her winningly, and Roxy couldn't believe her ears.

"Tessa, please, listen to me," said she, walking up to Tessa. She took one of Tessa's hands in hers. "I admire you so much, and this play, too. The whole project is amazing, and I wish I could be part of it, but...I can't. I can't do this."

Tessa looked confused and a little hurt.

"Can you think about it before saying no?"

Roxy sighed. She had no idea how thinking about it was going to help, but she also didn't want to embarrass Tessa in front of her colleagues. "Okay, I'll think about it."

"Great!" said Tessa with a smile. She turned back to Lisa and Roger, and they began discussing rehearsal schedules.

After a moment, Roxy felt she was no longer part of the conversation and, in fact, Tessa was barely paying attention to her. She ignored the pang of disappointment and decided to leave and find Chayo.

The wood shop was blissfully quiet. Roxy found Chayo sitting at the one desk in the room, a pencil behind her ear.

"Hey, good to see you," said Chayo, and even that small greeting, so full of warmth, made Roxy feel better.

"You too," said Roxy. She looked around and noticed that the wood shop was mostly empty. They had built so much and now it was as though none of it had ever happened. "Where'd it all go?"

Chayo shrugged. "Most of it was destroyed, my friend. I'm sitting here trying to figure out what we could do instead. What's left of the budget will probably go for costumes, so we have to figure this all out on the proverbial shoestring."

"If only you were referring to a French fry," joked Roxy. She was rewarded with a smile and quiet chuckle from Chayo. "Was anything saved?"

"Oh! Yes, actually," said Chayo. "The throne. Thank goodness. I'd locked it in one of the spare dressing rooms at the end of that little hallway over there." Chayo gestured toward the hallway where Lisa had her personal dressing room. "I guess the vandals never made it down there or didn't find the keys or whatever."

"That's good," said Roxy. An idea was forming in her head as Chayo was talking. "Are you going to stick with the space theme?"

Chayo shook her head. "I don't know how we possibly could. It was a cool concept, but a pricey one. And the costumes are totally destroyed."

Roxy nodded. "Okay. I have an idea."

CHAPTER THIRTY-TWO—TESSA

Tessa was glad to be back in her element after two frustrating days that put them even more behind schedule. Finally, she could focus on getting back to rehearsals and making a new plan for the play.

She tried not to focus on the fact that they were going to have to come up with an entirely new theme for the play—or a new way of staging the original idea without sets or costumes. Tessa had seen an amazing production of *The Tempest* once where the entire stage was white with no props or scenery, and color gels were used on the lights to create interesting effects that reflected the emotions of the scene or characters. Only two characters in that production had had actual costumes, and everyone else was in more or less street clothes. There was a way to do things in a minimalist kind of way, she supposed.

Still, Tessa was disappointed. She'd wanted to do something really over-the-top, and it was clearly not happening.

She met with Joy and her two assistant directors, her stage manager, her lighting designer, her sound board technician, and her head of crew, and they'd brainstormed for two hours, but the best they could come up with was some version of the blank stage concept.

The afternoon was eaten up with a long conference call to the grants committee who had been more than fair in extending their sympathies to her for the situation, but who had been equally committed to shuttering the entire production. They had no confidence that Tessa would be able to do more than a staged reading at this point, which wasn't what the grant was for.

Tessa and Joy worked their asses off in that meeting to convince them that she was working on a new concept, and that everyone was on board, and rehearsals were going swimmingly.

At least the last part was true. The entire cast, except for maybe two people, was off book at this point, which had to be some kind of record for any production. The blocking for the play was also done. Everything had been going according to schedule until the destruction of their costumes and sets that weekend.

Tessa's heart was pounding by the end of her pitch, and she thought she was going to puke while waiting for the committee chair to get back to her. The chair called her a half hour after the meeting ended to say that the committee was willing to give them one more chance as long as she could submit a new concept to them for the play by the end of the week.

Great, thought Tessa, all she needed was a brand-new concept and theme for the play, to be completely re-imagined and written up in two days, when the original concept had taken her six months to perfect—and even longer to research.

Luckily, rehearsals distracted her until dinner time. Roxy had already put in an order for some takeout, and they picked it up on the way to Tessa's apartment.

They stuffed their faces in near-silence, both of them ravenous. Finally, Tessa felt full and she stopped stuffing pasta and garlic bread in her mouth.

She grinned at Roxy, "I guess we were both pretty hungry, huh?"

Roxy was using a finger to get the very last bit of vodka sauce out of her takeout container. She looked up at Tessa, "Hmm?"

Tessa laughed. "I said, we were both starving, huh?"

Roxy licked the sauce off her fingers and sighed with pleasure. "Indeed, my lady." She blew a kiss with her greasy-fingered hand and then waved lasciviously at her.

Tessa giggled. How good it was to laugh with Roxy. It was a relief to feel so comfortable with her after a long and frustrating day.

Roxy had attended part of the rehearsals, but she'd been with Chayo the whole time. They'd been sitting a few rows behind Tessa and Joy, whispering occasionally, but Tessa hadn't been able to hear what they were saying.

"So, what was all that whispering about with Chayo at rehearsal?" Tessa got up and poured them both a generous glass of some pinot noir, her red wine of choice.

Roxy took a swig of the wine and set it down again. She looked pleased as punch.

"Chayo and I have been talking about the concept for the play," said Roxy. She lifted her eyebrows hopefully. "Wanna hear it?"

Tessa was intrigued. "I want nothing more than to hear this concept."

Roxy paused for drama before throwing open her arms. "Mermaids, baby!"

"Mermaids?"

"Yes," said Roxy. "Think about it. You could set the action right here on Cape Cod and all the ye old whaling days stuff from the museum in town. That little museum is chockablock full of dioramas and stuff that could be props. And if you did a Cape Code maritime theme, there's probably other museums or historical societies that might have other stuff you could just borrow—"

"And local theaters, too," added Tessa, warming up to the idea. Why hadn't she thought of it herself? The idea was right there in front of her. Her grant was all about making Shakespeare accessible to as many people as possible, and what could possibly be more accessible than setting the play right in people's backyards? "Roxy, you're a genius!"

Roxy blushed with pleasure.

They spent the next hour brainstorming ideas and adding to the list that Roxy and Chayo had already started in their conversation earlier. The more they talked about it, the more enthusiastic Tessa felt about it. It was a great idea—much better than anything she'd come up with, and fairly inexpensive as long as they got some locals to help.

"That is a brilliant idea. But do you think Rhoda will want to help us?" said Tessa finally. "She seems a bit…cold. Prickly, if you know what I mean."

"Oh yeah," said Roxy, waving Tessa's concerns away with her hand. "I thought that too. But she's a real peach. She's just got that ice-cold vibe. Not unlike someone else we know around here."

Tessa laughed. "Yeah, Lisa is like that."

"Ice queen extraordinaire," said Roxy. "Is that what you like? Cuz you know I'm not like that."

"First of all, my dear Roxana," said Tessa with a smile, feeling a bit of a buzz now from the wine that she was drinking just a touch too quickly, "I like you. I love you. I love the whole package. I don't need an ice queen in my life right now. Or ever."

She leaned over and kissed Roxy on the lips before sitting back in her chair and sipping some more wine.

"And second?"

"And second," she continued, "Lisa isn't always like that. What I liked about her was when that ice queen outside cracked wide-open and she showed me she could be funny. Vulnerable. Definitely a weird sense of humor."

"Is that what that is?" said Roxy. "Because I wasn't sure when she suggested I should actually be in a production of a Shakespeare play. On stage. Cuz that is *not* my vibe."

Roxy said the words like it was a big joke, but Tessa couldn't help feeling hurt.

"It's *my* vibe, though," she said. "Maybe Lisa was joking, but I think it's a great idea."

Roxy, who had been rocking on the back two legs of the chair, sat forward now, all four chair legs on the floor with a thud. She leaned toward Tessa, elbows on the table, holding her wine glass and taking a sip before speaking again.

"Honey, I know you think I'm great at a lot of things—which I don't deny—but acting is not one of them." Again, Roxy was trying to make light of things, but it didn't sit right with Tessa.

"Roxy, you *are* great at a lot of things, and I think you could be great at Perdita, too," she said, trying not to sound too bossy or whiny. "Plus, you'd really be helping out the play. And me," she added, trying to keep her tone light like Roxy's.

But Roxy's brows knitted at those words, and she set down her wine glass. She sat back in her chair, arms folded over her chest.

"Tessa, please, listen to me." Roxy sighed. "I don't like being on stage. I tried it in high school, and I didn't like it. I...I don't have an easy time reading plays. Or memorizing stuff."

"That's okay," said Tessa brightly. "We can work on it together. And Perdita's part is small, you'll see." Tessa didn't understand why Roxy was making such a big deal about it. Didn't she want to help Tessa? She'd come up with a really great concept for the play, so she'd read the play and knew what it was about. She'd been to lots of rehearsals. And beyond that, hadn't she told Tessa about how she worked as a tour guide in Salem? Roxy had lots of public speaking experience. "Being on stage isn't that different from doing your tours," she added encouragingly.

Roxy's expression grew cloudier. "It's not the same at all. Why are you pushing me on this? I don't want to do it."

"Why are you being this way?" The words popped out of Tessa's mouth before she could stop them. "I didn't mean it like that. I don't understand—"

"Exactly," said Roxy, her eyes bright with tears now. "You don't understand. You don't know what it's like to…to…to be dyslexic and be dating a Shakespeare expert." She was crying now, and Tessa's heart was exploding in her chest.

How could she have been so insensitive, so clueless?

"Roxy, I'm sorry," she said, but it was too late.

"It's just like with the brewery job. You think you know what I want better than I do," said Roxy, the words cutting Tessa to the core.

Before Tessa could react, Roxy was already up and putting on her coat. "I've gotta go," she said. "And no, I haven't read the play, so don't ask me to be in it. I can't do that."

Just like that, Roxy was gone, and Tessa was left alone in the apartment, the quiet jazz medley playing on her little Bluetooth speaker as if everything were fine and dandy. She turned off the music. She couldn't listen to it, tinkling away all smooth and sexy while she ugly-cried and threw away the remains of dinner.

Finally, Tessa let herself flop onto the couch and have a good cry. She sobbed into a pillow until her mascara ran and she remembered these weren't actually her pillows—they were the pillows of a rented apartment for a play that was a hair's breadth away from being a disaster.

She was exhausted and overwhelmed. The events of the last four days were simply too much. How could any one human being deal with so much in so little time? Even without the drama at the theater, there was her relationship with Roxy, or what was left of it. They'd gone from dating to sleeping together to fighting magical monsters together to fighting each other in less than a week.

Tessa wanted nothing more than to blame Roxy, but she knew deep down that this was a problem of her own making. She's been carrying a torch for Roxy for nine long years, and it was hard not to build her up in her mind as this perfect person, capable of doing anything.

And they'd talked about this. Roxy had told her she was dyslexic, but had Tessa really stopped to consider what that meant for Roxy? No. Clearly, she hadn't taken Roxy's confession completely seriously—that maybe it wasn't possible for Roxy to enjoy reading the play that meant everything to her.

Tessa felt like a class-A jerk, especially after Roxy had come up with an amazing idea to save the production and help her out.

They would find someone else to play Perdita, even if Tessa had to play her herself—or use a blow-up doll like she'd seen used for Bianca once in an off-off-Broadway production of *The Taming of the Shrew*. The thought made her smile.

There would always be another solution. She checked her phone and there was nothing there from Roxy. Her heart hurt all over again. She wanted Roxy—needed Roxy in her arms. She needed to know she was forgiven. But she didn't want to cross any more lines that night.

Before bed, she sent Roxy the briefest and most heartfelt message she could manage, and then went to sleep. Exhaustion hit her like a truck, and she was out immediately, her last thought of Roxy, hoping she would forgive her.

CHAPTER THIRTY-THREE—ROXY

R oxy woke up the next morning feeling rumpled and sweaty. She hadn't even had that much wine to drink, but there was something about red wine that always gave her a headache.

She blinked in the sunlight and her sleep-addled brain wondered, briefly, why the curtains were pulled aside. She liked to sleep in total darkness and never opened the curtains next to the bed.

Memories of the night before filtered into her consciousness, and she groaned. She'd acted like a complete *baby*.

In the logical light of day, Roxy knew that Tessa had not meant anything insidious or mean by her comments. She was enthusiastic and dedicated to her work, and she wanted Roxy to be a part of it. This was her way of including Roxy in her passion project, and Roxy, instead of calmly explaining to her that reading and learning a part in a Shakespeare play was not possible for her due to her disability, she'd completely lost her shit.

And walked out on her.

Who *did* that?

Immature kids, that's who. It was dawning on her that maybe she hadn't had any serious relationships in the past because *she* wasn't being serious about those relationships. To be honest, she'd enjoyed flitting from one relationship to another because it never meant having to make up after a fight; it never meant considering how the other person might be feeling or what they might need or want; and it definitely never meant really talking about her dyslexia or any of her insecurities to another person— insecurities that had, if she was honest, kept her from returning to school or pursuing better-paying jobs. Casual relationships were casual because they didn't go deep.

But she wanted to go deep with Tessa. And if Tessa didn't know things about her that were important, then whose fault was that?

Roxy's.

She stretched in bed and rubbed her face. These were Big Thoughts to be having so early in the morning.

She glanced at the clock and was surprised to see it was after nine. She'd been asleep for nearly twelve hours. It was not "early in the morning" by nearly any standard.

"Oh my God" she mumbled. She picked up her phone and saw a message from Tessa flashing on the preview screen from around eleven the night before. She was probably thinking Roxy was ignoring her again and being even more immature.

Before Roxy could unlock the screen and respond to the message, she heard the clatter of dishes or pots and pans—something like that—in the kitchen.

She froze.

Someone was in her apartment.

All sorts of crazy scenarios filled her head—someone had broken in and was searching her kitchen for the best pot to kill her with. Wait, who killed someone with a pot? No, maybe it was an animal. She'd left a window open and an animal had gotten in. *Crap.*

Just as Roxy was starting to think she could use the bedside lamp as a weapon, a familiar face appeared in the doorway of the bedroom.

"Hello, friend!"

Mo!

"Oh my God, you're back!" Roxy hooted with joy and jumped out of bed, where she'd been sleeping in nothing but her underwear and undershirt, and threw herself onto Mo.

Mo hugged her fiercely and even lifted her feet off the floor an inch. "Of course, I'm back, you silly git."

"Put me down, you loveable weirdo," said Roxy. Mo obediently set her on the floor and Roxy took a step back, eyebrow cocked. "Why do you have a British accent?"

"Do I?" Mo looked genuinely surprised.

"Yes," said Roxy. "You most definitely do."

Mo shrugged. "I popped over to the Thames for a bit to visit my sister and decided I'd like to see London for a day. Must've picked it up over there." She cleared her throat and spoke again, this time sounding exactly like she'd sounded like before. "There. Is that better?"

Roxy nodded. "You sound like your old self," she said. Mermaid magic was something else.

"Ahhh! I can't believe you're actually here. I missed you so much," said Roxy.

Over breakfast, Roxy filled Mo in on everything that'd happened while she was gone, finishing with her concept for the play and her fight with Tessa about why she couldn't play Perdita. Mo didn't really understand what dyslexia was, but she listened with sympathy to her story.

"You will make it up with Tessa," said Mo. "Of course you will."

"I hope so," said Roxy.

"I like your idea for the play very much," said Mo. "And I have an idea of my own for Perdita, too."

She paused and gave Roxy a meaningful look, her eyebrows knitting together in consternation. "But why are you here, Roxy? By yourself? Where is Tessa?"

"I, uh...well, I might have walked out on her last night."

"Roxy!"

Roxy summarized for Mo what had happened between her and Tessa the night before. Mo sighed when she'd finished.

"Oh, Roxy. Why are you still here? You must go and find Tessa and kiss and make up. And I will do the same with Lisa. She must be very sad that her assistant has been gone all this time."

Roxy nodded, reflecting that in fact Lisa *had* been out of sorts for the last week, more irritable...honestly, more like the Lisa Collins who had shown up unannounced at Pride of Ptown at the start of January than the Lisa Roxy had gotten used to seeing around the theater, humming to herself or laughing while running lines with Mo in the greenroom. That was cute. Lisa and Mo were friends.

They left the apartment together, separating after a few blocks. Mo headed to the theater and Roxy walked briskly to Tessa's apartment, hoping to catch Tessa at home still.

She was in luck, as the door to Tessa's apartment swung open mere seconds after she knocked.

"Oh, Roxy, I'm so sorry."

"Tessa, I'm a jerk."

They spoke at the same time, and in no time at all, they were in one another's arms, kissing and hugging and apologizing.

Eventually, they found themselves in Tessa's warm little kitchen, enjoying hot tea, which was starting to grow on Roxy. She was especially partial to a tropical green tea Tessa had introduced her to.

"I should have told you sooner that I was never going to read the play. I guess I thought you'd figured that out the night I fell asleep trying to watch it," said Roxy. She still felt embarrassed about how she'd acted. "I don't like talking about being dyslexic. It reminds me too much of bad grades in school and college. But I want us to be open with one another. About everything."

Tessa smiled and put a hand over Roxy's on the table between them. "I appreciate that. But I'm also to blame here. I still have superstar crush-object Roxy in my head, as it turns out. I was wrong to pressure you like that. I'm sorry."

Roxy leaned in a kissed Tessa on the lips. It felt good to have things out in the open. To be honest. It was yet another new sensation in her life she'd need to get used to.

"I guess we're both having to figure stuff out," Roxy said.

"And there's no one else I'd rather figure it out with." Tessa smiled and her eyes danced, before the smile faded away, and a look of concern replaced her earlier levity. "But what will we do about Perdita?"

"I think Mo has an idea about that," said Roxy. She couldn't help grinning with secret knowledge.

"Mo!?"

Roxy nodded. "Mo is *back*. And she's got a plan."

CHAPTER THIRTY-FOUR—TESSA

O pening night of the play.

Tessa could hardly believe it was here—and then done and gone.

She stood in the lobby of the theater after the show and watched as the stars of the show greeted the audience, talked to them, shook their hands, and, in Lisa's case and that of some of the other more famous cast members, signed programs and took selfies as well.

Tessa had learned so much about herself, and about Roxy, over the course of the last three weeks. Ever since they'd made up, Tessa had been working on listening to Roxy—really listening—and not just hearing what she wanted to hear. By the same token, Tessa was working on moderating her expectations in *all* aspects of her life. She'd always been a people-pleaser, always wanting things to be perfect, including herself, her work, and her partners, and it was time to set aside those impossible standards.

It had been hard to accept some of these realities for Tessa. But she was working hard to set aside her aspirations for perfection. She was learning quickly that perfect was the enemy of happiness and, in some cases, like the play, what she'd *thought* would be perfect, turned out to be nowhere near the mark. In spite of what she'd originally thought for sure were huge compromises—losing the space concept and all the expensive costumes as well as her hand-picked actor for Perdita—the play was a huge success.

Tessa's heart swelled with pride. Opening night had gone *so well*. She could hardly believe it.

Mo had been incredible in the role of Perdita. So often, Perdita was a character without much to give to the play, the drama being so tightly wound up with Leontes, Hermione, and Polixenes in the first half, but Mo had given it her all, and in doing so, she'd brought Perdita to life in a way that Tessa could never have imagined.

Who knew a mermaid who'd never heard of plays and theater two months earlier could give such a heartbreakingly beautiful performance on stage?

Lisa, of course, had done a spectacular job. She'd brought her all to the role of Leontes, and she was perfect—terrifying in the first half, and gut-wrenchingly sad in the second half. There was a rawness to Lisa's performance that night that Tessa hadn't been expecting—and the exchanges between her and Mo on stage as estranged parent and child were especially moving.

Everyone had done a great job, and so many people were coming up to Tessa now to congratulate her.

The sets and costumes were getting a lot of praise too. Roxy's idea had been a smash hit. With Rhoda's help and permission, they'd used some of the backdrops from the dioramas at the museum, shifting the concept from space back to Earth and, specifically, New England during the height of the nineteenth-century whaling industry. Leontes and Polixenes were governors of Massachusetts and Rhode Island, respectively, and Hermione, in a stroke of brilliance, rather than being a statue for twenty years, lived out her exile as a mermaid in Cape Cod Bay.

That idea had been Mo's of course.

The theater in Harwich had recently staged the *Pirates of Penzance*, and so, with the additional help of some of the locals working on the set, they'd been able to borrow at low-to-no cost many of the costumes from that production, and some of the props as well.

It had all worked out brilliantly, and in some ways, Tessa felt that perhaps a concept closer to the hearts of the people on Cape Cod was better than her space opera idea anyway. It was a little hard to admit that, as she'd been so proud of the space idea, but in the end what mattered was that they had a concept and it'd worked out. Everyone praised it, and she loved getting praise, of course.

Her mother and father and sister would be arriving the next day to see the second performance, so they weren't in the audience that night, and Tessa found herself a bit disappointed. Her mother had suggested that they come for opening night, and Tessa had discouraged them, telling them it would likely be the worst of the performances and it would be better to come the second night.

But there was always something magical about opening night—no pun intended.

Tessa glanced up surreptitiously at the ceiling of the lobby and was relieved to see that her wards were still in their places after she'd re-hung them a few weeks ago.

"Tessa!" Mo's jolly tones broke in on Tessa's thoughts, and she turned to greet her budding thespian. "It was so good!"

Mo hugged her so tight she could barely breathe for a moment. Finally, Mo let go and Tessa inhaled deeply.

"Wow, Mo, that's some hug," she said.

"Oh, yes, I have been practicing with Lisa."

"With Lisa?"

"Yes," said Mo, suddenly very solemn. "She told me she needs good hugs to help her with her role."

Mo had returned to being Lisa's assistant for the last three weeks of the play, and they'd been spending a lot of time together. Tessa had been so busy with the preparations that she hadn't really had time to consider Mo and Lisa's relationship. Was there something going on that she wasn't aware of?

Before she could ask any more questions, Roxy appeared with Rhoda and Clare, the curator at the museum.

"Look who I found," said Roxy with a big smile. She put a quick peck on Tessa's cheek, but a glance at her eyes showed that she was definitely thinking the same thing as Tessa—they needed some sexy time, and soon.

On impulse, Tessa hugged Rhoda. "I'm *so* grateful to you, Rhoda. We really couldn't have had this success without your cooperation and the dioramas from the museum."

Rhoda looked surprised by Tessa's outpouring of warmth and affection. She straightened her glasses and pulled at her black leather jacket once they broke apart.

"You're welcome, of course," she said with a shrug. "The museum hardly gets any traffic this time of year. And of course, it's a write-off for us—"

"Oh stop it, Rhody," interrupted Clare, waving a finger at Rhoda as if she were a naughty child. "Be nice."

Tess and Roxy exchanged glances. What on earth was that all about?

Rhoda smiled, a little embarrassed. "Tessa, Roxy, please meet my mom, Clare."

Tessa's eyes widened and she looked at Roxy as if to say, *did you know this?* Roxy shook her head slightly. She was just as surprised as Tessa.

"A pleasure to meet you," said Tessa. She put out her hand to Clare, and Clare shook it.

"Oh, sorry," said Clare, sounding genuinely contrite. "Did you want me to, uh…?" She put out her hand again and Tessa did the same, and Clare slapped it gently with hers on both sides.

There was a pregnant pause in the conversation before all five of them burst out laughing.

"I see now how silly it looks here," said Mo finally. "But really, if you see it in the water, it makes much more sense. We do it with our fins."

Roxy slapped her forehead. "Of course. Why didn't I think of that?"

They all giggled again.

"Clare, what did you think of the performance?" said Tessa. "Rhoda, and you?"

"I thought it was lovely," said Clare. She patted Mo's arm gently. "This one here is a real winner."

"You can say that again," said Lisa, who had just walked up to their circle.

The theater lobby was emptying out. The only people left were some of the cast and crew, a reporter from the local paper—probably waiting to talk to Tessa one more time—and some friends and family of the production, like Clare and Rhoda.

"Ms. Collins, you were fantastic," said Rhoda, transforming before Tessa's eyes into the kind of fangirl that she never would have expected. Rhoda hardly knew where to look, but Tessa could see she really wanted to look at Lisa, of course. "Would you—"

"Sign a program? Take a selfie? Whatever you want," said Lisa with a smile.

"Rhoda works at the museum. She helped us the night of the break-in and then she helped us get the sets for the play, too," said Tessa to Lisa, who hadn't really been involved with that side of the production. She'd been more or less in character or running lines for the last three weeks.

Her eyebrows shot up at this news. "Really? Well then, I must thank *you* for helping out Tessa so much. You really saved the show."

Rhoda blushed. "It's nothing, really."

They stepped aside and took some photos, and it made Tessa's heart positively glow with happiness to see Lisa being her best self.

Soon Rhoda returned to the group while Lisa was assailed with more fan requests from some lingering theatergoers. Tessa had been chatting with Mo about her experiences of the first night. Mo had been shooting questions to her about various parts of her performance, and, to be honest, Tessa had no notes for her. She'd been perfect on her first time.

"Must be mermaid magic," said Tessa quietly.

"So weird to be able to say that word out loud," said Roxy. "I thought I was going to say it in my sleep at one point." She looked over at Clare. "That whole time Mo and I were at the museum, did you know who Mo was?"

Now it was Clare's turn to blush and look at her shoes. "Will you hate me if I say yes?"

Roxy chuckled. "You must have been pretty surprised."

"I didn't figure it out right away," said Clare. "It's been a while since I took a dip in the sea."

Tessa was surprised to hear this—not because of what Clare was saying, but her tone. She didn't sound sad or angry or frustrated. She sounded…fine.

Her words appeared to remind Rhoda of something. She riffled through her large black leather purse and pulled out a small velvet drawstring bag.

She handed it to Mo, who took it automatically and then peeked inside it. She looked back up at Rhoda, confused. "What is this?"

"It's the bracelet of Gwenhidw," said Rhoda quietly. "I've been trying to give this to you for three weeks now. It's best if you can give it back to your people before the next full moon. We don't yet know if the Three Sisters are gone for real or if they're out somewhere gathering strength."

"But this bracelet is…garbage," said Mo. She pulled it out of the velvet bag and held it out on her palm. "It is not a mermaid bracelet. This is human trash. How could a mermaid even wear jewelry like this?"

Unexpectedly to everyone, Clare grabbed the bracelet from Mo's outstretched hand.

"Ma!" said Rhoda. "What are you doing?"

"What are *you* doing with *my* bracelet?" said Clare.

"*Your* bracelet? You were the one who told me it belonged to Gwenhidw."

"That was only a fairy tale," said Clare, her expression a mix of exasperation and affection. "I thought you knew that."

"Then why did the Three Sisters want it?" said Roxy. "Doesn't it have any magical powers?"

"Maybe," said Clare. "Anything given with love has magic within it."

"Ma, what are you saying?" Rhoda looked confused and impatient.

"This bracelet isn't yours to give away, and it most certainly wouldn't have helped the Sisters with whatever they wanted it for. Or maybe it would have. I suppose it's true. I don't know where your father found it."

"My father?"

"Yes, that is, your *real* father."

Chapter Thirty-five—Roxy

Roxy exchanged glances with Tessa. She, like Mo, was utterly rapt in the family drama playing out before them. It struck Roxy that perhaps this was completely par for the course after a performance of *The Winter's Tale*, with all of its family drama.

After three weeks of rehearsals, Roxy felt she knew the play better than if she'd read it. Best of all, she'd enjoyed the play. The language wasn't an issue once she could see it all in context. Seeing it all the way through tonight, she found herself moved by the play in a totally different way, and she'd been thinking a lot about the way the play represented family and relationships, the little misunderstandings that can turn into large-scale conflicts with far-flung consequences. It hit home for her—and clearly for Rhoda and Clare as well.

"I don't understand, Mother," said Rhoda, her voice wavering. "What is going on?"

"I wanted to tell you for a long time, but sometimes, so much time passes, that you don't have any idea of how to finally tell someone the truth. Especially someone you love so much," said Clare, looking at her daughter tenderly but also with concern. "Here, among these strangers, seems hardly the right time, but I suppose it's too late not to tell you."

"Mother!"

"I received this bracelet from your father when I learned I was pregnant with you. The very next day, I went for a swim round these parts, and I was trapped in a net—a magical net as it turned out—and brought to land. I had the bracelet with me, but I hid it in the rocks on the shore. The man you thought was your father was not your biological father."

"My father—my real father—is a *merman*?" said Rhoda, her voice barely above a whisper.

Clare nodded solemnly.

"Doesn't that make Rhoda a mermaid too?" said Roxy, unable to hold in her very loud thoughts any longer.

"Of course," said Clare gently.

"Hurray!" said Mo, jumping up and down.

Rhoda looked shocked to her core.

"Why did you let me think all this time that he was my father? This human who trapped you? Do you know how much it hurt to think that *he* was part of *me*?"

Clare patted Rhoda's arm gently. "He helped raise you. He *is* a part of you. And while I was angry with him at first, once you were born, it all faded. I grew to love you—and him."

"But why didn't you take us back? When you could? He was always traveling…we could have snuck away, gone home."

"It's not that simple. How was I going to leave your father here alone? It was getting harder and harder for me to shift my form, and I grew used to living here on land and…I liked it." Clare shrugged. "I liked living on land. I did send some messages to your biological father to let him know we were both all right. And he was okay with it. He had a couple other families by then. He was all right. There's no bad blood there." She recited this information in a manner so matter-of-fact, they were all speechless for a moment.

"The only thing that I was never sure about was your father's other daughter," said Clare finally.

"My father here on land?" said Rhoda quietly, as if her mind were still taking everything in.

Clare nodded, the only one of them acting as if this was all completely normal. "Yes. He had magical abilities, of course, as you know, being a magician, and he'd had a daughter before I came to him. She was being brought up by the mother, but occasionally the little girl would come to visit. Odd little thing, brightest red hair I'd ever seen, green eyes like a cat, and the biggest temper. I used to tell you both stories sometimes."

"I don't suppose you ever told them the story of Gwenhidw?" asked Roxy, whose brain was starting to put two and two together.

Clare nodded again. "Oh yes. I'm sure I did. That's a classic."

"And you showed them the bracelet?" asked Tessa, whose thoughts were going in the same direction as Roxy's.

"Very likely," said Clare. "Oh! I see where you're going with that. Yes. I suppose little Foo-foo might have taken it into her head that the bracelet was enchanted."

"Foo-foo?" said Rhoda incredulously. "I don't remember her at all."

"She stopped coming to visit when she started school. Her mother wanted her to study in Geneva. Of course, Foo-foo is just what we called her when she was little. You can't very well call a little girl of three or four *Faustina*."

Rhoda and Tessa looked at Roxy. It was almost too much to believe— Rhoda was a mermaid and Faustina Clerval was her stepsister?

"Why didn't you mention this connection when we were at the museum—and we saw her name in the register?" said Roxy, feeling rather indignant. Clare could have saved them a lot of time and energy if she'd filled them in on all these details six weeks earlier.

Clare looked confused. "But that was Faustina Clerval. I only knew Foo-foo as Faustina O'Connor." She paused and thought about it. "I suppose it's a unique name, but when she came to the museum, she didn't look like the little girl I'd seen back then. No red hair, no green eyes. Add to that a different last name, and I suppose I thought she really was someone else."

"Clearly, she's been incognito," said Tessa. "And I told you that the last name was a fake—a literary joke for fans of Mary Shelley."

"Right," said Roxy. Her mind was still stuck on the fact that Rhoda was a mermaid and Faustina was her evil sorceress stepsister. This was some messed up fairy tale shit, with a twist.

"But wait," said Mo. She looked at Clare. "You did not want to go back to the sea, okay. But what about your daughter? You never taught her to change to her tail?"

Clare turned to Mo. "No, I didn't. But to be honest, I didn't think it was possible. I'd taken her to the beach as a baby a few times and put her in the water—just her legs of course—but nothing ever happened."

Roxy looked back at Rhoda and was surprised to see tears filling her eyes behind their dark black glasses frames.

"I feel like I've lost something I never even knew I had," said Rhoda, sniffing, and Clare put her arms around her in a hug.

"Please," said Mo seriously. "Do not cry. All is not lost. All mermaids have within them the power to return to their first form."

"How can I return if I've never done it?" said Rhoda between sobs.

"She has a point," said Roxy to Mo.

Mo shook her head as if to shake away the idea. "It is inside you. You have this power. I can help you. I will help you both—if you want it."

Clare and Rhoda broke apart and looked at Mo. "Are you serious? Do you think there's hope for her—and for me?" said Clare.

"I know it, as you say, in my heart of hearts," said Mo. "At the next full moon, we will try it. I promise." She hugged them both in turn. "That is, of course, as long as Lisa is okay with it," added Mo. "It could be dangerous so I will explain to her."

"Huh?" said Roxy. She looked at Tessa. What did Lisa have to do with this?

Roxy felt like she was inside someone else's dream as she watched Mo go over to Lisa, who was still talking to one last fan. After snapping a selfie, the fan left, and they all watched Mo talk to Lisa, gesturing over at Clare and Rhoda. Then Lisa smiled and nodded and, of all things, put her arms around Mo and kissed her.

Dead on the lips.

Roxy sighed. The sight of Tessa's body never ceased to amaze her—or turn her on.

She cupped one of Tessa's breasts in her hand while kissing the other one, nuzzling it with her nose until Tessa giggled, then nibbling it with her teeth and sucking her nipple until it stood erect. She heard Tessa breathe in sharply, and she squeezed the other breast a little harder, teeth pulling on her nipple.

"Oh, Roxy," Tessa whispered.

They were naked in Tessa's bed, clothes thrown on the floor in uneven piles. Their bodies pressed together, and Roxy felt the heat in her body building like a slow fire.

She moved her mouth to Tessa's and kissed her, hard and deep. Tessa arched her back, pushing her body into Roxy, and Roxy dropped her hands to Tessa's soft backside and squeezed. Tessa began kissing her neck, leaving a trail of love bites there, each one inflaming Roxy's desire even more.

Roxy pushed Tessa down onto the pillows on the bed and began kissing her neck and breasts again, feeling her own body responding as she saw and felt Tessa's passion beneath her.

"Mmm, no, not like this," murmured Tessa. With a sudden, swift movement, Roxy found herself being rolled over so that Tessa was now on top of her, sitting astride her hips, with Roxy underneath her. She felt Tessa's hot wetness grinding into her pelvis, and it felt delicious. "I want to make you come," said Tessa and she grinned a naughty grin before leaning over Roxy and taking one of Roxy's nipples into her mouth.

The sensation was almost too much to bear. Roxy felt her entire body respond to the feeling of sucking and nibbling. After a moment, Tessa shifted to the other breast and administered her attentions there, and Roxy felt she could really see stars.

Roxy began to feel the start of an orgasm coming on, and she breathed deeply. It was too soon. She wanted this to last. She shifted them again so she was back on top.

Roxy pinned Tessa's hands with her own on either side of her head. "Give it up, baby. I'm on top now."

"So you think," said Tessa with a glint in her eye that made Roxy excited for whatever was coming next.

Roxy leaned over her and began to kiss her, sliding her tongue into Tessa's mouth. She used one arm to keep herself steady over Tessa, and the other hand she moved between Tessa's legs.

"Oh God, you're wet," she breathed before starting to kiss Tessa again. She slid her fingers between Tessa's hot folds, gliding in the wetness before circling her clit, which was already hard and erect. She plunged a finger inside her, and Tessa moaned into her mouth. "That's right, baby. I'm king today."

Tessa moaned again and then, unexpectedly, shifted herself again. One minute Roxy was on top, the next it was Tessa.

"Tonight, you come first," said Tessa, sliding down Roxy's body and positioning herself between Roxy's legs.

A second later, Roxy felt the delicious sensation of Tessa's tongue on her sex. It was indescribably hot, and Roxy had no idea how long she could hang on. Tessa's tongue moved over her expertly. She took her time exploring Roxy's center, her clit, her everything. Roxy moaned with pleasure. She'd never been with a woman who wanted to go down on *her*, and she relished the novelty yet again.

The steady, long strokes of her tongue began to increase, focusing more and more on her clit. Roxy felt want, desperate want for release building inside her, as if she were a string on a guitar wound too tightly. She wanted more, and Tessa could sense it. Tessa began sucking her clit just as she slipped a finger deep inside Roxy. The sensation deep within her spread outward, engulfing Roxy, and she felt that she was slipping over an edge in the dark, into a deep pool of release.

Roxy came hard and long, waves of pleasure crashing over her again and again until her body shuddered and came to a stop.

Tessa kissed her before lying down next to her on the pillow.

"Liked that, did you?" she said. Tessa's voice was still scratchy and low with desire.

"Mm," was all that Roxy could manage at that point. She was still relishing the sensations that Tessa could produce within her.

In so many of Roxy's previous relationships, she'd been on the side of providing pleasure. She was comfortable with that—and used to it. And while she'd had some partners who'd been willing to reciprocate, she'd noticed a pattern in which it was often far less than what she'd given them.

With Tessa, it wasn't like that at all. She gave pleasure—and she was given it in turn. It was a novel sensation, and she loved it.

They snuggled, pulling up the covers over them as their bodies cooled off from their exertion.

Roxy kissed Tessa gently. "That was fabulous."

"I wanted to do that," said Tessa. "Lisa—I mean my ex—"

"It's okay," said Roxy, with a laugh. "I know who your ex is."

"Okay, okay, it's just still a little weird," said Tessa. "Lisa didn't like that. She never wanted me to go down on her. So I'm glad you liked it. I liked it, too."

"That is just about the sexiest thing anyone has ever said to me," said Roxy, kissing her again.

Tessa sighed and lay back on the pillow. "Wow. What a crazy night."

"Seriously," said Roxy. Her mind was slowly returning back to the land of the living.

There was a pause, and Roxy enjoyed the warmth of their closeness, the security she felt with Tessa.

"What did you think of the play?" said Tessa after a moment. She rolled back on her side to be face-to-face with Roxy, and Roxy could see she was anxious.

"It was amazing," said Roxy truthfully. "I mean that. It was really *moving*. I don't get to see a whole lot of plays, but this was really something else. And to see a lesbian relationship in a Shakespeare play? Let's just say, it wasn't anything like my high school's production of *Romeo and Juliet*." Roxy mimed gagging, and Tessa laughed.

"So you liked it? Really?"

"Yes. And you should be really proud of yourself. I know I'm proud of you, proud to be your girlfriend," said Roxy, squeezing Tessa's hand gently. "You knocked it out of the park."

"Thank you," said Tessa.

They snuggled some more in the bed, and soon Roxy noticed that Tessa had fallen asleep. Roxy was feeling sleepy as well, yet somehow sleep wouldn't come. Slowly, it was dawning on Roxy that the play would be over in just ten days. Then there would be strike, of course, but that was only one day and then…what?

It was true that Tessa lived in Boston, and Roxy lived in Salem. That was a very doable distance for a relationship, but Roxy could already feel that it wasn't what she wanted with Tessa. And what about her future? Roxy kept wondering if it even made sense to return to Salem. She'd always loved living there, being from there, but Ptown had its charms too—but a commuter relationship between Ptown and Boston was logistically more difficult, and expensive, than Salem to Boston.

Roxy gazed at Tessa, trying to suppress her anxieties. Tessa slept very peacefully, and Roxy knew she was full of good ideas. They both were. She reminded herself that they would find a solution together.

The old Roxy would have thought about doing a cut-and-run in this situation. The stakes were high, emotions were intense, the girl was a keeper. In the past, her anxieties would have gotten the better of her, and she would have turned to self-sabotage.

Instead, Roxy thought about *The Winter's Tale* and about how much Tessa loved it and its themes of love conquering old injustices, and reconciliations even after many years. She thought, too, of Rhoda and her mother, and how Rhoda was willing to forgive her mother even when she learned she'd been keeping a massive secret from her for years. Those were all people dealing with way more drama than Roxy and Tessa, and they were making it work.

It was love, after all, that made it all worthwhile—and not the easy come, easy go kind of love. It was a deep, committed kind of love that could be both passionate and tender. Roxy wanted to be with Tessa for years, not weeks or months. And if that meant trying a new career or going back to school, then maybe that was okay. She was only twenty-eight, for crying out loud. They had the whole world at their feet, as long as they had one another.

Chapter Thirty-six—Tessa

A week and a day later, they found themselves yet again, on a beach at night in Provincetown.

Tessa marveled at how much had changed in just four weeks. Aside from the staging of the play and her growing and deepening relationship with Roxy, even the weather was changing. It was much warmer on the beach at night under the full moon in early March than in early February—even if it wasn't quite bikini weather. Tessa didn't relish the thought of getting into Cape Cod Bay, but Mo had assured her it wouldn't be for too long.

The run of *The Winter's Tale* was a smash hit, and the second and final week of performances was getting audience members from as far away as New York, Connecticut, and Vermont.

But tonight, with all but one performance left, Tessa was able to concentrate on something else—something wonderful and magical.

She and Roxy were on the beach with Lisa, Joy, Chayo, Mo, Rhoda, and Clare. As instructed by Mo, they'd all removed their shoes and joined hands. Mo was in the middle of their group, with Rhoda and Clare on either side of her. Tessa was next to Rhoda, and Roxy was holding hands with Clare. Joy and Lisa were on the other side of Rhoda, and on the other end of their line was Chayo.

Chayo had been very, well, Chayo, when Tessa told her she was a hedge witch and Mo was a mermaid.

"Girl, please, we Mexicans invented brujería. Ain't nothing you white girls got on us," she'd said with a smile. "Honestly, I'm a little miffed you didn't tell me sooner." She'd winked and given Tessa a hug, and Tessa knew they were good.

Lisa had already been initiated into Mo's true nature. Apparently, they'd been sleeping together ever since Mo had returned from the sea.

Tessa wasn't sure how to feel about their relationship. Mo was so different from Lisa, a free spirit to Lisa's type A control freak. She supposed, though, that as long as they were both consenting adults, no one else's opinions mattered, even if it *seemed* like the unlikeliest of matches. After learning Mo was a mermaid, finding out that Tessa and Roxy were both some version of witches was apparently NBD for Lisa.

The eight of them walked together into the water. The cold icy waves stung Tessa's legs for a moment before she remembered the spell she and Roxy had practiced with Rhoda to stay warm and keep the rest of their group warm as well.

Soon the water no longer felt cold to them, and they waded farther into the surf.

Tessa wasn't sure what to expect. Mo hadn't really been able to explain it to them; mermaid magic was beyond words, apparently.

After a moment, the sea became strangely calm around them, the full moon reflecting on the surface, a perfect glowing sphere. It was indescribably beautiful. Tessa breathed the refreshing night air deeply and felt a sense of peace settle over her. The stars twinkled in the sky like so many diamonds on black velvet, and just for a moment, it was perfectly silent.

Mo began to speak in her language. It was both strange and familiar, this speech of hers, and Tessa realized Mo was singing a beautiful though haunting melody. She and Roxy took that as their cue to channel spells for new beginnings and transformations, all the while holding onto Rhoda and Clare.

It was the work of a moment. One second, Rhoda was standing next to her, holding her hand, the next, she was under the water, and Tessa saw a flicker of a tail disappear beneath the unnaturally still surface of the Bay.

"Where'd they go?" shouted Joy, sounding panicked.

"It's okay," said Tessa. She pointed out toward the Bay to where the light from Long Point Light Station shone weakly in the distance. "Look."

Swimming some ten or fifteen yards in front of them were three mermaids—Mo, Rhoda, and Clare. Their tails flickered in the silvery light of the moon, and while they could not see the rest of them, Tessa recognized that this was a dance of joy and reunion they were witnessing.

Roxy waded over to Tessa and wrapped her arms around her. Tears were rolling down her face, and Tessa felt tears rising to her eyes as well.

"They're so happy," sniffed Roxy. "I want you to know, that's how I feel with you, too."

Tessa's heart skipped a beat. Roxy's words etched themselves into her heart. "Oh, Roxy."

They embraced, even as the cold of the winter was returning to them, their spell fading as they were distracted from everything else around them except one another.

"Hey, I'm freezing over here," shouted Chayo.

"Sorry," said Tessa. "We'd better get that spell going again or we'll all die out here."

"Truth," said Roxy.

They broke apart, except for their hands, renewing their spell to protect them all in the water.

There had been no sign of the Three Sisters, for which Tessa was extremely grateful, but it did no harm to be extra cautious.

The three mermaids were still swimming, frolicking with one another, and it was a joy to watch, but as the minutes ticked by, Tessa could feel the cold creeping back in, despite their spell work.

"Let's head back to shore," said Tessa to the others.

Slowly, they made their way back to shore, and Tessa was grateful to be out of the water. When she turned back, she saw Lisa still standing a few yards out in the water, looking out at where Mo was still swimming with the others.

She lifted a hand and waved to Mo, who, head above the waves for a moment, saw her and waved back, blowing a kiss. Lisa then blew a kiss back to her.

This was *not* the Lisa that Tessa was familiar with. But in that moment, she felt glad for Lisa. She'd found someone who brought out the best in her, and as Tessa reflected over the last three weeks of rehearsals, she realized that Lisa had been acting differently for a while. Tessa hadn't noticed it because Lisa's behavior had been…easier to deal with. Less diva-y. More content.

"They make a weird pair, huh?" said Chayo, coming over to stand next to Roxy and Tessa.

"They sure do," said Joy, joining them to look out at the water.

"I dunno," said Tessa. "They're happy together and that's all that matters."

"Amen to that, sister," said Chayo, patting her on the shoulder.

Tessa looked around her and felt a deep sense of contentment. Here she was, on a cold beach while it was still, technically, winter, but surrounded by her closest friends and the woman she loved, witnessing a startling and beautiful transformation that was part self-discovery and part reunion with family either left behind or never known. Love for Roxy, for her friends, for the whole world filled Tessa's heart, and she held that moment in her mind to look back on forever. It was one of life's few, utterly perfect moments.

EPILOGUE

Several months later

Roxy blew the whistle.

The squeak of sneakers and the distinctive plastic thump of many basketballs bouncing on polished wood filled the gym. Soon enough, there was laughter too, along with shouts of "Over here!" and "I'm open!"

The students completed the last of the drills quickly, and soon it was time for Roxy's favorite part—the scrimmage. Today she let them choose their teams, knowing that no one was going to be left at the end, unwanted. They were all friends, or at least friendly with one another—a fact that Roxy still marveled at.

When Tessa had first sold her on being a coach at her school, Roxy had resisted. She wasn't smart enough to be a teacher, or a good enough athlete to be a coach. She'd worried, too, that being among high school students would trigger some of her less fond memories of her own time in high school.

Roxy's fears had turned out to be completely unfounded, however. From the first day she'd been working with the students, she found herself completely in love with the job.

Being a coach was, in a lot of ways, very similar to being a kayaking or ski instructor. She'd never thought of those as "teacher" roles, but of course they were.

Now, watching the team split into two scrimmage teams go up against one another, Roxy realized she knew instinctively what the teams were doing well, and what they needed to work on. She could tell right away which positions each of the players would probably excel at.

She was, of course, only an assistant coach for now, working primarily with the JV team, but she didn't mind it one bit. Roxy found herself enjoying watching the head coach, Joel, work with the varsity team and learning from him by watching.

Once the scrimmage was over, Roxy talked over what she'd noticed with the group. Giving feedback to people who were listening to her was a strange experience, but again, a pleasant one. She'd never thought high school students would be so well-behaved, but she supposed that was one of the perks of working at a fancy private school.

Part of her had resisted Tessa's suggestion precisely because Roxy would be so far out of her own league at the school. It was the type of school her family could never have afforded—or so she thought. When she'd brought up her concerns, Tessa had explained that the school actively recruited talented students from low-income families with full scholarships. In fact, the school was committed to having at least a quarter of the students there on scholarship, and currently, that number was much higher, due to a generous donation from one of the school's main donors.

Of course, Roxy had been disappointed to leave behind Cape Cod and Provincetown—but only a little. She'd arranged to stay on at the brewery on a temporary basis, but by the end of June, the summer crowds were clogging the roads and beaches, and Roxy found herself missing the solemn quiet of Provincetown in winter.

Plus, she missed Tessa. Tessa had to return to her job in March after the show wrapped, and with only seeing her on weekends, it'd been lonely, to be honest. Roxy missed her—and Chayo and Joy and even Lisa.

Of course, there was still Mo. Mo and Clare and Rhoda had worked hard to make sure the waters around Cape Cod would continue to be safe for all magical creatures. Together with Tessa, they'd cast several powerful spells and enchantments on the Cape and its waters to keep the Three Sisters out for as long as possible.

Mo visited Roxy throughout the spring to keep her company between visits to her family below the sea and extensive time spent with Lisa in New York. The summer water traffic was too much for her, though, and starting in late May, her visits became rarer.

That weekend, though, they were all having a reunion meet-up out at the Cape. Lisa's Broadway show had just finished its limited run; Tessa and Roxy had a long weekend at the school; and even Hazel and Elizabeth were going to join them.

Roxy found Tessa in the school theater, reading through some plays for the following year.

"I'm done," said Roxy, leaning over to plant a kiss on her cheek. She was enjoying being in a normal, happy relationship. She felt safe and secure with Tessa, and it was a relief to feel that after the roller coaster of dating.

They walked out to the parking lot. They'd driven in together that morning, taking Roxy's truck to work so they could leave for the Cape right from school. It was already getting dark out, but Roxy didn't mind driving in the dark. Excitement for the weekend ahead was already giving her a buzz.

As they were exiting the parking lot, they saw Elizabeth waiting for Hazel to pick her up. Roxy drove over to say hi.

"This is so silly," said Elizabeth with a smile. "We should have all planned to drive there together."

"You two are still newlyweds," said Tessa with a laugh. "I'm sure you need lots of alone time." She gave Elizabeth a saucy wink, and Elizabeth laughed.

"Speak for yourselves," said Elizabeth, her voice full of gentle teasing.

Tessa and Roxy's PDAs were, in fact, a source of constant teasing in their friend group.

Roxy didn't know what it was, but she was utterly uninterested in what anyone had to say or think about her relationship with Tessa, or being out, and Tessa didn't seem to mind it either. Hazel was constantly warning her that it was risky, but Roxy enjoyed the recklessness of it. Let some old geezers or uptight Karens stare at them or glare or whatever. Roxy didn't care. She was in love.

The drive to Provincetown was uneventful, and soon they were pulling up to a beautiful clapboard house around the corner from the theater where they'd spent so much time together. Where they'd fallen in love.

The lights of the house were already on inside, signaling that Lisa and Mo had made it there first.

They'd found a vacation rental big enough for all of them, and it was going to be one big queer sleepover. Hazel and Elizabeth arrived not twenty minutes later, just as Rhoda and Clare walked over from their place. Lisa had put together a huge spread of food. Mo was bringing out the domestic goddess in her. She'd even managed to find some sushi that met Mo's high expectations but was still also appealing to non-mermaids.

They stayed up late into the night, talking, eating, laughing, and listening to music. Rhoda and Clare shared the good news that they were able to take over the running of Recovering Hearts since Isidora had hightailed it out of there. Madame Clerval's storefront was gone now too, replaced with a Mediterranean restaurant that was quite good. They all toasted to the good news.

Roxy was too wound up to go to bed, even when it was past three in the morning. She left Tessa fast asleep—that woman had *no* problems falling asleep, Roxy had noticed—and went outside. She always seemed to find herself outside at night in Provincetown. Hopefully, tonight there weren't any more enchanted mermaids to save.

There was a patio at the back of the house where Roxy settled herself, enjoying the view. The moon was only at the half, so that was a good sign in Roxy's book. Weird things tended to happen at the full moon.

Roxy was lost in thought for a moment, considering how much had changed since Hazel's wedding. It was hard to believe how much happier she felt, less lonely and less lost. Even materially her life had changed so much. The school paid a very decent wage, even for someone with a checkered work history and no prior coaching experience. And there were benefits. Benefits! She never thought she'd be excited to have dental insurance, but then again, she never thought she'd be working in a high school.

The sound of the patio doors sliding open and closed brough Roxy back to reality. A moment later, Hazel was sitting on the patio chair next to her wrapped in a thick blanket.

"Couldn't sleep?" said Hazel.

"Nope. You?"

"Nope."

"Too excited?"

"Exactly."

Hazel smiled at Roxy, and Roxy was reminded of all the times they'd stayed up late, talking about everything and anything.

"How are your powers these days?" asked Hazel.

After Hazel returned from her extensive honeymoon travels, Roxy had told her everything that'd happened in Ptown. Hazel had been nothing but supportive when she'd learned of Roxy's newfound magical powers. They'd had a real heart-to-heart about it, and Roxy had been proud of herself that she'd been able to ask Hazel about why she'd never mentioned that Roxy could do magic as a mortal without being accusatory or immature about it. She was extra glad because Hazel's reaction had been that of genuine surprise. She'd never heard of such a thing, but she was genuinely glad for Roxy. They'd always shared so much, and now they could share one more thing.

Of course, the irony was that Roxy hadn't been able to so much as summon a leaf off a tree since that night on the beach when Rhoda and Clare learned how to become mermaids again.

Roxy sighed and shrugged. She'd been thinking a lot about her powers and what they meant to her—how just a year earlier, getting powers and then losing them again would have made her desperately angry and upset. But now? With Tessa in her life, teaching her the ways of hedgecraft, being in a happy relationship, starting a new and rewarding job…the magic felt more like a bonus rather than a necessity.

"Sometimes I'll feel a little flicker of it," said Roxy. "It's like when your foot falls asleep, but somewhere further inside me."

"Have you tried to use it again?"

Roxy shook her head. "Tessa and I have talked about it. We both agree that maybe it was something that I was able to use because of the Three Sisters. The threat they posed. My powers were amped up because we needed them. Now things are good, so they're fallow. That's what Tessa calls it."

"Are you okay with that?" Hazel looked at her, concerned.

"Honestly, yes," said Roxy with a smile, and it felt like the truth. "It's fine. I'm really happy with my life right now. And just knowing that I was able to do all that…that's enough. For now, anyway."

Hazel smiled. "That's really good to hear." She paused. "You seem really happy. With Tessa. With the school."

Roxy smiled. "I was just thinking the same thing. I can hardly believe how much has changed since January."

"I'm really happy for you, Roxy," said Hazel. She reached over and squeezed Roxy's hand.

"Thanks," said Roxy. "I'm happy for you too. You and Elizabeth seem really happy together."

Hazel nodded. "We are."

There was a pause again, and they sat together in companionable silence.

Hazel sighed and shifted a bit in the seat. "Roxy, I want to tell you something."

Roxy turned away from the night sky where she'd been looking, idly, for constellations she recognized. "What's up?"

"Elizabeth is going to be on sabbatical next year."

"Wow," said Roxy. "Congratulations to her." This was good news, as Elizabeth had been talking a lot about wanting a sabbatical to research her next book. She didn't understand why Hazel thought this was important enough news to share with Roxy before telling everyone else.

"Yes. It's perfect timing, really. For us," said Hazel. She paused and swallowed. She looked at Roxy, and her eyes glistened in the moonlight. "For the baby."

Roxy's eyes widened. It was then that she noticed Hazel's right hand, resting gently on her belly. The blanket had slid off her shoulders, and Roxy could see a small bump, barely there, where there didn't used to be one.

"What!"

"Roxy, shh, you'll wake everyone," said Hazel, but she was smiling.

"How? When?" Roxy couldn't believe it. She was surprised and a little shocked but also very, very happy. She had no idea Hazel had wanted to start a family so soon, but then again, it wasn't something they'd discussed. Roxy had never thought to ask Hazel about having kids, and now she was beginning to wonder why.

Hazel explained that they'd decided to start trying in the summer, knowing that she might not get pregnant right away. She was lucky that on the second try, it worked, and she was due in June, just as Elizabeth's school year would be ending.

"So how many months are you gone now?"

"It's not even months yet, Roxy, it's more like weeks. I'm right at twelve weeks."

"Are you going to tell everyone this weekend?"

Hazel nodded. "Yes. But I wanted you to be the first to know." She squeezed Roxy's hand. "You're my best friend. Forever and ever."

Eyes filled Roxy's tears and her throat closed up with emotion. She leaned over and hugged Hazel.

A realization hit Roxy.

"I'm going to be an aunt!"

Hazel smiled. "Yes, of course. Aunt Roxy. I'll be counting on you to spoil them."

They stayed on the patio a while longer, talking about Hazel and Elizabeth's plans for the nursery, how Hazel was feeling (lots of sleepiness but no nausea), if they were going to learn the sex ahead of time (they disagreed on that point), and whether they'd told their families (not yet).

Finally, the chill of the night chased them back into the house where they said good night.

Roxy slipped into bed next to Tessa, snuggling up against her warm body. She tried to still her mind, but it was full of new thoughts and questions. Would Tessa want to get married? How soon? Would she want kids?

Roxy had never really given a thought to starting a family of her own. Her experiences with divorced parents had soured her for a long time on the idea of marriages, weddings, and family building. Loving Tessa and building a mature relationship with her had changed Roxy, though. She realized, as she lay there, that she would like to marry Tessa. They loved one another, and nothing was going to change that.

As for kids, Roxy wasn't sure what she felt. Occasionally, Tessa's mother would drop hints into conversation about wanting grandkids, but Roxy generally ignored such comments. She wondered what Tessa thought about them.

To be honest, the thought of taking care of another human being, beyond herself and Tessa, terrified Roxy, but a part of her was starting to consider the possibility seriously. If Tessa wanted a family, maybe that was something she could be on board with. More importantly, Roxy understood that these were the kinds of conversations they needed to have—that Roxy *wanted* to have with Tessa. In the past, something so serious would have terrified her, but now, she welcomed these new thoughts and possibilities.

Roxy spooned Tessa and slipped an arm around her. She breathed in the smell of Tessa and let her thoughts and worries float away. What was there to worry about when you had the love of your life to worry about it with you, after all? Roxy smiled into Tessa's hair and let the deep satisfaction of that thought comfort her as she slipped into sleep.

THE END

About the Author

Ursula Klein is originally from Maryland, where she grew up and attended university. She taught ESL in Europe after college, then returned to the United States and pursued graduate studies in New York. She has since lived in Tennessee, Texas, and Georgia before landing in her current location, Wisconsin. Ursula loves reading fantasy, romance, science fiction, and mysteries; she also enjoys crocheting, traveling, and spending time with her wife and young son. She is a huge fan of dressing up in costumes, loves celebrating Halloween, and was probably a witch in a past life.

Books Available from Bold Strokes Books

All Things Beautiful by Alaina Erdell. Casey Norford only planned to learn to paint like her mentor, Leighton Vaughn, not sleep with her. (978-1-63679-479-2)

Appalachian Awakening by Nance Sparks. The more Amber's and Leslie's paths cross, the more this hike of a lifetime begins to look like a love of a lifetime. (978-1-63679-527-0)

Dreamer by Kris Bryant. When life seems to be too good to be true and love is within reach, Sawyer and Macey discover the truth about the town of Ladybug Junction, and the cold light of reality tests the hearts of these dreamers. (978-1-63679-378-8)

Eyes on Her by Eden Darry. When increasingly violent acts of sabotage threaten to derail the opening of her glamping business, Callie Pope is sure her ex, Jules, has something to do with it. But Jules is dead…isn't she? (978-1-63679-214-9)

Head Over Heelflip by Sander Santiago. To secure the biggest prizes at the Colorado Amateur Street Sports Tour, Thomas Jefferson will do almost anything, even marrying his best friend and crush—Arturo "Uno" Ortiz. (978-1-63679-489-1)

Letters from Sarah by Joy Argento. A simple mistake brought them together, but Sarah must release past love to create a future with Lindsey she never dreamed possible. (978-1-63679-509-6)

Lost in the Wild by Kadyan. When their plane crash-lands, Allison and Mike face hunger, cold, a terrifying encounter with a bear, and feelings for each other neither expects. (978-1-63679-545-4)

Not Just Friends by Jordan Meadows. A tragedy leaves Jen struggling to figure out who she is and what is important to her. (978-1-63679-517-1)

Of Auras and Shadows by Jennifer Karter. Eryn and Rina's unexpected love may be exactly what the Community needs to heal the rot that comes not from the fetid Dark Lands that surround the Community but from within. (978-1-63679-541-6)

The Secret Duchess by Jane Walsh. A determined widow defies a duke and falls in love with a fashionable spinster in a fight for her rightful home. (978-1-63679-519-5)

Winter's Spell by Ursula Klein. When former college roommates reunite at a wedding in Provincetown, sparks fly, but can they find true love when evil sirens and trickster mermaids get in the way? (978-1-63679-503-4)

Coasting and Crashing by Ana Hartnett Reichardt. Life comes easy to Emma Wilson until Lake Palmer shows up at Alder University and derails her every plan. (978-1-63679-511-9)

Every Beat of Her Heart by KC Richardson. Piper and Gillian have their own fears about falling in love, but will they be able to overcome those feelings once they learn each other's secrets? (978-1-63679-515-7)

Grave Consequences by Sandra Barret. A decade after necromancy became licensed and legalized, can Tamar and Maddy overcome the lingering prejudice against their kind and their growing attraction to each other to uncover a plot that threatens both their lives? (978-1-63679-467-9)

Haunted by Myth by Barbara Ann Wright. When ghost-hunter Chloe seeks an answer to the current spectral epidemic, all clues point to one very famous face: Helen of Troy, whose motives are more complicated than history suggests and whose charms few can resist. (978-1-63679-461-7)

Invisible by Anna Larner. When medical school dropout Phoebe Frink falls for the shy costume shop assistant Violet Unwin, everything about their love feels certain, but can the same be said about their future? (978-1-63679-469-3)

Like They Do in the Movies by Nan Campbell. Celebrity gossip writer Fran Underhill becomes Chelsea Cartwright's personal assistant with the aim of taking the popular actress down, but neither of them anticipates the clash of their attraction. (978-1-63679-525-6)

Limelight by Gun Brooke. Liberty Bell and Palmer Elliston loathe each other. They clash every week on the hottest new TV show, until Liberty starts to sing and the impossible happens. (978-1-63679-192-0)

Playing with Matches by Georgia Beers. To help save Cori's store and help Liz survive her ex's wedding they strike a deal: a fake relationship, but just for one week. There's no way this will turn into the real deal. (978-1-63679-507-2)

The Memories of Marlie Rose by Morgan Lee Miller. Broadway legend Marlie Rose undergoes a procedure to erase all of her unwanted memories, but as she starts regretting her decision, she discovers that the only person who could help is the love she's trying to forget. (978-1-63679-347-4)

The Murders at Sugar Mill Farm by Ronica Black. A serial killer is on the loose in southern Louisiana and it's up to three women to solve the case while carefully dancing around feelings for each other. (978-1-63679-455-6)

Fire in the Sky by Radclyffe and Julie Cannon. Two women from different worlds have nothing in common and every reason to wish they'd never met—except for the attraction neither can deny. (978-1-63679-573-7)

A Talent Ignited by Suzanne Lenoir. When Evelyne is abducted and Annika believes she has been abandoned, they must risk everything to find each other again. (978-1-63679-483-9)

An Atlas to Forever by Krystina Rivers. Can Atlas, a difficult dog Ellie inherits after the death of her best friend, help the busy hopeless romantic find forever love with commitment-phobic animal behaviorist Hayden Brandt? (978-1-63679-451-8)

Bait and Witch by Clifford Mae Henderson. When Zeddi gets an unexpected inheritance from her client Mags, she discovers that Mags served as high priestess to a dwindling coven of old witches—who are positive that Mags was murdered. Zeddi owes it to her to uncover the truth. (978-1-63679-535-5)

Buried Secrets by Sheri Lewis Wohl. Tuesday and Addie, along with Tuesday's dog, Tripper, struggle to solve a twenty-five-year-old mystery while searching for love and redemption along the way. (978-1-63679-396-2)

Come Find Me in the Midnight Sun by Bailey Bridgewater. In Alaska, disappearing is the easy part. When two men go missing, state trooper Louisa Linebach must solve the case, and when she thinks she's coming close, she's wrong. (978-1-63679-566-9)

Death on the Water by CJ Birch. The Ocean Summit's authorities have ruled a death on board its inaugural cruise as a suicide, but Claire suspects murder and with the help of Assistant Cruise Director Moira, Claire conducts her own investigation. (978-1-63679-497-6)

Living For You by Jenny Frame. Can Sera Debrek face real and personal demons to help save the world from darkness and open her heart to love? (978-1-63679-491-4)

Mississippi River Mischief by Greg Herren. When a politician turns up dead and Scotty's client is the most obvious suspect, Scotty and his friends set out to prove his client's innocence. (978-1-63679-353-5)

Ride with Me by Jenna Jarvis. When Lucy's vacation to find herself becomes Emma's chance to remember herself, they realize that everything they're looking for might already be sitting right next to them—if they're willing to reach for it. (978-1-63679-499-0)

Whiskey and Wine by Kelly and Tana Fireside. Winemaker Tessa Williams and sex toy shop owner Lace Reynolds are both used to taking risks, but will they be willing to put their friendship on the line if it gives them a shot at finding forever love? (978-1-63679-531-7)

Hands of the Morri by Heather K O'Malley. Discovering she is a Lost Sister and growing acquainted with her new body, Asche learns how to be a warrior and commune with the Goddess the Hands serve, the Morri. (978-1-63679-465-5)

I Know About You by Erin Kaste. With her stalker inching closer to the truth, Cary Smith is forced to face the past she's tried desperately to forget. (978-1-63679-513-3)

Mate of Her Own by Elena Abbott. When Heather McKenna finally confronts the family who cursed her, her werewolf is shocked to discover her one true mate, and that's only the beginning. (978-1-63679-481-5)

Pumpkin Spice by Tagan Shepard. For Nicki, new love is making this pumpkin spice season sweeter than expected. (978-1-63679-388-7)

Rivals for Love by Ali Vali. Brooks Boseman's brother Curtis is getting married, and Brooks needs to be at the engagement party. Only she can't possibly go, not with Curtis set to marry the secret love of her youth, Fallon Goodwin. (978-1-63679-384-9)

Sweat Equity by Aurora Rey. When cheesemaker Sy Travino takes a job in rural Vermont and hires contractor Maddie Barrow to rehab a house she buys sight unseen, they both wind up with a lot more than they bargained for. (978-1-63679-487-7)

Taking the Plunge by Amanda Radley. When Regina Avery meets model Grace Holland—the most beautiful woman she's ever seen—she doesn't have a clue how to flirt, date, or hold on to a relationship. But Regina must take the plunge with Grace and hope she manages to swim. (978-1-63679-400-6)

We Met in a Bar by Claire Forsythe. Wealthy nightclub owner Erica turns undercover bartender on a mission to catch a thief where she meets no-strings, no-commitments Charlie, who couldn't be further from Erica's type. Right? (978-1-63679-521-8)

Western Blue by Suzie Clarke. Step back in time to this historic western filled with heroism, loyalty, friendship, and love. The odds are against this unlikely group—but never underestimate women who have nothing to lose. (978-1-63679-095-4)

Windswept by Patricia Evans. The windswept shores of the Scottish Highlands weave magic for two people convinced they'd never fall in love again. (978-1-63679-382-5)